THE HOLLAND F. ....GA

PART TEN

COLD CHILI

By

CLEVER BLACK

This is strictly a work of fiction. Any references to actual events, real people, living or dead, or actual localities, is to enhance the realism of the story. Events within the novel that coincide with actual events is purely coincidental.

ISBN: 978-0-9892445-9-6

CHAPTER ONE

FLIRTING WITH DISASTER

"I have no idea where Reynard Jacobs is at this moment. He never came here," thirty-four year-old Siloam Bovina stated to Bianca Jacobs as she stood outside of Moses' pen.

Bianca Jacobs, a tall, dark-skinned woman aged twenty-eight years, with micro-braids flowing down the left side of her face, stood before Siloam eyeing her with disdain. "I don't believe you at all," she told Siloam while looking her square in the eyes. "My father was coming here to see you and you only because you two were having an affair. I was the only one he told about this trip. Mary and Dimples didn't even know. Now, as an investigating officer of the law, I ask you again…what happened to my father?"

Siloam picked up right away the fact that Bianca was trying to intimidate her by using her credentials as a Vegas detective, but she be damned if she ever spoke on what she knew to be the truth concerning Reynard. The tanker truck had done its job by sucking up his remnants, and there was no further evidence left behind on the ranch. "Your guess is as good as mine," she said to Bianca over the tanker truck's engine.

"My guess is that he ended up here and you did something to him," Bianca remarked as she eyed the hog pen and grimaced over the rotten stench.

Siloam kept her eyes on Bianca as she watched her eyes dwell over to the hog pen at her back. Whether she could discern the pong of rotting flesh or not was not her concern. The only thing that mattered was that she not uncover the truth about Reynard. Bianca didn't know it, but she was flirting with disaster as Siloam Bovina had had her first taste of blood and she wasn't afraid to give herself another helping of homicide, if only to keep her transgressions against Dimples concealed for all times.

"Let me see your credentials, detective." Siloam remarked in a cold manner as she stared into Bianca's eyes.

"What?" Bianca asked as she chuckled slightly and looked away from Siloam.

"Look at me!" Siloam barked, forcing Bianca to whip her neck around and face her head on. In an instant, the tables had been turned and there was an immediate shift in power. Bianca had ridden onto the ranch with a cavalier attitude, but Siloam had been a part of the land for nearly two decades. Here, she was untouchable and she knew it. "You're a detective investigating a missing person. I'm willing to help you in any way I can, but I need to see your credentials first," Siloam stated while gazing hard at Bianca without blinking or flinching. "Show me your shield—detective."

"I left my shield back in Vegas," Bianca replied. "I'm here on unofficial business."

"Unofficial business is no business in my book, detective. Prove yourself to me. Then we will talk. Until then? Stay outta my way—before you yourself become a mystery," Siloam warned as she began removing her hazmat suit while walking off from Moses' pen.

Bianca walked off from the pen, climbed back into her truck and rode over to the guest house. She'd spotted Dimples walking into the home on her way in and sought out her sister after her less-than-favorable conversation with Siloam. She tapped on the door and Mary opened a minute or so later. She recognized the woman right away as she'd seen her on pictures courtesy of Reynard. "What are you doing here?" she asked with contempt in her voice.

"I came to see Dimples. Is she around?"

Mary hadn't time to answer before Dimples came to the door. "Momma, who at the door?"

When Dimples saw her sister standing on the porch looking all glamorous, she screamed joyously and brushed past her mother. "Bianca, what you doing here?" she exclaimed. "You could've called me! You come up from Texas?"

"No, Vegas," Bianca smiled. "I had some time off. Two weeks to be exact. Thought I'd spend them here with you so we can get to know one another better. Have you seen daddy?"

"Nooo," Dimples sang. "I been wondering where he at because he took some..." Dimples' voice trailed off at that moment as she didn't want to tell Bianca what her mother had told her the night Spoonie was shot, which was that her father had borrowed money from Mary and disappeared. "Come in out the cold! You hungry? We were fixing breakfast!"

"Yeah. I could use a bite to eat," Bianca spoke humbly as she walked into the home and removed her coat. "I didn't have time to book a room, sister. Can I stay with you and Takoda until I'm able to check in?"

"You don't need a hotel room, Bianca," Dimples stated happily. "There's a spare bedroom in me and my husband's home. You can stay with us while you're in town!"

"You sure? I don't wanna impose."

"Too late for that one," Mary sassed as she grabbed her wool trench coat, preparing to leave the home.

"Come on, momma!" Dimples complained.

Mary donned her coat, tied the belt, and said, "You know where I stand about your father's people, Regina. I don't like them in the least and have no interest in getting to know them. This is your," Mary caught herself before she spoke the word 'affair' as she didn't want to give Bianca an easy segue. She knew the woman's reason for arriving to the ranch the time she'd opened the door, but she chose not to speak on the matter. "This is your business to handle with this woman," she told Dimples. "Keep me out of it. Now, I'm going see Francine and have a cup of coffee with her. When I return? I want this woman out of my house and off this property. She's not welcomed here," she ended as she left the home.

****

Mary drove her F-150 over to the back side of Ponderosa where she climbed from the truck and slammed the door under the falling snow. She stormed up the stairs, furious over Bianca's arrival to the ranch. The doors on the patio were being guarded by a couple of ranch hands with assault rifles strapped to their backs and the family's ranch hand in charge after Flacco, a Mexican named Montenegro, was guarding the front while sitting out in his Nissan Titan. The family wasn't taking any chances after the incident with Spoonie, but the real threat, if Mary had to tell it, had already penetrated the property.

One of the guards opened the door for Mary and she stepped into the home and absorbed the smell of vanilla and mocha pouring from the kitchen area. Francine was over to the island counter pouring herself a cup of brew when she eyed Mary. "Morning, love," she smiled as she set the coffee pot back down onto the coffee maker. "What brings you over this early?"

"Dimples' sister arrived over to the guest house this morning," Mary sighed as she walked over to the counter, grabbed a mug and poured herself a cup of coffee.

"That's great!" Francine snapped as took a sip of her hot liquid.

"It isn't great, Francine," Mary politely retorted. "She's here to cause trouble…just like Reynard."

"Aww, that's not good. Cause trouble how?"

Mary walked towards the open area of the kitchen and Francine followed. The two entered the hall and walked towards Naomi's private room. "What I'm about to tell you can't be shared with no one, Francine," Mary spoke as the two entered the private room where Francine closed the door and Mary began to break down the fact that Siloam and Takoda had had an affair.

6

"Oh my. Now that's terrible," Francine placated towards Mary with shifty eyes while sipping her coffee.

"I'm not sure I should be telling you this, Francine." Mary remarked as she sat down on the couch.

"Mary?" Francine remarked as she took a seat on the couch beside Mary. "I knew all of the family's business before I ever met you. There are things that I could tell you that would make you vomit onto this very floor. But…you need not know those types of things. It's none of your business, but if and when it concerns the family? I make it point to make it *my* business. Now, what's going on with Reynard's daughter exactly?"

Just then there was a knock at the door. Mary eased up from the sofa and answered, only to see Siloam standing out in the hall in her denim outfit. "I just came from the guest house, Mary. I wanted to tell you that Regina's sister's here on the property."

"Why is everybody up in arms over the Jacobs family? They're, they're nobody to us!" Francine complained. "I was aiming to have a good cup of coffee and watch Good Morning America before Malaysia and Malara are brought down and all of a sudden everybody's snooping around over some bimbo belonging to a man no one gives a shit about!"

"She's a detective," Siloam stated upon locking the door.

Francine and Mary froze in their tracks at that moment. "She's a cop?" Francine questioned. "Well, this puts everything into new perspective," she stated as she walked around the room while holding onto her mug of coffee. "It's a good thing Siloam got rid of the body, or else we would be in big trouble here."

"You knew?" Mary asked towards Francine.

"I know just about everything, okay, Mary? But that's neither here nor there. What matters is that this woman not know. And the only way she'll know if is someone were to tell her. We all are going to keep quiet on this."

"What about the affair? She's sure to speak on the affair." Mary remarked.

"Dimples may have to eat that one. If her old man had kept it in his pants this wouldn't even be an issue. This is what cheating gets you sometimes in life," Francine replied matter-of-factly as she set her coffee down.

"I'll call and let Naomi know what's going on," Siloam remarked.

"And I'm going kick her off the property."

"No!" Francine protested. "We would want to keep an eye on her."

"But if she stays she may tell Dimples about me and Takoda. She may have already told her by now." Siloam fretted.

"Like I said, Dimples may have to eat that one. You, too, Siloam. And Naomi has enough on her plate to deal with down in Oklahoma City with Spoonie and the new businesses. Don't call her at this early hour with that nonsense," Francine objected as she picked up her cell phone. "This is a matter the three of us can deal with. We'll just have to play Reynard's daughter's game until we figure out our next move. What's her full name?" she asked as the phone to The Cicero Hot Dog Deli back in Illinois began to ring.

CHAPTER TWO
CHERRYVALE CONFESSIONS

November 1992

"That was some run you managed to put together from the French Quarters to the river's edge," Sheriff Rance Olsen stated out of breath to Faye Bender as he hopped into the driver's seat of his patrol car and looked over to the handcuffed woman sitting across from him. "What the hell were you thinking of doing? Swimming the entire span of the Mississippi River?" he asked as he pulled his door shut.

Faye was out of breath herself. She sat with her hands cuffed behind her back while eyeing the sheriff. "You said, you said Sascha sent you. What is this about?" she asked as sweat ran down her temples.

"We have a thousand miles to cover, Miss Bender. Sit back and enjoy the ride and I'll explain everything to ya'." Sheriff Olsen remarked calmly as he placed his car in drive and led the Iowa caravan out of downtown New Orleans with the flashers atop his brown and yellow patrol car blaring as he and his caravan of four blew through the red lights spanning Canal Street while making a beeline for Interstate-10 west.

Nothing was actually said between Sheriff Olsen and Faye Bender during the first half hour or so of the ride. The two just sat side by side, Faye staring off into blank space as the sheriff drove with a dead stare while looking straight ahead as a sea of concrete whizzed by at a high rate of speed.

"Williams Boulevard. That's the last exit out of this town," Sheriff Olsen remarked as the car glided over the overpass spanning the last street inside the city. *"This here is actually the town of Kenner, but it's all the same. It's all New Orleans. Nothing but miles of swampland ahead of us now,"* smiled as he reached for his lukewarm coffee and took a long sip.

"You people sure have a way of dodging what really matters in life. Everybody back in Patterson acts as if nothing's wrong up there. Like it's all good up there," Faye stated as she eyed the sheriff with disdain.

"Patterson was made ugly by three men, Faye," Sheriff Olsen remarked calmly as his car cruised up onto an elevated portion of Interstate-10 that spanned the vast swamp surrounding the city to the west. *"Made ugly by three men you killed during your time there. Can't say I blame you for what ya' did, though. Murder and incest? It's enough to sicken any good man's heart—and I'm a good man."* Sheriff Olsen's voice crept louder as he declared, *"I've been ordained by people who have your best interest at heart to bring you in alive and that's what I intend to do! The town owes you,"* he then added as he lowered his voice. *"Owes you for freeing them of an ugly secret that one man, that one man being Corey Mobley, held over the heads of his flesh and blood."*

"Everyone that cares about me is locked up."

"Sascha's not operating alone. Hell, she couldn't even sanction such an undertaking, but she got in contact with the mayor back in Patterson and I got the order. Didn't agree with it in the beginning, but after learning the truth? I had no choice."

"Mary Beth," Faye remarked as she looked to the floorboard of the patrol car.

"And the Senator." Sheriff Olsen followed.

"Mabel?" Faye asked surprised.

"That's right. You have powerful allies and don't even know it, young gal." Sheriff Olsen smiled as the murky waters of Lake Ponchartrain came into view.

"*You were one of the good guys. What's bringing you over to our side?*"

"*Money, hell!*" Sheriff Olsen remarked as he looked over to Faye while smiling. "*Mable and Mary Beth have basically retired my ass for bringing you home alive. But if you wanna go further? I've always had it in me. I just didn't think Corey was the right outlaw to lead the bunch.*"

"*Why didn't you kill him yourself?*"

"*I'm not the killing type. Just a man who knows how to play his position. Besides, I had you to do the dirty work,*" Sheriff Olsen remarked seriously as he eyed Faye. "*I could've busted you the night Jeremy and Wendell went missing because I knew where you'd run to even if Corey didn't. Corey gave Franklin the benefit of the doubt the night you crashed into Franklin's cornfield, but I knew there was no other place for you to hide other than that farm. I knew if Corey caught up to ya' he would kill you, so I let the investigation unfold on its own, hoping you would get away. And ya' did.*"

"*Did you know about Wendell and Jeremy?*"

"*I never knew of the Mobley brothers' intent that night. When Corey announced that they were missing the following morning? That was unexpected. Mary Beth told me just days ago what actually happened. You handled that well, Faye. Ya' did Patterson a favor ridding us of those two sexual deviants some years back,*" Sheriff Olsen stated proudly.

Faye wasn't feeling the Sheriff's sentiment, however. She wondered how people sworn to uphold the law could allow a man to run freely just because he held a badge. Corey was pure scum in her eyes and deserved his comeuppance. "*He had help you know?*" she said to Sheriff Olsen.

"*She's a federal agent now. Untouchable in our eyes,*" Sheriff Olsen responded. "*She'll be expecting retaliation. It's best to let that situation die down for the time being.*"

"*What's going to happen to me in the meantime?*"

"*You'll have your day to exact revenge on that federal agent that killed your family if that's what ya' wanna do, but as for now? We have to figure out a way to clear you of the charges you're up against because in the eyes of the Iowa justice system? You're the one they believe that is behind the Patterson massacre."*

"I didn't kill my family!" Faye shouted.

"I know. Everyone involved knows that, Faye, but it's no walk in the park. We'll work it out," Sheriff Olsen responded as he picked up a box of Krispy Kreme donuts. "Care for one? There's a couple of raspberry jellies in there if you care for a taste."

"I don't wanna puke on myself," Faye responded as she laid her head back and eyed the bald cypress trees that jetted out from the white caps of the grey, brackish waters encompassing Lake Ponchartrain as the patrol car cruised over the elevated portion of Interstate-10.

"Suit yourself," Sheriff Olsen replied nonchalantly as he set the box of donuts in between him and Faye. "We have another four hundred and fifty miles to go outside of fuel stops before we stop for the night so you might wanna partake of the breakfast being offered here."

"Just wake me when we get there," Faye countered as she rested her head against the window and closed her eyes while pondering what possibly lay ahead for the remainder of her life...

..."That's some story, Faye," I told the woman after she shared with me the day she was captured down in New Orleans.

"There's more, Mister Holland," she told me. "And now that I've shared a little of my past, tell me a little bit about yourself. Are you a married man?" she asked me as we continued walking side by side up the road that cut through the middle of her land.

"Married with two kids and an extended family that contributes greatly to the population percentage of this nation." I smirked as I reached inside my trench coat jacket and pulled out a cigar.

"Marriage is a beautiful thing. So is raising a family," Faye said to me as she looked back over her shoulder and smiled. "You've already met Maggie. That woman who offered your friend a light is my sister Bonita, the other one is a woman by the name of Sascha Merkendorf. The woman in the third patrol car is our friend Cikala."

"All y'all German?"

"Not Cikala. She's a Native American. We have blacks inside our outfit as well as you already know. Ours is a multicultural organization, Mister Holland. One can never be close-minded in this deadly occupation. It helps to have people from all walks of life, as I'm sure you can attest."

"I definitely can relate," I responded as I bit the end of my cigar and lit the opposite end.

Faye paused and turned to face her mansion sitting across the snow-covered land towards the east. "I have really come a long way, Ben," she remarked with a proud smile on her face. "After getting arrested, I was taken to Iowa and charged with murdering my own family. It was a big deal back then."

"How you beat the rap?"

"Let's just say it took eight years and involved politics and a disappearing act on an old ally of my sister. This woman Isabella sold me out after she was busted inside the prison with drugs she was smuggling in for Bonita. That's how I was caught. We got her back a few years later, though. That job was Boogie and Maggie's first hit as a matter of fact. Have you ever done time, Mister Holland?"

I nodded my head while looking to the ground. "I was dead behind bars, Faye," I admitted. "I was caught inside the airport down in New Orleans back in ninety-nine going after this guy who basically wiped out my whole crew. Me and my boys killed him and his brother right before they boarded a plane. I caught two life sentences, but I had a beast of a lawyer who gave back all that time."

I ran down further details on how Dante` beat Lisa Vanguard during my retrial over a course of thirty minutes or so. The

13

only name I gave up was Lisa's, but Faye knew from jump the relationship I had with the woman.

"I faced the same circumstances, Mister Holland," Faye remarked after I completed my story, "but my journey back to freedom was a little different. Would you like to hear it before you leave? After all, it has been a long drive for you. Would you like a meal before you go? It'll give us time to become better acquainted now that we will be doing business together."

"I'm not hungry, but I wouldn't mind listening to what you have to say."

"Good. I have an open fireplace on my patio behind my home. We can sit there and talk," Faye replied as she turned around whistled by placing two fingers beneath her tongue. "To the home!" she yelled aloud. She then turned back to me and said, "You and I will walk. Your friend can walk with Bonita as well as they seem to be into one another."

"My boy Vic into women, period."

"And Bonita likes…well…she likes whatever gets her off." Faye stated through a chuckle. "Here's the deal—you've told me about your previous incarceration, and now it is my turn. We enter into a pact now. I believe that you and I are both reasonable people that are able to resolve conflict without bloodshed. We sit at the front of our organizations and are the first line of defense in this delicate dance amongst murderers."

"It helps to know one's past." I remarked as I climbed over the fence.

"In order to better decipher one's future moves," Faye followed as she eased under the top rail.

"And to avoid unnecessary conflict." I replied as I extended a hand out and helped the woman right herself.

"Also to alert one of future actions that may be detrimental to the alliance formed." Faye remarked as she smiled over to me. "You really are a gentleman. It is an honor to have met you today."

I smiled inwardly as me and Faye walked side by side while staring down at the snow. This woman had a mind incomparable when it came to the business. That I knew, but she was willing to allow me to know more about herself, and I was willing to listen and learn. "What's your story? How'd you beat your rap?" I asked as we walked up onto patio.

Just as Faye was about to began her story, we both noticed a plane coming in low on the horizon from the west. It looked like it was going to crash into some trees at the edge of the property, but the Cessna coasted over the forest and touched down on a runway that I thought was just a driveway at first. The engine grew louder as the plane approached the back side of the home and looped around on a wide, circular concrete slab. The propeller slowed its rotation and the engine died just as a middle aged woman with brown hair and grey eyes, and another younger woman similar in appearance, climbed out of the plane.

"Governor Mobley. Delilah. What brings you two to Cherryvale?" I heard Faye ask the older woman who'd coasted the plane onto the property.

"Beverly Battle never called you? That coke head," Governor Mobley stated dejectedly as she climbed the stairs. "Mother's sick. She's on her death bed back in Patterson. She asked for you this morning."

"Mabel's dying?" Faye asked stunned as I sat listening to the women. "Why am I just hearing about this? I was there a month ago and she was fine!"

"Grandma didn't want you to worry," Governor Mabel's daughter, Delilah, assisted. "Maggie had been shot, RJ was killed. She kept her heart disease a secret believing she would get better. We all prayed she got better. I guess God was too busy to listen to what we were asking."

I noticed the facetious attitude the younger woman carried at the moment. Delilah came off like she was angry at the world. And it was clear to see that she was upset at God. Her and Governor Mabel looked like they came from wealth. The Governor was alright, but her daughter gave off negative vibes for some unknown reason.

"You'll have to excuse Delilah, Ben," Faye said, shaking me

from my thoughts. "Unlike her mother, she doesn't believe in God."

There it is right there. But I can't judge Delilah. All the crazy shit going on in this world it's not hard to understand why some don't believe in a higher source.

"Ben? You wanna fly to Iowa with us?" Delilah asked me. "If you and Faye still have business you can talk on the plane and we'll get you back here." At least she was cordial in her atheism.

"Nah, we done with business for now," I told the young woman. "It's probably best we get on the road anyway."

"Right. We may be there for some days making arrangements anyway," Faye followed. "Sorry, Ben. I guess I'll have to tell you the rest of the story another time, but today, we part ways in peace and as partners in this business. You know how to contact me. My sister will see you and Victor out," she told me while shaking my hand.

CHAPTER THREE

HER ANGLE

Me and Vic left Cherryvale I guess around the noon hour. Faye had put me up on some game as to how politics and crime go hand in hand. It would've been good to hear how she beat the rap exactly, but the main goal, that of preventing an all-out war, had been accomplished.

Interstate thirty-five brought us thirty miles close to Ponderosa so I decided to stop in and see how everything was going on the ranch being that most of the family was still ninety miles or so down the road over to OU Medical Center with Spoonie. I rode by Mary's produce store after crossing Kaw Lake, checking it out briefly to make sure it was secure. From what she told me during Christmas, this winter was to be the last winter she would close because she was going into year-round production this spring. Mary doing it big with her produce now. She got her onions and tomatoes up in grocery stores throughout the Midwest, got her own fleet of trucks, and raking in close to seven figures a year thanks to Naomi.

Riding up on the ranch around six in the evening, I see for the first time that the gate was closed and padlocked. I look around and all I see is snow-covered ground, snow-capped barns off to the east and silhouettes of dead hickory trees to the southeast and west. I can't see the houses from here and I'm not sure who on the property so I pull out my cell to call Naomi and find out what's up. Before I could even dial her number, a black Quad cab pick-up truck rode over the hill and

17

slowly approached the gate with its bright lights on.

"Here the fuck we go again. They gone do us like they did in Kansas," Victor sighed from the passenger seat.

I laughed a little. "Nah, brer," I said to him as I opened the door and placed a foot to the ground. "I think after that thing with Spoonie the family ain't takin' no chances, ya' dig? They done put security in place look like."

"That's what's up," Victor nodded as I stood up outside the Maserati.

I remain silent as I watch the pick-up creep to a halt. The doors opened slowly and Siloam and a Mexican ranch hand I knew to be named Montenegro emerged from both sides. Montenegro was Flacco's right hand man on the property. He was a little shorter and stockier than Flacco with brown, low-cut hair. He had thick eyebrows that shielded dark eyes and a thick, handle-barred mustache. He often wore a baseball cap and seemed to be frowning most times.

This man here rarely spoke, but when he did, you knew he was in the room. He was a stern individual. Direct and to the point and fiercely loyal to the family was what Dawk told me. Seeing Montenegro climb from the pick-up was no big surprise. He looked the type willing to move up into security. Why Siloam was with him I had no clue, though. She seemed out of place at the moment.

"Senor Holland," Montenegro said to me as he rounded the front of the truck with a .226 rifle strapped around his shoulder. "I was not expecting anyone else here tonight. You should call when coming. No disrespect—it just makes things less tense for me—especially after the sun goes down."

"This how you run detail?" I asked trying to get a feel for how things run now.

"Si. I am in charge of security now per Senorita Dawkins' orders." Montenegro told me. "Siloam is helping me for a while and I'm showing her the ropes of the detail on her and Flacco's orders."

I looked over to Siloam somewhat puzzled. I mean, this

wasn't a demotion or anything, I just never knew her to get down like this here. She was always the rock and roll chick to me. "Who all here, Montenegro?" I asked while eyeing Siloam inquisitively.

"Most of the family is still in Oklahoma City," Siloam answered on Montenegro's behalf. "The kids are all here. They're over to the mansion with DeeDee, Twiggy and Sharona. Mary, Martha and Dimples are here also…along with Dimples' sister."

"Dimples sister?" I asked as Montenegro walked over and unlocked the gate.

"Yeah. She arrived earlier today. They're over to Mary's home," Siloam stated as she walked back to the pick-up truck. I could tell something was on her mind heavy. Maybe her new assignment for the time being or whatever. I don't know.

"In another week or so we'll have an electric gate installed on both entrances. Here, and where the tractor trailers come in on the north side, Senor Holland," Montenegro spoke aloud, breaking my chain-of-thoughts. "Things'll be a whole lot easier then. Monitors and electric fencing and what not. All the bells and whistles," he stated proudly while smiling and twirling his fingers beside his large head. "Come on! Let's get out this cold! I'll guide you over to Ponderosa."

"Nah," I rebutted. "We gone head over to the guest house first. Everything secure on the front, but y'all might wanna keep an eye on Kaw Lake. If anybody come? That'll be the way in."

"We have the lake covered with two guys on detail until Dawk's home is erected," Siloam remarked. "Come on and follow us to the guest house."

Me and Victor trailed Montenegro and Siloam over to Mary's house. The Mexican blew the horn as he and Siloam rode off from in front of the home. As me and Vic were climbing out of the car, Mary pulled the door open. "Ben? Come on in outta the cold, baby! Oh! You have Victor with you! Come on in, you guys!"

Me and my dog stepped off into the home and right away it was like we were thawing out. It was frigid cold out and standing out talking to Montenegro and Siloam didn't help none. We removed our coats over the smell of cabbage and fried chicken.

"We shoulda stopped and got something eat, Ben. I'm starving, man." Victor stated, loud enough for Mary to hear.

"Yes, Victor. You can have some cabbage and fried chicken," Mary remarked through laughter. "All you had to do was ask and not drop hints to my nephew," she added as she walked back up the aisle leading to the elevated kitchen while shaking her head.

"You wasn't even slick, fam," I chided as me and Vic headed towards the kitchen.

I climbed the stairs and saw Martha sitting at the island counter picking at a large chicken breast with a plate full of cabbage and ham before her and a piece of cornbread off to the side. "What's happenin', Ben?" she asked while eyeing me and Vic as we made our way over to the counter.

Mary and Martha both had these brown eyes that bore into your face. Whether they were excited, saddened, worried or angry, their eyes always remained the same. Mary had that easy disposition. She was easy to read most times.

Martha, however, was hard to decipher. You never knew where she was mentally until she spoke most times. She continued watching me and Vic with those brown eyes until we neared. "You the one was checking me out in my sleep back at the hospital?" she asked Vic the time he nodded towards her. "I'm woke now. Why you nodding your head and shit like you can't speak?" she chuckled while picking at her meat, pulling a few strands and easing it in her mouth.

"Nah, it wasn't even—"

"Like that?" Martha smiled. "Typical male answer. Now I feel kinda bad."

"Why?" Victor asked while smiling and bumping his fists together.

"Because I thought you was checking me out. But since it ain't like that…" Martha's voice trailed off as she eased off her stool with her plate of food. "Hollar at me before you leave, Ben," she stated as she headed for the den.

"Ben! What's up, man?" Regina said as she trotted down the stairs with a female a little taller than she on her heels.

Dimples was pulling this woman along like a child. She was all smiles as she shoved her in front of me. "This is my sister, Bianca!" she stated proudly.

"Right. Bianca," Mary spoke dryly as she walked off from the counter while curling her lips. "Ben, you and Victor are welcome to eat. I'll put fresh towels in the bathroom for you two while the food is warming," she added as she went and turned the stove on.

I shook Bianca's hand briefly and Victor followed. She was tall, nearly six feet, with micro-braided hair. She was easy on the eyes with her radiant brown skin that was near Katrina's complexion. She resembled her father a lot, but I hope she don't carry his ways because dude was a snake the little I knew about him. "You come down with Reynard?" I asked her.

"No," Bianca smiled back at me. "I just came to hang with my sister. My father told me of her and we met briefly down in Texas, but I never was afforded the right amount of time because of my career. Now, I'm here to bond with my blood," she stated as she looked back and ran her hand over Dimples' arm. "We're having fun catching up."

"We are!" Dimples said in this happy tone. "We'll be back down later. Come on back upstairs, Bianca."

Right out the gate something about Bianca didn't sit right with me. I don't know if it was the fake smile she put on or what, but I was getting bad vibes from the woman. She didn't appear to be having fun to me. It was more like she was tolerating the situation. I wonder what's her angle. "Ben? Are you gonna eat?" Mary asked, shaking me from a deep thought about this Bianca chick that done just popped up on the ranch.

"Yeah. Vic? They got a couple of bathrooms off to your

right, fam. Mary, can you fix my plate? I'm going talk with Martha for a minute." I remarked as I headed for the den.

Martha was sitting on one of the couches before a marble table inside the den. This here was a comfortable room with a sixty-three inch flat-screen TV in the far corner to my right. A fireplace was in between two leather sofas off to my left and a bookshelf and computer stand was on my immediate right inside the overly-large carpeted room. The spare staircase was just ahead on my left opposite the corner from the TV, and pictures of the family were all around, on the walls and sitting in a few expensive curio cabinets.

There wasn't much light inside the room and Martha had the TV off. I clicked on a tall lamp near the entrance as I closed the door. Martha got up and did the same to the door leading to the spare staircase, using a napkin to twist the door and lock it. We met in the center of the den and stood face-to-face.

"That bitch a police," was the first thing Martha said to me while wiping her hands free of grease.

"Police?"

"Umm, hmm. She went at Siloam when she first got here this morning. Told her she knew about her and Reynard fuckin' and Oklahoma City was where he told her he was going before he left."

"All that's true?" I asked as I stood with my hand underneath my chin, slowly digesting the seriousness of the situation.

"I checked with Mary and she said it was true. Siloam and Reynard had an affair. Mary tried to put her out, but Francine told her it's best we keep Bianca close for the time being in case she try and pull something. Francine running her credentials, too. She using some of the old law on the payroll from Cicero to check her background. Until then, ain't shit we can do."

"What happened to Reynard?"

"Siloam told me she killed the man because he was bribing Takoda and extorting her for sex, but it's more to the story."

I listened as Martha ran down to me all what Reynard had done and was trying to do to Mary. Feeding him to the hog was the best thing for him in my book. As of now, only me, Martha, Siloam, Mary, Flacco, Francine and Naomi knew what had happened to dude. I can't see nobody talking about that there because we all got too much to lose, the only problem was the fact that Reynard daughter done put her chips on the table. She might lay up there and tell Dimples about Tak and Siloam just to cause problems, and her being a cop don't help none at all. It's a good thing Reynard done up and disappeared, but Bianca was right, his trail ended right here in Oklahoma so that in itself was a potential powder keg.

A soft knock on the door at that moment sent Martha that way. She opened and Mary stepped into the room. "I take it Martha told you about Bianca?" she asked me as she closed the door halfway, leaving me a view of Victor, who sat at the counter stuffing his face.

"Yeah." I responded as I eyed Mary.

"I do not like that woman. I don't want her here. And I wish she would just leave." Mary stated in an exasperated manner as she threw her hands up even with her shoulders. "It's only a matter of time before this whole thing blows up in Dimples' face."

"She can ask about Reynard all she want to towards Dimples. Dimples don't know nothing about what happened. So long as everybody keep quiet, her investigation ain't gone never gain ground."

"Martha said the same thing, Ben," Mary said to me as she placed her hands on her hips and looked to the floor. "But after what Reynard tried to do to me and what Spoonie is going through right now, I just don't trust Bianca. I really don't care to know anything about Reynard and his family, but Regina feels different."

"This here is the oddest of circumstances," Martha remarked as she began pacing the floor in deep thought with her hands on her hips while looking down at the floor. "We got Dimples and Bianca, biological sisters just connecting. Their father all but vanished and—"

"I know what happened to the man," Mary sighed, finishing her twin's thought as she began to pace the floor opposite Martha, still holding her hands to hips with her head bowed. "Nobody won't tell what happened to Reynard but—"

"Bianca may figure it out." Martha and Mary spoke simultaneously. They shook their heads in unison as they passed one another headed in opposite directions, steadily pacing the floor.

"But even if she don't figure it out," Mary remarked. "If she doesn't figure it out, what's to stop her from—"

"Telling Regina that Siloam and Takoda had an affair," she and Martha replied in unison once more.

Martha nodded and said, "If she knows what's good for her —"

"She would leave." Mary interjected, finishing Martha's thoughts as the two eyed one another and shook their heads in agreement.

For the first time in my life, I got a chance to see Mary and Martha work in tandem. It was as if for a brief moment, they'd become one. They mirrored one another's movements and finished each other's thoughts with ease. Having watched these two, I saw something in Mary—she had a willingness to protect the family—and I liked what I saw. I knew how far Mary would go, though. She wouldn't pick up a gun and kill— at least I don't think she would. She was more like a spy to me with that easy-going, naïve spirit. That demeanor gave her permission to ask random questions and report back to the family on this Bianca chick. I could just look at Mary and Martha as they paced the floor and could tell that they were going to do all they could to prevent Bianca from ever learning the truth about Reynard Jacobs—cop or no cop.

"Look like y'all got it under control for now. If y'all need help let me know what I can do," I told my aunts.

They both looked over to me and nodded in unison. "I think we'll be okay," Martha remarked. "I'm gone stay here on the ranch and send Twiggy down to help Bay and T-Top run loads. We gone get to the bottom of this here."

"Naomi know about this woman?"

"Francine gave her a heads up earlier. She said let it play out. Bianca ain't kicking up no dust right about now, but she may. She just may," Martha ended as I nodded and headed towards the kitchen to have dinner before resting up for the night.

We all returned to the den and Victor was shaking his head with a face full of food. "Whoever did this here know what they hell they *doing*!" he emphasized.

"Thanks, man." Martha smiled.

"Stop taking false credit, Martha." Mary chuckled.

"See? I'm tryna earn some cool points and ya' killing my vibe, Mary." Martha replied as she opened a bottle of wine and poured Victor a glass.

"Thanks, Martha," Victor stated as he held the glass. "Now, about me checkin' you out? You can't blame a man for eyeing a thing of beauty. A work of art."

Martha like them young boys from what I heard. I ain't gone even say nothing because I know she know how to handle her business. Victor got a few ladies out in Arizona, but it's nothing serious, just like I suspect nothing too lasting to go down between him and Martha.

"He leaving with me yeh, Martha?"

"Not until I'm done with 'em, though, nephew."

"Lord," Mary dragged as she shook her head and poured a glass of wine.

"What, Mary?" Martha chuckled. "We all grown."

"He's younger than your niece, Martha," Mary said before sipping her wine.

"I know where all his blood flow with his age," Martha replied while nodding her head through a naughty smile. "Let me stop playing before this man think I'm for real."

I could see the disappointment in Victor's eyes as Martha walked off, being sure to add a bit more sexy to her walk. I sucked my teeth and shook my head at my dog. "She way out your league, player." I told him.

"That's what your mouth say. Just give this man some time," he told me as he resumed eating.

An hour or so later, Regina and Bianca came back down the stairs. Nothing seem to come out the deal as far as her mentioning that she knew Tak and Siloam had slept together and they seem to be getting along. When Regina told me Bianca was planning on sleeping over to her house, I put that on hold by asking her to play Spades with me, Martha and Victor. I didn't feel comfortable with Bianca leaving with my cousin knowing she was suspect of the family. For all I know, she could've had it in for Dimples.

I grabbed a bottle of wine and Mary and Martha scooped some glasses and we all headed over to the den and set up a table and turned on some music. Before long, we were busting decks and cutting suits. The whole time I had my eye on Bianca, watching her moves and listening to her convo, none of which I liked because she seemed phony than a mutherfucka.

Dimples couldn't see it, but this chick was trouble. Sooner or later, she was gone blow up my cousin spot by telling her what she knew about Tak and Siloam, the only question was when. I wasn't sure how that was gone go down, but I wasn't gone let Regina leave with this woman tonight, especially with Takoda being out on a run over to Tulsa to pick up a few junked cars. She can go when he get back tomorrow morning because I had plans on serving her plenty wine to keep her in the guest house this evening. That way, me Martha and Vic can all keep an eye on her and Bianca.

****

I awoke the following morning a little after eight after getting about five hours of sleep. Shit went well last night. I managed to get Dimples to consume four glasses of wine before it was all said and done. She tried to leave, but Martha

26

chimed in about what'd happened to the Langelys. She came outta left field with that one, but it worked. Dimples stayed put. While the women were playing Spades, me and Victor went up and checked Bianca's bags to make sure she didn't have a burner hidden somewhere. Call me crazy or whatever, but I ain't tryna get killed in my sleep, ya' dig? Especially by some skank off the streets looking for a come up on my people.

I walked out the den in my gym shorts and t-shirt and saw Victor moving about the kitchen. This dude here done made his self at home major. He was setting up a tray of coffee and had a couple of eggs boiling with some toast going. "What up, nephew-in-law?" he said to me with a smirk on his face.

"Stop playing with me, brer," I joked with him as I went and grabbed a couple of towels out the laundry room. "You checked on Dimples and Bianca for me, fam?"

"Yeah. They still knocked out," Victor said as he set up the breakfast tray. He looked around the island counter and grabbed one of Mary's roses and laid it across the boiled eggs and toast. "Now, if you excuse me, I'm going serve Martha breakfast in bed."

"Where you slept last night, dude? Last I remember you and Martha was chilling in the living room looking at some scrap books."

Victor looked at me like…*Where you think I slept?* while heading for the main staircase with the tray.

"Victor, what's taking so long with my breakfast, boy?" I heard Martha yell from the top of the stairs. "Nephew? I be in Martha room if ya' need me," he stated through laughter as he disappeared from sight.

That was fast. I knew Martha and Vic was hitting it off, but Auntie, Auntie wild…I shook my head with a smile over what'd gone down. Martha can handle her biz, though. And Victor my dog. I just wish they'd been more…fuck it…that's on them. I went on and washed up and dressed in some baggy jeans and a long sleeve Polo. By that time, Mary had awakened and was in the kitchen hooking up some grits and fish.

Before long, there was a knock on the door. I got up and answered and saw Tak standing on the porch. This the dude I been needing to talk to. I opened the door and stepped out onto the porch out in the cold. "You heard Bianca was in town, fam?"

"Nahh. I just got back from Tulsa. I was coming to pick up Tacoma when I saw Dimples truck over here." Tak answered as he looked at me surprised. "She said anything?" he then asked, almost whispering.

"She ain't say shit yet, whoa. But that's gone happen sooner or later, ya' dig? You gotta figure out what you gone do when it come up."

"I'm gone tell her today, Ben. That's all I got right now is the truth."

"The truth?" I asked Tak seriously. "You shouldn't say nothing until Bianca bring it up, brer. She might not even get a chance to say nothing. I think you should keep quiet on it."

"Really? You think that's the best move?"

"For now," I answered. Under any other circumstances, I would've been in agreement with Tak. I mean, had him and Siloam not fucked, we wouldn't even be in this jam. Reynard would still be alive and we wouldn't be tap-dancing with this shit and going back and forth on what to do with Bianca exactly. To be honest, I don't believe Bianca the police at all. She don't act like the law, but that's not saying much and we have to take her at her word for now until Francine can find out about the li'l chick. If we was to get rid of her and she was the actual police, this here place would be filled with law. They'd set up a substation right on the ranch tryna find out what happened to Bianca.

"I'm gone take your advice for the time being," Tak remarked, shaking me from my thoughts as he walked into the home.

"Bianca still in there, brer." I told him.

Tak paused and said, "I'm gone have to see her eventually. Might as well get that initial contact over with, right?"

I nodded and followed him inside to see how things would unfold when Bianca laid eyes on him for the first time since she'd arrived on the ranch.

"Coming out the academy four years ago my first radio call was an armed robbery in progress at a credit union in North Vegas, girl," I heard Bianca telling Dimples when me and Takoda walked into the kitchen. "Heyyy, brother-in-law!" she blurted out as she stopped talking and ran up and hugged him.

I walked on past them two and went over to the stove. "You want me to fix you something, Ben?" Mary asked me.

"Nah, I'm good, Auntie. I'm gone make a western omelet. You got some ham and bell pepper?"

"Can I have one, Cousin?" Bianca directed her question towards me.

I looked down at Mary then over to Bianca. "I'm a leave everything out for ya'," I told her.

"I'll make three for us," Takoda said, keeping things polite.

"Thanks, brother-in-law," Bianca smiled. "Regina letting me stay with y'all. I hope that's not a problem?"

"No it's not a problem at all," Takoda smiled to Bianca before walking off with a sullen look on his face.

"Good, because that woulda been messed up to deny family. Regina, what you do for fun, girl? This look like a town where people sleep around with one another. You don't run with them kind of people do you?"

"What?" Regina laughed as she set the table. "What makes you ask that crazy question? We, no...we don't do that in this family."

"Oh, I just was asking based on past experience 'cause you know daddy cheated on my momma with her best friend. That's why they divorced. He could never stay faithful. Like a lotta men in this world," Bianca spat as she eyed Takoda on the slick.

"That's not my problem," Dimples stated in a proud tone as she wrapped silverware up in cloth napkins. "And daddy told me that him and your mother was just having problems. He never said that's what it was. Enough of all that infidelity talk. Finish telling me about your first radio call."

I could see Bianca's angle right away. Boy, she was gone torment the hell out Takoda and tease him on the slick by making subtle implications about the time he and Siloam slept together. Unless she said something outright, Takoda may survive this deal. Can't say the same for Bianca, though; because I know if she play games like that with Siloam after knowing what Martha told me she did to Reynard, it's gone be a totally different outcome because Siloam was willing to kill to keep her business from gettin' out. If Bianca knew what was good for her, she'd take her propaganda and blow town, or at the very least shut up about shit. She looked like the type that gotta learn the hard way, though, so we just gone have to wait and see what happen with that there situation.

CHAPTER FOUR

SAVE YOURSELF

An alabaster white Mercedes S-class had just pulled up to the police headquarters in downtown Oklahoma City just a few minutes after Tak had arrived on the ranch back up in Ponca City. Tonto Jamison sat behind the wheel of his luxurious ride as he dialed a number. When the line picked up, the voice on the other end asked, "Son, where are you? I've been worried sick!"

"I'm about to turn myself in, momma. I fucked up," Tonto glumly stated.

"Did you talk to your brother?"

"Kahlil ain't fuckin' with me!" Tonto barked. "What, what I'm gone say to him? What he gone say to me?" he angrily asked as he patted the leather coat covering his chest.

"You should at least apologize, Tonto. Apologize to Kahlil and that family."

"Ma, in this life? For what I did? An apology ain't gone cut it. The safest place for me is behind bars right now."

"For what you're charged with you may never come home," Miss Jamison remarked sadly as she readied herself for work over to the entertainment complex the Holland family owned up in Ponca City. "I can talk to them for you. Not Dawk or Naomi, but there's someone I can talk to."

"You do what you want to. I'm going get this over with,

31

though. I have an idea how I can help myself get out this jam."

"I get off at seven. You be sure to call me." Miss Jamison stated before ending the call.

Disappointed would best describe forty-three year-old Hakiba Jamison as she moved about the single wide three bedroom trailer, but the feeling she carried wasn't new to her. Ever since she'd left her estranged husband behind in Muskogee, Oklahoma eighteen years ago, Tonto had been nothing but a malcontented child that somehow managed to make the wrong decision each and every time he approached the figurative fork in the road of life.

When confronted with a moral dilemma, Hakiba's oldest son almost always made the wrong choice. Like the time he'd obtained a job at a local gas station in Ponca City his junior year of high school. He was the town favorite during that time, appearing in the local newspaper on a weekly basis, and his highlight reel was being played every Friday night during the news' sports broadcast.

When the 2001 football season ended, word got around that Tonto was looking for a job. The manager of a small convenience store hired him before he'd even filled out the application. Two months later, Tonto was fired because he'd begun giving away free gas to his football teammates who had cars, and free beer to a few of the girls around town in exchange for sexual favors. The gas station had turned into a local hangout not even a week after Tonto had taken the job. Small time dealers soon began peddling weed and meth right in front the store, and the restroom had turned into a shooting gallery and romp room.

Tiva had even had sex in the store once with Tonto during that time. It wasn't her proudest moment, either, but that's another story entirely. The week before Tonto was fired, a sophomore student was stabbed to death inside the store after confronting a woman high on meth and had accused the woman of shooting up dope inside the bathroom. The meth addict went into fit of rage and stabbed the high schooler over fifty times. It was Ponca City's most tragic homicide to date.

For Hakiba, the only right choice Tonto had made was to play football; something he was good at, but he still found a way to foul up his reputation by constantly getting into fights and fueling rumors of him being a drug dealer. He'd carried the bad boy image so well, that by the time he reached NFL potential, he was damaged goods. After sinking his own career in sports, Hakiba watched as her oldest son took to the streets. She knew all what Tonto was involved in, but she never figured he'd go so far as to kidnap one of the daughters belonging to the wealthiest family in Ponca City, and one of the most powerful families in the state with a violent history that was known around town.

Fearing for her son's life, Hakiba sought to make the peace. The petite, light brown-skinned Oklahoman with short, black hair finished dressing, climbed into her minivan and drove towards town. She didn't feel comfortable approaching the family on the ranch, so she sought out an easier route that would hopefully bring about a peaceful resolution over her sons' transgressions.

****

Meanwhile, down at police headquarters, Tonto was busy talking to a federal agent. He was wanted on a kidnapping and attempted murder charge, both of which were federal charges under Oklahoma law, and the story he was telling, was much different than what'd actually gone down, but the law had nothing to go on at the time except his unsolicited testimony.

"You were just the driver, Tonto?" a lone federal agent approaching retirement age asked as the two sat inside a small interview room. A lone deputy of Native American descent stood by in a corner listening to the conversation as he kept an eye on Tonto.

"That was all I did, man," Tonto stated. "See, Chablis? The dude that got killed that night when he got ran over by Kimi Dawkins? He, he told me we was just gone ride over there and he was gone talk to his girl Koko Dawkins," he remarked while tapping the table with the fingertips of his shackled hand.

"Koko Dawkins. The one you and your crew tried to

kidnap," the federal agent remarked as he jotted down notes.

"That's not my crew, man. And I ain't have nothing to do with no kidnapping. That was on Chablis, and that boy Chauncey Gainey."

"We got a shooting victim named Chauncey Gainey over to Saint Anthony Hospital. Did you know that?"

"Yeah, I dropped him off over there the night it went down. Chablis and Chauncey came running out the house with this girl Koko and put her in the car. Chablis hopped in and pointed the gun at me and told me to drive. So I drove."

"Umm, hmm," the federal agent remarked dryly, not believing a word of Tonto's statement as he'd gotten a full report from Kimi Dawkins during an interview in the lobby of OU Medical Center the night her sister Shima 'Spoonie' Dawkins had been shot. "Did you ever enter the Dawkins residence?"

"I never walked into that house, sir." Tonto stated in all sincerity. "I was in the car listening to music when they ran outta there with Koko and threw her in the car."

"What you're telling me is not adding up, Tonto," the hoarse-voiced, bald-headed slender Caucasian remarked as he eyed his suspect with apprehension. "According to the report, you were the ring leader."

"Chablis set the whole thing up, man! I knew nothing about it!" Tonto pleaded.

"The ole pin the rap on the dead guy routine," the federal agent remarked matter-of-factly. "You may have turned yourself in, Jamison, but that just made my job that much easier. I don't believe a word you've spoken this morning, and if you don't give me a bone to gnaw on soon, you'll never see the light of the day."

Tonto leaned back in the chair with his hands still cuffed to the table. "I can tell you that Gainey was the one who shot Spoonie after Koko rolled out my car, and my brother Kahlil shot Gainey while I was driving off. I didn't do no shooting. I was only the driver."

"Kahlil shot Chauncey," the federal agent remarked. "The Oklahoma State star football player is involved in a shooting is what you're telling me?"

"Everybody saying this chick Jordan Whispers shot Chauncey. They only saying that because the gun was registered to her. But Kahlil was doing the shooting and I saw it," Tonto admitted. "And I saw the bullet Chauncey fired into Spoonie. Now, that boy got a rap sheet longer than the end of a Kung Fu flick. I'm willing to get on the stand against that fool for what he did. That gotta count for something."

"It's good enough to get you a bond," the federal agent remarked. "You'll be placed on house arrest, but I'll need an address."

"A Bond?" Tonto fretted. "I, sir, I don't want a bond. I'm good where I'm at. I rather stay here until I go to trial. But if you want me to testify against Chauncey you gotta promise me something in return."

The federal agent ignored Tonto's plea to remain behind bars and said, "Of course you won't walk scot free, but if I can match fingerprints to the tech nine that was fired by Kahlil, and the gun Chauncey used to shoot Spoonie, I can get you ten years and you'll be out in six and a half. In return, you'll help me put Chauncey Gainey away for life. And I'm a Sooner fan, so taking down Kahlil will be the icing on my cake as I sail off into the land of retirement."

"We got a deal," Tonto remarked somberly. "Look man, I missed breakfast. Anyway I can get a meal? I mean, for my unsolicited testimony?"

"We can manage that. Deputy? Can you escort Tonto Jamison to a cell? There's a diner up the street. Get 'em some breakfast. Make him comfortable and whatnot the duration of his stay."

"I'll get him processed and changed out, but I have another detail I can't miss within the hour," the deputy remarked as he unshackled Tonto's hands from the table and secured them behind his back.

"Oh boy," the elderly agent remarked as he ran his veiny hands over his wrinkled face. "Where's good help when you need it? Change him out and I'll send out for his breakfast."

Tonto was all smiles on the inside. The lies he'd told was mixed with plenty truth and were becoming more and more believable was his belief. And his testifying against Chauncey would mean nothing. He was always a hothead and Tonto knew it. Going in, he never had intentions on harming Koko. When she rolled out of his car, he was prepared to let her go, only Chauncey had gotten trigger happy and started busting at everybody and had inadvertently shot Spoonie in the process. The entire plan had ended in a huge disaster and Tonto was now trying to save his own skin. And the only way for him to do that, in his mind, was to sell everyone involved down the river, including his own brother.

After changing out into an orange jump suit and being taken to a private cell that had a TV, Tonto settled in with a Waffle House breakfast consisting of grilled chicken, grits and hash browns. There in jail he knew he was out of harm's way. The Holland family would not be able to touch him as long as he was locked up, which was why he refused a bond hearing, but the law is the law. And unbeknownst to Tonto, his cooperating with the feds based on the story he was telling, would backfire in a way he'd never expected.

CHAPTER FIVE

THE GOOD WIVES CLUB

Downtown Ponca City was just beginning to stir awake shortly after nine in the morning, a little under an hour after Hakiba had talked to her son Tonto. Main Street was where an assortment of privately-owned businesses lined a four-lane street with wide sidewalks on either side. Cars traveling into the shopping district parked right out in front of the one and two story decades-old buildings that lined the avenue. In the middle of the sleepy town's small business district, on the east side of the street, sat a two story brown-bricked building with four large glass panes, two on the first floor and two on the second floor, and there was a hanging sign out front that read, *Holland Antiques and Interior Designs.*

Holland Antiques and Interior Designs was Oneika Brackens and AquaNina Mishaan's businesses that had been started by their respective lovers, Dawk and Bena Holland. The two had started out in separate buildings, but soon merged when it became clear that many of the people purchasing new homes on the town's budding east side often perused both their businesses to have their newly-built homes decorated.

Twenty-three year-old Oneika Brackens was an excellent interior design specialist. From her second floor office, the brown-haired, brown-eyed, high-yellowed-skinned Creek Indian and Caucasian young woman held presentations for first-time homeowners. The Associate's degree in Interior Design she'd obtained from Pioneer Technology Center was serving her well in life. Barely two years in, Oneika Brackens had become the top home décor consultant and interior designer in and around Ponca City.

Twenty-four year-old AquaNina Mishaan, meanwhile, was a force to be reckoned with when it came to valuable antiques and artifacts. From her first floor showroom, she would sell old western relics ranging from furniture to plates, and even old diaries and pictures once owned by pioneers of the west who were claiming stake to the area long before the Oklahoma land rush of 1889.

In a predominately white town, AquaNina and Oneika's business was often frequented by many a Caucasian who had a love of old relics, and many of the Native Americans who lived in the city often sought to have their heirlooms appraised and put up for sale or auction. Some of the items fetched upwards of $40,000 dollars on the open market. No matter the sale price, AquaNina would always pull down a ten percent commission for negotiating the deal. Her skill didn't come from a college like Oneika, to the contrary, AquaNina Mishaan just had a natural ability to recognize the value of vintage items that captured the hearts and minds of collectors from across the country. She and Oneika were pulling in just under a quarter million dollars a year with their business venture and were on an even keel.

AquaNina was setting up the store's window display with carved buffalo horns and decades old topaz neck clutches when she eyed Hakiba's Windstar minivan pulling up out front. She called for Oneika as she walked over and unlocked the front door.

Oneika, now five months pregnant with Dawk's child and showing, eased down the staircase and went and stood beside AquaNina just as Hakiba walked into the business. "Can we help you?" she asked Tonto's mother in a kind, but cautious manner.

"Yes," Hakiba responded in a stern, but respectful manner. "I was wondering if there was a way for my family and the Holland family to come to some kind of a resolution over what Tonto has done."

Oneika and AquaNina looked at one another perplexed. Neither viewed themselves as having the authority to speak on what'd gone down with Spoonie, let alone come to some form of 'resolution' on behalf of the family. "Can I ask why you're coming to us, Miss Jamison?" Oneika inquired. "We have no say so on what the family decides to do."

"But I know it's Dawk and Bay that I should be worried about, Oneika. I'm not…crazy. Me and a whole lot of other people around town know what it is that your family does for a living. They kill people. That's why Doss was killed in Missouri. I don't wanna see anything happen to my son. Spoonie lived. And my son didn't pull the trigger."

"Then who did?" Oneika asked as AquaNina stood beside her in silence.

"If I tell you, what can you do to help me save my son's life?"

Oneika shifted her weight and said, "There's nothing I can do except relay a message to my fiancé."

"And, and we don't know what if anything Dawk and Bay are up to. It may be nothing," AquaNina chimed in.

"Not with that family. There's always something." Hakiba retorted.

"But if Dawk and Bay were planning on doing something to Tonto they would—"

"They wouldn't think of doing such a thing." Oneika interrupted, realizing AquaNina was on the verge of talking a little too much.

"Let her finish her thoughts," Hakiba said to Oneika. The woman was viewing AquaNina as the weakest link and was trying to get her to reveal what, if anything she knew concerning the family's plans for Tonto. "She obviously has more to say."

"She's done talking," Oneika declared as she stepped in front of AquaNina. "Like I say, the family wouldn't think of doing such a thing to Tonto. If they wanted to hurt him, they would've done it already. And at the very least, they would've fired you from the entertainment complex but they haven't. They're letting the police handle matters. Tonto's fate is in the hands of the law, not the Holland family. Now, can I help you with anything else this morning?"

Hakiba understood at that moment that she would not get any answers to her questions from Oneika or AquaNina. Oneika was mum on the matter and AquaNina was following lead. She left the shop with an incredulous feeling, one that was telling her that her oldest son was on borrowed time and she was powerless to do anything about it.

Feeling she had no other choice, Hakiba rode over to Kay County Sheriff's Office and requested to speak to Sheriff Glenn Nimitz. Nimitz had a rapport with the Jamison family going back several years. He was a huge high school football fan and had supported Tonto early on when he began playing for Ponca City High School. Nimitz was the man who'd kept Tonto's jacket clean in his youth. Auto theft charges were reduced to joyriding. Charges of grand larceny were rescinded and reduced to petty theft. Because of Nimitz, Tonto was allowed free reign over the streets of Ponca City. When he moved on to Oklahoma State, however, Nimitz was unable to protect Tonto from his own recklessness. Through it all, he still had an affinity for the lad he'd grown fond of over time.

Hakiba had an ally in Nimitz and she knew it. She waited in the lobby of the medium-sized, marble-floored police headquarters until Sheriff Nimitz, a burly, bearded man of sixty years standing 6'1", and weighing two hundred and seventy-five pounds, walked out into the lobby. "Miss Jamison? What brings you here at this early hour?"

Hakiba rubbed her hands together and said, "I think my son's life is in danger over this thing with Naomi Holland-Dawkins' daughter Shima. Tonto didn't do anything and I don't wanna lose him. I don't wanna lose him," the woman cried.

"I heard about what Tonto did down there," the sheriff remarked. "Whether he was involved or not it serves the Holland family right. They may have the town's people fooled, but not me. How can I help you?"

"Can we talk in private? I have some information I want to share with you about the Holland family."

"Well now," Sheriff Nimitz smiled as thoughts of past dealings with the Holland family crept into his mind.

His name was Garland Smith. A pack rat-of-a man and a Vietnam veteran who wanted nothing more than to farm catfish and work land he'd purchased that abutted Kaw Lake on the east side of town. Smith had complained to Sheriff Nimitz about the family next door stealing his fish back in September of 1997. The old man was too little too late, however, because he had no fish left in the pond he'd erected, and even though Sheriff Nimitz had staked out the land, there was never a sign of a thief on the property after the report had been filed.

Garland Smith was found dead inside his home in January of 2003. Autopsy reports stated he'd died of thirst after suffering a broken hip from a fall inside his home. Shortly thereafter, the family he'd been having animosity with since the day he'd purchased the land, the Holland family, had obtained his property. Garland Smith's death may have been ruled accidental, but one couldn't tell Sheriff Nimitz that the man hadn't met his demise at the hands of the Holland-Dawkins family someway somehow. And because he and Garland were friends that had served together during the Vietnam War, Sheriff Nimitz took it upon himself to hear what Hakiba Jamison had to say, if only to settle an old score for a man who'd been his friend.

Unbeknownst to all, the pact that Hakiba Jamison and Sheriff Glenn Nimitz would forge on this early morning in late January of 2009 would eventually set the wheels in motion for a future violent act that would shock Ponca City to its core.

CHAPTER SIX

TWO WAYS TO PLAY IT

Spoonie had been in recovery down at OU Medical Center the past three days and all was well with the seventeen year-old who was now sedated and resting peacefully in her recovery room with her mother at her side.

Naomi sat calmly in a chair beside her daughter's bed a couple of hours after Hakiba Jamison had talked to Sheriff Nimitz. The room was dim, save for a lamp she'd placed on the sink inside the bathroom to provide some light as she remained at her daughter's side peeling the pages of one of eight photo albums she'd had retrieved from Ponderosa at her request the day before. The picture books were handcrafted leather bound albums that had the names of her beloved eight inscribed on the front and chronicled their years from birth to the present.

All of Naomi's children were in and out of each other's picture books, but in each book that held their respective names, each child was the star. The albums told a story of progression, some more impactful than others; like Bena Holland's album, which chronicled the story of a daughter who was caring and kind, but also revengeful and sneaky in her youth. Hers took a dark turn once images of her laying in recovery inside of Ponderosa were added to her picture book. Looking back, one may have seen it coming with Bay given the countless pictures of her holding various assault weapons and rifles the family owned, but one would have to know her full story to envision and understand why she'd been shot and nearly killed.

Tiva's photo album was identical to Bay's right up until the time AquaNina Mishaan started to appear in Bay's album. Her story broke off into her talking on the phone and dressing up to go to the movies with different boys around town. There was even a picture of Tonto in T-Top's album on the night she'd gone to Junior Prom with him, which was the same night she'd given him her virginity. A husband named Junior Cernigliaro was in her picture story, but his images faded away in the year 2006 and were now dominated by her family along with a set of identical twins named Malaysia and Malara. Hers was the story of a daughter who adored her family, took risks and lived a life of loyalty to those who earned her trust.

Kimi and Koko's albums showed their progression from that of debating, yet thoughtful sisters who meddled in all of their siblings' affairs and had to be right at all times. Over time, they matured into that of settled, sophisticated prima donnas that were mathematical geniuses. Birthday parties dominated their albums, happy times, as they were the most fun-loving of Naomi's eight.

Dawk's album was that of a young gentleman. He was often in pictures with his father, either working on some home project, or with an occasional shotgun draped across his shoulder while sitting atop a horse. His latter pictures showed a man about his business, an alpha male with a family on the horizon with Oneika Brackens now filling many pages of his picture book.

Walee had a picture book that was filled with moments that made one laugh as they looked at the images and recalled days long passed. An investigative lad, many of the pages inside his picture book were filled with him holding mysterious bugs, baby birds, amphibians and small mammals that he found while exploring the land. Images of him scaring Spoonie and Tyke with his biological discoveries lined page after page. Other pages showed the three sharing meals, and many had Walee out in front leading his youngest sisters along like a proud Boy Scout. This was the one photo album where Spoonie and Tyke began to emerge onto the scene and one could easily tell that these three were joined at the hip.

Spoonie and Tyke's picture albums, when one opened either book, had an aurora of innocence personified that reeked of Teddy bears, blood hound puppies and softball. Identical doll outfits for these chocolate, Afro-sporting beauties, who could melt hearts without having to speak a word.

Flipping through the pages of Spoonie's album, Naomi's heart grew fond as she eyed images of her daughter standing in her Oklahoma State uniform holding onto a bat that was pointed to the ground. Her eyes watered under the soft light of the recovery room and the steady beep of her daughter's heart monitor. Like the many albums before hers, Spoonie's album reflected pain more than once. Naomi's eight all had pictures that showed their pain on the day their father was buried; it was the one moment of agony they all shared, but only Bay and Spoonie had pain inflicted upon them that was captured for all times.

"Lord, I thank you for not taking the innocent and blameless from my life," Naomi prayed silently just as the door to Spoonie's room was eased open accompanied by a soft tap.

"Momma?" Dawk asked lowly.

"Yes, son. Come on in, love," Naomi replied softly as she wiped her eyes and closed the picture book.

Dawk entered the room and walked over and knelt down beside Naomi and eyed Spoonie resting on her back with her arms at her side. "How she doing?" he asked in a near whisper as he reached out and touched Spoonie's hand.

"She's resting comfortably," Naomi responded in a tender voice as the monitor kicked up a few paces and quickly returned to normal. "Doctor Duchene says she'll have to remain off her feet for about four to six months so as not aggravate her pelvis. She can't put any pressure on her legs during that time."

"She get to get carried around. She gone love that," Dawk chuckled.

Naomi looked down at her son as she sat Spoonie's picture

book on the nightstand beside the bed while reaching out her other hand to run it over his thick head of hair. There was a look of contentment on her face as she smiled down at her firstborn with admiration. Having him around was such comfort. "I wonder over your father's feelings if he were here at this exact moment."

"I imagine he would be feeling rage," Dawk remarked in a low tone as he kept his eyes on Spoonie. "That's what I feel every time I think about what went down."

"At the outset he may be, but not now," Naomi whispered. "If he was here at this moment, he'd be where you are. Kneeling beside me and watching his daughter in reverence and thanking God that she survived. You're a good proxy. You and Ben both."

"I got big shoes to fill," Dawk remarked as he picked up Spoonie's hand and kissed it before standing to his feet. He went over to a corner and turned on the warm water and wet a towel and walked back over to Spoonie's bed. "I got some news to relay," he said as he patted his sister's forehead and cheeks tenderly and handed a small bag to his mother.

"What is it?" Naomi asked as she pulled an orange Oklahoma State softball cap from the bag and looked at all the signatures adorning the wool material.

"Got word from a deputy working a detail in the lobby that Tonto turned himself in a couple of hours ago. He got booked with one count of attempted kidnapping and one count of attempted murder. Chauncey Gainey is the other guy involved. He being treated over to Saint Anthony Hospital and gone be booked with attempted murder and kidnapping."

"We need them on the streets," Naomi replied as she eyed the bandages around Spoonie's stomach and handed Dawk the hat. "We have no one here that can touch him in the manner in which we reached out to Bahdoon LuQman in Illinois."

"I know," Dawk said as he took the hat from his mother and placed it at Spoonie's side. "The entire softball team signed this hat yesterday," he then added. "A few of the girls gave it to me when I went and checked on her and Tyke's dorm room apartment last night."

"Did Tonto offer a statement?"

"This deputy told me Tonto willing to take the stand on Chauncey for a ten year deal that'll have 'em out in six. Chauncey got a long rap sheet and he won't get a bond. He looking at life, but Tonto another story. He gone get a bond according to the deputy. If he do, it's two ways we can play it."

Naomi knew what Dawk was getting at when he spoke of 'two ways to play it'. Nothing could be done about Chauncey as the family hadn't the reach inside the jails. As powerful a family they were, for the Holland family, killing Chauncey in Oklahoma would be too much of a risk. Naomi's gut was telling her that she shouldn't corrupt the system in her own backyard in the manner in which the family had gotten to Bahdoon 'Q-man' LuQman up in Illinois, but Tonto could be touched, if only he were on the streets. And the way Naomi saw it, Chauncey wouldn't even be a factor in the big scheme of things had not Tonto set the wheels in motion.

"Let the courts deal with Gainey. Get Tonto," was her order just as Spoonie stirred awake.

"Momma?" the wounded seventeen year-old called out weakly.

"I'm here, baby," Naomi remarked lovingly as she placed the back of her hand to Spoonie's cheek. "How're you feeling now, love? Is the pain medication working?"

"Yes, but," Spoonie swallowed hard and said, "I'm thirsty. And where's everybody?" she panted.

Dawk picked up the hat given to him by Oklahoma State's softball team. "The family been here the whole time, li'l sis. Even your friends on the softball team," he remarked as he set the softball cap near Spoonie's left hand. "They gave me this hat to give to you. Said they dedicating the whole season to ya'."

"After I thank them, I'm going to tell them to just play. I hate it here," Spoonie answered in a low tone before closing her eyes and drifting off to sleep once more.

Spoonie had awaken the night before, twelve hours before the affects of her forty-eight hour induced coma was to wear off. During that time, she was able to see the family and friends that were on hand briefly. They'd gone in in groups of three and wished her well, only able to spend a few minutes to allow others time before she dozed off again. Spoonie couldn't remember talking to anyone, however, as she was highly-medicated, but her early awakening, and now her having the ability to express what was ailing her exactly, signified to all involved, including her caregiver, Doctor Duchene, that she was on her way to a full recovery. All she needed was time to rest and heal.

"I'll get one of the nurses to give her another IV," Dawk remarked as he headed for the door.

"Dawk," Naomi called out.

Dawk looked back at Naomi. "Yeah, momma?"

"Ben called and said he be in within the hour. That thing with Tonto? Get it done," she commanded for a second and final time. Dawk merely nodded as he headed out the door to secure a nurse to tend to his wounded sister.

CHAPTER SEVEN

THE HUNT IS ON

I'd made it over to OU Medical Center just after the noon hour. When me and Victor walked into the recovery unit we saw Walee and his crew milling about the lobby area. Looking at all these youngsters sitting around remind me of the day me, Oscar and Jason went after Damenga. This here bunch wasn't on that level, though, and I'm glad they not given what happened to me and my boys.

"Cuz? What it is?" Dawk spoke out as he walked up the hall holding onto six bottles of sodas.

"I got some news, fam. We need ta' talk."

"Follow me back downstairs," Dawk remarked as he passed the drinks around to everybody.

We rode the elevator down to the lobby and Dawk walked over to this security guard I'd seen on the way in. "You got a minute?" he asked the man.

"Yeah, bro. What you need?" the security guard asked.

The three of us stepped off into the hospital parking lot and climbed inside one of the Suburbans. "That boy Tonto turned his self in this morning," Dawk said to me as he started the car and turned on the heat. "This here security guard gave me the low down on dude."

"Tonto gave up some info?"

"He saying this dude Chauncey Gainey was in on it," Dawk said to me. "Chauncey got shot. As far as the law know, Jordan was the one who did the shooting, but Tonto willing to testify that he saw Kahlil shoot Chauncey."

"We need that gun," I told Dawk as I sat in the backseat.

Dawk looked over to the security guard and handed him a grip. "We done, fam. Thanks for the information."

"Anything else?" the guard asked us as he reached for the door handle.

"Nah, we done for now." Dawk told him. "If I need you again I'll be in touch. And if you ever need a favor or got more info you get up with me, alright?" Dawk went silent as the cop/security guard nodded and climbed out of the ride.

When dude cleared out I turned to Dawk. "What's up with that? We need that gun outta evidence, fam," I told him.

Dawk chuckled and said, "I know you and your people back in the N.O. used illegal burners back in the day. We do too, but that tech-nine registered to Jordan. Her finger prints the only one on it."

"That's what's up. Think she gone be able to get on the stand and tell a story?"

"If it get down to it she would. She won't have to, though—not if we get rid of Tonto before his sentencing date."

"He got a bond?"

"Yeah. He just need somebody to bail him out. His momma ain't got that kind of money."

"But we do," I told Dawk as I nodded my head, now fully understanding the plan he was putting together.

"I'm gone be leaving for Mexico in a couple of days," Dawk remarked, shaking me from my thoughts.

"And I gotta get ready for this trip to the Cayman Island," I stated.

"While that's happenin' we can get Lee to do our friend Tonto a favor'." Dawk stated as we began running down exactly how we was gone get at Tonto Jamison.

CHAPTER EIGHT
POKING AND PRODDING

"This herbal tea will make you all better," Sergeant Sandra Cordova said to Special Agent Laddy Norcross as she sat on the edge of the bed inside his suite inside the Millennium Hotel in downtown Saint Louis. It was two days after Naomi had given Dawk the order to take down Tonto Jamison.

Laddy was in the process of recovering from a terrible cold that had sidelined him for nearly a week. Sandra was there every step of the way to coax him back to health and now the two were set to embark on what they both viewed as the case of a lifetime. The federal agent sat up in the bed and took the tea from Sandra. The voluptuous Hispanic woman couldn't help but to admire his biceps and broad shoulders cutting through his white silk wife beater as he leaned to one side and took a sip.

"I wanna thank you for being a good host, Miss Cordova," Laddy remarked as he set the cup down and flipped the covers off his legs.

"Think nothing of it," Sandra replied. "SpongeBob pajama pants?" she then giggled lightly as Laddy stood up and stretched.

"My wife brought me and my son matching sleeping pants for Christmas. Little fella's not even a year old and she dresses him up in all these costumes and takes tons of pictures. She *insists*," Laddy emphasized as he went over to the closet and pulled down a dark brown silk suit, "she insists that the three of us dress alike in our night time apparel. I guess I've become accustomed to the ritual, even when they aren't around."

"I have a morning ritual too," Sandra remarked.

"And that would be?"

Sandra smiled and shook her head while looking away from Laddy. "You're a married man," she stated as she smiled back over to Laddy. "I wouldn't dare."

Laddy merely smirked as he headed for the bathroom.

"Throw me your suit! I'll iron it for you, agent!" Sandra called out.

"It's already pressed! Thank you anyhow!" Laddy yelled out loud before closing the bathroom door.

Sandra sighed and laid back in the spot where Laddy once lay. *"Why are all the good ones taken?"* she asked herself as she sniffed the pillow where Laddy's head once rested an inhaled his manly scent.

Twenty minutes later, Laddy emerged from the bathroom freshly shaved and dressed. He walked into the room and saw Sandra snoozing where he once slept. He stared at the woman in silence for several lingering seconds, admiring her beauty and thick frame. Her breasts moved up and down at a gentle pace and there was a look of contentment on her face as she slumbered in street clothes that consisted of a beige loose-fitting business suit, white blouse and black ankle-length boots with a shoulder holster carrying her government-issued .40 Glock.

"It's all business, agent." Laddy said to himself just before he kicked the edge of the mattress with his wing tips. "We're on the clock, Sergeant!" he stated loudly.

Sandra stirred awake and smiled over to Laddy. The dream she'd had of the two of them being intimate left her happy and ready to face the day. "Where're we headed first?" she asked as she jumped up from the bed and grabbed her coat.

"Going see the doctorrrrr," Laddy sang while laughing.

"Okay, Mister Kool Moe Dee," Sandra quipped. "You all right, agent," she added as she gathered her purse and tailed Laddy out the door.

****

Doctor Obadiah Wickenstaff was sitting in his corner office inside Mercy Hospital lining up his staff for an upcoming surgical procedure on a patient by the name of Guadalupe Cruz when his secretary tapped on the door and eased it open. "Doctor Wickenstaff? There's a Laddy Norcross and a Sandra Cordova here to see you?"

"Norcross? Cordova?" Doctor Wickenstaff pondered as he checked his itinerary. "I have no one scheduled by that name."

"They're FBI and State Highway Patrol, sir," the secretary remarked. "Is everything okay? Should I let them in or send them away?"

Right away Doctor Wickenstaff's mind began to race. His latest patient, Guadalupe Cruz, was having her final procedure paid out-of-pocket by his friend of nearly two years, Naomi Holland. The good doctor knew from times past that Naomi and her family were involved in illegal activity, only he didn't know any of the intricate details of said actions. All he knew was that the family paid handsomely on tax free money in the low six figure range. So what if a couple of detectives came poking and prodding. As far as he was concerned, the law had nothing on him. And if they did, he was definitely going to find out how much they knew, if they knew anything at all to begin with.

"No, no. Send them in," Doctor Wickenstaff finally told his secretary as he closed his notepad and stood up behind his marble desk. He waited patiently as a brown-haired, blue-eyed man in a dark brown suit and black trench coat being followed by a Hispanic woman in a beige business suit and black three-quarter length cashmere coat walked into his office.

Laddy eyed the slender Native American standing before him in a black silk suit with a stethoscope draping his neck and was immediately impressed. In his assessment, the doctor before him was a man of honesty and would readily answer any question he posed. "Good morning, doctor," he said to Obadiah as he and Sandra walked up to the man's desk.

"Morning, umm?"

"I'm Special Agent Laddy Norcross and this is Sergeant Sandra Cordova from the Missouri Highway Patrol," Laddy clarified as he put his badge on display. "We're here to ask about a Bena Holland?"

"Bena Holland was a patient of mine back in two thousand seven. She received a shell fragment to her skull. I remember because her family agreed to allow MIT technicians to conduct a study on patients that'd received brain trauma. Can I ask what this is about?"

"We want to know what you know about Bena Holland. What, if anything you can tell us that led to her being shot that night back in two thousand seven?" Laddy asked.

"Forgive me, Agent Norcross, but all I do here at Mercy Hospital is treat the patients that are brought in. There isn't much that I can tell you about the patient Bena Holland except for the fact that she was injured in a shooting. Saint Louis is one of the most violent cities in the nation and I've saved many lives. Never have I asked the reasons why a person was harmed. I file the necessary reports with the proper authorities and operate within the realms of the law so there isn't much more I can tell you about Bena Holland. And according to federal law, a patient's health records are unredeemable unless one has a warrant."

"Are you protecting the Holland family, Doctor Obadiah?" Sandra asked bluntly as she moved to stand before Laddy. "Because we have every right to believe—"

"That Bena Holland is Naomi Holland's daughter!" Laddy interrupted as he placed a hand to Sandra's bosom and nudged her back. "That's all we want to know right now. Is Bena Holland Naomi's daughter, Doctor Wickenstaff?"

"That she is," Obadiah agreed.

"Excuse my colleague. She has a certain itch that needs to be scratched," Laddy remarked as he eyed Sandra harshly.

"That's a sexist remark, guy." Sandra retorted with a smirk. "No offense to the true statement, though." Laddy again stared Sandra down and she relented as she turned and walked over to Doctor Wiceknstaff's bookshelf. "Okay, okay. Carry on," she remarked as she picked up a medical magazine and began flipping through the pages. "Men," she said under her breath with her back turned.

"Thank you," Laddy replied while shaking his head and giving a slight smirk over to his impromptu partner and budding sidekick's backside. "Now, Doctor Wickenstaff," he stated as he got back into focus. "Have you been in contact with Naomi Holland since Bena Holland's release?"

"I was in contact on occasion," Doctor Wickenstaff replied. "But it was only to make sure my former patient had recovered completely. Bena is no longer part of the MIT study, which ended over a year ago and we have had no further communication since that time."

"And you are certain that you haven't had any contact with the Holland family in over a year. You're certain of that fact? You haven't forgotten a moment have you, doctor?" Laddy asked seriously while staring into Wickenstaff's eyes.

Obadiah remained silent. After several seconds, Sandra began humming the theme music the Jeopardy game show.

"Quiet!" Laddy grimaced as he eyed the doctor and stepped closer. "Are you sure about your answer, Doctor Wickenstaff?" he asked sternly as he placed his hands on his hips and eyed the physician. "Because if I find out that you've lied to me today? I *will* come back with a warrant and confiscate your computers and every single document you have on record. I'll go so far as to subpoena your bank records and every phone call you've made going back three years. If there're dots for me to connect? I will find them. And when I take down the Holland family? Count on being a part of the chain gang."

"I have not had any more contact with the Holland family since the day Bena Holland was released from the MIT study. I did my job and moved on." Doctor Wickenstaff adamantly stated.

Laddy stared Doctor Wickenstaff down for nearly a solid minute. "Okay!" he finally quipped as he turned and headed for the office doors with his hands still on his hips. "Sandra? Let's leave the good doctor be."

Sandra rolled her eyes as she sashayed away from Obadiah's bookshelf. "You know he's being dishonest with us don't you?" she asked once the two were outside of the doctor's office.

"I know that, Cordova, but we haven't grounds for a search warrant. What are we gonna do? Tie the guy up and force him to tell us what he knows?"

"I wouldn't be against it. What about you?" Sandra playfully asked. Laddy looked over to his impromptu partner without smiling as the two left the office entirely. "It was just a joke, Laddy. You need to loosen up," she quickly defended. "What's our next move?"

"I looked into the neighborhood where Bena Holland was shot back in two thousand seven while in the hotel. There's a deli there," Laddy stated as he pressed the elevator button. "Let's have us some breakfast and watch the neighborhood. See if we can pick up on anything," he ended just as the elevator doors opened.

Obadiah, meanwhile, was inside his office pondering the visit he'd just received from Laddy and Sandra. He knew he was being dishonest, but the Holland family was a meal ticket. He hadn't forgotten the payout he received for treating a man who'd been shot in the spleen named Victor back in 2008, and he knew, given the family's occupation, that he could very well be called on again. With the intent of keeping his meal ticket valid, he began searching his desk drawers for a phone number he had tucked away for safekeeping.

****

"I've had a dekko at the most recent job report for the month of December, Misses Dawkins and Crikey Moses, it doesn't look good from me vantage point. Yeh nation has loss over five hundred thousand jobs in one of the most profitable months on the United States' fiscal calendar. Me and my

58

investors would be off our trolley to agree to such terms," Dunkirk Fraser, a fifty-five year-old black British man, stated as he sat before his three-man team of investors inside his London office.

"Mister Dunkirk, I can assure you that with Holland-Dawkins Enterprises taking control of your company here in America, you'll have access to a strategic marketing campaign focusing on the young and wealthy—actors, singers, and your everyday rich clientele that are weathering the financial crisis the United States is facing," Naomi told her potential seller as she sat in her executive, high-back chair inside her main office inside the Kerr-McGhee building in downtown Oklahoma City.

"Actors, singers and by George the everyday wealthy bloke," Dunkirk lampooned as he and his counterparts laughed amongst themselves. "Naomi, all the titles you've listed are spending peanuts in yeh country. The real money lies here in Europe given yeh nation's distress."

Kimi and Koko both were flipping through a book that broke down British terms and scrambling to write down notes to place before their mother as she conducted business.

Dekko means they had a look, Kimi's note read.

Crikey Moses means they're surprised, was Koko's note. More importantly, Koko had jotted down the fact that Greece was on the verge of a financial collapse according to the World Bank.

"I see," Naomi replied as she read the notes and shifted in her seat.

The Holland family was in the process of trying to secure several shopping malls that were spread out across the country. The malls were held by Fraser Company, Dunkirk's business. The main problem the family was facing was uncertainty on the part of Dunkirk Fraser that the family would be able to weather the recession that had befallen the United States while rebuilding the malls' profitability. Fraser Company was not only negotiating with the Holland family, however; they were in negotiations with a Grecian-owned investment company who was promising more financial backing, and Naomi knew it.

Having read Koko's last note, Naomi sought to persuade her potential sellers and gain leverage in the on-going negotiations. "The company, or rather the nation you're leaning towards, Mister Fraser, is not even listed in the top twenty as far as voting power is concerned according to The World Bank," she let it be known. "And in spite of a recession that hasn't been seen since the nineteen thirties, the United States remains at the top of international banking and investments. Nations all over this planet are still investing in America. We may be down, but we're not out. Our dollar is still the standard around the globe."

"Yeh make sense, Misses Dawkins," Dunkirk remarked as he read over a report from The World Bank announcing Greece's instability and a potential economic collapse. "But the Grecian investors have offered us twice the amount you're offering. It makes no difference to me whether the Grecians succeed or not. We just as soon take the money and run."

"One hundred million dollars looks good on paper," Naomi remarked as Kimi slid a note before her face that read, *Use the phrase Dog's dinner—it means to make a mess.* "But what good is the money if the buyers are bankrupt, Dunkirk? You would have to resell your company for a third of its value. It'll be a dog's dinner for you and your partners if you all not make the deal with Holland Dawkins Enterprises. You would run the risk of losing sixty million dollars at least on a failed investment because of the devaluation of the Grecian dollar. And even if you were to, 'take the money and run'? How would that look in the eyes of future buyers and investors interested in doing business with Fraser Company? The deal with the Grecians, should it fail, would say to the world that Fraser Company is in the business of selling bad investments."

Dunkirk took a sip of his whiskey and puffed his cigar as he leaned back and stared at the speaker phone resting atop his large, circular marble table. "As the saying goes, a sucker is born every minute," he stated. "Say what yeh want, but one hundred million dollars is worthy of my attention, Naomi. And the failing company I would maybe be selling is on the private market, which is far different from an IPO. International laws of commerce have no bearing on such deals of a private nature. I may be creating a big mess for me self, but, I'm willing to give my potential Grecian investors some more time."

"How much time? Because the clock is ticking, Mister Fraser."

"Ninety days. Give me another three months, Misses Dawkins. Then I'll make my decision."

Naomi looked over to Kimi and Koko and shook her head somberly. "My offer of fifty million dollars is final, Mister Fraser," she declared as she stood up from her desk and looked out towards the Oklahoma City skyline. "If you make the deal with your Grecian counterparts? It's all but a given that you'll be back at HDE's doorstep and we will be obliged to offer a lower buying price. I'm showing you 'love' as we say here in America, but the love I'm showing today won't be as sweet the second time around."

"Misses Dawkins, yeh have me respect," Fraser remarked as he let soak in what his American counterpart had just said to him. "Whatever the outcome of our deal? I'll be sure to be in kind heart next time we speak. Cheerio," the Brit stated as he ended the call.

Naomi stood with her back to Kimi and Koko as she reflected on the stalemate she and Dunkirk were now in. As of now, the entire deal she was trying to forge was out of her hands. She could only go on what bankers in New York were speculating on, which was the belief that Greece's economy would soon collapse under financial strain. These were facts that Naomi knew Dunkirk understood, but he was still willing to hedge a bet that Greece would not falter, thereby earning his company an additional fifty million dollars on the sale of three shopping malls.

It was a bet worth hedging against America on Dunkirk's part, but Naomi resided in the country in which Dunkirk was betting against, and things were looking pretty good from her point of view. The family didn't need a total falter of the Grecian economy, just a down-tick in their overall budget within the next month to force Fraser to look back towards

American shores and give control of their shopping malls to HDE, and if Naomi had to tell it, Dunkirk would definitely come knocking on her doors once again.

This entire deal had brought about some sorrow to Naomi for the simple fact that she was gambling on the failure of others in order for the family's enterprise to succeed. Lives would have to be ruined in some part of the world in order for HDE to come out on top. *"Be with those in Greece who haven't any power, Jesus,"* she silently prayed just as her cell phone vibrated across her desk.

Kimi looked down at the number and said, "That's Bay's old doctor calling, momma."

"Wickenstaff?" Naomi asked bedazzled as she walked back over to her desk. "Kimi? You and Koko go on and look over the time limit on those leases on the anchor stores inside those malls while I take this call," she requested as she picked up the vibrating phone. "Obadiah?" she asked somewhat apprehensively as Kimi assisted Koko to her feet and handed her a set of crutches. The two then left the office and closed the door behind them.

"I have some news for you. Naomi," Doctor Wickenstaff remarked over the phone. "Today I was visited by a federal agent Laddy Norcross and a Missouri patrolwoman by the name of Sandra Cordova. They inquired into Bay's shooting and asked if we were in continuous contact. I denied everything."

"Federal agent," Naomi asked rhetorically as her mind went into overdrive. Right away she knew the authorities were inquiring into the Saint Charles shooting, but there was more to the story she knew without having to be told. The area where Doss and Bay were shot also held the bar where Lucky, Mildred, Benito, and Coban were killed. The three men were known made guys. She began to wonder if they were now investigating more than just the shooting. "How much do they know?" she asked Obadiah.

"They know Bena is Doss's daughter is all I understand, but just their presence poses a problem, Naomi. What I am going to do is decline payment for Guadalupe Cruz until a later date while reserving the right to file payment from Medicare. I'm sorry this has happened."

"No, no, you'll get your money and we'll bear the weight of it all. If you hear anything else, anything, you notify me immediately, Obadiah."

"You have my word, Naomi. Thank you," Doctor Wickenstaff assured before ending the call.

Naomi walked around her office in deep thought as she contemplated her next move. She now knew that the FBI was in the family's backyard. On top of that, they had her and Bena's name in their files. Naomi knew the family had a crew over in Saint Charles that had the job of watching out for the feds, so she gave Dawk a call and informed him of the news and requested that he get in touch with the crew from Saint Charles to put them on alert.

****

"You like this dick, huh, ya' sexy mutherfucka?" Jay-D asked in a raspy voice as he slow-dicked his lover from behind inside his bedroom.

"You know I do, Jason. It's all I ever wanted," a soft, feminine voice replied. *"You feel good inside me, baby. I love you."*

Jason pulled on his lover's long, black silky hair, tugging her upwards to draw her in for a kiss as he stroked her long and deep in the doggy-style position. When his lover turned around and looked him in the eyes and he saw who it was actually, Jay-D began throwing punches as the sound of his ringing cell phone filled his ears. He quickly jumped up, grabbed his phone and sat on the edge of the bed while running his hands over his braids as he answered. "What up?" he groaned.

"Got word them alphabet boys in town," Dawk stated in reference to the feds. "They might be watching the block. Be careful how you move and find out what you can."

"I'm on it." Jay-D groggily replied before ending the call and tossing his phone aside. He then stood to his feet in his boxers and wondered how he could have a dream about him fucking Kree and really had no answer. They were friends, and that's the only way he saw it as he brushed the matter off and grabbed a fresh set of underwear and headed for the bathroom.

After showering and changing into a pair of brown silk slacks and a long sleeve, white turtle neck shirt with a pair of white suede shoes, Jay-D trotted down the stairs. He'd put the dream he'd had out of his mind until he spotted Kree sitting before the home computer with his niece Nancy Cottonwood standing behind her leaning over her shoulder.

"And you saying, this Facebook shit here better than MySpace was and they have way more people on they web site?" Jay-D heard Nancy asking Kree as he crept back up the stairs.

"Yeah," Kree remarked happily as she clicked on pictures of her family down in Sao Paulo, Brazil. "I have two cousins back in Sao Paulo that I communicate with now. I haven't seen them in like six years or so. We went to this private academy together in over in Portugal my senior year of high school. I'm three years older than them so I graduated before they did. They graduated with marketing degrees from the University of Barcelona and work for my mother and father now in the coffee business is what they told me."

"That's what's up. I'm happy you able to talk to some of the people in your family after the way your parents dissed you, homegirl," Nancy remarked as she stared at the images on the PC screen. "Now let's see if this Facebook gone help me and my uncles find my auntie. Type the name Katrina Sanders in that mutherfucka and see what happen."

Kree blushed and typed in another name on the computer screen instead. Several seconds later, a dark-skinned man with a tapered afro and neatly-trimmed beard appeared. "What you think?" she asked Nancy.

"That nigga look like Alonzo a li'l bit. Who that?"

"This boy I met in the mall last week. His name is Michael Hammond. He's new to the lifestyle, but he's willing to be open with me after a while."

Nancy stood upright and rolled her eyes. "Over and over you deal with the same type of niggas, Kree. Them niggas on the low!" the sixteen year-old boomed. "Niggas like that don't want nobody to know about what they doing with somebody like you!"

"What you mean somebody like me?"

"You know what I'm saying, girl. Them niggas just wanna fuck."

"Sex has nothing to do with it, Nancy," Kree retorted. "Michael sees me as a person he can love. He just needs time," she added as she retyped the name Katrina Sanders into the system.

Nancy looked at the back of Kree's head while shaking her head in disbelief. Although young in age, she was still able to recognize the mistakes others years her senior were making in life. She was the type to poke her nose into the business of everybody involved her life in order to understand their reason for being.

Kree, in Nancy's young, yet, mature mind, was once again, on the verge of making a costly mistake. This Michael character was taking the same route as Alonzo Milton, wanting to keep things undercover until the appropriate time, but that time never came. In Nancy's eyes, Kree was on the verge of making the same mistake she'd made with Alonzo with Michael.

Nancy had taken a liking to Kree, however; the two were often in one another's company being Kree styled her hair inside Bangin' Heads salon. The sixteen year-old had made up her mind to stick close to Kree and look out for her. She wouldn't dare force her opinion, but she would do what she could to make sure Kree not become a victim of circumstance over her own blind heart.

"Enough of your boy Michael for now," Nancy stated to Kree. "What names we got? Anybody from Arizona?"

"Nothing from the area we looking for," Kree responded as she scrolled down the list of names. "I see names from Rhode

Island, Indiana, Florida…places like that. Nothing from Arizona. Sorry."

"Aww, it was worth a shot. We gone keep looking, though," Nancy remarked as Jay-D descended the stairs.

Jay-D had remained hidden on the staircase after he'd peeped Kree inside the living room. His first thought that his dream had some merit being Kree was the first person he'd seen at the day's start. He walked down the remainder of the stairs and stood outside the living room where he asked, "What the fuck you doing here, Kree?"

Kree looked over to Jason with a smile, but she quickly changed her demeanor when she noticed his cruel gaze. "I, you asked me to set up a Facebook account to track down your sister the night I braided your hair, remember?" she stated. "I had to travel with Kantrell to a hair show in DC and I been going see Loopy every day. Today was the first day I had free. I didn't mean to take so long, Jason. I'm sorry if I made you mad."

"That was over two weeks ago and you just showing up? We don't need you for that shit right about now! Get the fuck up out my shit!" Jay-D scoffed as he slammed his fists together.

"The fuck your problem is?" Nancy asked in defense of Kree. "She just explained everything that went down, man! You trippin'!"

"I ain't tryna hear that shit," Jay-D complained as he pulled the front door open and remained silent while staring at Kree.

Kree's eyes watered at that moment. Jay-D hurt her constantly, but it was always with a brushing off of the implicit affinity for him that she carried in her heart. It was a fun game, one of possible fulfillment, a possible dream come true, but his statements on this day had taken on new meaning, that of an all-out disdain towards her existence. "What did I do to make you talk to me like that, Jason?" she asked as she leaned down and gathered her over-sized leather purse.

"It's you," Jay-D declared while walking off. "Just the sight of you pisses me off! Nancy, lock the door after she leave," he

66

ended as he stormed off towards the kitchen.

"You told that nigga, big brother!" Dooney snapped as he sat at the kitchen table chomping down on a piece of fried catfish with a dish of cheese grits on the side. "That boy thank he gone come in here and make his self at home and get close to ya', fam."

"Why you ain't send her away when she first got here?" Jay-D scowled as he looked into the pots the stove, only to find that the contents inside were mere scraps left behind that were not sufficient enough to coat his empty belly.

"When *he* first got here," Dooney emphasized as he picked at his fish, "I was the one to answer the doorbell. I open the door and his fuck ass was standing there smiling and shit."

Nancy walked into the kitchen at moment and said, "Dooney asked her what she was doing here and I told him she was here to set up that Facebook account Uncle Eddie asked me to do to look for y'all sister Katrina. She *had* ta' come in on that shit because if I got a aunt out there I wanna know."

"Nancy took it upon herself to go 'head with that bullshit you asked Kareem to do the night he braided your hair. She was good setting up that Facebook shit or whatever today, but you ain't had ta' let that fuck nigga braid your hair that night. I still can't cipher why you even allowed that shit that night— friends or not, that was a fuck move on your part!"

Jay-D hauled off and slapped the piece of fish out his brother's hands. "You calling me a fuck nigga?" he asked enraged as he grabbed his brother around the neck.

Dooney jumped up from his chair and flung Jay-D down. He jumped back up to his feet and charged at his brother. The two had moved the table out of position and had knocked over a couple of chairs while grabbing at one another. "If you got feelings for Kareem that's on you, nigga! Deal with it!" Dooney, who was the stronger of the brothers being he carried more weight, yelled as he pinned Jay-D to the kitchen door and drew back his right arm, preparing to land a blow to his brother's face.

"No!" Nancy yelled as she ran up and grabbed Dooney's arm. "Y'all brothers and y'all fighting?"

"Over Kareem!" Dooney snapped as he brushed Nancy off and backed away from Jay-D. "This here all over Kareem faggot ass! Because Jay can't deal with the way he feel about that dude!"

Jay-D moved away from the door and pulled up on his slacks. "You the only one that disrespect her, Donnell. It ain't about me, it's about how you refer to Kree."

"How I refer to Kree," Dooney laughed as he minimized his brother's comeback. "The fuck difference it make how I feel, Jay? I'm me, nigga!" he stated in defense of himself as he pounded his chest with a balled fist. "You can't and you *ain't* gone change my stance on homosexuality, big brother! I see Kareem for what he is from *my* point of view! *My* point of view, nigga! Regardless of how you feel about that gay shit!"

"Everybody deserves respect, Dooney!" Jay-D angrily defended. "It ain't about somebody being gay, it's about respect for people!"

"I don't know how to give that kind of respect, bruh," Dooney replied as he slid the kitchen table back into place and patted the sides of his gym shorts. "Not on some bullshit like that! I see it for what it is between you and him, though!" he ended as he hurried out of the kitchen.

Jay-D placed a hand to the edge of the stove as he looked the floor. "It's not even about me liking Kree," he said to Nancy, who'd remained behind after Dooney had stormed off.

"You the only one outside of them girls in Bangin' Heads that stick up for that chick," Nancy stated. "Don't ever change that, Jay. People are people. And I like Kree, too, man. You know how Dooney is—always the hard ass in the family after Eddie Junior, but I can tell he wouldn't go against you if you if you was…was to hook up… hook with…"

"Hook up with Kree?" Jay-D asked as he looked over to Nancy. "Would I be wrong?"

"Why mutherfuckas older than me have the hardest time

making their own decisions in life?" Nancy asked aloud of herself as she looked towards the ceiling. "What's wrong with you and Kree, man?" she asked her uncle. "Love is love! That girl love you, Jay-D! She better than any of them other women you deal with out here! You can't even trust them other hoes enough to let 'em know where we stay! But Kree done been here more than once and now she over here setting up online accounts on our computer to help us find about Katrina! Fuck Dooney! He gone get over his feelings!"

"I'm going to the deli up the block," Jay-D remarked as he walked out of the kitchen. "Y'all ain't save a nigga no breakfast and I'm hungry."

"You can run all you want, Jay, but the heart don't lie!" Nancy barked as she knelt down and started picking up the dishes.

Jay-D soaked in his niece's last statement as he stepped out onto his front porch. He was about to descend the stairs when he noticed an unmarked patrol car sitting across from Bernadette's, the deli owned by the mid-fifties Caucasian woman for some years now that sat in the middle of the block on Elm Street. He backed back into the home's foyer and dialed Kree's number without giving it a second thought.

Kree eyed her phone laying on the front seat, recognizing Jay-D's number as she stared at the screen. She was put off by the way he'd talked to her, but she couldn't deny the man who held her heart captive. "Hello?" she answered after several rings.

"Yo, where you at right about now?"

"Going pick up Jessie from Fox Park. I'm already two hours late so I gotta hear it from Kantrell this morning. What's up?"

"I need you to double back to Bernadette's and order something and meet me over to Jaycee Park up the way."

"You right there on the block. Do it yourself," Kree snapped.

Jay-D nodded inside the pristine foyer while fully understanding that Kree's standoffishness was emanating from the way he'd disrespected her minutes earlier. "My bad on how

I treated you this morning," he stated. "I just had a lot on my mind when I woke up."

"Did it have anything to do with me?" Kree pondered to herself as she reflected on the numerous dreams she'd had of her and Jay-D being intimate, but she dare not ask. "I understand, Jason. Your life isn't an easy one to live, and neither is mine. I understand. Although we live under different circumstances? We face the same pressures."

"What you mean?" Jay-D asked.

"We have to do what others expect of us," Kree responded. "People like us have to live a certain way in order to appease those whose opinion matters the most just to gain their approval."

"I'm not 'people like us'."

"Neither am I, Jason. I'm just a human being with the same feelings as any other person living on this planet. I want what everybody else want out of life, which is to be loved and respected for who I am. Nothing more. Now how can I help you this morning?" Kree asked as she turned onto a block and began guiding her luxurious Maxima back towards Elm Street while Jay-D ran down to her what he needed her to do exactly.

CHAPTER NINE

WHITE BOOTS AND NEW CARPET

"When the world is on your shoulder...gotta straighten up your act and boogie down...if you can't hang with the feeling...then there ain't no room for you in this part of town..."

While Jay-D was trying to figure out if the feds were indeed on his block, back over to Ponderosa, Naomi's private room was lit up with the groovy sounds of Michael Jackson's song *Off The Wall*.

Francine Cernigliaro was enjoying time with the youngest ones in the family by hosting a singing party. At age seventy-five, she was still very much a vibrant woman. Her grandchildren, as well as Tacoma and now Doss III kept her soul young. The joyful woman pranced around the room in her white three-inch heels, white silk blouse and pink hip-huggers while clapping her hands in rhythm as Malaysia and Malara followed her lead. Across the way, seven year-old Doss III stood in a white suit wearing a pair of sunshades, looking like Elvis Presley in his thick buck shoes as he danced by himself.

"Come on, Malaysia and Malara!" Francine yelled over the music as she began stepping in place. "Sing with grandma! This is our part."

"Ife ain't swo bad at umm...wive ya' wife off the wall..." the twins sung in unison with Francine as they stood side by side staring up at their grandmother while rocking side to side.

71

"Life ain't so bad after all…live your life off the wall is how it goes," Francine laughed as she corrected the twins while boogying in place.

The early morning disco tech was in full swing as Siloam Bovina walked into the room. "You wanted to see me, Francine?" she asked over the music as she walked up to the gyrating woman. Francine raised her hand to silence Siloam before grabbing Tacoma's hand and dancing with the eight year-old briefly while singing to him… "*'Cause we're the party people night and day…living crazy that's the only way… So tonight…gotta leave that nine to five upon the shelf…*"

"*And just enjoy yourself…*" Tacoma sang as he rocked out to the music alongside Doss III.

Siloam stood smiling as she watched the gang of five bouncing and rocking, Francine in the middle of the kids as she swayed her hips while snapping her diamond-clad fingers and wrists above her styled, frost-white hair.

"Okay, Malaysia and Malara, it's your time!" Francine laughed. "Little Doss, help the twins out why don't ya'?" she joyfully requested.

Doss III did the Chuck Berry over the floor and eased up behind Malaysia and Malara just as the song broke down. Together, he and Malara sang out…"*Life ain't so bad at all… live your life off the wall…*"

Malaysia fell out at that moment, dropping down on her rear end. She'd grown upset that someone had sung with her and her sister. She sat on the floor kicking her legs while scream-singing…"*Live your life wof the wall!*"

"There! You said it by yourself, Malaysia! You can get up now, sweetie!" Francine laughed while breathing heavy as she moved to take a seat on the couch and turned the music down with a remote control. "Tacoma? You and Little Doss go into the kitchen. Sharona's in there with Irene and they should have your biscuits and gravy ready. Malaysia and Malara? Hit the fridge!"

Tacoma and Doss III ran out the room chasing one another

as Malaysia and Malara skipped over to the small fridge Francine had installed in the lower shelf inside Naomi's bookcase. Malara pulled the small door open, leaned down and grabbed a cup of pudding and handed it to her twin. "Not, not the chocolate, Malara! Get you and Malaysia the fruit cups— the ones with the pretty flowers on it that I put in there for you twos last night. We'll have the pudding after dinner later on this evening," Francine called out while waving her arms in protest.

Malara graciously set the pudding down and grabbed the two flower-patterned cups of crushed fruit and handed one to her twin. The two walked over and nuzzled up against their grandmother and handed her their cups to open. "Siloam, come and have a seat," Francine requested while patting the soft leather cushion beside her.

Siloam, dressed in a stonewashed denim skirt, and wearing a matching wool jacket with white cotton around the collar along with a pair of white knee-length boots and a white, leather sombrero, walked over and grabbed the cup of fruit from Malaysia's tiny hands and pulled the lid off. "Montenegro said you had some news to share with me today?" she asked as she handed the aluminum can back to the toddler.

"Yes," Francine replied as she pulled the top on Malara's fruit cup. "Go and get your plastic spoons, babies. They're over in the plastic bowl beside your fridge," she added as she set Malara's cup down on the coffee table. "Now," the loving great grandmother remarked as she turned her attention to Siloam. "Earlier this morning I got a call from the boys back in Cicero concerning our guest Bianca Jacobs," she let it be known just as Malaysia and Malara returned to with their pink plastic spoons and began eating at the coffee table.

"Bichanca Shacobs," Malara innocently repeated while scooping up a portion of her crushed fruit.

"Yeah, Bitchanca," Francine slyly mocked while eyeing her great grandchildren with admiration. "Siloam," she then said. "Bianca came here under the guise of being a detective from Vegas. Truth is, she's a life insurance agent living in Texas."

"Shexas," Malaysia repeated as best she could.

"Malaysia, how about you and Malara go and watch the television," Francine ordered in a serious tone as she picked up the TV remote control and turned on the small flat screen atop Naomi's desk. The twins went silent and curled their mouths into the 'uh oh' position and looked at one another while walking off, as if they knew they weren't supposed to hear what 'grandma-ma' and Siloam was talking about.

Once the twins were out of earshot, Siloam resumed the conversation. "This entire extortion racket Bianca's running stems from Reynard setting up a life insurance policy on Mary," she told Francine as she began mapping out what she was going to do to Bianca exactly now that the truth was known.

"Right," Francine remarked. "And guess who set up the policy?"

Siloam looked over to Francine without replying to her question as she already knew the answer. "I have to keep her from telling Dimples. That's my main concern."

"Well," Francine remarked as she scooted to the edge of the couch and rested her elbows on her skinny kneecaps. "I have a way to help you out, but you'll have only today to do the job."

"What do you have in mind, Francine?"

"Mendoza's RV needed to be serviced, but it could only be done down in Oklahoma City. I got Takoda to take it down there this morning and had Dimples join him. Bianca is here in Ponca City all by herself until tomorrow morning." Francine remarked as she eyed Siloam, her eyes silently saying, '*you know what you have to do now.*'

"I'll just go and have a talk with Bianca," Siloam casually remarked as she eased up from the couch.

"Hey!" Francine called out in a stern, commanding voice. When Siloam turned and looked down at her, the longtime mafia wife rose to her feet and pulled a .22 semiautomatic handgun she had tucked in her back waistband and said, "In order for you to keep this thing away from Dimples, you'll

74

have to make Bianca disappear for all times. Her body cannot be discovered ever. And from this day forth? Let the pussy you give away, not belong to any married or taken man inside this family," she adamantly stated while staring into Siloam's eyes.

"I've learned my lesson," Siloam replied as she walked up and took the gun from Francine.

"Let's hope so. You call Montenegro when you're finished and he'll help you out," she ended as she turned her attention back to Malaysia and Malara and allowed Siloam to leave the room.

****

Back over to Saint Charles, Jay-D was sitting inside his Navigator in Jaycee Park, just a short distance away from Elm Street, thinking hard about the fight he'd had with Dooney. Why he defended Kree always was a question he had no answer to, save for it was the right thing to do in his eyes. Kree was a person deserving of respect in his mind—but he couldn't but wonder if there was more to his reasoning.

While lost in his own thoughts, Jay-D spotted Kree's white Maxima making its way through the lightly falling snow. He quickly got back into focus as the car slowly winded through the park and backed in beside him. He and Kree let their tinted windows down at the same time when the cars came into close contact. Kree leaned over the passenger seat, smiled up at Jay-D and said, "I got you some breakfast. I know you didn't ask, but your brother and niece ate all the fish and grits we cooked."

"Like you ain't have nothing to do with that," Jay-D quipped. "Come on in," he added as he nodded his head towards his passenger seat.

Kree climbed from her car with a styrofoam plate and trotted around the front side of Jay-D's ride. He eyed her in her yellow knee-length leather skirt, black knee-length heeled boots with her short, hooded black leather jacket and yellow fur hat. The thing Jay-D appreciated about Kree was her courage to be herself, but in his mind, a person living her lifestyle shouldn't have to be brave. They should just be able live without being judged. No one that knew of his occupation or his reputation ever judged him for the things he did to people—things far worse than someone like Kree, who wouldn't hurt a soul and would give her last if it meant helping someone in need.

The heat was going inside the SUV and Lil Jon, Usher and Ludacris' song *Lovers And Friends* had just come across the radio as Kree climbed into the ride. "I got you fried catfish and cheese grits from Bernadette's," she stated as she set the plate on the dashboard.

"That's cool. Thank you," Jay-D replied over the music as he draped an arm over the seat and took in Kree's appearance. "What you find out over there?" he asked while checking her out.

Kree removed her yellow fur hat, shook her shoulder length coal black hair free and said, "When I got there, the man and lady you described to me was sitting inside eating. They had some folders on the table with pictures but I couldn't see what they were looking at. They look like police to me, but I can't be sure. You gone have to check it out yourself."

"You got that for me?"

"Yeah," Kree answered as she handed Jay-D a slip of paper with the license plate number belonging to the only unidentifiable car on the block.

"That was my bad on how I came at ya' earlier." Jay-D stated while eyeing the numbers and letters Kree had written down. "I owe you for this here."

"Jay, why you so nice to me sometimes and other times you treat me like dirt?" Kree asked as the music played on.

Jay-D leaned back in the driver's seat and looked straight ahead. "You know this started out with you keeping quiet on Alonzo," he remarked.

"All this time and I haven't said nothing. You think I would tell on you? That's why you keeping me around? So I won't ever snitch on you?"

"Nah," Jay-D answered. "Sometimes I just feel sorry for you, Kree. I don't like how people treat you out there in that world. You deserve better treatment."

"Especially from the people that really matter to me." Kree stated as her brown eyes bore into the side of Jay-D's face. "I would never hurt or betray you, Jason. Because, whether you know it or not? I love the hell outta you, boy. I dream about you. I fantasize about us being together," she confessed as she opened the door slightly. "I did what you asked me to do this morning. Now I'm on my way to work to hear Kantrell rip into me for being three hours late instead of two."

Kree closed the door in seemingly slow motion. In all honesty, she was hoping for the 'baby come back moment'— that moment when the man she loved would call her back and share his feelings with her—no matter the outcome—because she was simply tired of being kept on a string by Jason David Cottonwood. She had a man wanting her in a another guy she'd met and was ready to walk away from Jason on this cold winter's day in January of 2009.

Jason heard the door shut gently. He watched as Kree walked in front of his ride with her head bowed. Her eyes had spoken volumes the time she spent inside his Navigator. The pain he'd put on her heart was undeniable and he felt bad over the anguish he'd brought into her life over a murder he'd committed against a man she'd once loved. The fight he'd had at the home ran through his mind as his brother's and niece's voice echoed in his mind…*"If you got feelings for Kree that's on you, nigga! Deal with it!"* his brother Dooney's voice.

"Love is love! That girl love you, Jay-D! She better than any of them other women you deal with out here! You can't even trust them other hoes enough to let 'em know where we stay!" his niece Nancy's voice.

"Yo, Kree?" Jay-D called out the time he let the window down.

Kree raised a hand even with her shoulder as she tilted her head to the sky and rolled her eyes. "Jason, I have to get over to my job. I don't have time for this. What do you want from me now?" she complained.

"You said I owe you for what you did today. How can I pay you back?"

"Really?" Kree asked somewhat apprehensively. She was ever-optimistic over her and Jason, and the littlest gesture from him meant the world, but still, she would remain reserved in her feelings. "Are you willing to do anything I want?" she asked curiously.

"Anything within reason." Jay-D remarked seriously.

"Okay," Kree replied, deciding to test the waters. "Dinner… at my place…if it's okay with you?"

Jay-D rubbed his chin in deep thought. He'd been to Kree's house on occasion, but never in an intimate setting. He knew the implications and the possible outcome, but he wasn't turned off by it. "I can see that there happening," he remarked while looking straight ahead.

Kree was giddy beyond words. Her heartrate kicked up a few beats and she actually felt herself becoming aroused. "Let me know when it's convenient for you," she calmly stated as a warm, fuzzy feeling encompassed the pit of her stomach. "Just don't make me wait too long, Jason."

"Let me handle this business with the family and we gone make it happen," Jay-D responded as he placed his Navigator in drive and eased off.

"Okay! And I'll keep looking for your sister, Jason!" she yelled out loud while watching the love of her life drive away.

****

Back over to Ponca City, inside Dimples' home, Bianca Jacobs was inside the spare bedroom preparing to leave the home momentarily to head into town to retrieve a package of stew meat and potatoes in order to make a crock pot of beef stew for dinner later on while she parlayed inside her sister's home for the day. She grabbed her set of keys containing the spare to Dimples' home and entered the hall where she paused and looked over to her right. Just down the hall lay Dimples and Tak's bedroom.

Bianca had been snooping around the one story, sprawling ranch home on the north side of town trying to find any proof of what had happened to her father, but she'd been coming up empty-handed. She'd searched the closets inside the bedroom she'd been sleeping in since the day after her arrival, along with the office Dimples had set up in the living room, all while her sister and Tak slept soundly in the night.

Going in, Dimples' bedroom had been off limits for Bianca as she didn't want to violate her sister's personal space, not to mention she'd never been afforded the time as Dimples was always around, having taken off from Mary's Produce to spend time with her. Drastic times call for drastic measures, however, was Bianca's reasoning as she twirled her keys in her hand several times while looking up to the vaulted ceiling. *"She'll never know,"* she finally convinced herself as she walked to her right and entered her sister's bedroom and began rummaging through the closets and drawers with the hopes of finding a lead on her father's whereabouts.

There was nothing inside the home that gave Bianca a clue as to where Reynard had gone, but she did come across financial statements belonging to Dimples after searching one of her dresser drawers. If Bianca had to tell it, Regina was doing okay in life with a bank account approaching a quarter million dollars. She began thinking of ways to siphon money from her sister just as she heard a knock at the front door, a knock that'd startled her to the point that she'd dropped her set of keys onto the floor. She knelt down to look for the keys and saw that they'd fallen under Dimples' antique dresser with the raised legs, but she couldn't reach them unless she slid the dresser away from the wall.

The doorbell rung at that moment, followed by a knock and then a second ringing of the doorbell. Bianca was forced to leave her personal set of keys behind for the moment. She returned to her feet and placed Dimples' financial statements back into their proper position inside the drawer; she then straightened her clothes and trotted out of her sister's bedroom to see who was knocking like a mad man. She was surprised to see Siloam Bovina standing on the porch when she pulled the door open.

"What do you want?" Bianca asked Siloam dryly as she stood in the doorway with her arms folded.

"We need to talk. Can I come in?" Siloam asked meekly.

Bianca backed away from the door and Siloam entered the home where the two adjoined to the carpeted dining room. "What's keeping you from telling Dimples about me and Takoda?" Siloam asked as she removed her wool coat and pulled out a chair. "I mean, that's why you're here, right?" she followed up as she took a seat.

Bianca pressed her hands to the table and said, "I'm here to find out what happened to my father, Siloam. I know you know, so why don't you just tell me?"

"If I don't?" Siloam asked as she rested her elbows on the table and looked up at Bianca.

"I'm gonna let this whole family know what you've done." Bianca sassed as she raised her hands to her sides.

"Is there anything I can do to have this not get out?"

Bianca paced the plush fuchsia carpeted floor in her stilettoes, rubbed the side of her face and smiled slyly. "You can pay me to keep quiet," she stated. "How much are you worth?"

"She just like her daddy. A dead beat," Siloam said to herself as she began to seethe on the inside while staring Bianca in the eyes. "To say you're a cop, you don't carry your badge with honor. You would take a bribe? How honorable is that?" she questioned through squint eyes of disdain.

"It's a lot of us cops that have no honor. I threw decency out the window along with protocol when my father came up missing. And ya' know what?" Bianca asked matter-of-factly as her voice went up a few octaves. "I really don't want your money. What I want is what I'm getting from you right now— to see you squirm. How does it feel not to know what will happen?"

"You sure you wanna play this game with me?" Siloam asked in a casual, but serious tone as she righted herself in her seat and looked down at the new carpet Dimples had placed inside her dining room.

"I'm not playing any games, Siloam. Before it's all said and done I'm going to ruin you. I'm gone make this family hate you so bad you're gonna wanna run away and hide forever— never to be seen again. Then *you* will become a mystery."

Siloam crossed her legs and stared up at Bianca from her seated position. "If you care about Dimples you wouldn't dare bring that up," she explained while cracking her knuckles.

"This isn't about caring," Bianca scoffed as she placed her hands on her hips. "This isn't even about Dimples."

"Then what is it?" Siloam asked in a nonchalant manner as her eyes scanned the fuchsia carpet inside the lavish dining room for a second time.

"I'm not going to repeat myself. You have until Regina gets back tomorrow morning to tell me what I wanna know about my father. Otherwise? Prepare yourself for shame."

Siloam stared coldly into Bianca's eyes as she contemplated on what she was preparing to do, but before she went through with her plan, she decided to bargain with her one last time in order to see if she could get the woman to maybe reconsider her actions. "I'm going to be fair with you," she stated. "If you go and pack your things right now, I'll buy you a plane ticket back to Texas, or Vegas…or wherever the hell you come from. But if you stay? You'll come to regret it today."

"I'm not going anywhere!" Bianca retorted. "I'm here to expose your ass so deal with it!"

Tears of anger filled Siloam's eyes over what Bianca was forcing her to do. "Please leave," she suggested once more. "This is my last time asking you to…to just leave."

"Fuck you!" Bianca laughed as she grew giddy over Siloam's plea. "Now, excuse me. I have to clean up around here and go to the grocery store back in town. You worry about that shit you, Takoda and my daddy did," she ended as she turned to leave the room.

"I have some cleaning and prepping of my own to do today," Siloam stated as she rose from the chair and went behind her back.

Bianca was in a braggadocios frame of mind when she

turned to face Siloam in preparation of hurling another threat. When she laid eyes on the handgun the Cherokee Indian was gripping, however, she quickly shifted focus and did her best to bluff, despite her being fearful of the weapon aimed at her torso. "I'm a fuckin' police, bitch!" she yelled. "If anything happen to me the entire Vegas police department gone be down here! They know where I'm at, Siloam, so put the gun away before you ruin your life!"

Siloam licked her lips as she smiled inwardly over to Bianca. This was to be the crowning moment in her months-long saga of having to cover up her transgressions against Dimples. All the free fucks she'd given up to Reynard, and the countless lies she'd told to keep her betrayal from crossing Dimples' ears in order to keep the backstab a secret was about to payoff. Francine had given her an outlet, and it was understood fully by the Cherokee that she had to capitalize on the opportunity at hand because this day may never present itself again. Yet, in spite of the obvious, Siloam couldn't help but to gloat and milk Bianca's comeuppance to the fullest extent by running down the undeniable facts.

"You're a life insurance agent working for Prudential, Bianca. You're a fraud," Siloam corrected as she held the gun on her nemesis.

Sexing Takoda and having her secret uncovered by Reynard had brought out the ugly in Siloam, a hidden dark side that she was growing to not only to understand, but to also love and accept as it felt so good to win. Killing Reynard was exhilarating. And now, the feel of taking a life, especially that of those who posed a threat to her existence and that of the family's well-being set right in this budding assassin's heart as she continued to read Bianca. "Did you really think I wasn't going to look into your background the time you arrived and announced who you were? Reynard took out a life insurance policy on Mary and tried to kill her. You were in on it because you were the one who drew up the documents. I know everything," she confessed while looking at Bianca out the corner of her eye.

Bianca was left stunned over Siloam's revelation. All the

power she believed she was holding since her arrival over to the ranch had been drained from her psyche after Siloam had spoken. The jig was now up and she knew it. To save face, she became a compliant citizen hoping not to become a murder victim as she knew her rouse had just run its full course. "I'll, I'll go and pack my bags now if it's okay," she relented. "And I won't say anything to Dimples. I'll even give you my work number and home address if you don't believe me."

Siloam was unfazed by Bianca's concession, but she was willing to exercise mercy, if only for the moment. "Good. I see you have some sense about yourself." she nodded as she waved the gun towards the living room. "Let's go and pack your bags so you can get the hell out of Oklahoma for good."

Bianca walked through the living room with Siloam on her heels. "All I really wanted to know is what happened to my father. Did, did he ever come back here?" she asked humbly.

"He came back and borrowed money from Dimples and disappeared. Guess his gambling debts caught up with him." Siloam lied as she tailed Bianca into the spare bedroom.

"He was always a snake," Bianca stated, trying to sell her father down the river and endear herself to Siloam. "I knew when he wanted me to draw up those life insurance policies on Mary that he had something low down planned," she added as she pulled a dresser drawer open and grabbed a few of her folded clothes.

"Umm hmm," was all Siloam said as she hovered over Bianca, making sure she didn't reach for a gun of her own while gathering her clothes. She followed the woman's every step as she packed two suitcases.

"That's all you have to say is 'umm hmm'?" Bianca asked, panting heavily as she threw clothes into her first suitcase. "I'm trying to tell you that it was my father who was behind all of this mess. He forced me to conjure up that life insurance policy I didn't want nothing to do with it," she said in one breath.

"Why did you come here with the attitude, Bianca?" Siloam inquired as she walked around the room in her white leather boots with her hands tucked behind the back of her stonewashed dress. "You could've kept things peaceful by stating your case to me, and getting to know your sister, but you tried to ruin me instead. I regret the day I slept with Takoda, and for that? I owe you an apology. I hope you and Dimples can really get to know one another as time goes on."

"Really?" Bianca smiled as she threw clothes into her second suitcase. "Is that still possible? I thought you would—"

"You getting to know your family is not my concern. Dimples is a good woman," Siloam interrupted as she stopped pacing the floor and turned to face Bianca head on. "I won't interfere in you and Dimples' affairs. All I ask is that you not say anything about me and Takoda. I want the peace we share to remain intact and not have Dimples lose trust and faith in me over a mistake me, your father, and Takoda made."

"I won't say a word." Bianca replied as she placed the last of her clothing into her first suitcase and zipped it. "I just want you to know that it's not because you have that gun that I've changed my mind. I can be flip at the mouth a lot of times and I'm not good at all at handling animosity. You should hear how I talk to some of the customers who call the insurance company I work for," she laughed. "I'll go back home and rethink things and come back with a new attitude I promise."

"I understand what you're saying," Siloam remarked as she donned a friendly smile. "We'll purchase your ticket when we get to Oklahoma City. You have everything you came with?" she asked as Bianca zipped the last suitcase.

"Yeah," Bianca replied in a humble manner. "Siloam, I want you to know that I'm sorry for—"

Bianca was halted in her speech and screamed aloud when a bullet slammed into her right thigh. She fell to the wooden floor clutching her wound as she looked up at Siloam. "What are you doing?" she cried aloud.

"I needed you out of the dining room. Didn't wanna leave blood on the new carpet," Siloam coolly stated as she aimed the gun at Bianca's head.

"Siloam, no! Please! I was ready to leave! I'm done with everything my father wanted me to do!"

"And I'm done with you, Bianca Jacobs. I killed your daddy and he was fed to that hog you saw when you first got here. The stench you smelled? That was the last of Reynard's remains being sucked into a sewerage truck!" Siloam revealed as her voice hit an angry crescendo. "You wanted to know what happened to your daddy? Now you know! And now I'm gonna do the same thing to you!"

Bianca vomited onto the floor as she convulsed in pain. "I wasn't, I wasn't gone hurt no one," she cried aloud. "I wasn't gone hurt nobody!"

Siloam knelt down and stared at Bianca without an ounce of concern for her troubles. "My reputation means everything to me," she declared. "You came here to ruin me. I'm not certain what you intended on gaining by telling Regina what you knew about me and Takoda, but it's worth me killing you to keep that part of my life hidden. Your being alive poses a threat not only to my existence, but that of my prosperity. I won't be able to sleep well at night just knowing you're alive. Wherever you are in this world!" Siloam laughed.

Bianca reached out a bloody hand, but Siloam fell back, preventing her from staining her clothes and boots. "Help meeeee! Lord, no! Help meeeee!" Bianca screamed aloud as she reached out for Siloam. "You don't have to this! Just let me go! Let me go!"

Dimples resided in an area where the homes were spaced out nearly a half football field apart. No one could hear Bianca's screams whatsoever, let alone the gunshots. Siloam, knowing Bianca's cries for help were going unheard, said nothing as she took to one knee and fired two more rounds from the gun. The bullets landed in Bianca's chest and she fell onto her back. She began gagging as blood poured from her mouth and nostrils. The gurgling sounds she made were soothing to Siloam, who was unwilling to do anything to end the woman's suffering.

Kneeling down just outside of the pool of blood that was gathering around her second murder victim's body, Siloam let the gun hang loosely from her hand while remaining on one knee and said to Bianca, "The mistake you made was not telling Dimples the very first day you got here about me and Takoda. You would've won. But, now? Regina will never know. I've won the cold war between you and I, girlfriend. You breathe easy now. I'll wait while you die a slow death, but then again." Siloam stated as she looked at the gun in her hand, then looked back over to Bianca while slowly raising the gun.

Bianca was trying to speak, but the blood collecting in her throat prevented her from doing so. She began fading in and out as she looked Siloam square in the eyes. Her last thought was that of wonderment. How on earth did her game of manipulation end with her being shot to death inside her sister's home? It was an outcome she'd never even contemplated. The mortally wounded woman soon entered into a state of shock as thoughts of her father having been killed at the hands of the woman who'd just shot her ran through her horrified mind. The last thing she would see would be that of a barrel of a gun aimed at her face, and then a quick flash of light.

Siloam stood to her feet and stared at the bullet she'd planted into Bianca's forehead. The job had been done. Her secret would remain intact for all times was now her belief. After calling Montenegro, she set about removing Bianca's clothes in preparation of the gory task that lay ahead. She ran out to the garage and grabbed a roll of poly and a razor blade and darted back to the bedroom barefooted. She had to get Bianca's body onto the waxed plastic to prevent it from soaking into the wood.

After spreading the wrap out, Siloam rolled Bianca's corpse onto the plastic facedown. Her blood was steadily soaking into the wood so she frantically pulled down a suitcase, unzipped it and began dabbing the blood with some of Bianca's clothes. It was more blood than she'd calculated, but time was on her side as Dimples and Tak wouldn't be back in town until the following morning.

The ringing of the doorbell startled Siloam as she dabbed Bianca's blood. She ran to the front door and peeked out and saw Montenegro and pulled the door open.

"Did you not kill her on the carpet?" was the first thing the Mexican asked as he walked into the home while looking the place over.

"She's in the bedroom. Some of her blood got on the wood, but I wiped it all up."

"It will get into the cracks, Senorita Bovina." Montenegro replied as he looked down at the wooden floors inside the foyer. "Is all the wood the same in the home?"

"It's all oak."

"Oak," Montenegro mimicked as he tapped the wooden floor with the tips of his boots. "What we will do is chop the body up into pieces inside the tub to where Moses can feed. Afterwards, we'll go into town and get replacement boards and pull up the old boards. That way the blood won't show up in the cracks. Dimples will certainly want to know why her sister left all of sudden so we have to cover all the angles should the law become involved. We have the entire day, so let's get to work," he ended as he and Siloam set about their gory task.

CHAPTER TEN

POUNDS OF FLESH AND MONEY

It was nearing the midnight hour when we pulled up on the ranch, the same day Siloam had killed Bianca Jacobs. After chopping up the woman's body and wrapping her remains in plastic, Siloam and Montenegro redid the floors in Dimples' spare bedroom was what we was told. The wood looked as if it hadn't been touched given their fly-by-night renovation job was what me, Naomi and Dawk had observed when we went and surveyed the crime scene before heading back over to the ranch. All that remained now was for Bianca's remains to be discarded.

Siloam and Montenegro had waited until nightfall to remove Bianca's body parts from Dimples' house. They'd placed her remains into the back of Montenegro's Titan and had driven them back to the ranch and we'd all arrived at the same time over to Moses' pen.

Naomi hopped from behind the wheel of the Suburban we rode up in and Dawk climbed from the passenger seat as I eased from the back passenger seat. The three of us was dead tired as it had been a long day of planning and plotting. Planning on Naomi's part for a trip she would have to make to Mexico to get Flacco and his family in line before meeting with the Devereaux family in order to secure a deal for land in Brazil that was ripe with cocoa leaves, and waiting on me and Dawk's part because we were anticipating the moment Tonto Jamison's bail would be posted.

Everybody had all gained ground on this day. The Devereaux family had agreed to meet with Naomi and discuss the offer of buying three thousand acres of land at a set price of $10.5 million dollars. She and Dawk was headed to Mexico City on a commercial flight the day after tomorrow. From there, they would meet up with Flacco's family and fly to his homeland to meet his people and then hold talks with the Devereaux family.

As far as myself, I'd put up the $250,000 dollar bail on Tonto Jamison. His accomplice Chauncey Gainey was looking at a life sentence because of prior charges, but Tonto was set for bail. I did him that favor so we could get him back on the streets where we needed him, ya' dig? If I coulda got at dude myself for what he did to my people I would do it no doubt, but I was scheduled to take a flight down to Cayman Island tomorrow afternoon and secure the family's first major solo deal with Rafael Gacha.

While me, Naomi and Dawk were away, my plan was to give Lee Sato the greenlight on Tonto Jamison. He was bringing Amber and Tre' up to Ponca City the following morning so I would break down what I wanted done when he arrived over to the airport back in town. This job would a tricky one because it would have to go down in our backyard so-to-speak, and Lee would be expected to have the job done while Naomi and Dawk were out of the country because that there would give them both a good alibi. The police would be sure to check with them on that deal being Tonto had tried to kidnap Koko was what we were presuming.

Naomi walked over to Moses' pen where Montenegro was dumping a couple of limbs over the fence. This here wasn't new to me because I done chopped up a body myself in the past. Some people might be grossed out by it all, but everybody was at ease with what was going down. Just another day's work.

The hog was chomping into the flesh being scattered around the snow and mud. I watched as he chomped down on a mangled piece of Bianca's flesh. Then, he did the oddest thing. After devouring a large chunk of flesh, this here hog turned around and let a pile of shit, but he wasn't through. I was standing thinking about the humiliation of a human having being eaten and then shit out when Moses dropped down flat onto his belly atop the manure he'd just released. It was like he took joy in his antics. I mean, he was rolling around in a shitty Bianca like he was, like he was in hog heaven for lack of a better choice of words.

"Chomp, chomp!" Montenegro commanded as he threw more of Bianca's remains into the pig sty. Moses stood up and ran back towards the wooden fence, intentionally ramming it before standing strong and strutting around in a perfect circle. His eyes were focused on the flesh that lay in the muck inside the pen as he pranced around the hunks of flesh. Soon, he nudged it with his nostrils, getting it into what I could only guess was the optimum position before gobbling up what he could into his mouth. Blood and bits of flesh ran down his chin as he stared at us while munching on Bianca's flesh. It was a hard way for anybody to go, but to be honest, I feel no way about it. She shouldna came to the ranch with her bull shit. Now, she will remain for all times.

"It's gonna take most of the night for Moses to devour Bianca, but by the time he's done there wouldn't be much left except for a bit of undigested flesh that would be rinsed into his bin, Naomi," Siloam stated, shaking me from my thoughts.

"Good," my aunt replied casually as she turned away from the pen. "Your next assignment is to oversee the property while I'm away. Roofers will be here the day after tomorrow to put the finishing touches on Dawk's home. Check them out. Make sure they are who they say they are."

Just then, Dawk's phone rung. He picked up and walked off a ways for a minute. When he came back, he had this look of disbelief on his face. "Ma? Ben? We need to talk," he stated.

The three of us left Siloam and Montenegro to their business and rode back to Ponderosa. Along the way, Dawk dropped some info on me and Naomi. "That was Jay-D on the line. We just got confirmation on what Doctor Wickenstaff told you earlier, momma. Sandra Cordova and Laddy Norcross was on Elm Street this morning. Feds in town." he remarked somberly as he guided the SUV across the land.

Naomi had told me and Dawk earlier in the day what Doctor Wickenstaff had relayed to her. Jay-D's info only confirmed things. Hearing Laddy's name was not good in no form or fashion. We had a shipment coming in in a few weeks and a club opening soon, but we were up on things. With the feds in town, though, we had to be extra careful.

"We gone have to keep Bay and T-Top out of Missouri for now," I remarked as we all climbed from the SUV and headed up the theatrical stairs under the dark, cold skies.

"They gone handle things down at the Valley Brook warehouse for the time being," Dawk said to me as we approached the patio doors of Ponderosa.

"I want to know why this State Trooper has linked up with Laddy Norcross. I'll get with Francine and see if we can get the Cannapolis family in Chicago to pull some strings," Naomi stated as a couple of guards opened the doors for us.

Immediately, Naomi was greeted by Tacoma, Doss III, Malaysia and Malara while Irene and Sharona busied themselves with putting away a few dishes. I watched as they all ran up and gave my aunt hugs around her waist and knees. "Aww, my babies," she spoke in a joyful tone. "What are you four doing up at this late hour?"

"It's Friday!" Tacoma stated. "No class tomorrow and we was able to have a party! We getting ready to watch another movie after we load the popcorn machine!"

"Did you use Kimi and Koko's ice cream maker to make your own ice cream today like we talked about over the phone earlier?"

"My momma and Miss Irene did it for us!" Doss III remarked. "They made lemonade ice cream and it was off the chain! We ain't save nobody nothin'!"

"I tried to save you some, Auntie," Tacoma chimed in. "But it was too good."

Naomi laughed and asked, "Well, did Malara and Malaysia get some of that ice cream?"

Tiva's daughters shook their heads, saying no as they planted their faces in Naomi's slacks and left wet marks on the silk. She eyed Tacoma and Doss III, her eyes asking if Malaysia and Malara were speaking the truth.

"They didn't ask for any!" Doss III defended.

"We have more for the twins. But not tonight. They are hyper enough and we tryin' to put these puppies to bed," Sharona remarked out loud from the kitchen. "Would you like some, Naomi?"

"No, thank you. We're going to convene to my private room for a while. Is Francine awake?"

"She had her coffee and went down a couple of hours ago." Irene said to Naomi while placing silverware into one of the cabinets.

"Okay. If you need us you know where to find us." Naomi remarked as she eased on through the kitchen.

My Aunt had the ability to navigate through all the diversities of the family like that of a ship sailing smooth waters. She was the type to never be overwhelmed no matter the circumstance, in my book. As I look back over time, coming to know what I know about my people, no one outside of Eileen Holland had my aunt's ability. Ruth may have had it, but she never got the chance.

I know it's odd, but as I traverse through these rough seas with my family, I tend to draw off family history, mine included, and the facts can't be ignored: me and my people so deep into this game that two of the feds who are investigating us is on our hit list. Angles were swirling like crazy and the pace was hectic. My mind going off in a thousand different directions. I can't help but to think that I'm missing something here with the feds, but I can't quite put my finger on it just yet. Instincts were telling me that the Germans knew more than what they were speaking on being we had such a close connection to Lisa Vanguard. Not that they were hiding anything for their own benefit, they just didn't know.

I was vaguely listening as Dawk and Naomi discussed the

family's next move over in Saint Louis. I'd seen it coming given what we'd just learned. Dawk was going to move over to East Saint Louis and link up with Natalia III and Malik for the time being, and Jay-D was gone hug the block over in Saint Charles on Elm Street and keep an eye out for the feds.

My plan for the time being was to make the trip down to Cayman Island and secure our first major score and get up with Faye Bender when I made it back stateside. On top of that, Lee had to take care of Tonto. We got a full plate ahead of us, but if we can maneuver through the fog of the streets, we gone be the ones to come out on top. I excused myself from Naomi's and Dawk's discussion after receiving a text from Martha.

"I'm going check on that thing with Cayman Island," I told them both as I left the room and made my way up to Naomi's suite.

****

"I want the best people in the family with you when you make this trip tomorrow, Ben." Martha said to me as she banded a $50,000 dollar stack of hundred dollar bills laying out on a medium-sized, square, marble table. She placed the money onto a digital scale and saw that it weighed out at 1.1 pounds before tossing it into a duffle bag that rested at her side on the grey marble floor.

"My boys Tre` and Victor flying in with me. Should be a quick exchange on the runway, though," I stated as I weighed out a 1.1 pound stack of hundred dollar bills and tossed it into a duffle bag at my feet.

"I got my best drivers on the loads to Oklahoma City and Flagstaff. Dawk gone put another driver out Flacco crew to make the final run to East Saint Louis, the Flagstaff driver going straight through. He gone need a load going out from there," Martha let it be known as she grabbed another handful of hundreds.

"We'll have a load of grapes going to Napa Valley from the vineyards." I told her.

"Good. I'll link back up with him once he empty out in

California," Martha said to me. "Gacha's men gone have to give me the tracking numbers on the reefers they sending up to Laredo so I can send 'em to a bonded warehouse and have Tropicana sign off on those two refrigerated units with the Department of Agriculture," she then let it be known.

"How that work?" I asked as I shuffled a pile of hundred dollars bills into a uniform stack.

"With a bonded warehouse, imported goods are barred from search and seizure by the federal government until the bond is paid in full or the goods have been delivered domestically."

"How you gone play it?" I followed up while placing the stack of hundreds inside a money counter and letting it click away.

"We gone pay the cost of the bond upfront the day before the shipment hit Laredo," Martha replied. "It'll show up as a paid bond when my drivers hit customs and they'll flow though unchecked."

"Why not pay it after they hit U.S. soil?"

"Because by securing the bond beforehand, the shipment will be transferred to Tropicana itself and our containers will enter under a Trusted Trader agreement. Tropicana is a trusted company and they make these kinds of deals all day every day. Our trailers won't warrant search under the Tropicana label being they're a Trusted Trader with Homeland Security."

"Right up under their nose, huh?" I stated casually.

"Yes, sir," Martha smiled. "Slovak Vineyards and Saint Charles Ave Cold Cartage is what's being printed on the manifests and entered into the system. HDE won't even show up and data processors with Tropicana merely signing off on refrigerated units coming in from Venezuela via computer."

"How long before Tropicana pick up on what we doing?"

"Naomi estimating eighteen months, but by then we'll have our own orange grove going down in Brazil if the Devereaux deal go through. And if Tropicana ever pick up on loads they aren't shipping, it'll be Ernestine Maxwell that would make the inquiry. She and Naomi seem to be getting along pretty good after the presentation Kimi and Koko put down so we good for a year at the earliest."

"Cool," I remarked as me and Martha continued counting out the monies needed for the family's first major score.

CHAPTER ELEVEN

BANK BUSINESS

Ben and Martha were holed up inside of Naomi's office on the second floor of Ponderosa counting out $5.7 million dollars, the agreed upon price for three hundred kilograms of cocaine being supplied by Rafael Gacha, in fifty thousand dollar bundles that weighed 1.1 pounds.

Martha had just broken down to Ben the intricacies involved in international drug trade in brief fashion. She was the family's Transportation Coordinator—the person responsible for making sure the cocaine shipments arrived on time and was void of inspection when crossing over into America. Hers was a just a spark plug in the big scheme of things, however; because above Martha Holland, were two individuals who were the metaphoric pistons inside the family's high-powered engine.

Across the way, inside the same room, twenty year-olds Kimi and Koko were at their mother's desk working on the paperwork needed in order to make the upcoming deal look legit in the eyes of the federal government. The family's middle set of twins were involved in a delicate undertaking. One in which all international banking laws had to be strictly adhered to in order to avoid the raising of flags that would catch the eyes of the U.S. Treasury Department, Internal Revenue Service, U.S. Customs and the Federal Bureau of Investigations.

Kimi and Koko were gathering data and conducting research on *BNP Paribas Bank & Trust Cayman Limited*, one of the largest banks in the world. Paribas Bank was based in Paris, France, but the financial institution had a major branch located on Cayman Island where the twins had set up the family's offshore account.

The printer was working overtime printing out files Kimi and Koko were downloading for an upcoming presentation both had to make before their mother inside Holland-Dawkins Enterprises (HDE) concerning the movement of incoming cocaine profits that the family would soon start dropping off for rinsing. The twins were studying international banking transaction laws and memorizing the rules on how to route monies deposited into Paribas' Cayman branch and move it overseas to Paris, France where it would sit idle for three business days before being deposited back into HDE's coffers back in Oklahoma City—this would be the rinse their mother had been training them for over the past six years or so.

Although in the midst of a crisis involving what had gone down with Spoonie, the family was still conducting business. Millions of dollars' worth of cocaine was preparing to be shipped from Venezuela via railroad. Each cocaine transaction could only be made from the Cayman Islands in person by a courier as Gacha now dealt in cash and cash only.

Kimi and Koko would never have to touch the money nor meet with Gacha's men, as that was Ben's job. Once the drop was completed, the twins would receive a phone call from Ben giving them the go ahead to remove $5.7 million dollars from the books and get the ball rolling on future deposits that could then be done from HDE's headquarters in Oklahoma City, or any other computer the family had linked up to the main office.

With the cash deal in place and the family's money in good hands, Kimi and Koko turned their attention to their next task, which was a monumental one that would test their skills like never before if it was even possible given all they'd accomplished thus far. The twins had had a conversation with their mother the day before concerning the setting up of new avenues in order for the family to rinse the bulk of their cocaine profits clean. They'd asked their mother how to go about setting up new businesses, but Naomi merely responded by telling her daughters to conduct their own research and get back to her on February 9th, which was a little under three weeks away.

Ever loyal, and rapidly becoming key players inside the organization literally overnight, Kimi and Koko left OU Medical Center the night before, returned to the ranch and immediately went to work. Setting up the Paribas transfer was child's play. After learning the procedures, all the twins had to do was link the Paribas account to HDE's account, an action that would not raise federal eyebrows as they'd learned that it was standard banking procedure that fell within the guidelines of federal tax codes concerning offshore books.

"I can't find what momma's asking us to do with these new ventures, Kimi," Koko complained to her twin as they both stood over their mother's marble desk with both of their Accountant books spread open along with their laptops fired up.

The major problem the twins were having was that of establishing new venues to rinse the dirty money, which was a conundrum neither could figure out completely as of yet.

"I think I found one way we can do part of it," Kimi remarked while staring at her computer screen. "Let me go and check something with Dawk," she added as she leaned down and placed her heels back onto her feet and grabbed a pad and pen.

Kimi made it down to the first floor and tapped on the door leading to her father's private room. Samantha answered and Kimi entered and eyed an arsenal of semi-automatic weapons and banana clips spread out on the bar counter. Dawk was sitting on the edge of the couch loading shells into a couple of clips he had in his lap with the aid of latex gloves.

"Kimi, you want a rib eye steak, sister? What about Koko?" Samantha asked as she ran back over to the skillet that was just beginning to sizzle as a light mist rose up into the air.

"Not right now, girl. We way too caught up in this

99

brainteaser our momma dropped on us. You got everything set for this flight down to Cayman Island tomorrow?"

"Yes, ma'am. Plane's been checked out and the flight plan is already filed. Tre` and Amber be in tomorrow on a commercial flight to join us," Samantha replied as she dumped a bowl of chopped white onions and sliced bell pepper on top of the steaks she was grilling.

"What's up, Kimi?" Dawk asked casually as he looked over to his sister while sliding shells into a curled magazine.

"I have a question about the...about the thing over to Cayman Island." Kimi stated as she held onto her notepad and pen.

"Like what?" Dawk asked as he continued sliding shells into the clip.

"We know the numbers but, how long will it take y'all to move it?"

"Six weeks max. Expect a drop between every four and six weeks over a three day period." Dawk answered as he slid a clip into an AR-15, set it aside and then picked up another clip and began loading it up with .762 millimeter shells.

Kimi jotted down a few notes and looked to the ceiling. "Six weeks," she sighed. "We need another bin to drop money in because tax rebounds won't be enough."

"That's gone be a problem?"

"Perhaps, Dawk—but I have an idea on another way we can channel funds and earn points on the money. Momma got the final say so on it, though. I'm just scared to even mention this one here."

"What's the other way?" Dawk asked as he slid a fully-loaded clip into an AP-9 semiautomatic, set it down and picked up another clip belonging to the family's beloved Chicago Piano and started filling it up with .9mm bullets.

"We can loan money." Kimi responded as she jotted down more notes.

"To who?" Dawk asked perplexed.

"The federal government," Kimi remarked as she walked off, leaving Dawk and Samantha behind looking at one another in stunned silence.

CHAPTER TWELVE

I AIN'T A KILLER BUT...

The morning after Bianca's remains had been fed to Moses found Lee Sato getting ready to pick up Amber Slovak from Will Rogers International. He'd camped out the night before over to Udelle's dorm down in Norman and the two actually kicked it off pretty good. Udelle was a wealth of information concerning Koko for Lee. He'd broken down Koko's relationship with Chablis and what led up to the night things went down with Spoonie. He also expressed his excitement over his and Kimi's upcoming marriage the night before.

"You coming down to the island when me and Kimi get married, dude?" Udelle asked Lee the night before as the two sat in the living room drinking cognac while watching old weather reports that Udelle had linked up to the flat screen TV.

"Yeah, yeah. Whatever," Lee remarked half-drunk and uninterested as he laid back on the couch and plopped his feet up on the wooden table and topped off his glass. "Udelle, let me ask ya' somethin'. Why, why we sitting here like a couple of geeky ass mutherfuckas watching weather patterns in the Pacific Ocean? This, this shit is boring as the fuck, dude," he declared as he passed the bottle.

"Because, man," Udelle laughed as he took the bottle from Lee and poured himself another shot. "Me and Kimi gettin' married in the Solomon Islands come September."

"Way over there? What's the reason for that move?"

"Man, Kimi said she wanted to go somewhere far the fuck out. She looked at Bora Bora, Tahiti and Fiji, but she said too many rich folk have weddings over there. My baby just wanted to be different."

"It don't get no different than the Solomon Islands." Lee appreciated as he sipped his liquor. "That place, that place has a lot of history. Tragic history."

"I read up on that," Udelle remarked. "They gotta lot of ships sunk from the war with Japan. People go scuba diving there now."

"September is usually the wet months over there. There may be be bad weather 'round the time you and Kimi marry."

"August is the driest month on the calendar," Udelle said to Lee before downing his shot of cognac. "October be like one of the wettest months, so we cuttin' it close going with September. The rain really don't start until October, but ain't no telling," he added as he passed the bottle of cognac back to Lee.

"Temperature good, though. It average out about seventy-six degrees." Lee remarked as he reached over and grabbed his glass off the end table.

Udelle looked over to Lee surprised. "How you know the average temperature over to the Solomon Islands?"

"My grandmother and grandfather, who never met beforehand because they lived in different cities at the time back in China? They were both enslaved by the Japanese and taken to the Solomon Islands to help build an airstrip for those communist mutherfuckas during World War Two," Lee responded as he poured himself another shot. "They met and became lovers inside an enslavement camp and gave birth to a son. Through all that shit, they helped one another survive the hell they were in—working in the hot sun barefoot on hot gravel and sand under the threat of being beaten if they ever grew tired while keeping the man who eventually became my father alive the whole time."

"Damn," Udelle responded as he rubbed his chin and eyed Lee while sitting on the edge of the couch. "Shit ain't to different from what a lot of black folk went through here in America during slavery, bruh."

Lee downed his shot of cognac and set his shot glass back on the end table. "My mother and father lived a hard life, man," he admitted as he rubbed his chin and briefly reflected on his family's history. "But in spite of being poor? My parents taught me the value of family and friendship. They taught me not to see color, but to stick close to those who stick close to you. It's been that way all my life since I touched down in Oakland," he expressed through a deep sigh as he looked off into nowhere particular and thought about the many friends he'd loss to the streets.

Udelle wasn't naïve by a long shot. He knew Doss Dawkins was a gangster, the same way he knew Dawk Holland was a gangster. He also knew Ben Holland wasn't to be played with on any level. And truth be told, Udelle had never ruled out his woman Kimi, nor that of Koko, being involved in the same occupation as their father to some extent. The only thing he was certain of was that Spoonie and Tyke had no ties to illegal activities. Walee was out there he could tell by simply observing, but he wasn't involved in what all the rest of the family had going on.

Lee had come down shortly after things had gone down with Spoonie. To Udelle, that wasn't a coincidence, but at the same time, he wasn't bothered by the drama swirling around Lee's presence. He'd talked to Kimi earlier in the day and she'd told him that Lee was going to be staying the night over to his dorm while she returned to Ponderosa to handle some business for the family and he was free to use the Maserati as he pleased.

After talking to Lee for a while, Udelle understood that his woman was actually placing a bodyguard on him to keep him safe. He understood clearly the fact that he had a Boss chick on his arms and it made him feel proud to have a woman of Kimi's caliber loving and caring for him without asking for anything in return other than for him to be loyal to what the two of them had going on, which was good sex and *commitment through marriage while pursuing their life goals.*

Understanding what he had in Kimi, unlike the failed relationship between Chablis and Koko, Udelle had decided to get down with the family and be in it for the long haul. From that moment forth, after chopping it up with Lee Sato, unless Kimi herself decided to share, Udelle promised himself that he would not dip into his woman's affairs. Instead, he would give her the love and support she needed to best be able to handle business on behalf of the family. The aspiring meteorologist also had enough ambition within himself to pursue his own goals in in life, thereby bringing something to table and contributing to the Cause.

Unlike Chablis, Udelle had not the jealous streak in him that would surely lead to calamity. He was confident in Kimi, a woman fast becoming about the world of finance that not only met with, but was related to people of great wealth and power. At the end of the day though, Udelle knew where his woman's heart lay. He felt not threatened by her occupation, but honored and hadn't a worry in the world. Kimi wasn't the type to fuck her way to the top. Instead, she and her family were laying down the rules. Why not support his future bride and ride the rungs of the ladder of success was his reasoning.

"When the Americans took control of the Islands in nineteen forty-three, my grandparents returned to Beijing with my father and married," Lee stated, removing Udelle from thoughts of the life he saw on the horizon.

"What happened after that, homeboy?" Udelle asked as he eased back onto the leather couch.

"Some years later, my father met my mother at a fishery and they married. I was like ten when my father returned to the Solomon Islands to the very place he was born. I never forgot that trip because it was like an escape from poverty. I respect that place because although I wasn't born there, it was where I actually originated. It was where me and my parents vacationed every other year right up until we landed in San Francisco. I know the Solomon Islands well." Lee remarked as he eased up to the edge of the couch and poured himself another shot.

"Say, Lee? You wanna be in my wedding?" Udelle asked seriously.

Lee looked over to Udelle and laughed lowly. "The fuck you want me in your wedding for?" he questioned in a protested tone. "You barely know me. I'm just here to...I'm just here, man," his voice trailed off as he had no intentions on revealing exactly why he was camping out at Bay's condo.

"You here to look after me huh, bruh?" Udelle asked as he placed his slipper-clad feet up onto the table. "I got my own protection, though," he added as he looked over towards a teal and white box resting on the end table to his left. "I respect what you doing to the fullest, though, cuz," he said as he turned back to Lee. "You down, homie. I can have it to where you and Koko walk up the aisle if you want to, ya' feel? How fire would that be?"

Lee looked off from Udelle with a smile on his face. He adored him some Koko, but he didn't want her taking things the wrong way. "Women," he said as he looked over to Udelle. "Women have this thing about weddings, man. If me and Koko were to walk down the aisle she might get to thinking we next and that's not in our future right now."

"What y'all doing then, brother?"

"We're just kicking it right now."

"I feel ya' on that," Udelle remarked casually while nodding his head. "But check this, Kimi gone no doubt want her sister to walk the aisle. And it's a damn good chance that Koko gone be her maid of honor if she don't ask Naomi or Bay. So, if that happen? Who gone walk with Koko?"

"You got me there," Lee replied as he pointed over to Udelle while holding onto his shot glass. "But the maid of honor walk with the best man in a wedding, right?"

"You up for the job, my dude?" Udelle asked.

Lee had to sit upright on the couch after hearing Udelle's reply. He set his glass of cognac down and waved his hands outwards with a puzzled look on his face. "You asking me to be the best man in your wedding?" he asked through a chuckle that hinted at his surprise and disbelief. "That's like the best friend's job. And I ain't near 'bout your best friend," he added as he grabbed the bottle of cognac off the table and readied himself for another shot. "Enough drinkin' for you tonight. You done had enough liquor to last well past September."

Udelle laughed as he slammed a backhand into Lee's chest and inadvertently knocked the bottle of Louis XIII from Lee's hand, spilling the liquor onto Lee's silk shirt and shorts in the process.

"What the fuck?" Lee exclaimed as he jumped up from the couch and balled his fists up at Udelle. "Your drunk ass need ta' go to bed!"

"We both drunk!" Udelle quipped as he sunk back into the couch. "But, I ain't a killer but don't push me!" he added as he laughed aloud, having quoted Tupac's opening lyrics to his hit song Hail Mary.

"What that's supposed to mean?" Lee asked as he walked into the kitchen and grabbed a wet rag to wipe down the leather couch.

"I'm just tryna put you on with the family without you having to off somebody, man!" Udelle stated as he stood up and faced Lee while wobbling slightly. "Maybe asking you to be my best man was a bit much. But Dawk getting married in April and I know Koko walking. You can at least do that, right? You walk down the aisle with Koko in Oneika's wedding? Man, you in with the family!"

"I been in with the family!" Lee retorted as he reflected on the job he and Victor Felix pulled off in East Saint Louis against the Charles brothers, and the job he himself pulled over in Denver against the witness who was going to testify against Asa Spade and his crew. In his mind, those events had brought him into the family so he saw no need to participate in any wedding just to earn stripes as he felt he'd already proven his loyalty.

"You in with the family based on what you did in the streets, Lee! On the streets!" Udelle reiterated as he headed for the kitchen and grabbed a slice of pizza he and Lee had ordered

earlier in the night. "I know you out for Tonto, fam," he said before chomping down on a slice of meat lover's from Pizza Hut. "If I knew where he was I would tell you so you could earn them there stripes. Chablis was my best friend once upon a time—but I can't feel bad for 'em now given the thing he co-signed on with that fool Tonto."

"Tonto better hope and pray that the police catch up to 'em before I do," Lee let it be known. "But on some other shit? You want me to replace your dead best friend by being the best man in your wedding?" he asked disdainfully as he began cleaning up Udelle's mess. "That ain't gone do nothing for me or the position I hold."

Udelle regained his composure after coating his stomach with a few bites of pizza and walked out of the kitchen and stood before Lee in the center of the living room. He knew Lee was gunning for bigger status within the family, but to him, this deal with Tonto, should Lee take matters into his own hands, would be nothing more than a detriment to everything the family had going on. "Sometimes it's not about who or how many people you kill for the people you working for, but the manner in which you treat the ones the family deem indispensable," he told Lee.

"I ain't never kill nobody," Lee responded as he looked way from Udelle.

"I'm not gone even go there with you, Lee. And I would never ask you about something as deep as that because it's none of my business. What I'm tryna tell ya' is that Kimi and Koko is indispensable. And I know for a fact that you love my ole lady twin. You should be in Oneika's wedding not only for Koko, but for yourself, man. And then think about being my best man. You should be around to see the end result of what the family got going on instead of being somebody that they talk about after it's all said and done. Tonto ain't worth it. Think about how you starting off with Koko, my dude. You wanna lose her over some shit that was going on long before you even knew who she was? Some shit you know the family can already handle?" he questioned as he stared Lee in the eyes awaiting a reply.

"Maybe this here a deal the family don't wanna touch because it's too close to home. Ever thought about that shit, weather man?" Lee asked as he stared Udelle in the eyes.

"I see your point," Udelle responded. "Do what you do, homeboy. But, just be in Oneika's wedding. I really want you to help me out with me and Kimi wedding, but I'm willing to let that go for now. Being in Oneika wedding would be good for Kimi and especially Koko, though. She would enjoy that, man. That's all. Do that favor for me. Be in Oneika's wedding."

Lee let what Udelle was asking of him soak in as he finished wiping down the couch. He would indeed have to lay low after killing Tonto and as far as he knew, he would have a clear schedule. After completing what could be one of his most difficult tasks to date, he himself began to believe that a new and legitimate assignment would be just what he needed. On top of that, he would still remain close to Koko given the job Udelle was asking of him.

"You already know I'd love to walk with Koko, man. I can do that. But planning a wedding for you? I don't know," Lee remarked.

"Okay! Okay!" Udelle exclaimed in a happy tone. "Think about being my best man! But I can count on you being in Oneika wedding, right?"

Lee ran his hands over the sides of his silk shorts, smiled and said, "I'll do it, man. I'd be happy to participate in that wedding. That shit'll be tight. Only, only if Ben says it's cool and I get to walk with my baby Koko, though."

"That's what I'm talkin' 'bout! You gone walk with Koko no doubt, man!" Udelle responded in jubilance as he pointed over to Lee. "You and me? We got the princesses in our palms, bruh! Enjoy this shit! Let Dawk 'nem know what it is in the morning. But in the meantime, though, fam? I'm going throw up this slice of pizza I done ate? And pass the fuck out!" he ended as he ran out the living room headed towards the bathroom in the hall where he closed the door and began oiling up everything outside of his vital organs.

Lee reflected on the night before as he finished up a plate of shrimp and grits before leaving to pick up Amber and Tre`. Together, the three rode up to Ponca City in a rental car Lee was wheeling and made their way over to the airport on the west side of town. Samantha, Ben, Vic, Kimi and Koko were already on hand when the trio pulled up, Ben sitting inside the plane going over in his mind the final details of the upcoming deal and texting Katrina while Samantha walked around the G-550 corporate jet doing her preflight check as Vic and Tre` stood talking beside the plane.

Lee climbed from behind the wheel of his Hyundai rental car and went and hugged his woman briefly as she stood on her crutches beside the family's bulletproof Escalade where Siloam and two Mexicans dressed in denim outfits and sporting denim trench coats and ten gallon hats stood at the rear of the vehicle looking off into the distance. "Your man is a bit off," he told Kimi while hugging Koko amidst the heavy security.

"Let me guess, he ran you crazy talking about weather?" Kimi laughed.

"That too," Lee laughed. "But he want me to be the best man for you and his wedding."

Kimi's eyebrows raised. "I thought it woulda been this dude Devin from our Accounting class," she remarked. "Why you?"

"That's my question. I told 'em I'd think about it. But I do wanna be in Oneika's wedding with my baby," he smiled as he leaned into Koko and kissed her neck, forcing her to giggle into the frigid morning air.

"I was gone ask you, baby! My foot should be well by then! Thank you, Udelle!" Koko screamed out loud, even though Udelle wasn't on hand to appreciate her gesture.

"Don't let me down, Lee." Kimi smiled. "You'll make a great best man. Help my future husband out, player."

"Alright, Kimi. Let 'em know I'll do it," Lee laughed. "You gone be okay, baby?" he then asked Koko.

"Yeah," Koko replied lovingly while staring up into Lee's

eyes. "I got you a room in my name at the Hilton not too far from here, but I can't visit right now because I have a boat load of work to complete."

"I saw that place. You gone tuck me in later?"

"If not? I'll see you tomorrow morning. I hope you're not disappointed? I just got a feeling I'll be working late and it's supposed to snow today. I'll come soon as I can."

"What?" Lee asked, waving Koko's statement off. "I know what you do, baby. And you know what I do, right?" he then whispered into her ear.

"Be careful, love," Koko whispered back into Lee's ear.

"Always," Lee smiled as he backed away from his woman. He then nodded over to Kimi before turning and trotting up the stairs of the G-550 in his grey silk suit and black mid-length leather jacket. "Boss?" he said as he peeked into the plane.

"Come in, fam," Ben remarked as he set his phone and a folder aside. When Lee sat before him, Ben leaned back, crossed his legs and said, "Tonto bail was put up last night by an anonymous source on some untraceable money. My people got word that his momma, Hakiba Jamison, caught up with Oneika at her shop downtown yesterday morning. She tryna make a deal to save her son, ya' dig? But the family not letting what that boy did slide. We want Tonto taken care of, but don't touch his mother."

"I'm gone do what I can, boss, but if his mother gets in my way…"

"Lee," Ben remarked calmly as Samantha and Amber walked past him, heading towards the cockpit. "This thing with Tonto is delicate, brer. His brother Kahlil know what's going down. Dude really don't care about that there because his brother done became his enemy, but if we touch his moms, brer? That's gone create a whole new set of problems for us."

Lee leaned back and crossed his legs T-style and analyzed the situation. Tonto was a done deal already, but he could see how killing Kahlil's mother would cause problems for the family. Kahlil and Walee would fall out if that were to happen and the friendship the young baller had with Spoonie and Tyke would be damaged as well. Killing Hakiba would do more harm to the young ones in the family than anything else, and the last thing Lee wanted to do was to be the one to bring about disharmony within the family.

"I see what you saying, boss," Lee remarked as he leaned forward and rested his elbows on his knees. He looked Ben in the eyes and said, "Hakiba won't be touched at all, but I'm not sure if I can get the job done in a day, man. I gotta at least study dude and pick up a routine. That's gone take time."

"Naomi and Dawk gone be down in Mexico for a few days. When we done in Cayman Islands, me, Vic and Tre` flying back to Arizona. Naomi and Dawk won't return stateside until you off Tonto," Ben remarked as he looked out the window and watched as Siloam and a ranch hand helped Koko back into the Escalade. He remained silent as he watched his family pile into the SUV and ride off from the airport. "Here Tonto address," he finally said to Lee. "He gone be staying with his momma while he under house arrest," he added as he slid Lee a sheet of paper. "They stay on the west side of town in a trailer park. Morning time be the best time to pull it off from what Dawk saying, but that's at your discretion."

Lee plucked the paper and memorized the address before handing it back to Ben and scooting to the edge of the leather seat. "I won't let you down, boss," he stated as he reached out and shook Ben's hand.

"If we remain true to what we doing we gone all walk away from this thing with Saudi money, fam," Ben remarked as thoughts of his old crew ran through his mind. "I'm able to see better given my past mistakes, but I still need people I can trust gone be loyal to this here thing in order to succeed."

"You know I'm with you," Lee stated, steadily looking Ben in the eyes as the engines on the plane revved up. "Until the end of the line," he professed. "Udelle asked me to be the best in his wedding last night," he then added. "I told Kimi I'd do it, and I wanna walk with Koko in Oneika's wedding."

Ben laughed lightly over the jet's vibration. "I was expecting you to be in Oneika's wedding because I knew Koko was gone be in it. I can see that. But I think you being the best man for Udelle would be something good for you and Koko, brer."

"I ain't never done no shit like that in my life, Ben. And then I'm thinking he did it more to keep me from killing Tonto more than anything else."

"We know that there ain't gone happen," Ben remarked. "But you gone have to lay low after this here deal anyway so that'll be a good way to occupy your time. You got my blessing on both those deals. Koko told you the hotel," he stated in an assured tone. "Here your key. Check behind the headboard for the piece you gone use on the job. Go on and kick back and do your thing, fam. This an all-expense paid venture and you got everything you need."

Lee took the hotel key from Ben, nodded and stood up and shook his hand just as Samantha stuck her head out the cockpit. "We ready for takeoff!" she called out.

Ben pointed to Lee and said, "You on the clock, fam. I'm counting on you to get it done."

Lee threw up a peace sign and emerged from the plane. He trotted down the stairs and made his way over to his Hyundai and climbed behind the wheel and made his way over to the Hilton in order to set up and go after Tonto.

CHAPTER THIRTEEN

WHO CAN YOU TRUST

Samantha had touched down on Cayman Island just after seven in the evening. Swan and Monty, the two cops I had on the payroll back in the day down in New Orleans, was on hand to greet me as I stepped off the plane. I handed over two briefcases to Swan and he passed them along to two Colombian foot soldiers and nodded towards a limousine. "Wait for us in the car," he told the guards accompanying him. When the men cleared out, Swan looked me in the eyes and said, "I got some news that may be of benefit to your family later on down the road, Ben."

"What's up?" I asked.

Swan looked me over for a quick second and whispered, "Gacha got word a new cartel in America based out of San Antonio, Texas is trying to establish ground. He wanted me to make you aware."

"Who are they?" I whispered back.

"A bunch of misfit louts operating out of San Antonio. They call themselves the Eagle Pass Cartel."

"I appreciate the info on these thugs, but I'm not seeing how this affects my family. We don't operate in Texas and not planning to." I spoke lowly.

"It doesn't impact your family for now, but if this cartel plan on expanding? It could lead to trouble. You have to find out who they are and eliminate them. That's what Gacha is asking. That's what he wants done."

"He not giving us much to go on, Swan. I mean, how we gone find these people?"

"Gacha only has the name of the cartel and the city where they're based because it's all he knows. He likes your family, man!" Swan emphasized towards me. "And he wouldn't be sending the message if he didn't think it was of any importance to ya'. Find out who these people are and kill them! Because it's only a matter of time before they start gunning for you and your people!"

"I'll see what I can find out and handle that as soon as possible."

"Good," Swan sighed as he ran his hands over his thinning grey ponytail. "No need to contact us until it's done. If we find out anything beforehand we'll let you know." he ended before walking back over to the idling limousine.

I watched as the tail lights on Swan and Monty's limousine lit up the runway as they rode off. When they cleared out, I whistled for Victor. He was from Mexico and might know something about these people. I met him halfway down the runway and asked, "What you know about an Eagle Pass Cartel?"

"Eagle Pass Cartel I know nothing about, but Eagle Pass is a city on—"

"The Texas-American border in south central Texas." I remarked, cutting Victor off as my mind began working overtime. To me, this situation was reminiscent of the Lapiente` family. Any organization crossing over into America from Mexico had to be moving major weight. And if they were being backed by Gacha that meant they had money and men behind them—enough strength to wage war in our own backyard of they wanted to.

"Everything okay, boss?" Victor asked me, shaking me from my thoughts.

"I gotta make a few moves when we get back to Arizona." I

said to Victor as I made my way back to the jet.

The deal down in Cayman went unhinged for the mast part. It wasn't a drug deal gone bad, but I can't help but to feel anxious over what Swan had told me as I trotted up the stairs leading back to Samantha's plane while sending an all-clear text to Kimi.

"How'd it go?" Samantha asked as she sat before a small table with Amber, the two of them playing poker with Tre` as I stepped onto the plane.

"We good. Let's fly," I told Samantha as I went over to the bar and poured myself a drink. My glass wasn't half full before the stairs to the plane were being raised.

Within minutes, we were prepared to make the flight back to America. "Control tower, this is Ponchartrain One requesting take off on runway two." There they go with lingo again. Listening to Amber and Samantha make flight preparations was like a lullaby to my ears and relaxing to my soul as I knew I was in good hands.

I laid my head back and closed my eyes while planning a trip up to Florence, Colorado once we landed back at the airport down in Phoenix. Swan had given me a heads up, but there was one person I knew I could talk to and get not only a leg up on the budding problem, but also obtain further insight into the mind of Gacha and how the man operated his organization.

****

We made it back to Arizona just after eleven after a four and a half hour flight. If you've never flown over the open ocean under clear skies at night during a full moon I suggest you do it. You'll gain a greater appreciation for a higher source, or at the very least recognize the awe-inspiring power that mother nature welds over the Earth.

Tired, we all off-boarded the jet and headed home. Victor went to his place after we made sure that Tre`, Samantha and Amber were locked away inside Samantha's home over to Tempe. I took my sister's Caprice and headed home to the

Mesa mansion I shared with my wife. I'd texted Katrina and told her I was on my way and to have it ready for me and she knew what I meant.

"It's been ready, baby. You better come get it." Katrina texted back. That's how we get down ya' dig? I can picture my wife setting up a bath for us, her brown-skinned body soft to the touch, sexy lips waiting to be kissed with a moist pussy ready to be licked and fucked to satisfaction.

I entered the mansion with a clear mind, in spite of the info Swan had dropped on me back on Grand Cayman. Home was where I could put the business out of my mind for a while. Family time, ya' know? And it'd been a while, nearly a month since I'd seen my wife. I'd gotten tied up with what'd gone down with Spoonie and the Germans and had to make sure the family was straight before I sought my way home. Along the way, I'd secured the first deal for the family's first big shipment so we good for the foreseeable future, but I still had a few loose ends to tie up before I could really fall back— namely, the situation with this unknown cartel.

Feeling good about the current circumstances, I detached myself from the game by grabbing a bottle of champagne from the fridge and made my way upstairs. My dick was already hardening as I thought about sexing Katrina in our jacuzzi after we'd smoked and drank and just kicked it. All that shit went out the window when I walked into the bedroom and saw Henrietta sitting on the bench at the foot of my bed with Kenyan in her arms bouncing up and down on the mattress.

"Ben, I'm glad you're home," Henrietta said to me. "I think Kenyan has a tummy ache. I heard him crying and came to see what was wrong and he was just a wailing away."

I ain't gone lie, I booted my youngest son up like he was some dude off the streets as he lay in Henrietta's lap heaving while running his hands over her chin. This dude here, I don't know if he lived before or not, but every time I stay away for a while and me and Katrina make plans he act up. He don't be sick, just be missing me and wondering where I'm at. Henrietta play right into his li'l act, too. She fall for it every time, but I'm a sucker for my sons as well. I love him and Ben Junior to death. If my youngest flesh was uptight and wanted his daddy because he ain't seen me in so long, then that's what it is.

"I got 'em, Auntie," I told Henrietta after setting the champagne bottle down on a shelf. I walked over and scooped my crying son up into my arms and placed him over my shoulder. "Daddy, got ya', brer. Ya' good?"

"Dada," Kenyan cried as he laid his head on my shoulder and hugged my neck tenderly. My son's entire body relaxed as I began walking around the master suite with him tucked away in my arms while gently patting his back.

"How's Spoonie?" Henrietta asked me as I rocked my son to sleep.

"She good, Auntie. She be home soon. The family planning a big welcome home party. We all invited. I'll let y'all know when it is."

"That's wonderful, Ben," Katrina said to me as she entered the room on the tail end of the conversation. "I got the menu ready, by the way."

"For the restaurant in Saint Charles?" I asked.

"Yeah. I'm 'bout ready to bring the final menu for the café forth. I'll be flying out there next week to meet with the interior designers."

"That's cool. You sure you can handle that, girl? You gone be feeding like a hundred people on opening night," I joked.

"That's all?" Katrina shot back. She then smiled and nodded over to Henrietta, who was busy working the remote control to set up some cartoons for Kenyan, as she held up a pack of grape Dutch cigars in one hand and a bag of bubble gum weed in the other with her silk robe open, displaying her voluptuous body. Needless to say, I wanted all that over there in my life.

"Henrietta, I think Kenyan gone be all right," I told my Aunt while smiling over to Katrina on the slick. "You wanna lay my boy in his crib?"

"Sure, Ben. The monitor is on in both bedrooms. Hopefully he'll sleep through the remainder of night," Henrietta said as she took my sleeping son from my arms.

"I got a surprise for you, Auntie."

"What's that, Ben?" Henrietta asked as she held onto my son.

"We going up to Florence, Colorado day after tomorrow. Going see Yiska."

"Ben! You tell a story!" Henrietta exclaimed happily. "Really?"

"For real."

"I'm going to do it!" Henrietta said as she looked around happily. "You only live once, and I'm going to see that man live if it's last thing I do. I won't waste this opportunity."

"What you gone do to Yis like that?" I asked Henrietta with raised eyebrows.

"Take your mind out of the gutter, young man," Henrietta laughed as she stepped back and looked me up and down with one leg extended out before her body while holding onto Kenyan. "We're going to have a picnic during our visit. Can I do that for Yiska?"

"I'll make it happen, Auntie," I stated.

"Good. You two enjoy yourselves now," she said with a sly smile as she turned and walked out of the bedroom with my son's head resting on her shoulder.

I closed the door behind Henrietta and turned back to Katrina. She was already headed to the bathroom and was running water in the jacuzzi and had disrobed. I watched from across the way as she turned to the side with a remote in her hand. Katrina got this complex about her weight and her past, but you know what? We all make mistakes. I mean, me and my wife didn't have a normal childhood coming up. My parents were killed early on and her mother was a dope fiend that sold her for drugs. All Katrina wanted was love, and all I wanted was a family to replace the one I'd lost. After the dust had settled, we found each other in the chaos. I loved this woman before I even loved myself, and she gave me a family, two sons, before I ever knew of my father's people. No matter what, we here, brer. We in it for the long haul.

It wasn't long before a song I hadn't heard literally in years encompassed the entire suite. I could see Katrina setting up champagne glasses and an ashtray beside the spa. I grabbed the bottle of champagne I'd set on the shelf earlier just as the O'Jays' song *Stairway To Heaven* came over the speakers.

This was my wife and this was why I loved her so damn much. She was able to touch my heart like no other. I removed my suit jacket while walking towards the bathroom with a proud smile on my face, humbled over the beautiful specimen of woman that had chosen to love me unconditionally as the song played on while we began to kick back and relax.

****

The following morning I was up as the six 'o' clock hour approached. Tre` and Victor had opened the detail shop so I was good on that. I made a call up to Nevada and got in touch with the Asians and notified them of the fact that I needed a face-to-face with JunJie and they signed off on it. Before we hung up, I had them notify the guards and inform Yiska that my Aunt Henrietta was wanting to bring in a picnic basket. It took about ten minutes for everything to clear, and Yiska was now preparing himself for a visit.

I dressed up in a khaki Dickies outfit and black Soldier Reeboks inside my bedroom suite and left the room seeking out my sons. They were down in the dining room being served breakfast by Celeste and Henrietta. A plate of grits and cheese with hot sausage links was slid before me as I took a seat at the breakfast table. I was about to start feeding Kenyan myself because I knew how he could get with a plate of food in front of his face, but I was distracted by a phone call from Dawk. I didn't get up with him when I touched down in Arizona and I knew he was calling for an update. "Yo," I answered.

"What it is, fam?"

"It's all good, cuz. Still on the clock with that thing," I told him, referencing the situation with Lee and Tonto. "We meet back up once things get taken care of, I'm gone be here in AZ for the time being. Should be another couple of days or so at the latest for that deal with that boy, though."

"Cool. We meet back up after that there get taken care of. You be in for Spoonie return? She should be home some time April."

"I'm gone have ta' see you before then, fam."

"What up?"

"Got wind of some info down in the islands. With that there news, I'm going check something out in ADX and I'm a fill you in once I get things straight with that there, ya' dig?" I said as I reached out to pull the bowl of grits from in front of Kenyan.

"Already," Dawk stated before ending the call. By that time I was too late. Kenyan had slammed his hand down into his grits and flipped the whole bowl over. Grits splattered everywhere. My chest and chin was covered in goo. My oldest boy, Ben Holland Junior, had a forehead full of grits that was dripping down over his eyebrows and running down the sides of his nose. IIe sat calmly as the particles slid down over his light skin with a look on his face that said, "*Dad, check that fool,*"

"Kenyan don't know no better, son. He gone get better with time," I told Ben Junior, who reached for a napkin and handed it to me before sticking out his face. Spending time with my sons was the favorite way to start my day, ya' dig? After getting them cleaned and fed, I headed on out the door to start my day wondering how Lee was making out back up in Ponca City.

CHAPTER FOURTEEN

SOME REAL SUGAR

Lee Sato awoke inside his suite inside the Marriott over to Ponca City a few minutes after Ben had left out to head to his detail shop back over in Arizona. He checked the time and saw that it was 8:30 in the morning as he walked over to the mini fridge in the nude and pulled it open. He had plans on warming up the ribs and chicken he'd bought before Kimi and Koko had dropped him off the day before, but the food had been left out overnight. He cringed upon seeing the plate of food sitting atop the mini fridge as he walked over and flipped the lid open on the styrofoam plate. "Come on, man. Way to starve yourself, Lee," he sighed as he poked at the dried out ribs and tough chicken with a side of cold macaroni. The tall, slender, tatted up Asian walked back over to the bed and checked the .9mm on the nightstand while turning on the television to check the weather.

Snow was in store for later on in the morning according to the weather channel, so Lee went and peeked out the curtains. The skies were grey and flurries were already sparsely dropping from the clouds. Lee didn't like how the day was starting out. He was sporting a dreadful feeling for reasons unexplainable as he opened the playlist on his phone and flipped through the selections. Upon finding a song to amplify his melancholy mood, he grabbed his gun and overnight bag from the bedside and launched himself into a shit, shave and shower as rapper Pastor Troy's song *We Ready* began playing on his cell.

He emerged from a steaming hot shower ten minutes later and was drying his spiked hair when he heard a knock on the door. Flinging the towel aside, he shut his phone down, grabbed his .9mm off the sink and tiptoed over to the door. "Who's there?" he asked as he hid in an open closet near the room's entrance.

"It's Koko."

"Koko?" Lee whispered to himself as he moved to crack the door. "Who's with you?" he asked in a low tone as the door shielded his naked body and the gun he was gripping.

"I'm by myself." Koko responded as she brought a brown paper bag into view. "Hungry?" she asked mischievously while revealing her pearly whites.

"You came here by yourself?" Lee questioned as he unchained the door and pulled it open. "Baby, you in no shape to be out here on your own!"

Koko laughed as handed Lee the paper bag and guided herself into the room on her walking stick. "I told you I was coming yesterday, boy. I'm safe here in my hometown, Lee," she remarked as she eased around to face her love interest head on.

"Really?" Lee asked casually as he closed and chained the door. "There're dangerous people in your hometown, Koko. I don't want you to ever make that mistake again."

"You're not dangerous to me, Lee. And I'm not making a mistake," Koko retorted. Lee had an angry look on his face she suddenly noticed. It was a look she'd seen before, one that intimidated her as flashes of Chablis and his male aggression towards her crossed her mind. "I didn't mean to upset you so I'll just go now," she remarked in an attempt to free herself from Lee's ire.

"No, no, no!" Lee pleaded as he set the gun and paper bag aside and grabbed Koko's hand. "I'm not trying to boss you around or anything like that and I'm not angry for you being here, but look at you, baby. You're barely able to walk. You could slip and fall and it has to be hard to drive like that."

"You sure that's all there is?" Koko asked cautiously as she shifted her weight on her walking stick.

"I don't," Lee ran his hands over his spiked hair and walked off in frustration. "I don't wanna see nothing happen to you, alright?" he grumbled. "And you're over there gettin' mad at me because I care what happens to you?" he asked as he turned and faced the woman he adored.

"I'm fine, Lee," Koko comforted through a smile. "I didn't drive and I didn't come alone. Siloam is waiting for me in the Suburban back downstairs. I brought you breakfast. My grandfather and Francine fixed a helping of chocolate chipped pancakes for the children this morning. I had them fry up some bacon and scrambled some eggs to go along with it and brought you some lemon tea too. They don't have room service here and I thought you'd be hungry waking up."

Lee placed his hands to his hips and eyed Koko as he stood in all his nudity with a smirk. "You, you did that for me, baby?"

"I did." Koko remarked as she looked to the floor and contemplated her exact reason for visiting Lee at such an early hour. Setting caution aside, she raised her head slowly and smiled again. "Lee," she began, "The entire time you've been here has been wonderful. My family likes you and I care what happens to you. I'm just trying to make what you do as easy as possible. Bring some normality to it if that makes sense."

Lee eyed the specimen of woman standing before him in her tight-fitting light-brown silk dress and white mink coat with specks of light-brown mixed in. A leather knee-length light brown boot was on her left foot and a stylish light-brown leather medical boot covered her fractured right foot. Loyal she was to his Cause he now understood. To hurt this sweet, gorgeous woman was something he could never fathom doing in life. He'd rather walk away from it all and sacrifice his own life if it meant her living. Koko may not have been willing to say it, but nothing was stopping him from expressing what was

125

on his heart.

"I'm not afraid to say I love you Koko Dawkins," Lee admitted as he stepped closer.

Koko looked away and pressed her lips together as her eyes watered. She was feeling it too, but for her, it was too soon. "I can't say it back. Not at this moment, as much as I'm feeling it in my heart I can't. But that doesn't mean I don't have feelings for you," she admitted as Lee wrapped his protective arms around her shoulders and drew her head into his tatted chest.

"You don't have to," Lee responded as he nudged Koko's chin upwards and stared into her watery brown eyes. "So long as you know where I stand that's all that matters. I'm not worthy to even stand in your shadow right about now, but here I am—loving on you like I've never loved any other woman in my life."

"I missed you last night. Just wanted to be near you," Koko confessed as she closed her eyes and began rubbing her face up and down on Lee's chest while unrepentantly allowing her lips to linger over his flesh as she began planting soft kisses on his rugged flesh.

"What you got in store for me, girl?" Lee asked in a sexy, raspy voice as his hands slide inside of Koko's mink coat where he gripped her firm, round ass.

"Give me some time and I'll show you. Nothing stopping me from starting with this, though," Koko responded lovingly as she raised her head and kissed Lee passionately.

Lee kept a firm grip on Koko's ass while tonguing her as he gripped the silk that was clinging to her voluptuous body. The two flicked tongues as he began pulling Koko's dress up towards her hips. "Baby, my foot. I can't," Koko protested as her hand slid down Lee's body.

"That's why you came here wearing no panties and standing there stroking my dick with your bare hands?" Lee asked as he pulled Koko's dress up and over her wide hips and palmed her bare ass cheeks.

"The pancakes aren't that sweet. Thought you might want to

taste some real sugar before you go to work this morning." Koko answered as she pulled back from Lee and let her coat fall from her shoulders to the floor.

Without saying a word, Lee stepped up and nudged Koko around. "Sure you can handle it?" he asked.

"Don't brag, boy. Just do it," Koko replied as she grabbed the end of the wooden circular table inside the room and bent forward while spreading her legs with the ends of her silk dress curled up over her waist.

"Don't say I didn't warn you," Lee boasted as he knelt down behind Koko.

Koko had her eyes closed and wasn't anticipating Lee's move. "It's wet and ready for—" she paused midsentence and gasped when she felt Lee's tongue penetrating her inner folds. "Baby," she moaned as she stretched her arms out and laid her stomach flat on the table top.

"Umm hmm," Lee declared through a mouth full of pussy as he sucked Koko's clitoris from the back. His tongue stroke made its way to her opening and he began darting it in and out as he curled the tip, licking her warm, wet insides.

Koko was trying to pull away as the pleasure was too intense, but she was held back by Lee's hands that were planted on the front side of her hips. "Bring it to me," he demanded as he kissed, sucked and licked on his woman's pussy while pulling her back.

"Lee," Koko moaned as she reached back and pulled her cheeks open and pushed her ass back into his face. "You gone make me come like this!"

"No I'm not," Lee stated as he removed his face from Koko's crevice and stood up.

"Don't you do this to me! Don't you—God!" Koko cried out as she felt Lee's dick sliding into her slickened pussy. His dick went on for what seemed like an eternity before his pelvis bumped her ass, forcing her face into a contorted display of amazed delight as he began stroking her long, deep, hard and fast. "Take me!" she cried out loud.

Lee was a man of little words that possessed a big sword. He knew how to please a woman when it got down to it and his dick always did the talking. The sight of his rod sliding in and out some of the best pussy life had to offer as it creamed all over his cock grew him more rigid as he began slapping the sides of Koko's soft butt cheeks. "Fuck!" he growled as he kept his eyes on the pretty pussy that was delivering ecstasy incomparable.

"You making me come! I'm finna come!" Koko cried out as Lee's dick hit places she never knew existed. "This better than the time in Arizona! This better than Arizona!"

Sweat was forming on Lee's chest and back as he pummeled Koko from behind, but while in the midst of fucking her into oblivion and taking his self over the edge in the process, he couldn't help but to think about Koko's fractured foot for some odd reason. A few more strokes was all he needed, but he had to make sure his woman was satisfied. "Are you there, Koko? You coming, baby?"

Before Koko could answer, there was a knock at the door. "Koko, this Siloam! Are you okay in there? It's been some time now!"

"I'm coming, Siloam!" Koko screamed aloud as she rose up and looked back at Lee while grinding down onto the good dick he possessed. "I'm coming!" she screamed out a second time as she stared back into her lover's eyes. "I'm coming!"

Lee gritted his teeth and heaved as he drove into Koko and rested his dick deep inside her gaping pussy. He then pulled out when he felt his dick convulsing and shot his load all over her wide ass.

Koko's legs were trembling as an intense orgasm coursed through her body as Lee's hot semen coated her ass and backside. "Boy," she laughed as laid her head on the table and planted her face in her arms with her ass in the air.

"This my pussy," Lee gasped as he used the tip of his dick to spell out his name on Koko's ass with the semen he'd spilled onto her flesh. "L-E-E-," he panted. "Signed, sealed, delivered, baby—"

"I'm yours," Koko finished as she rose, turned around and smiled at Lee while palming the back of his head to draw him in for a deep, sensual kiss to close out the act.

"Koko?" Siloam called out, breaking the trance.

Lee and Koko blushed at one another as they embraced. "If I could spend the entire time here with you I would," Lee admitted.

"I know," Koko remarked as she draped an arm over Lee's shoulder. "But you have a job to do. I hope I've put your mind at ease?"

"What pancakes?" Lee asked seriously as he walked over and grabbed a cotton robe to cover his naked flesh. "I done had my breakfast, baby," he stated as he walked back over to Koko.

Koko blushed as she lowered her dress and grabbed her walking stick. "I know you can eat me to satisfaction and get full, but man can't live off pussy alone," she remarked seriously. "Eat your breakfast before you leave. Tonto ain't going nowhere so take your time with that, and call me if you need me."

"Koko!" Siloam boomed as she knocked on the door again.

"I'm coming now, Siloam!" Koko yelled back as Lee grabbed her coat and placed it back onto her body. "See you later, love," she added as she tilted her head back and gave Lee a final kiss before reaching out to pull the door open.

"What were you two doing?" Siloam was heard asking as Koko wobbled out into the hall.

"I was giving him his breakfast like I told you," Koko was heard saying by Lee as he eased the door shut.

Alone in the empty room, Lee checked the time and saw that it was just after nine 'o' clock. The dreadful mood he'd been harboring had been vanquished by Koko's visit and he now went about the remainder of his routine unabashedly as he knew nothing, not even that of having to kill a man, would stand in the way of him ever seeing Koko Dawkins again.

CHAPTER FIFTEEN

SOMETHING BAD HAPPENED

"Dammit!" Hakiba scoffed as she stared at the water backing up into the washing machine inside her single wide trailer.

While Lee set about his day, Hakiba Jamison, the hardworking matriarch of the Jamison family, was attempting place a load of clothes into the washing machine for cleaning before she left for her job over to the Holland family's entertainment complex, but water from the home's sewer line was backing up into the machine. The smell was nauseating for Hakiba, and she didn't have time to drain the line as she was already running late for work.

"Tonto!" Hakiba called out as she kicked aside a basket full of dirty laundry. "Tonto, get up!" she yelled as she marched up the narrow hall and pushed Tonto's bedroom door open.

Tonto jumped up and reached for a .9mm he had resting in a folding chair beside his bed. He eased up when he saw his mother standing in the doorway with her arms folded. "If you're going to be in this house until your trial you're going to have to pitch in with the chores," Hakiba complained.

"I never wanted to come back here!" Tonto complained as he flung the covers off his legs and reached for a half-smoked blunt sitting in an ashtray on the floor beside his bed. "I'm still tryna figure out who bailed me out. I know it was Dawk!" he boomed. "I oughta steal a car or something so they can lock me back up."

"Way to make it easy on yourself," Hakiba stated in a sarcastic manner as she placed her hands on her hips. "The police down in Oklahoma City is giving you a break for what you've done. Be happy!"

"Momma, I'm a sitting duck here! You can't see that?" Tonto scoffed as he raised his leg and put his ankle bracelet on display. "I can't go a hundred yards from the house. That's not even far enough to walk to the corner store to get some beer or blunt wraps," he added as he grabbed a lighter and lit his blunt.

"If beer and blunt wraps is all you're worried about given all that's going on with you, you're already way behind on life, Tonto," Hakiba retorted. "That ankle bracelet you're wearing goes far enough for you to walk to the laundry room at the center of the complex and put a load of clothes into the wash. When you're done with that, come back here and call maintenance so they can come and drain the sewer line. The washer's backed up again."

"Why don't you get your favorite son to do it? He came back here last night after working out down in Stillwater, you know?" Tonto asked rhetorically as he took another toke of his blunt.

"Kahlil's home?" Hakiba smiled as she placed a hand over her heart and took off running to Kahlil's bedroom where she eased the door open.

Kahlil was sleeping with his back to the door with an orange handkerchief covering his head. For Haikiba, that meant her youngest son had gotten his hair braided the day before. She folded her arms and leaned on the threshold and simply admired her progeny as he slept. Kahlil, for Hakiba, represented hope and a better way of life, not for herself, however, but one for his own financial stability.

Wooden panels, dingy furniture and minimum wage jobs had been Hakiba and her sons' lot for as long she could remember. She'd tried to do her best and she did. Never had a day gone by without a meal. Never was a bill missed and never had the family been homeless, although coming close on several occasions. Tonto had the vision, but somewhere along the way, he'd lost focus and had all but given up. Kahlil, however, Kahlil was able to see better days ahead. He kept the vision and had never given up.

Hakiba smiled as she reflected on thirteen year-old Kahlil telling her that he was going to be a first round draft pick like his older brother someday back in the fall of 2004. *"That way, you'll have two rich sons to take care of you, momma,"* he told Hakiba as he sat on the floor before the family's rickety coffee table eating a grits and gravy dinner as she sewed the holes on the sides the worn cleats her son used to play middle school football.

Hakiba also remembered the day Kahlil came home and told her about the cool family he'd met at Kaw Lake Park back in the summer of 2001. *"My new friend Walee and his younger sisters Spoonie and Tyke is big Oklahoma State fans, momma! We all gone go there someday!"*

"I don't know if I'll be able to afford that college, Kahlil," Hakiba remembered telling her son on that hot summer day back in 2001.

"You won't need money, momma. I'm gone be the best safety around here. Northern Oklahoma is Oklahoma State's recruiting ground and they offer full scholarships All I have to do is get them to notice me, and I'm gone do that by working out every day and making the middle school and high school teams."

Hakiba smiled proudly as he kept her eyes on Kahlil. He done everything he'd said he was going to do up until this point. He'd made the middle school team and became the best defensive player in the region and had earned that scholarship he'd spoken of nearly nine years earlier. She'd seen his highlights on ESPN and had heard broadcasters from across the country speak well of her son and it warmed her heart each and every time.

"Momma, Kahlil done put his dirty sweats in here and I ain't washing none of his shit!" Tonto yelled from the front of the trailer home, shaking Hakiba from her brief moment of reflection.

133

"Tell Tonto he ain't gotta touch my clothes I'll do my own laundry," nineteen year-old Kahlil groggily stated as he rolled over and placed his feet to the floor. "He barely do stuff for the family anyway besides cause problems," he added as he leaned forward and grabbed his calves.

"No, baby," Hakiba stated lovingly as she walked over to her son and knelt before him. "You just rest. Tonto said you were working out last night in Stillwater. How did you get here?"

"Spring training coming up and I wanna be ahead of the pack. I came back to grab my gloves and ankle weights in Spoonie and Tyke car. I don't think I need the weights because I overexerted myself on the leg compresses last night. I barely made it here driving they was cramping up so bad."

"Stay here. I'll go and get you some Biofreeze to put on your legs."

"It's my calves," Kahlil grimaced as he laid back on his full-sized bed.

Hakiba left Kahlil's side and entered the bathroom and pulled open the medicine cabinet. She searched for the ointment she kept stored but saw that it was missing. "Tonto, have you seen the Biofreeze?" she asked aloud.

"Used it all last night!" Tonto yelled back as he checked the washing machine while toking his blunt.

Hakiba stormed out of the bathroom and walked to the front of the home. "That was a half full bottle I had for Kahlil and you used it all?"

Tonto waved his mother off as he blew smoke from his nostrils. "It's always about Kahlil with you," he stated as he eyed his mother with disdain. "You don't care what happen to me. No one cares what happens to me. Why you even let me come back home?"

"You're still my son, Tonto. You think I want to see you go to jail or worse? Well, I don't, but sometimes you create your own problems. You haven't done anything for yourself the past few months except to break the law and this is where you are right now." Hakiba stated as she went into the kitchen and grabbed a jar of Vick's vapor rub and walked back down the hall towards Kahlil's bedroom.

"I'm here for being a man! A better man than you think, than you think Kahlil is above me!"

Hakiba reemerged from Kahlil's bedroom and walked up to Tonto. "This is not a competition between you and your brother! Had you done what you were supposed to do in life this would not be happening to you, Tonto!"

"Funny how you do nothing to stop it, momma," Tonto retorted. "You act like you don't understand what's going on. Like you don't care what can possibly happen to me."

"I never stopped caring, Tonto," Hakiba spoke lovingly. "But you can't kick a sleeping giant and not expect it to awaken and look around for the person who upset it. This is your bed! You've made your bed and you have to sleep in it! I have Kahlil to worry—"

Hakiba's speech was cut short when Tonto clasped his hands to her neck and pressed his thumbs to her esophagus to cut off her breathing. "I could kill you right now and disappear! Where's your favorite son to save you now, huh? Laying back rubbing his thighs like a fuckin' bitch why you in here praying that I not do this! That I not kill you this morning?" he scoffed lowly as he shook his mother.

Hakiba shook her head in protest as her eyes watered. Her tongue was forced out of her mouth as she continued slapping at Tonto's wrists.

"That's right," Tonto whispered. "I'm your problem child. And as long as I'm around, you'll never have peace—you and your son will never have peace! He stole my dream! *My dream*!" the jealous-hearted young man ended as he let go of the grip he had on his mother's neck.

Kahlil had just walked into the hall when Tonto let go of Hakiba. He sensed something was not right, but wasn't sure. "Everything okay, momma?" he asked as he eyed Tonto while standing in the hall.

"Yeah," Hakiba coughed as Tonto leaned down and picked up Kahlil's sweats off the floor and tossed them into the basket.

"Ain't nothing, li'l brother," Tonto quickly followed with a smirk on his face. "Just sorting the laundry. Right, momma?"

Hakiba checked the time on her watch and said, "I have to get going. Tonto, do what I ask you to do. Kahlil, you be careful around here and I'll see you this evening," she stated, doing her best to hide her fright and anxiety.

"I'm not staying here, momma. I be gone once my clothes dry."

"That's good to know, son. Call me the time you get back to Stillwater. I have to go now because I'm running behind," Hakiba replied as she headed for the front door.

"Go on clock in for your slave masters the Holland family," Tonto sighed as he took another toke off his blunt and slammed the lid on the washing machine.

"What's your deal, man?" Kahlil scoffed as he walked into the kitchen and opened the refrigerator.

Tonto appeared in the threshold. "My deal?" he asked rhetorically. "I don't have no deal. Look like you the one gone be gettin' a deal…baller!"

"Maybe so," Kahlil answered as he pulled out a pack of bacon and grabbed a skillet from the dish rack. "If it happen, we outta this tin can hut we living in," he added as he turned on the gas stove.

"Gone move on up like the Jefferson's, huh? Maybe move on over to the east side where your people living."

"Wouldn't be a bad move," Kahlil replied as he began placing strips of bacon into the skillet.

"You better be careful on that field. Be a shame if somebody was to go after your knees, twist your kneecap towards one of the sidelines, or, or maybe they'll break your neck like you did Chablis. Remember him?"

"You talkin' about the fuck boy you got to help you try and

kidnap Koko? He right where he belong now," Kahlil laughed as the bacon began to sizzle. "And I ain't even worried about what happen on the field. The whole world respect me and my game, bruh. You the one gotta be worried," he added as he turned back towards the refrigerator.

Tonto was already on edge given what he was up against. He knew his time was short, and it angered him to see his brother's football career expanding before his very eyes. Kahlil was the college star he'd wanted to be. He was the big man on campus Tonto had dreamed of being a few years back, and he was the one whose name was often mentioned on ESPN in talks of the Heisman trophy. No longer able to conceal his jealous rage, Tonto ran into the kitchen while screaming aloud.

Kahlil was expecting his brother to try something. Before Tonto got near him, he pulled the refrigerator door open completely just as Tonto dove for his knees and slammed it against the top of his head. "You crazy, boy?" he growled as he slammed the door shut and stared at his brother.

Tonto rolled over and stood to his feet and threw his hands up. "This been in the makin', potna! You and momma? Y'all no longer mean shit to me! I'm just fuckin' here!"

Kahlil pulled a butcher's knife from the dish rack and held it out towards Tonto, freezing him in his tracks momentarily. "You ain't got the heart to jug me, li'l brother!" he seethed as he charged at Kahlil.

Tonto was right. Kahlil hadn't the heart to stab him. He dropped the knife as Tonto rushed him and tackled him around the midsection and forced him down onto his back inside the kitchen. A blow to the left side of his face stunned Kahlil to action and he retaliated with a punch to Tonto's rib cage. The older brother let go of a guttural sound as he covered his torso and leaned back against the lower cabinets.

Kahlil righted himself just in time to see his brother go for the knife he'd dropped. Knowing Tonto was a force to be reckoned with, he scurried out of the kitchen just as Tonto took another swipe at his knees with the blade. "I'm gone end your career, li'l brother! Slice your knees up, homie! You ain't gone see a fuckin' NFL field ever in life!"

It's fair to say that Kahlil was frightened out of his mind over his brother's aggression at that moment. All that mattered was him preserving his knees, which was the essence of his life. Tonto had become the bane of his existence and all he wanted to do was get as far away from the place that left him feeling like a prisoner since his junior year in high school. He'd regretted returning home on this day. His actual intent was to make peace with Tonto and let him know he wasn't mad at him over what he'd tried to do to Koko and was taking no sides in the matter. His brother attacking him, however, had just forced him to choose sides. He knew where the winners lay, and he was riding with the Holland family until the very end.

Amid Tonto's incoherent rage, Kahlil darted from the home and ran out into the courtyard. In just his white and orange Adidas slippers, orange nylon gym shorts and white Adidas tank top, he ran through copious amounts of snow and made his way to the front of the trailer park. A road leading to the corner store gave him relief from the fracas as he made his way up the block.

Tonto, meanwhile, had regained his composure. He rose up from the linoleum floor and removed the smoking bacon from the gas stove just as the smoke detector sounded. "God, I hate this dump!" he seethed as he fanned the grey smoke and made his way over to the bathroom in order to clean himself up.

Back out on the block, Kahlil had just made his way over to the corner store. In a haste to get away from Tonto, he'd left behind his cell phone, the keys to Spoonie's car, and warm clothes. He didn't want to call the police on his brother, so he decided on calling the only person he could rely on in times of trouble. He jogged into the business and made his way over to the counter just as a navy blue Hyundai cruised by headed towards the trailer park. "I need a phone!" he stated in desperation as he ran up to the female cashier he'd gone to high school with.

"Not my problem, Kahlil. You know the rules. Pay phone is outside," the cashier rebutted as she stood behind the counter taking drags off a cigarette.

"Carla, please," Kahlil pleaded. "One call and one minute. That's all I need!"

Carla removed some of her stringy auburn hair from her chubby, freckled face and smiled as she put out her cigarette. "You're lucky I know you, boy," she sighed as she went into her jean jacket and handed Kahlil her cell. "Make it quick!"

****

"Them cheerleaders on your softball squad get down or what, Spoonie?" Walee joked with his sister as he sat beside her bed inside OU Medical Center.

"Boy," Spoonie laughed. "My girls ain't about that life. Leave them be. The football cheerleaders, though?"

"They bout it?" Walee asked seriously.

"Yeah, and I don't want Kahlil near those girls," Spoonie stated in a slightly disappointed manner just as Walee's phone rung.

"Speaking of," Walee replied as he answered his cell. "What up, my brother?"

"Dog, how long before you can make it up to my house in Ponca City?"

"Couple hours max. What the deal?" Walee asked as he snapped his fingers and got Jordan's attention.

"Just come, bruh. Tonto up here trippin'! I be at the corner store by my house waiting." Kahlil responded before ending the call.

****

Tonto, meanwhile, had just wiped himself clean and was preparing to busy himself with the laundry as he had nothing else to do being he'd run Kahlil off. He walked past his bedroom and heard a report on the morning news that'd caught his ear when he heard his accomplice's name. Backing back down the hall, he walked into his bedroom and picked up the remote control and turned the volume up on the TV. The news was running as a bandaged Chauncey Gainey came into view.

Tonto's coconspirator was flanked by two federal agents while being escorted into the Oklahoma City Police Department headquarters in downtown Oklahoma City. He was draped in a black trench coat and Tonto could tell that his left arm was in a sling. The night they'd tried to kidnap Koko, Chauncey had been wounded in the shoulder. As they fled the scene of the botched attempt, Tonto had pushed Chablis' corpse out into the street over Chauncey's agonizing screams. OU was the closest hospital to get help for Chauncey, but Tonto knew the Holland family would be going there with Spoonie, so he headed south to Saint Anthony's Hospital and let him out in front of the emergency room before peeling out.

By law, doctors are required to report all gunshot victims to the authorities. Chauncey's case was no different. When asked what happened by investigating detectives, Chauncey had stated that he'd gotten caught up in a shootout between rival gangs outside of a night club and had caught a stray bullet. Officers investigated and found no reports of a shooting in the area in which Tonto mentioned, but being some shootings went unreported in certain instances, the law had no choice but to take him at his word. That was until Walee and company arrived over to OU with a wounded Spoonie and Koko.

The law was able to corroborate Koko's statements with what they already knew concerning Chauncey and he was placed under guarded condition pending ballistics from the gun Jordan Whispers had allegedly fired. Bullets matched and Chauncey became a person of interest. Authorities were waiting to question him upon release, but Tonto had accelerated things with his given statement that Chablis and Chauncey were the orchestrators of the botched kidnap attempt.

Tonto watched as Chauncey ignored all questions from reporters as he walked in between the arresting officers with his head bowed. He wondered briefly what Chauncey would have to say about the kidnapping, but he wasn't at all worried, though; he had plenty dirt on Chauncey—enough to buy his self a deal given the bodies his accomplice had under his belt.

The murders from Texas to Kansas that Chauncey had perpetrated would surely earn him a lesser sentence was Tonto's reasoning as he finished his blunt, donned a dark blue velvet jogging suit and placed a pair of black Timberlands onto his feet and sought out the laundry basket while tucking a . 9mm Berretta into the front of his waistband.

****

Lee Sato was pulling up to the trailer park at the same time Tonto was leaving the trailer. He swerved into a parking spot inside the sprawling, flatland complex, climbed out and walked in between a couple of single-wide trailer homes. The trailer park had homes spread out in rows on either side of a courtyard. To the left was a wooded area, and to the right was the laundromat that sat in the center of the courtyard, and there were more homes behind it that lined another separate courtyard where Jane Dow once lived with her mother. Lee eyed the trailers from across the way until he saw the numbers that matched the address he was searching for on the home of the trailer furthest to his left near the woods.

Lee was only there to map out a way to get in and out of the trailer park on this day as his plan was to pull a kick door in the late night hour. A dark figure out the corner of his right eye quickly caught his attention just before he turned to leave, however; he looked around and recognized Tonto right away and quickly summed up what was going down when he eyed the empty clothesbasket Tonto was holding onto. Sooner or later, if Lee had to tell it, his mark would have to return to the laundromat to retrieve his clothes. He crept back down in between the trailers, hid behind one, and watched as Tonto returned to his home.

The weather began to change as the nine 'o' clock hour approached. Skies darkened and a steady snow began to fall as Lee made his way over to the laundromat a few minutes after Tonto had gone into the home. Dressed in an all-white leather, hooded jumpsuit, white leather boots and white gloves, the Asian assassin laid down beside the tin structure of the laundromat and covered his head with the hood on his jumpsuit. He wore white goggles with tinted lenses and was gripping a black, pearl-handled .45 semiautomatic.

The snow that was already covering the ground camouflaged Lee well, and the constant falling ice added to his cover as he lay in wait like a Bengal tiger preying upon its next meal. Stealthy could best describe Lee Sato. He was a cunning murderer that dared to test the limits of one's abilities to take down a mark. He lay in wait for nearly an hour, more than the allotted time for a dryer or washer to complete its cycle. As he lay waiting, several tenants had run from their trailers to retrieve clothes, a couple of them running right past him as he lay buried in the snow, only the tint of his goggles, which looked like mere rocks or small patches of dirt was visible.

Lee kept his eyes on the trailer at the opposite end of the sidewalk on his right for another fifteen minutes when the door finally opened. Tonto appeared holding onto that same empty close basket. He readied himself by easing further down into the snow, and as Tonto neared, he tilted his gun, which had been cocked for nearly ninety minutes, to an upward angle. When Tonto grew near the entrance to the laundromat, Lee pulled the trigger. To his dismay, however, the gun didn't fire. He kept his eyes on Tonto, who hadn't noticed him, as he repeatedly squeezed the trigger.

Laying in the snow for over an hour in cold temperatures had frozen the grease lining in the chamber of the gun Lee was planning to use. He could only remain hidden and watch as Tonto walked into the laundromat. Two choices were now put before Lee. He could abort the mission and let Tonto go on home and return with a better gun, or he could ambush him and use a more hands on deadlier approach. Lee was capable of doing both, but this was an opportunity not to be missed, and it was far less dangerous than pulling a kick door. Deciding to go through with the job, he rose up from the ground. Snow poured off the back of his jumpsuit as he trotted into the laundromat with the jammed gun draping his side.

Tonto felt someone approaching him from behind and he went for the .9mm tucked in his front waistband. He was bum rushed just as he was turning around and was whacked across the head with a metal object. He fell back against the washing machine as his gun fired off a round. The bullet slammed into the side of the appliance and a stream of water began to spurt from the front of the unit. A second blow to the temple weakened Tonto and he let go of his weapon. With both hands free, he grabbed his goggled-faced attacker around the neck and began squeezing hard.

Lee was forced back against the wall beside the entrance to the laundromat. Tonto was stronger than he'd given him credit, but it was no surprise given his 6'4" one hundred eighty-plus pound physique. He could feel the air being squeezed from his lungs and his muscles began growing weak. Refusing to concede, he mustered up the strength to raise his arms and pressed his thumbs into Tonto's eyes, detaching one from its socket in the process.

Tonto screamed and fell up against the washing machine inside the enclosed area. He turned his back on his attacker and grabbed his face as he began coughing and gagging.

Lee, in turn, was gasping for air as he searched for Tonto's gun. Unable to find it, he picked up his own jammed pistol, walked over to Tonto and shoved him around and stared into his one open eye.

"What the, what the fuck is this about, man?" Tonto asked through his pain.

Lee didn't respond. He merely hauled off and backhanded Tonto with the cold steel, breaking his jaw with the powerful jab. When Tonto fell to the floor, water from the washing machine began coating his velvet jogging suit and spreading his blood around. Lee leaned down and picked him up by the collar and began beating him across the face with the jammed pistol.

Tonto was panting hard as he suffered blow after blow to his face and cranium. Lee had become enraged. Images of Koko sitting in that hospital waiting room with a cast on her foot while Spoonie endured a long, agonizing surgery was forcing him to want to literally stomp the life out of one the people responsible for bringing pain to the family. He bit his bottom lip through his mask as he threw Tonto's unconscious body to the floor and began stomping his head with the heel of his leather boot in angered silence.

Tonto's arms were stretched out upwards and his fingers were spread out; it was an involuntary reaction to the brain trauma he was suffering at the behest of his assailant. He lay with his eyes open in stunned silence as kick upon kick landed upon just about every spot above his neck. His face had become bloody and swollen, his hair was matted to his skull and a thick, red, mucus-like fluid had begun seeping from his right ear.

Lee kicked and stomped Tonto for nearly two minutes until one stomp went down further than all the previous ones. He recognized the sound of crushed bone right away and stopped to check the damage. When he looked down, he could see brain matter seeping from the top of Tonto's broken skull.

Covered in blood all the way up to his knees, Lee removed his boots, so as not to leave a blood trail, and quickly darted out of the laundromat with his jammed pistol and a plastic bag. He made it back to the rental car unseen and hopped inside after placing his bloody boots inside the plastic and backed out of the parking spot. He drove barefoot while wiping himself clean with baby wipes with the intent of heading back the Hilton to change clothes and blow town.

Just as Lee was exiting the trailer park, he lost control of the car and it swerved off the road where the right wheel became stuck in a snow bank. He hopped out in his socks after placing the car in park and ran around to the front of the car in an attempt to lodge it free as a rumbling sound was heard thumping inside a grey, four door old school Lincoln...

"*...Let me tell ya' the meaning of coming through...when the seats all cream and the candy's dark blue...approaching downtown...knockin' doors down...ten, eleven slabs in a single file line...*" Pimp C's song *Knocking Doors Down* was jumping from the interior of Bay's Lincoln as Walee let the driver's side window down. "Yo, dog, you need some—" Walee spoke no further words as he recognized the man standing in front of the Hyundai. He hopped out with the quickness and ran over to Lee. "What happened?" he asked.

"Just help me move it," Lee answered, ignoring Walee's question.

Walee looked at Lee, noticing the sprinkles of blood on the front of his jogging suit. He then looked back down towards the trailer park before looking back over to the Asian. "He dead?" he asked, understanding the reason why Lee was present.

"Let's get 'em outta here!" Kahlil snapped, shaking Walee from his thoughts as he ran up to the car.

"Fam," Walee stated lowly. "We can handle—"

"I'm good, man!" Kahlil retorted as he eyed Walee with tears forming in his eyes. "I know what he did, bruh! Let's just get 'em outta here, fuck! Jordan, get behind the wheel and put it in reverse!"

Jordan hopped into the Hyundai and placed it in reverse as Lee, Kahlil and Walee grabbed the front bumper, lifted and pushed the car back. After several lunges, the Hyundai became dislodged and rolled backwards.

Lee dusted his hands and stepped in between Walee and Kahlil. "I shouldn't say it, but I am," he remarked as he turned around and faced the boys. "The three of y'all never saw me. This," he said as he pointed towards the Hyundai, "this never happened. If you get questioned, it never happened."

"I'm good on that. And my main chick behind the wheel ain't see shit," Walee remarked as he looked over to Kahlil.

Hearing Lee speak on keeping silent had brought everything home for Kahlil. His brother was dead, and he'd just helped free the killer. Tonto had had it in for him, though. The way he swung that knife at his knees and the rage he held in his eyes while doing so had dissolved the last vestiges of reservation and compassion he held in his heart for his blood brother. He quickly eyed the people around him, starting with Walee.

For nearly a decade the man standing beside him had been his brother through thick and then. When his family had no food, it was Walee who'd gotten his aunt Mary to buy groceries for Hakiba. In his eight grade year, in order to play football, Hakiba could not afford the fees needed to cover medical insurance and uniforms. Again, Walee came through by asking his father to sponsor Kahlil. And when he couldn't afford to cover dorm fees after receiving a scholarship to Oklahoma State, Walee gave Kahlil a job as camera man when he was just beginning to film Jordan having girl on girl sex and he'd earned enough to cover his dorm fees and then some. He now had money to blow because of his friend, who never asked for nothing return as it was all unconditional.

Then there was Jordan Whispers. She was the big sister inside Walee's crew. A defender and supporter of he and Walee's antics, more times than not joining in herself to help them run game on women they were interested in getting on camera or just for the sheer sexual pleasure. But more importantly, Jordan was willing to take the stand and say she was the one who'd shot Chauncey in order to preserve Kahlil's freedom and career.

Lee was the last person Kahlil eyed as the thoughts he carried played out in milliseconds. A guy he'd only met the night Spoonie was shot had made his way to Ponca City and handled a matter he was incapable of dealing with despite his knowing what needed doing. When it got down to it, the people before Kahlil were his family, not Tonto. "My moms?" he asked as he looked Lee in the eyes.

"I never saw her, Kahlil. I was told not to harm her and that's what I did." Lee stated as he headed for the driver's seat and climbed behind the wheel.

"Where you going now?" Walee asked.

"Back to my hotel. I have to change and leave."

"Nah," Walee objected as he went into his coat pocket and pulled out a set of keys. "It's best you keep going, fam. This the key to my apartment down in Oklahoma City. Jordan, write the address down for 'em."

"I have shit I gotta move outta there," Lee remarked as he took the keys from Walee.

"Gimmie the hotel key and me and my people gone pack all

your stuff and bring it to you," Walee stated. "I got some Windex in Bay ride. We gone wipe everything down for ya' before we head back down there."

Lee nodded his head in a thankful manner. "He's in the laundromat. Tell Koko I'm sorry I didn't get to say goodbye," he requested as he took the paper containing Walee's address from Jordan, and closed the door, keeping in mind to call Ben the time he touched down in Oklahoma City.

"I'll tell her you gone see her later," Walee responded seriously. "Go on, fam. We got it from here."

Lee threw up a peace sign as he placed the car in drive and slowly rode off. Walee and company, meanwhile, climbed back inside of Bay's Lincoln and rode down into the trailer park and entered the premises. The three were all looking over to the right where the laundromat lay as their stroll began to slow. From a distance of a hundred feet or so, they could see a pair of black boots sticking out of the doorway. It was a sight eerie enough to force them all to remain silent for several lingering seconds as they walked across the snow-covered courtyard.

"We all thinking it," Jordan finally spoke up. "Y'all wanna go and see it up-close?"

Walee looked over to Kahlil, who had tears pouring down his face. "I'll let the police tell me what happened to 'em," he stated as he began jogging towards his trailer home. "I'm just going get my ankle weights and gloves, change my clothes and grab Spoonie keys! What I wanna see that for? I ain't gone make me feel good!" he yelled out.

Walee and Jordan shrugged the matter off as they ran and followed Kahlil home. They waited while he changed clothes and gathered a few things. He'd just grabbed Spoonie's car keys and the three were readying to leave when they heard a woman scream. It was a shriek that came from the direction of the laundromat, one they need not investigate as they all knew the source of the belligerent woman's cries of help.

Before Kahlil could make it to the front door, there were several knocks. He opened to see three people from the residences bundled up with scarves and hooded jackets. "Where's your mother?" a middle-aged Caucasian male asked. "Is everything okay with you, son?"

"I'm good. Why you ask?" Kahlil answered as blue and red lights came into view. Several officers dressed in all black appeared on the scene as they sloshed through the snow, making their way over to the laundromat.

"You should come!" the man suggested as he looked over to laundromat, then back at Kahlil. "Something bad happened to your brother."

CHAPTER SIXTEEN

WELCOME TO THE FAMILY

It was nearing the noon hour as a dozen or so children, all no older than the age of twelve, lined a dirt road that was bordered by lush greenery leading up to a wooden gate that had a single topless U.S. Army jeep parked out front as a caravan of five vehicles, two black on black bulletproof H-1 Hummers, followed by a bulletproof, black on black BMW limousine with mirror tint, that was being tailed by two more bulletproof H-1 black on black Hummers, whizzed by at a hurried pace.

The gates were immediately closed and the jeep fell in line as the children all took off running behind the caravan of vehicles as it made a beeline for a three-story white-stone villa trimmed in black oak.

Paraiso was the town's name. Located in the state of Tabasco in the country of Mexico on the state's northwestern tip, this small town consisting of 87,000 residents thrived off of agriculture, livestock and forestry. It was one of the poorer towns in the state of Tabasco, and Mexico itself. Given its close proximity to the Gulf of Mexico, this low-laying town's acreage consisted of over fifty percent swampland and marsh. Many residents took to fishing and would transport their daily haul back to Villahermosa, Tabasco's capital, to sell in order to support their families.

Those types were the working stiffs, however, because when it got down to it, Paraiso was a town that thrived off of another profitable industry—that industry being that of cartel security. Although there were several families who earned a living providing protection for various drug organizations, no other family was more feared nor respected than that of the Ramirez family—Flacco's people.

Flacco and his clan were the richest of the wealthiest inside a city that lived according to its own laws. This was outlaw country. A land where whoever possessed the most money and held the biggest gun called the shots. And as of date, the Ramirez family was Jefe de Jefes (Boss of Bosses). The Mexican crime family wasn't a self-made clan, however; and unlike the others who shared the same occupation, this particular family had ties to an American cartel who paid them handsomely for their services. Whereas the other families got mere scraps from other cartels, the Ramirez family was made rich by the Holland family. American dollars untraceable had made them rich beyond compare and they'd used the monies coming in from the United States to build their own empire.

Inside the pristine BMW limousine sat Naomi, Dawk and Flacco. Mother and son were taking in the scenery as Flacco sat with a proud smile on his face. They'd traveled through many a poor area where citizens were holding up American flags and screaming aloud *"Ramirez familia es la familia mas fuerte!"* (Ramirez family is the greatest family!)

"This is all because of your family's doing, Naomi," Flacco had remarked during one stretch of the ride. "Because of your family, my family has respect and live a life many of the people who admire us can only dream."

Naomi had remained silent during that time as she stared at the worn down houses and people wearing rags for clothes while waving tattered American flags through her sunshade-covered eyes. She'd imagined what she would encounter traveling down to Mexico, but her imagination had done her a disservice. She really didn't like what her eyes were witnessing. There were just too many poor people around for her liking. Poverty breeds animosity. And the moves the family was planning on making would fuel envy towards the Ramirez family was her belief, if there wasn't any conflict on hand at the present.

Dawk was thinking on a whole other level, yet similar to his mother. He sat beside Naomi with a PPD-40 automatic in his lap as flashbacks of the night he and his father and sisters had taken down Carmella Lapiente' and her soldiers south of Brownsville, Texas ran through his mind. Mexico was a country that played by a totally different set of rules, he knew. Just like Naomi, Dawk saw that there was too much poverty. No way could the family operate in this lawless land without having to wipe out dozens. The good thing was that the family was aiming to set up in Brazil, and not Tabasco, so that offered some relief to his anxiety.

"We have to discuss security a lot more with this move we about to make, Flacco," Dawk remarked as the caravan traveled over the land. "With more money, that's gone bring more problems. What kinda plans your family have for the future?"

"I understand your worry, Senor Holland," Flacco remarked. "It's easy to look at all the poor people and worry that they would revolt. But my family takes care of many. You will see," he added. "We have plans, and when you expand in power, so do we. Paraiso is our city. There is nothing to fear. I assure you."

Just then, Dawk's phone rung, he recognized the Connecticut area code as that of Ben's cover phone and picked up. "Yo?"

"That thing with ya' boy is done, brer. We met up with a li'l problem, though. The younger one know what happened," he stated in reference to Kahlil.

"How?" Dawk asked he ran his hand over his PPD-40.

"Big boy tried to stab the younger one and he ran out the house and called your li'l brother from that corner store. My man got stuck in some snow on the way out and li'l brother rolled up when he was trying to free the car. The young one put two and two together and everything got exposed. Dude solid, though. Police asked him if he knew what happened they all said they was just there to pick up some things to take back to

151

the dorm room like they never even knew what happened. Police buying it."

"That boy used that chick phone at the store?" Dawk asked.

"Yeah, but she ain't talking and she gave the phone to ya' brother, ya' dig. He got rid of it."

"We know where our weakness lay," Dawk remarked.

"True that, but so long as the li'l chick don't talk it'll be hard to connect the pieces. We really can't do nothing if they subpoena her phone records, but that'll be on a hunch and I don't think the law playing it that for out. Either way, y'all free to head back whenever because the heat ain't on y'all."

"That phone call worrying me. We gone have to keep tabs on that chick," Dawk stated seriously.

"The slim chick gone hang 'round Ponca City while the investigation going on," Ben said in reference to Jordan Whispers. "Ole girl up to the store did a flick with her not too long ago so she know how to play it."

"Already. Cut ya' man a check and I pay you back when we meet up again. It's all good down here so far. I be in touch," Dawk replied before ending the call. "Tonto out the picture," he then stated to Naomi and Flacco as the limousine came to a halt in the semi-circle cobblestone driveway before a three-story white-stone villa trimmed in black oak.

Flacco had barely opened the door when, "*Es que mi segunda mujer norteamericano favorito dentro de ti coche, ¿no?*" (Is that my second favorite American woman inside thee car, no?) was heard coming from beneath the breezeway.

"*Ya que cuando llegué a ser su segunda mujer norteamericano favorito, Hollywood? Y que me ha sustituido?*" (Since when did I become your second favorite American woman, Hollywood? And who has replaced me?) Naomi remarked through a smile.

"*Su nombre es Michelle Obama! Lo que una mujer tiene su país para una primera dama! Si pudiera tener, yo he votado por el presidente dos veces sólo por su esposa!*" (Her name is Michelle Obama! What a woman your country has for a first lady! If I could have, I would've voted for your President twice just because of his wife!) the short and stocky, raspy-voiced Mexican remarked jovially as he tugged down on his cowboy hat and walked up and hugged Naomi.

Altoona 'Hollywood' Ramirez was a forty-nine year-old stunt pilot and driver that'd spent time in the United States— Hollywood to be exact—which was how he'd earned his nickname. He was Flacco's only uncle, and a man of many aspects if Naomi had to tell it. He'd worked on several major motion pictures around the world at the turn of the century, and was the owner of a popular night club down in Buenos Aires, Argentina called *The Hollywood Hut* where many American singers, bands and actors often hung out when in town. He was also the pilot of the plane that had landed on Little Cayman when the family had met Rafael Gacha and received the Levamisole formula.

Several more men approached Naomi and Dawk as they stood outside of the limousine before the villa; one was a man who needed no introduction in Naomi's eyes, as he was an honor to have met in times past. His name was Edgar Ramirez, a slightly-balding, slender, thick-mustached man like Flacco. The two were similar in appearance because Edgar was Flacco's father.

"How are you, Senorita Dawkins? Senor Holland?"

"Better now having met your presence," Naomi smiled as she leaned in and hugged the Ramirez family's patriarch.

"You flatter me with your words, but it is I who am honored. We've prepared such a fiesta for you and Senor Dawk. Come!" Edgar said as he stepped aside and extended his hand, welcoming Naomi and Dawk into the family's compound.

Edgar Ramirez Senior was a physically fit sixty-three year old ex-military man that'd been a part of the Special Forces Unit for the Mexican Army up until 2004, when he retired with honors. Edgar was a man of adventure. His many missions with the Mexican Army had taken him into the jungles of Guatemala where he and his platoon battled para-military groups who were kidnapping prominent Mexican citizens and holding them for ransom.

During his career, Edgar Senior was recognized nationwide for his successful missions. To go along with his military credentials, there were also people involved in less savory businesses who sought Edgar's services. And while still part of the Mexican Army, he'd taken on side jobs for various cartels by providing security. Other times, he went into hostile territory, including the state of Colombia, and destroyed cocoa processing plants and disrupted routes of rival cartels.

Like many of the families in and around Tabasco, however, the Ramirez family knew they were being given pennies on the dollar for what their work was actually worth. It was only when the Holland family began funneling money into the family's coffers during the mid-to-late nineties that they actually began to see the fruits of their labor come to full harvest. The duplex where the family of over two dozen previously resided was given away the day they were able to buy the ranch at the turn of the century.

Livestock was soon brought, Hollywood was able to live out some of his dreams after obtaining a green card with Naomi's help and with each passing year, as the Holland family grew in wealth and prosperity, so did the Ramirez family. Although living thousands of miles apart, these two families had grown together in wealth and power over the years in their respective lands. The Ramirez family, to put it plainly, was the Mexican version of the Holland family—Holland south so-to-speak.

Flacco was the second to youngest of Edgar's five children. There were three more siblings ahead of him consisting of one brother and two sisters, the oldest being a sister age forty-five and the youngest being that of a brother age nineteen. Like Hollywood, Flacco's two brothers were involved the security business. They were weapons experts with hearts of stone and ready to take down their opponents. A true asset and loyal ally to the Holland family they were.

After a short walk in between a row of stone columns, the group of two dozen or so emerged out into a courtyard that had a low-lying wooden stage lined with lights and banners all around. An all-female Mexican band of four decked out in sundresses and sombreros were cueing up guitars and brass instruments, and several tables covered in satin clothes was spread out before the platform. Countless silver trays were on the tables along with bottles of wine on chilled ice.

Hollywood scooted past the crowd and began walking backwards with his arms spread and said, "My daughters over there are going to play for us in a little while, but first, first we are going to have us a little snack, Naomi! You like the group ABBA?"

Naomi walked over to the tables and eyed the dishes. "Haven't heard them in a long while, but they're okay. What is all this food, Hollywood?" she asked with a wide smile on her face. "This is beyond a snack."

Hollywood walked over and stood beside Naomi. "Noo," he sang as he turned around and eyed the food spread out on the tables while pulling up on his one-size too big, black silk slacks. "This, this here is like I said. A snack to hold us off until after the meeting with the Devereaux family later. If you think this is a lot of food you should see what dinner looks like around here."

"Well, what is this 'snack' as you like to call it?"

"Nothing much, Naomi," Hollywood replied in his raspy, comical voice. "Just some pork tacos, huaraches, steak gorditas, menudo, queso flamedo, a uhhh, a dish of toasted chocolate-covered grasshoppers and sheets of marinated beef with some Veracruz-style red snapper and caramel empanadas." The happy-go-lucky Mexican took a deep breath and continued with, "We got some dulce de leche, which is like your Bill Cosby's Jell-O pudding, no? We also have bolillos, that's your salty bread right there. There's beef tamales, steamed rice with onion gravy, turnip greens with ham hocks, deep-fried chicken wings, picadillo, chimichangas, steak fajitas and three pans of lasagna. That's all—just a little something we threw together."

"This is beyond lunch and something thrown together," Naomi chuckled. "Some of this food, forgive me for saying it, but I refuse to eat some of this food."

"That would be the toasted chocolate-covered grasshoppers that you will be refusing to eat today," Hollywood remarked as he walked over and grabbed the silver tray of chocolate-crusted insects and passed it off to his youngest nephew. "Take that shit away," he mockingly scoffed while staring him up and down.

"I thought they would be willing to experiment with a new cuisine, Uncle Hollywood," the nineteen year-old remarked, slightly embarrassed.

"New cuisine and Uncle Hollywood my ass! I told you you would scare Naomi and Dawk off with those things," Hollywood snapped while watching his nephew walking off with the toasted bugs. "No one but you and I—correction! You're the only one who eats those things, Edgar Junior. Put that shit away in a hurry because you're embarrassing us. And why are you a junior when you're the last of the boys born to your father leaves me to question whether Flacco and the other one…who barely talks mind you…are truly the legitimate sons of Edgar Ramirez Senior and my honest nephews. Your mother has some explaining to do in time let me say that much."

Naomi and Dawk laughed to themselves as activity continue to unfold inside the lavish courtyard of the villa. The Ramirez family was nearly twice as big as the Holland family. Flacco's two sisters had eleven kids between them and his oldest brother had three kids of his own. His younger brother also had a newborn baby and a pregnant wife. Ramirez family members ranging in age from sixty-three to three months were on hand to host Dawk and Naomi. The younger kids ran around, chasing one another in a frenzied game of tag while the older ones set up tables, hung more banners and tuned instruments.

After saying prayer, the three dozen or so people all took seats and began sharing the large meal. Wine was poured up, pleasantries were exchanged and jokes abounded. Hollywood kept everybody laughing with his self-deprecating wisecracks and Naomi told stories of life back in America to some of the kids, who were mainly interested in movie stars and musicians back home.

"You can ask about the Justin Biebers and Miley Cyrus's of

the world until you're all blue in the face, my sobrinas (nieces) but your aunts, my hijas (daughters) are the real stars!" Hollywood said to several of his young nieces as his four daughters excused themselves from the table and took to the stage.

"Naomi, you told us about Jane Dow back in the states. She sounds like a star on the rise, but you haven't heard Hot Tabasco yet. They may change your mind, no?" Hollywood remarked.

"No!" Naomi laughed as she stirred her lemon water.

"Okay, I just have to make you a believer now. Girls?" Hollywood smiled as he extended his hand towards the stage. "Smoke session's in the back for all interested parties!" he then yelled out loud.

Hollywood's four daughters, his 'gorgeous princesses' as he'd referred to them often during the luncheon, readied themselves before their instruments on stage with five of their younger cousins as several adult members of the Ramirez family excused themselves and convened at a table further back from the rest of the group that had a pound of marijuana waiting to be rolled.

Hot Tabasco readied themselves; the quartet of voluptuous, sundress and boot-wearing tan-skinned vixens with stylish black heads of hair and perfect makeup began checking the volumes on their guitars, drums and keyboards while allowing time for drinks to be poured and marijuana to be rolled and toked. Naomi was on her second glass of lemon water as she watched the entire group of nine cue up. She was a fan of live performances and was playing close attention to the women as they went about their duties. They weren't ones to talk much, unlike Jane Dow, who always had something to say while tuning her instruments back on the ranch she noticed, and she also wondered how they would sound.

When the smell of marijuana coaxed past Naomi's nostrils, Hot Tabasco began their act. A single, diamond-clad hand was waved over the keyboard and the guitars and drums quickly followed. The younger ones began shaking maracas and tapping tambourines and a perfect rhythm was established as the entire group of none let loose into the open air with…"*Se puede bailar… usted puede jive… teniendo el tiempo de tu vida(oooohhhh)… ver a esa chica… ver esa escena… cavando el baile de la reina…*" (You can dance…you can jive…having the time of your life(oooohhhh)…see that girl…watch that scene…digging the dancing queen…)

Splendid. That was the first word that'd come to mind when Naomi heard the Ramirez family harmoniously singin ABBA's song *Dancing Queen*.

"The Spanish version to this song way better than any American version you can think of!" Hollywood yelled over the singing as he rose from his seat and grabbed one of Naomi's hands. "*Hermosa mujer que debe bailar conmigo mientras mis hijas cantan!*" (Beautiful woman you must dance with me while my daughters sing!)

"*No tengo! Ha sido un tiempo!*" (I haven't! It's been a while!) Naomi laughed over the music. "*Creo que he perdido mi ritmo!*" (I think I've lost my rhythm!)

"I was born without rhythm but it never stopped me, Naomi! Come on! Aren't they gorgeous? Isn't this a gorgeous moment?"

Naomi looked over to Dawk, who was smiling while shaking his head. "Dad won't be mad, momma. Enjoy the moment like he said," he leaned over and stated.

"I know. I just don't want to look like a fool!" Naomi responded over the singers.

"You won't be alone! Come on!" Dawk said out loud as he took Flacco's mother's hand, stood up and led her out into the center of the courtyard where a good portion of the Ramirez family was either partnered up or dancing in groups before the stage.

Hot Tabasco seemed to take it up a notch as they continued singing in perfect harmony… "*Con un poco de música… todo está bien… Estás de humor para un baile… y cuando tienes la oportunidad… tienes el baile de la reina… joven y dulce… sólo diecisiete..."* (With a bit of rock music…everything is fine… you're in the mood for a dance…and when you get the chance…you are the dancing queen…young and sweet…only seventeen…)

It didn't take long for Naomi to get in rhythm. She hadn't lost her touch after all. Alright, now!" she laughed as clapped her hands while swaying her hips.

"Beautiful!" Hollywood exclaimed joyously over his daughters' angelic voices as he twirled Naomi around. The two danced the entire song before Naomi broke off and returned to her seat with a contented heart. She really needed that release, if only for the moment.

The group was mingling a couple of hours later, Hot Tabasco in the middle of playing another disco hit, when Flacco had gotten the word that the Devereaux family was nearing the compound. He stood up and clapped his hands. Immediately, the band ceased to play, the dancing was halted and the tables were cleared. Foot soldiers inside the Ramirez family grabbed their AK-47s and climbed into two Suburbans and rode down to the ranch's entrance that lay a quarter mile away. The gate was pulled open just as two Cadillac Avalanches with dark tint rolled to a halt.

The lead SUV's window slid down and a tan-skinned man, rugged in appearance, with a neatly trimmed mustache wearing a sombrero and sunshades came into view. He was Flacco's oldest brother, fifty-eight year-old Juan Camilo Ramirez Senior. Juan was a man of few words that spoke little English, and was more than adept at making his presence felt through his violent disposition. He nodded in silence through his sunshade-covered eyes and ran his hands over his sideburns, signaling to Flacco that everything was good on his end.

"We have the Devereauxs in the Cadillac behind us, Uncle Flacco," twenty-four year-old Juan Camilo Ramirez Junior, better known as Camilo, stated from the passenger seat as he leaned over and eyed Flacco.

"¿Tienen alguna dificultad en sus ojos, Camilo?" (Are they of any trouble in your eyes, Camilo?) Flacco asked in a near

whisper.

Camilo pulled down on his snap back Dodgers baseball cap as reflections of the moonlight jumped off his diamond-clad wrists. *"Almorzamos con ellos dentro del aeropuerto en la Ciudad de México, mientras esperaban en las aduanas para aprobar sus visas. Están demasiado confiar en si me preguntas. Llegaron solos. Sea cual sea Naomi quiere hacer esta noche debe ser fácil. Los Devereauxs son presa fácil."* (We had lunch with them inside the airport at Mexico City while they waited on customs to approve their visas. They're way too trusting if you ask me. They came alone. Whatever Naomi wants to do tonight should be easy. The Devereauxs are pushovers.)

Flacco eyed his oldest brother and nephew in silence as he digested his nephew's assessment, believing fully the report Camilo had given him.

Juan Camilo and Camilo Junior oversaw the Ramirez family's intelligence gathering unit. Camilo was the brains, having studied Computer Science at New Mexico State University on a visa and earning his degree two years prior.

Juan Camilo was the muscle inside the Ramirez family. While Flacco and Altoona went on to pursue American dreams of wealth, Juan Camilo had opted to stay behind in Mexico as he'd always viewed himself of being that of the family's protector. He was the only capable male during the early nineties while Flacco, Altoona and Edgar Senior were away and he'd handled his job well by preventing any cartel from establishing roots in the town of Paraiso.

Juan Camilo was a name that sent chills up and down the spines of Paraiso residents as he was known to chop the heads off of leaders of families who stood in the way of the Ramirez family's profits. He would place the decapitated heads on wooden sticks and plant them in the town's center as a warning to all who dared to challenge the Ramirez family's authority. *"La familia Ramírez come primero,"* was his motto when it came to the competition down in Mexico and everybody around town knew it more than they cared to express.

After several minutes had gone by, Flacco nodded and walked over to the second Avalanche. The driver's side window rolled down and his youngest sister, thirty-seven year-old Luciana Ramirez came into view. Luciana was a buxom woman with curly, long, black hair and slender, silky eyebrows. Dark-eyed and seductive, she was the woman who had aided Juan Camilo during his numerous campaigns of violence. She could best be described as a lure and was a rival's worse nightmare given the cunning and seductive prowess she possessed.

Knowing Luciana possessed the gift of gab, Flacco put on a smile as he touched his sister's chin and eyed a young Brazilian sitting in the passenger seat. "I'm Flacco Ramirez," he stated calmly. "On behalf of the Holland family? I would like to welcome you to our homeland, senor."

"My name is Cristian Devereaux," the man responded. "My aunt, Barbara Devereaux, is present, and ready to negotiate on behalf of the Devereaux family tonight."

"Let us began," Flacco responded as he extended a kind hand to the young Brazilian. "You will follow us to the meeting place."

Flacco walked back over to Juan Camilo's Avalanche and climbed into the backseat. As the vehicles began to move forward, he texted Naomi a message stating, "*It's your call.*"

The vehicles were waved through the gates as Juan Carmilo and Luciana drove the Devereauxs over to a second, smaller villa used as a guest house. The Ramirez guest villa was more like a saloon. It was a two story stone building that sported worn wooden floors throughout. The second floor was an arms locker where countless machine guns and other weaponry, including that of grenades and a flame thrower were stored. The first floor had a bar counter that faced saloon-style doors used to enter the establishment.

Naomi and Dawk were seated at a large wooden table when three Brazilians walked into the dilapidated villa that had a nineteenth century western American appeal. Flacco walked in and stood before the group and introduced Cristian, Savio, and

Barbara Devereaux.

Cristian was a young man in his mid-twenties with dark eyes and was well-built with thick biceps and muscular legs that showed through his silk suit pants. Savio was on the slender side with stringy, brown hair and dark eyes and was in his early twenties. The Devereaux men were sharp in appearance, but it was Barbara Devereaux, a late-fifties tan-skinned Brazilian with crystal grey eyes and brown hair that flowed down her back that was obviously calling the shots as the men seemed to defer to her by standing behind her with their hands clasped together.

"I was expecting something more grandiose than just a simple room with no artwork or other interesting features," Barbara remarked as she looked around the living room with obvious disregard. She flailed the silk scarf around her neck as if she were fanning dust away from her face before looking over in the direction of the three people seated at the table to her right. "And you people are?"

Dawk rose from his seated position and said, "We're the Holland family. I'm Dawk. This is my mother Naomi and this is our trusted associate Flacco. The three of us are acting on behalf of the Holland family—the family that the Devereaux family has agreed to sell three thousand acres of land to at a set price ten and a half million dollars."

"Ohh, that," Barbara remarked nonchalantly as she looked away from the three people on the opposite side of the table. "Some thing has come up. I'm not sure we can make this deal today."

Naomi remained seated as she eyed Barbara with derision. From the time she'd laid eyes on the woman, she'd begun receiving negative vibes. The way Barbara had pranced into the villa with her smug demeanor, as if the people around her were beneath her family didn't sit right with the matriarch of the Holland family. If she was more of an unreserved person, Naomi would've read Barbara her rights after her last remark, but she could see the woman was trying to play hard ball, which was a game she knew how to play with the best of them.

"Why would you travel all the way here to Mexico just to decline an offer, Misses Devereaux?" Naomi inquired.

"I never said I was declining the offer, Naomi. I said 'some —thing', not 'something', has come up. In fact, I'm willing to offer a lower price to your family—but it comes with a favor that must be done on my family's behalf."

"Why don't you all sit and discuss the deal over drinks," Flacco suggested as he got up and walked over to a cart containing several bottles of chilled champagne.

Barbara took a seat across from Naomi and Dawk while Savio and Cristian stood behind her. There was a brief period of silence as Flacco wheeled the cart over and popped the tops on two bottles of champagne and poured.

Barbara eyed her glass cautiously before cutting her eyes over to Naomi. "Why don't you drink first?"

"You're an untrusting group of people," Naomi observed as she picked up her glass and took a sip of champagne. "Do you really think we would stoop so low as to poison you? What would we have to gain?"

"In this business I've learned to trust no one," Barbara replied as she ran her index finger over the rim of her glass and checked it for residue. "We have something very valuable that you want," she added as she pulled out a strip of lye and ran her finger over the surface. When the impromptu poison inspection came back negative, only then did Barbara partake of the champagne she'd been offered.

"Are you selling the land to us or not?" Naomi asked as she grew a little inpatient over Barbara's over-exercising of caution. "No one here has it in for your family. This is a simple purchase of land for private use."

"A private use of land that will net your family millions upon millions of dollars given its crop. And I'm not talking orange harvests, Naomi." Barbara responded in matter-of-fact tone as she took a second sip of champagne. "There're cocoa leaves that grow unchecked on the land we own, is that not your family's main objective? To gain access to those cocoa leaves?"

"What we do with the land is of our personal business." Dawk stated.

Barbara smiled with confidence. "By law," she began, "by law I have the right to inquire into what will be the specific use of the property. And if I deem the use—"

"Of said property could be of a detriment to your government or pose a threat to the future profits of your business the Devereaux family has the right to decline the offer without the Holland family having the ability to file an appeal with the International Commerce Committee unless we face full disclosure," Naomi interjected as she shifted in her seat and crossed her legs. "But I know you would not have come this far to present to us the laws surrounding an international business arrangement. So get to the point of you having made this trip."

"Okay," Barbara stated as she removed her scarf. "And this is off the record, just the same as what I know to be true about the reason behind your family wanting to purchase land dominated by cocoa leaves will be off the record." Naomi nodded and Barbara continued. "As you know, our coffee enterprise's stock has been dwindling, but we have another venture that is proving to be lucrative and we feel that your family has the capability of advancing our Cause, which would be to both of our benefit—if you help us solve this little issue."

"That little issue being?" Naomi asked.

"There's a Jamaican family that has bombarded their way onto the New York scene with a boat load of heroin. Should they be removed, my family is prepared to offer the land in Brazil at a wholesale price of five million dollars, less than half of what you've offered."

"You're asking us to do a hit on your behalf for five and a half million dollars." Naomi stated as Dawk leaned over and whispered in her ear, *"The Germans want in on New York. Heroin is their market, we can get them to do it."* Naomi nodded in agreement over her son's remark. "Barbara, who are these Jamaicans?" she asked.

"Their names are Jaffrey and Theron Fischer. They're white Jamaicans operating in Brooklyn—Manhattan to be exact," Barbara remarked as she handed two photographs to Naomi and Dawk.

"How long on the job?" Dawk asked as he looked over the two white Jamaican men in the photographs.

"Before summer's end," Barbara remarked. "That'll give us time to arrange shipments from our warehouse."

"What about the deal on the land in Brazil?" Naomi inquired.

"The deal is contingent upon completion of the contract," Barbara replied.

Naomi placed a finger to her temple and eyed Barbara cautiously. She saw something in the woman that Barbara couldn't see in herself and she was aiming to expose it. "You people don't seem like the type to peddle drugs and engage in violence. I'm suspecting that there is more to this story," she propagated.

"More? What would ever give you that impression, Naomi?" Barbara inquired as she facetiously laughed, a move that hadn't gone unnoticed by Naomi and her team.

"Don't patronize me and my family, okay?" Naomi sternly stated. "You walk in here and ask us to kill two men for you and we're not supposed to ask why? What did they do exactly?"

Barbara took another sip of her champagne and said, "They, they killed my husband. He went to New York City to discuss a marketing strategy with people he thought were allies, but they killed him instead and mailed his head back to us inside an ice chest and told us to stay away. Now we're in possession of nearly five hundred pounds of heroin and we can't move it."

"Are you afraid?" Naomi asked as she nodded, knowing she was getting to the gist of the matter behind the New York hit.

"No," Barbara replied meekly, yet failing to convince Naomi. "We just haven't the muscle to strike back and we know no one in the states. Our family is a family mainly of logistical types. We know shipping and have government contacts in Brazil. You do this job for us in New York? We'll make the shipping of your refined cocoa leaves a priority. Maybe you can help? And in return? We offer all of our resources."

Naomi knew from past conversations with Flacco that the Devereaux family was going to allow them to ship their cocaine north into Venezuela on trucks that they owned. The route through Brazil would be a better option, however, but Martha would have to set up an exact route, and that could take months. The family would have to move the freighters owned by Phil and Grover to Sao Paulo or some other port on the east coast of South America. From there, they would need a port of entry into the United States. If both families worked together, however, the profits would be incalculable, Naomi knew, but the shrewd businesswoman also knew more, as the Devereauxs had just exposed their entire hand. They were in a weakened state and Naomi saw an angle that could be played in order to gain leverage.

"This is an unforgiving business we're involved in—a business that you and your family have chosen to involve yourselves in without fully understanding its possible repercussions, I don't think," Naomi remarked as she began to lay out her counter offer. "We will get you your revenge, but in order for that to happen, you must give us the land you're attempting to sell us."

"That is the deal. We will give you the land for less than half the cost of the initial deal of ten and a half million dollars," Barbara replied as Dawk and Flacco chuckled to themselves.

Naomi looked over to Dawk and Flacco with a sly smile on her face before placing her gaze back upon Barbara. "I don't think you're understanding me correctly," she stated in a serious tone. "We will get you your revenge, and you will give us the land—free of charge," she declared.

"No way," Barbara said as she leaned back in her chair.

"Again, I don't think you understand the nature of the business you're involved in, Barbara. The people that killed your husband? It's a good chance they now know how much heroin your family is sitting on. Your husband may have gone so far as to tell them everything under the belief that he was making an American connect."

"I'm not understanding," Barbara countered as she held her hands open in wonderment. "What does one have to do with the other?"

Naomi didn't respond right away. She uncrossed her legs, rested her elbows on the table, clasped her hands together and said, "Barbara? Your family's coffee business is on the verge of collapsing and your government contacts have nothing to offer by way of muscle. With five hundred pounds of heroin in your possession and no way to move it? You're ripe for a band of sting kings to swoop in and overwhelm you with brute force. The people your husband tried to make a deal with cut off his head and mailed it back to you. They may very well come for you. Cut off you, Savio, and, I'm sorry, what's your name, sweetie?" she asked as she peered over Barbara's shoulder and eyed Cristian, whose name she hadn't actually forgotten, but only wanted to use the move to diminish the Devereaux family's worth to her and the family altogether.

"My, my name is Cristian, ma'am," the young man replied, obviously bothered over what he'd heard Naomi tell his aunt given the way he continuously swallowed the lump in his throat as his face glistened with sweat.

"Right. Cristian," Naomi remarked as she eyed Savio, who was just as tense as his older brother, with a wide smile on her face. "*¿Está bien allí, hermano?*" (You okay over there, brother?) she joyfully asked, knowing she now had the Devereauxs completely by the nut sack.

"*Estoy bien. Acaba de tomar detrás todo.*" (I'm fine. Just taken back by it all.) Savio remarked as his hands trembled.

"*Como debe ser.*" (As you should be.) Naomi stated as she dropped her smile, leaned back in her chair and crossed her legs once more while staring at Barbara with a scowl on her face. "You three are novices—*novices*—and you come here to our compound alone after the head, and, please, forgive me for lack of use of better words, but you come here unprotected after the head of your family has been killed in America and try and set the terms? You can't do that. Not with this family," she added just as Hollywood and Edgar Junior walked into the villa with AK-47s draped over their shoulders.

Barbara's heart sunk to the pit of her stomach. "We don't want any trouble!" she screamed in all out horror. "You can have it! Take the land if you want! Just let us go!"

Knowing she now had Barbara and her nephews' full and undivided attention with the presence of Hollywood and Edgar Junior, Naomi sought to finalize the deal on her terms. "I'm not going to take your land in that manner, Misses Devereaux. I know what's that's like," she stated as she briefly reflected on the tragic events that unfolded within her family in Sylacauga, Alabama back in 1962. "But what I will do," she said as she leaned down and picked up a briefcase. "What I will do is have you sign it over to me for not five million dollars, but for two and a half million dollars instead," she remarked as she opened the square box and slid documents over to Barbara that prescribed the transferring of three thousand acres of land located in Boa Vista, Brazil.

"You're not going to kill us and your counter offer is half of the offer I've made. Why, and I'm just asking…why should we agree to these terms?" Barbara asked anxiously as she looked back at the two men who'd walked into the living room to make sure their rifles weren't aimed at her or her nephews.

"Guys?" Naomi said to Hollywood and Edgar Junior, coaxing them to leave the room. Once the men cleared out, she looked back over to Barbara and said, "It was never my intention to kill neither you nor your nephews. Be thankful that it is my family that you've met with today because there are many other families who would've taken you for everything you have. Your heroin business? We can help you with that. We have people that know how to move that product. Until then? You'll need protection from these Jamaicans because they may be after you. If not them, someone will be soon enough."

Barbara swallowed and nodded as she stared Naomi in the eyes. "We have a factory that produces heroin. There can be much more."

"I know," Naomi whispered through a naughty smile as she stared at Barbara. "If you agree to these terms I'm about to lay out? You will come under the control of the Holland family. Anybody that touches your family touches us all and we will retaliate on your behalf. These are the terms, are you ready to hear them?"

"I'm listening," Barbara replied like that of a student in the throes of receiving a mathematical formula from its esteemed professor.

"Okay," Naomi replied as reached out her hands and turned her palms upwards.

Barbara complied by placing her palms in Naomi's palms as the two women stared into one another's eyes. "These are the terms," Naomi stated. "Any move that the Devereaux family makes will have to be sanctioned by the Holland family. You're not to kill or negotiate any more deals from this day forth on your own. We will need your political contacts after we take care of business in New York. You are not to use our name under any circumstances until given permission to do so and we command a twenty percent tax on any venture, deal, contract or any other transaction your family makes. Understood?"

"Thank you," Barbara said as she nodded while holding onto Naomi's hands.

"Welcome to the family," Naomi smiled. "I would propose a toast, but let us go and prepare a large dinner to celebrate instead. An escort will take you back to Mexico City tomorrow afternoon," she added as the meeting drew to a close.

CHAPTER SEVENTEEN

MENAGE A TROIS` NOT

It was the morning after Naomi had brought the Devereauxs into the family fold down in Mexico. Being that Ben was headed up to Florence, Colorado to visit JunJie and Yiska, Tre` Mitchell was left with the task of opening up H.O.U.S.E. of I.D.E.A.S. and stand in as acting manager. He eased from beside Samantha and climbed out of bed and headed for the bathroom, taking a quick glimpse back at the two beauties laying in his king-sized bed before somberly shaking his head and walking into the bathroom and slamming the door shut. The noise startled Samantha, who shot her eyes open as she lay on her back beside Amber.

Amber was awakened herself. She rolled over onto her back and lay beside Samantha, the two of them staring up at the ceiling. "Well, that didn't go as planned last night," she remarked as she wiped sleep from her eyes and yawned.

"I know," Samantha sighed. "Everything was set up perfect. I think we caught him off guard or something. I don't know."

"It was a definite blow to his ego I can tell ya' that." Amber replied matter-of-factly. "Maybe it'll work next time."

"Maybe so," Samantha stated as she looked over to Amber and planted a tender kiss on her forehead. "You were fantastic last night, though. At least we had fun."

"Yeah," Amber smiled. "But it could've been much better."

"We'll get there. A lot of men believe they want a ménage a trois—not!" Samantha laughed as she climbed from bed and headed for the bathroom.

When Samantha opened the door, Tre`, who was having a long, uplifting talk with his dick, righted himself and turned on the sink faucet. "What's up, baby?" he asked as he placed a towel under the running water.

Samantha walked up to her husband and hugged him from behind. "You okay, Tre`?"

"Yeah, yeah I'm good." Tre` remarked as he wrung the towel and wiped his face. "You know I was a bit sleepy last night, right? Put in like thirteen hours at the shop. Then went and grabbed the twins, fixed dinner for 'em, cleaned up the house a bit."

"I know. I know, baby. It's not a big deal. I thought we'd surprise you with it."

"Oh, I was surprised big time."

"Next time we'll plan it. Maybe the night the club opens in Saint Charles. Or just let it happen naturally. I don't know."

"Saint Charles would be cool," Tre` remarked. "I gotta redeem myself."

"You will," Samantha comforted as she moved to turn on the shower. "And you can start right now," she ended as she pulled off her panties and removed her bra.

****

Tre` left his home an hour later. The time spent with his wife was hot beyond compare, but he still felt embarrassed over what'd gone down the night before with her and Amber. He made it over to H.O.U.S.E. of I.D.E.A.S. and spoke to the fellas briefly before pulling the day's first work order. He and Victor would be working together on a '72 Chevy Caprice that needed an overhaul on its engine before being taken over to Lee and ran through the paint shop.

All morning, Victor had been noticing the glumness coming from Tre`. He talked about the time he and Martha had spent together before he left Oklahoma and how Lee had taken on the job of being the best man in Kimi's wedding, but Tre` had nothing more than a 'yeah, that's cool' for a reply each time.

"You all right, bro?" Victor finally asked Tre` as the two knelt under the engine of the Chevy tinkering around with its carburetor and spark plugs.

"Yeah, I'm cool, bruh."

"No you not," Victor retorted as he looked over to Tre`. "Your ass been down in the dumps since you walked in here. What's up, fam? Everything all right on the home front?" he asked seriously.

Tre` looked around the busy shop to make sure no one was close by to listen. "Remember, remember the time Kimi and Koko came into town and I ran down to you what Samantha and Amber was trying to set up that night?"

"The three-way?" Victor asked with a wide smile as he reached for a ratchet wrench.

"Yeah," Tre` responded as he loosened the top on the carburetor and removed the lid. "They came in last night with it on their mind, fam."

Victor eyed Tre` as he began loosening spark plugs on the engine. He needed no further information as thoughts of what Tre` had gotten into the night before with Samantha and Amber ran through his mind. The cloth on the front of his Dickies began to tent as he asked, "What y'all do?"

"Shit," Tre` remarked dejectedly.

"Say what now?" Victor asked as he removed a spark plug and dropped it into a plastic bucket situated at his feet.

"I know I told Samantha that was like my fantasy and shit, man, but I couldn't go through with it, you know?"

"Why?" Victor asked casually as he silently began wondering what was wrong with Tre`.

"Because I felt like I woulda been cheating on my wife. That shit sound crazy, fam?"

173

"Nah," Victor replied nonchalantly as he removed another spark plug and dropped it into the bucket. "Tell ya' what, though. Next time Samantha and Amber wanna get a three-way going and your punk ass chicken out? Give me a call. I'll show you what to do with them two fine ass mutherfuckas."

Tre` looked over to Victor without saying a word.

"What?" Victor looked up and laughed. "I'm tryna help you out and you over there getting upset and shit? Boy, you better man up and get in there! You in a position so many dudes wanna be in, fam," he added as he shook his head in dismay.

"Not every man want that there, though, Vic. My wife all I need. And the thing is, I think she more into Amber than anything. It's like I'm a side item and Amber the main course."

"I'd be a side item all damn day, homeboy. You see your wife? You see Amber? Better get over your reservations and handle your business. I wish I had a li'l hoe like Saman—I wish I had a woman like Samantha looking to get down like that."

"You called my wife a hoe?" Tre` asked with a hint of anger in his voice as he rose up from underneath the hood.

"I ain't, I ain't saying your wife a hoe," Victor laughed as he crept from under the hood of the car and backed away from Tre`. "The umm, the situation is hoe-like, though, I ain't gone lie. But that's what dudes be wantin', bruh! Ain't nothing wrong with it! I'm just…never mind. Don't listen to me, homie. Do what you think best," he suggested as he went back up under the hood. "Pass me the five-eighth socket over there."

"Grab that shit yourself," Tre` snapped as he pushed the hood of the car down on Victor's head. "Try and have a man-to-man talk with this mutherfucka and he got jokes early in the morning," he complained while walking off.

"Hey!" Victor called out as he lay underneath the hood planted on top of his back while laughing. "I ain't mean that shit, Tre`! Your wife not a hoe! Tre`? Tre`!"

"Fuck you I ain't got shit ta' say to you the rest of the mutherfuckin' day!" Tre` snapped as he walked out of the garage.

Victor laughed to himself as he raised the hood and resumed working on the Chevy. There was nothing behind his remarks about Samantha as he loved her like a sister. For whatever reason, though, Tre` always sought him out about relationship advice and each time, Victor would clown him on how he dealt with Samantha. He would never stoop so low as to try and get with his homeboy's wife, Amber neither, for that matter, but clowning Tre` was something he simply couldn't resist doing whenever the two talked as he knew how much his boy loved Samantha. *"He be all right with that. Happens to the best of us,"* Victor remarked to himself as he continued working on the vehicle by his lonesome.

CHAPTER EIGHTEEN

THE GURU

Samantha and Amber had flown me, Katrina, Henrietta and my sons and nieces into the small airport in the town of Florence, Colorado two days day after I'd returned from the Cayman Islands. Henrietta had visited Yiska on several occasions, but it'd been nearly four years since I'd seen the man who was like a father to me. I feel bad not having visited Yis since my release, but I was so caught up in finding Samantha, building a life and then learning about my father's people. Not makin g excuses, though, because I shoulda been made a trip to see the OG.

We hopped into a van we'd rented and made our way over to ADX and prepared to enter the prison. The place still looked like the fortress it was as me and my family walked in the cold air underneath the caged fence leading to the prison. The houses of confinement were off in the distance. I could see the building where I was once caged over to my right and the very window where I witnessed Katrina hold up the sign that read, *"Hello from Arizona. I love you."* I had no idea at that time just how much that woman would change my life and the blessings that would soon follow.

This was a happy day. It'd been some months, nearly a year since Henrietta had visited Yiska and he'd never met my sons or my sister. Yis had said to me a while back that he didn't want to see me get into another jam. I knew from letters he had written to me that he already knew what was up with me,

177

though, because I was the one who'd sent JunJie Maruyama his way when the Asian touched down. I can only imagine the war stories the men shared over the few months JunJie had been on the inside, and I wonder what advice the old timer would have for me knowing I was back doing the same thing that'd put me behind bars in the first place. I feel no shame about the matter, and I would hide nothing from Yiska because he like the father I never had.

We reached the main building and I was glad to see that there weren't many visitors on this cold, winter weekday in the month of January, just a couple of single women, an elderly white couple and a Hispanic family with three children. Henrietta sat beside me with this big wicker basket full of food that lit up the entire waiting area. Small talk was made up until the time we were all called in.

"How do I look, Ben? Am I presentable?" Henrietta asked me as she smoothened out her black cashmere coat.

I walked over and straightened the wool safari hat she wore and touched her cheek with the back of my hand. "Sixty looks damn good on you, Auntie. You look younger than the day you stood outside this prison and welcomed me home back in two thousand five."

Henrietta smiled up at me and ran her hand across my heart before walking off. I know my Aunt. I can tell by the look on her face that she was hoping that I wouldn't end up back inside this place over what I was doing. It was an unspoken concern that she would bring up on occasion, but I, like she, knew this was neither the time nor the place. We walked through the security area, the officers on duty checking Henrietta's picnic basket and the babies' diaper bags before allowing us to enter the visiting room. We set up at three tables and prisoners began filing in. JunJie emerged first. Nobody with me paid him no mind as they didn't know who he was.

"Mister Holland," Maruyama spoke aloud as he clapped his hands together and made his way over to our seating area. "How is life on the outside?"

"Life is good, Mister Maruyama. I want you to meet my

family."

"Ahhhh! The kids, the wife and the sister," he stated in an amazed tone as he nodded towards Henrietta and Samantha. "I have heard so much about you all. I'm pleased to meet you all."

Henrietta and Samantha were greeting JunJie when Yis walked in. He stood inside the double doors looking over to me with this wide smile on his face and placed a single finger over his lips as he crept around the tables and eased up behind Henrietta and tapped her on the shoulder.

Henrietta was enthralled in conversation with JunJie, enamored by his mannerisms and accent when she looked around to her left. She saw no one. When she looked to her right, there stood Yiska, smiling in her face. "Am I smelling a pot roast with scalloped potatoes, young lady?" he asked with a twinkle in his eyes.

"You, you said you'd want to enjoy it in the free world," Henrietta remarked meekly. "But, we aren't getting any younger. A while back, you said I should live for the moment. Why shouldn't *we* live for the moment? Holding on for a day that may never come is a waste of time."

"Are you saying I shall never see a day outside of these walls?"

"Not saying that. But why wait?" Henrietta asked as she smiled up at Yiska while placing a tender hand to his face. She then leaned in, raised up on the tips of her boots and kissed his lips tenderly.

The two remained lip-locked for a minute or so before Yiska pulled back. He ran a hand through Henrietta's slightly-greying brown hair and gave a nod of approval. "You've won me over, woman. How could I refuse such a sweet offer? I can't. Thank you for doing this."

"How you doing, pop?" I asked, breaking the trance between my aunt and Yis.

"Ben," Yiska smiled. "How are you, son?"

"Holding strong, brer," I smiled. "Holding strong. I told you about Samantha. Here she is, man. My heart and soul."

Yis breathed in deeply and exhaled. "My goodness. Pictures do you no justice, Samantha," he smiled as he hugged my sister. "The night Ben learned you were alive changed him *forever*!"

"It changed my life, too, Mister Hoka," Samantha stated as she held onto the man. "I owe you."

"Owe me?" Yis asked as he leaned back while holding onto the sides of Samantha's arm. "What do you owe me for?"

"For helping my brother to not give up on life. He could've just become a convict, but you made him a man."

"It was always in him, Samantha. I just spoke the words he needed to hear at the right time that's all."

"Heyyyy!" two little voices interrupted.

I watched as Yis looked down and saw Gabby and Tabby standing before him waving up at him with happy smiles on their faces.

"The babies," he smiled as leaned down and tugged on their tiny hands. "I'm so glad you two have one another, Samantha! Let's all sit! Tell me some stories. Good stories while we share this wonderful dinner my lady has prepared." I heard the OG say as Samantha handed Gabby to him while Henrietta picked up Tabby and brought her close to his side.

While Yis got acquainted with my family, I turned my attention back to JunJie. He motioned for the soda machine and we headed that way. "Do you have a single bill?" he asked me.

I slid a dollar in the machine and JunJie selected a can Coke. "Thank you, young man. I love the way this drink fizzles," he stated through a smile as he popped the top. "It's one of the new and simple things I've learned to enjoy on the inside. Reminds me of champagne in an odd way."

"It's a long way from what it really was." I told him.

"Yes it is, Ben. The businesses, the mansions, the cars and… ahhh…the women," he added as he closed his eyes and chuckled to himself. "As much power as I held, I can't get a single woman behind these bars. If I could have that? My march towards death behind these walls would be a pleasant journey."

"Don't talk like that, JunJie. You'll be around for years to come. And you still have value to this organization."

JunJie took a sip of his soda and said, "My son Phillip tells me you have a budding problem with a cartel down in Texas?"

"I got word from a friend on Gacha's security team that somebody may be moving in on our territory in the future." I said to JunJie as we walked over and stood before a window in an isolated portion of the visitor's room. "They call themselves the Eagle Pass Cartel. Ever heard of 'em?"

"Can't say I have heard of Eagle Pass Cartel. Is your guy reliable?"

"I trust 'em. I mean, he didn't have any reason to lie to me or anything like that."

"Okay," JunJie remarked. "Something's astir here, Mister Holland."

"I'm thinking that too, just can't put my finger on it."

JunJie set his soda on the edge of the window and tucked his hands inside his orange jumpsuit. "I know nothing of this Eagle Pass Cartel. But if what your guy told you is genuine? I would guess it to be someone from within our own inner circle," he said to me.

"Who in the circle could it be? If that's what it is?" I asked.

"Could be anybody, Ben. We know it's neither your family or that of my son or godson, so that narrows the scope. Who could it be?" he pondered out loud as he stared out the window with his hands behind his back.

"Somebody that's been around for a while, or maybe somebody that know how we operate," I told JunJie.

"Righhhttt," JunJie nodded as he looked up at me. "But, what if Gacha knows about the deal down in Brazil with the Deveraux family? What if this was like a subtle warning he's sending us and just threw out the name Eagle Pass Cartel to throw us off until he arranges our demise. It's a tactic I would use."

"The Deveraux family want these two guys Jaffrey and Theron Fischer killed up in Manhattan. Maybe that's an angle. They could be working with Gacha for all we know."

"That angle doesn't have a feel of deception or cold-calculation, Ben. I believe the Devereaux family to be sincere. But...why do I feel as if I've heard the name Fischer before?" JunJie asked me as he rubbed his chin while looking down to the floor. "Fischer. Fischer," he pondered. "I, I can't recall everything."

"You know of these guys?" I asked.

"There was a Jewish guy by the name of Iiayad Sheinheimer that did business with Gacha back in the early nineties that mentioned somebody named Fischer to me once I think, but we talking fifteen years ago and I really can't remember," JunJie told me. "What I do remember is that Sheinheimer was in on a hit against an American Ambassador by the name of Sanjar, his son Sanjar Junior, and one of the top hcroin suppliers in the nation down in Caracas when Gacha was just establishing himself. A man named Alfredo Lowes."

"Lowes?" I asked as I looked over to JunJie.

"You've heard of him?"

"Alfredo was connected to the Germans I made the deal with on behalf of the family to take down Tammy Moto."

"The Weinberger Family? That's who put the hit out on Tammy?" JunJie asked me.

"How you know the Germans?"

"I know them in name only, Ben, because of the Sanjar hit down in Caracas. How much have you talked with the Germans? What do you know about them exactly?"

"I talked with a woman by the name of Faye Bender. She gave me the rundown on Lisa Vanguard. Lisa killed her best friend's parents back in the late seventies and did some other shit, too. Faye and Lisa have an old score to settle, but she want Tammy Moto out of the way for setting up a faction of their crew. Tammy and Lisa used the cocaine Laddy Norcross busted you with and then ripped the Germans out of nearly four million dollars with the same product and sent two of their people to jail over in Philadelphia. They gotta pay for that one."

"And Phillip and Grover are taking the job to avenge what Lisa has done to me." JunJie nodded in his understanding.

"It's a tic-for-tac play. We get Tammy Moto for the Germans and they've agreed to do an international hit in return or take down three marks here in America. Three hits per agent."

"The one international hit? Is it Gacha?" JunJie asked as he looked over to me.

"I was actually thinking about pulling the hit off the table and calling for another sit down, but what if you right? What if Gacha got it in for us?"

"It's not adding up, Ben," JunJie said while shaking his head in disapproval. "If Gacha wanted to off our organization, he would've done it on Little Cayman Island. Instead, he gave you the Levamisole formula. That meeting on Little Cayman was only months ago. Gacha would've already had the hit in place beforehand and would've never shared that formula with us."

"We should just stick with the Germans and say fuck Gacha." I couldn't help but to acknowledge.

"We don't wanna jump the gun here, Ben," JunJie counseled. "There's more to the Germans. That I know."

"I'm listening."

"This guy Alfredo Lowes, he had a woman by the name of Tanya Weinberger. That's who pulls the strings for the Germans now. Talk to her to get a better understanding."

"The Germans have a lot of political connections that could be of value to us later on down the road."

"That they do, Ben. But it is a most delicate alliance. The Germans could go either way. They could endear themselves to us, or become our most dreaded enemy ever."

"We have a leg up, though, on some old shit."

"Right," JunJie remarked. "The Germans know nothing about Iiayad Sheinheimer, the man who supplied the C-4 used to kill Alfredo Lowes back in nineteen ninety-two down in Caracas. Give them that information, and in return? Ask them to use their political connections to look into the Eagle Pass Cartel for us. I have a gut instinct that's telling me everything will be brought to light fully once we find out who they are exactly."

"Done deal," I told JunJie. "You okay with your sons going after Tammy Moto?" I then asked. "It's gone be the most difficult hit the family ever pulled off and they may not recover from it."

"Phillip and Grover are aware that this may be a one way ticket, Ben. But we're too far gone to turn back. Whatever happens, we will not hold the Holland family responsible. This deal with Lisa and Tammy is ours to deal with. You focus on the Eagle Pass Cartel and work on unifying the family with the Germans. You were right about that. We need to unite. Leave the federal agents to Phil and Grover," JunJie said as he turned to me and extended his hand, the two of us sealing the deal with a firm handshake before rejoiningthe rest of the family.

CHAPTER NINETEEN

LINING THEM ALL UP

It was three days after I'd talked to JunJie Maruyama. The former boss of the organization was a treasure trove of wisdom and information. Meeting that man there was the second-to-last piece needed in order for me to gain a complete understanding of the entire operation my family was running. The only person I haven't met yet was Asa Spade, but given what I'd been told by Naomi and JunJie, Asa nothing more than a cog in this well-oiled machine. Don't get me wrong, he important to the family and he gone be straight when he get out, but my assessment of the situation is that although my people and the Italians were running entire cities just a couple of years back, it was JunJie who pulled the strings during that time.

My family became the stronger force, however, and rather than to concede to infighting, JunJie had the wisdom and humbleness to give power to the next capable crew in the organization he controlled—that crew being that of the Holland family.

I'm working with some real gangsters that's 'bout nothing but that paper right here. Top tier hustlers that'll kill anybody that stand in their way—even the feds. Which brings me to Cincinnati, Ohio while we talking.

During our talk, JunJie mentioned to me that the family should be on the lookout for a hit that could possibly come from someone that was either close to us, or knew of us that was involved in the same business. *"It could be anybody behind the Eagle Pass Cartel, Ben. And by anybody, I mean other organizations that have just as much power as we do, or someone inside our own family who has much to gain,"* was what he said to me as we continued our discussion.

JunJie not only gave me the plan needed to get a leg up on a possible hit on the family during my visit to Florence, Colorado, he also gave me the name of the potential target. It all made sense when you look back on it, I mean, who else would our enemies go after if they wanted to get at us and hit us where it hurt?

With those thoughts in mind, I got in contact with Faye Bender over to Kansas and was able to set up a meeting in Cincinnati on this here day. JunJie said I should meet with the people who really called the shots for the Germans and learn their intent and I was taking his advice. I had Samantha and Amber fly me and Victor into Cincinnati, Ohio were we landed at Cincinnati Municipal Lunken Airport under grey skies.

As Samantha brought the G-550 to a halt, a black four door 2008 Bentley Continental Flying Spur with black mirror tint pulled up alongside us. I looked out the window and saw two women step out the car. One was a slender, yet curvy tan-skinned female with a nappy tan Afro. She stood on the opposite side of the Bentley with a pair shades covering her eyes staring directly at the door on the plane as it slowly lowered. I couldn't see a weapon, but I could tell she was clutching a firearm given her stance and the way she kept her arms hidden in between the opened door and the interior of the car.

The other female, a slender pale-skinned woman with long, brown hair, climbed from behind the wheel in an all-white mink coat while scanning the area briefly. In her hand, tucked in the sleeve of her fur coat, I could make out faint traces of a chrome gun that looked like a Uzi with a black silencer over the barrel. I rose from my seat and pulled a couple of pictures from the inside of my suit jacket and took in the images before looking out the window once more.

Faye said these were the women that were going to meet me and the images matched the pictures. Despite them having guns, I only reached down and unshackled the AK-47 I had resting on the back seat and removed the .45 caliber from my waistband and set it in the seat next to me. I emerged from the plane unarmed once the door was lowered and trotted down the stairs while scanning the area for anything that looked out of place. All seemed to be on the up and up. No strange cars off in the distance rolling our way or stragglers milling about in the hangar off in the distance.

"Mister Holland. I'm Tanya Weinberger," the woman said to me as she extended a hand.

"Faye speaks well of you, Tanya," I remarked as I walked down the last couple of stairs and shook the woman's hand.

"And she has done the same in reference to you and your family, Mister Holland. The silent one back there is my daughter Helen. I know she's a cause of conflict within your family, but she's my American Express and I never leave home without her."

"That's an issue that still has to be worked out with my people in Missouri, but that's not my business to deal with. My people in Saint Louis gone handle that in due time." I told Tanya as my eyes continued to scan the area.

"Helen is willing to resolve the issue and she has my blessing and approval to keep the peace. I understand it's a delicate nature and hope we can start to fully unite here and now. Faye tells me you have a problem that we may be able to help you and your family resolve?" Tanya asked as she stood face-to-face with me and stared into my eyes with her hands clasped behind her back under the grey skies and blowing, cold wind.

"We've agreed to take down Tammy Moto," I stated. "What I'm asking for in return is an improvised hit to take place in Manhattan before Tammy goes down. Do you have any business there?"

"Not yet, but Faye informed me that she told you of our plans to move in on the heroin market in New York—which we will—but our agreed upon contracts on your family's behalf were scheduled to take place once Tammy Moto is eliminated, not before, Mister Holland."

"This job needs to be done while we in the process of going after Tammy."

"What you're asking for is a charity hit, Mister Holland," Tanya said to me as she casually looked me off. "That is a form of business we do not do. We aren't into donation murder so my answer is no. We will do the prearranged number of kills on behalf of your family *after* Tammy Moto is killed not before. If you want this Jamaican job done in Manhattan by my family before Tammy is killed you'll have to pay for it."

"What if I told you the people involved were the top suppliers of heroin to Brooklyn and the Bronx?"

"Makes no difference to me. After we take Philadelphia we will move in on New York. We will find out who controls the market on our own and remove them ourselves."

"With these names you can bypass Philadelphia and go straight for the grand prize."

"Nothing you're saying to me will convince my family to do a job for free, Mister Holland. You and I have nothing further to discuss until the Moto job is done," Tanya said to me as she turned and reached for the door handle on her Bentley.

"His name was Iiayad," I stated to Tanya as she held her back to me.

"Excuse me?" she asked as she turned and faced me once more.

"Your man Alfredo Lowes? I know who killed him."

I could tell that I'd sparked interest in Tanya with my last remark by the way she raised her eyebrows and the sudden attentiveness of Helen from across the way. The li'l chick rounded the car speaking German and I hadn't a clue what she was saying. "*Wenn Sie wissen, wer mein Vater tötete, was Sie uns sagen müssen! Dies ist eine unfaire Schnäppchen!*" (If you know who killed my daddy you must tell us! This is an unfair bargain!)

188

"Helen!" Tanya screamed as she shoved her daughter back. "It is not an unfair bargain!"

Victor stepped off the plane at that moment with the .50 caliber I knew he was packing tucked behind his backside. "Everything good, boss?" he asked, a little on edge as he eased halfway down the stairs with his eyes focused in on Tanya and Boogie.

"We good, fam." I coolly stated, knowing I had Tanya right where I needed her to be with her emotions. "We just wrapping up things with this deal in New York," I added as I stared back at Tanya and Boogie with a hidden smirk.

My intent was to get the Germans to do the hit on behalf of the Devereaux family on consignment. JunJie had given me the plan to work, but I was tweaking it to perfection because I was able to see things the Asian couldn't see being he was locked up. It was all but a given that Tammy was going down, we just had to wait until after Asa Spade's trial to fulfill the contract. I was trying to get the land the Devereaux family owned down in Brazil into my family's hands as quick as possible, though, only Tanya had a certain kind of obstinacy about herself that I hadn't anticipated. I had no choice but to pull out my ace-in-the-hole to get the ball rolling on the Jamaicans in Manhattan.

I stood and watched as Tanya placed her hands to her hips and looked at the ground in deep thought. She choked back tears as she looked over to me and said, "Who it was that killed Alfredo has been fucking my head up for nearly twenty years, man. The name of his killer is worth us going after the dealers in New York. Who is Iiayad? Where is he from? What does he do for a living?" she asked in rapid succession.

"Iiayad is a marketing manager for a major corporation here in America. Word has it that he was in Caracas the day Alfredo Lowes was blown up back in ninety-two and then sat in on a meeting after his death." I told Tanya. "I'll give you his full name and location if you agree to the hit in New York. This could give your family a leg up on the market up there and you'll be able to get back at the man who was in on the hit against your man and Helen's father," I added as a bonus. "And you will still get Tammy Moto out the way on top of it all." I then threw in for extra measure.

Tanya looked back at Helen briefly. When she nodded her approval, Tanya turned back to me and said, "We have a deal. I can't give you a timeline until I check everything out."

"It needs to go down before the end of summer."

"If it's at all possible, we'll get it done before the end of spring. Now, the full name of the man who killed Alfredo?"

"His full name is Iiayad Sheinheimer. He living down in Boca Raton, Florida right about now and work for Tropicana."

"And who are these people you want dead in Manhattan?" Tanya asked as she pulled out a small notepad and pen.

"Their names are Jaffrey and Theron Fischer."

"Okay," Tanya nodded. "I'll check things out and get back to you," she ended before walking off.

Once the Germans cleared out, I climbed back up the stairs leading to the G-550. My job of getting things in order on old scores and upcoming hits that needed doing was now complete. As of date, Tonto had been taken down thanks to my boy Lee, and the Ponca City police were left clueless. Chauncey had copped to a sixty year sentence with a chance for parole after serving thirty-eight years so he was no longer a problem. And without even touching Tammy Moto just yet, I'd gotten the Germans to agree to do a hit in New York and to take down Iiayad Sheinheimer too, who was a budding thorn in the family's side.

When I stepped onto the plane, Samantha was there to greet me. She was clutching the AK-47 I'd unshackled. I never ask my sister to pick up a weapon to protect me when I'm working, ya' dig? It was just something that was understood between us —a responsibility she'd taken upon herself, but an action never denied because I knew when it got down to it, Samantha would bust on my behalf. So far, she ain't never been put in harm's way because we were landing in places were business was conducted right there on the runway and I was making it a point to be in and out during this period of time. Samantha and Amber may have been jetting me around from city-to-city and flying offshore, but I was making it a point to not have us leave any airport we touched down at in order to keep them both safe. Still, Samantha never failed to have my back no matter what.

"Where to now?" Samantha asked as the hydraulic door to the jet was raised by Amber from the cockpit.

"Ponca City. I gotta hollar at Dawk for a minute before we head back to Arizona," I said to Samantha as I walked over the wooden floors of the plane and took a seat while unbuttoning my leather trench coat and loosening my tie.

"I'll go and set the coordinates," Samantha responded as she eased passed me and handed me the chopper before heading towards the cockpit.

CHAPTER TWENTY

KNOW THY ENEMY

"I gotta take 'em out...if he live he'll confess...so eight ball you ready(yeah)...shoot 'em in his chest(I got 'em)...one mutherfucka dead over bullshit...guess he didn't really know the niggas he was runnin' with..."

Light traffic was out and morning skies were clearing as Dawk Holland and Natalia III cruised down I-44 in Natalia's white-on-white 2008 Expedition bumping Memphis rappers 8Ball and MJG's song titled *Niggas Like Us*. It was three days after Ben had talked to Tanya on the runway up in Cincinnati. The family's first shipment of cocaine was now days away from reaching the Valley Brook Warehouse and Dawk was in the family's main hub of Saint Louis in order to make sure the crews were up on their jobs.

Natalia III had mentioned to DeeDee that the family not forget about him when the two talked inside of The Cicero Hot Dog Deli the day after Mendoza had been killed, and he was told that he would be contacted once the rackets were back up and running. True to their word, the Holland family had placed the Italian back into his old position of providing security for the family's cocaine shipments along with helping to distribute the product.

Twenty-five year-old Natalia III had a crew of four Italians born and bred in Cicero underneath him. He could best be described as a thoughtful, yet cold and calculating man of

Italian descent with a fierce loyalty to rank and order inside La Cosa Nostra, and his three goons were just as loyal. Natalia's crew was made up of the grandsons of former Capos and Enforcers that ran other crews inside Twenty Third Street Mafia, grandsons who'd all sided with him when he went against his own father and Junior Cernigliaro during the failed coup that led to Doss Dawkins' demise.

The Cicero faction of the Holland family, when it got down to it, was pure muscle. With fourteen bodies under their belt going back to 2006, the next generation of Italians within the organization was more than capable of holding their own when it came to providing security for suppliers of large of amounts of cocaine.

The only problem for Dawk with the Cicero gang, however, was that he and Natalia III didn't always see eye-to-eye on matters. The Italian would sometimes question Dawk's judgement on certain matters when it came to running the cocaine operation. He and Dawk had gotten into a couple of heated debates over where Natalia was to distribute the family's product once he was done with his security detail. Natalia wanted to sell his bricks in the cities of Kansas City and Minneapolis. Kansas City was cool for Dawk, but Minneapolis was off the table for the time being.

Natalia couldn't understand Dawk's reasoning, but he agreed to obey the order. Some in the family down in Missouri, namely Jay-D, questioned Dawk over the reasons behind giving a newcomer like Natalia III such an important job when Malik Gomez was more than capable of handling that task.

Dawk's answer to that question was that it was better to keep one's enemies close. The reason behind his reply came shortly after Ben had touched down in Ponca City after his meeting with Tanya Weinberger. Ben had put Dawk up on game with the information he'd received from JunJie and the family was now aware of the budding problem; they also knew of Iiayad Sheinheimer's role and were anticipating his demise once Tanya Weinberger confirmed Ben's story.

As they rode, Natalia III pulled out a manila folder from under his seat and handed it to Dawk. "Check that out," he requested as he checked a text he'd just received that read... *Where u at?*

Dawk pulled the folder open and slid out a menu that had a picture of his father, Lucky, Mendoza and Zell Verniche` on the front cover. The four legendary gangsters were all seated inside Zell's booth wearing silk suits as they sat stone-faced with their hands resting on the table. They all sported diamond pinky rings, and Zell, Mendoza and Lucky were sporting fedoras.

Dawk eyed his father sitting beside Lucky. Doss was sporting a fresh bald-cut fade with a neatly-trimmed beard and a diamond earring in his left ear. He saw a lot of himself in his father, able to discern that he had Doss' eyes and his square jawline and both were ripped. The only difference Dawk could decipher was that he was taller and lighter than his father, and he wore his long black hair in a ponytail.

"I should get a haircut, a bald fade like my father," Dawk said as he stared at his father's image.

"That would suit you, il mio amico," Natalia agreed as he lay back in the driver's seat.

"I like my father's look. I get a bald fade, I would just be a lighter version of my daddy."

Dawk liked the thought. He and his father had a lot in common, not just that of being handsome, but also in the way they handled business and the love they had for family. Dawk was going to be a father within the next four months. He wished his father was still alive to be able see him marry and bring life into the world. Knowing he got the chance to be a grandfather when Tiva gave birth to Malaysia and Malara, however, had eased his mind. Not wanting to drift any further and dampen his mood, Dawk focused back in on the entire picture. It was a classic snapshot, a photo that captured the essence of a real gangster in every sense of the word and would keep the images of the men alive in one's mind for all time.

"I told DeeDee the day after we learned Mendoza was killed that was I going to create a menu for the Hot Dog deli back in Cicero," Natalia III stated as he sent a text back that read...*b up to McDs in about ten.* "That there is the prototype for the new menu complete with the new dishes for each of the bosses," he then told Dawk as he continued up the freeway.

Dawk pulled open the menu and saw a list of four meals under the heading *Cicero's Legendary House Specials* set against a dark brown and black backdrop. Given the table of contents, he could see that each of the four meals listed had their own page and all had a price sale price listed at $200 dollars, except for the last one, which had a sale price of $34.99.

The first meal listed was called *The Capo Dei Capi* (Boss of Bosses). Dawk knew that would be Zell's meal given the title.

The next meal listed was called *The Cernigiaro*. That left no guessing as to who that meal was dedicated to.

The third meal was called *The Enforcer*. Dawk had a guess as to who that meal was dedicated to, but he also began to question the names of the meals on menu as he read the name of the last meal which was called *The Working Man*, a meal that only had a $34.99 price tag.

Dawk kept his thoughts to himself as he flipped open to the first page of the menu. There sitting in his booth in his suit and tie under dim lighting, was a large picture of Zell Verniche`. He sat with his hands resting before a dish of scungilli, which was an Italian dish consisting of large marine snails drenched in marinara sauce and spread over pasta. Beside the gangster was a bottle of Rum and a slice of cheesecake.

"The Capo Dei Capi," Dawk stated seriously. "I figured that would've been Zell's meal."

"He loved him some mollusks," Natalia III replied as he got another text that read…*Max is waiting.*

You dumb fuck, he screamed to his self as he quickly read the text and bothered not to reply.

Dawk, meanwhile, had flipped to the second page of the menu. There was an image of Mendoza Cernigliaro sitting before a plate containing an Italian sausage dog with au gratin, a large order of fries and a Pepsi in a glass. There was a full bottle of scotch and a Duke of Devon Macanudo Cigar off to the side of the meal and a $200 dollar sale price.

"That was what Mendoza asked for as his last wish," Dawk nodded as he held the menu open on Mendoza's picture and wondered who *The Enforcer* was dedicated to.

At this point, Dawk was beginning to feel insulted by one name and one price—that of *The Working Man*. He didn't appreciate his father been listed last, on top of having received such a low title and cheap meal ticket. In his mind, there was the Boss of Bosses, The Cernigliaro and The Enforcer, a meal in which he assumed was Lucky's lasagna meal.

"You better not had put no fried chicken or nothing clichéd like that on the menu for my daddy," Dawk stated out loud to Natalia as he sat upright in the passenger seat and turned down the stereo.

"The fuck you talkin' about?" Natalia III asked as he sat up in the driver's seat and mean-mugged Dawk. "You think I would fuckin' insult Doss by doing some…eh…" the Italian paused mid-sentence when caught on to what he believed Dawk was implying. "You think I'm a racist, Dawk?" he asked in disbelief.

"I'm looking at the names, Natalia. I see respected names, and then I see The Working Man. Like my father was a helper or something. That's how I see it. That's how I see this menu. It was supposed to be dedicated to gangsters. Everybody on there was a gangster and deserve respect."

"So, the working man isn't to be respected," Natalia III stated in a matter-of-fact manner as he nodded his head up and down.

"I ain't say that there," Dawk retorted. "I'm thinking we should go with a different name for my father's meal and raise the price."

"Yeah," Natalia III responded casually. "Before you decide to change the name on The Working Man and raise the price, take a look at the last two meals and I'll explain something to ya' about Cicero when you're done," he suggested as he leaned back in the driver's seat and continued cruising down I-44 headed east.

Dawk flipped the laminated page and an image of his father

came into view. Doss was sitting in the booth before a plate that held a thick-cut rib eye steak and a fully-loaded baked potato with a side salad. There was a bottle of cognac off to the side and a Punch cigar on the table. The meal, like the previous two, also carried a $200 dollar price tag.

Dawk was now a little perplexed. "This not the order," he told Natalia.

"Order of what? How they died?" Natalia asked as he looked over to Dawk, now fully understanding his disapproval of the names of the last two meals.

"Yeah," Dawk remarked. "Zell went first, then Mend…" Dawk's voice trailed off when he realized his mistake. Lucky had died before Mendoza. His belief that the men were listed in the order of their deaths was off. He'd also had a moment of blind racism as he was more focused on his father being listed last with title of The Working Man and the cheap price tag rather than the titles of meals, which seemed to be the theme of the menu Natalia III had put together.

Dawk flipped the fourth page and Lucky's image came into view under a meal titled *The Working Man*. He was sitting before a plate of lasagna with a smaller dish that held a cut of filet mignon, and there was a bottle of red wine off to the side and the meal had a price tag of $34.99.

Dawk had just been embarrassed into silence. He'd had all sorts of negative thoughts running through his mind over a title, that, when it got down to it, deserved the most respect given the dedication it took for such a man who indeed had to work for a living.

"Back in Cicero," Natalia remarked, shaking Dawk from his thoughts. "Back in Cicero, because you weren't raised there to really understand how close the people are back there? Everybody, every man, no matter what he did for a living, so long as he didn't hurt any children? He was respected. But Lucky, Lucky was like a hero back there. He was the working man of Cicero—a man's man. People knew what he did for a living, but they respected him because he made a name for his self and looked out for people."

"That was Lucky," Dawk agreed. "I owe you an apoly—"

"Let me finish, Dawk," Natalia III interrupted. "I know you know your father better than all of us put together, but you don't know him how we knew him in Cicero. Your father was and is a legend up there. Doss had the ladies all over him, just like his father," he laughed. "But Doss Dawkins was all about his business. He never entertained any of those women and he was a man that could be counted on above any other Capo. He couldn't get made, but that was his unspoken title amongst the Italians just in case you didn't know. Your father was a Capo."

"I never knew that," Dawk remarked. "Before he became Boss he was—"

"The Enforcer." Natalia III remarked as he looked over to Dawk with a serious gaze planted on his face. "You should really come up and hang out in Cicero some time. Your family has roots there and you shouldn't let them die."

"I'm gone do that," Dawk remarked while nodding his head and running his hand over his goatee. "I'm gone get with you and set something up when the time right."

"Okay. Just make sure you leave the racism wherever that shit come from," Natalia III quipped.

Dawk laughed and said, "I deserve that and more. My grandfather gone love this menu, dude." he added.

"So I take it you like it now that you know the intent behind it," Natalia III replied as he exited onto Jefferson Avenue.

"It's one of the best gestures anybody ever made towards the family. You think you gone make money off it, though? Two hundred dollars a meal ain't cheap for real working folk."

"You kiddin' me?" Natalia III laughed as he turned into McDonald's on Jefferson Avenue. "That one booth is booked up for the remainder of the month and all the way into March. Ten to fifteen meals a day served alone off those dinners we're offering. It's a boom for the deli up there."

Dawk bothered not replying as he scratched his chin and scanned the area as Natalia headed for the drive-thru. This was the same McDonald's where Bay had caught Phoebe Perez slipping and nothing about the situation sat right with him in the least. "Yo, I know another McDonald's on the other side of Fox Park," he told Natalia. "This one here be fuckin' up the orders."

"Yeah? We'll pick up something on the way out then. I'm a just head over to Ann Avenue."

Natalia made the short drive over to Fox Park and swerved onto Ann Avenue. The block was quiet except for the three trap houses the family controlled. The day after Dawk, Bay and T-top and the Cottonwoods had killed Ya Murder and her crew, Dawk had given Malik Gomez the assignment of renovating the trap houses. He was on the block this mid-morning in early February to make sure what he'd ordered was being taken care of. Right away, he could see some of Malik's team making repairs to the traps. They all had brand new metal doors put up and security cameras were going up all around.

A couple of work vans had trailers loaded down with steel burglar bars and workers were busy unstrapping the wrought iron to place over the doors and windows on the first floors of the traps. The two climbed from the Expedition just as Malik emerged from the main trap in the center of the block.

"Homes!" Malik stated towards Dawk with a surprise look on his face as he walked up and gave him a quick hug. "I wasn't expecting, I wasn't expecting to see you so early."

"Just swingin' in to make sure everything going smooth. First load coming in soon and everybody need to be up on their job." Dawk stated while scanning the block in appreciation of what his eyes were witnessing.

"They on it, homes. It'll be another three days at the most before we're done. My guys have to make sure the cameras are in full operation and put the steel bars up on the doors and first floor windows. Come and check it out," Malik responded as he threw a thumb back at the trap and slammed his left fist into his right palm.

"Anybody need taken out in the Lou or elsewhere while that's going on?" Dawk asked as he and Natalia trailed Malik up the sidewalk leading to the main trap house.

"Not right now," Malik responded as he pushed the door open and stepped inside. "Things been quiet since Ya Murder and Juggie went down."

"That's what it is then," Dawk replied. "Malik? You ever heard of a Eagle Pass Cartel?" he then asked as he and Natalia walked into the trap.

"Eagle Pass Cartel?" Malik asked with a frown as he thought deeply while closing and locking the front door behind Dawk and Natalia. "I can't say I've heard of them before, boss. Is there something we should know about them?"

"Nah," Dawk answered. "It was just a name dropped on us. Nothing to worry about, fam. We don't operate in the same lanes from what I know. Just thought I'd ask around about 'em," he ended just as DeMarco emerged from the kitchen. "You got the money counters ready to go, 'Marco?" he asked as he walked into the kitchen and began an inspection by checking to make sure the windows were locked and the back door was solid.

"Yeah, they all hooked up, man. I was waiting on Max, but he ain't made it back from the store," DeMarco replied. "I got like five hundred in twenties on me, though. We can do a quick test on the machines if you want."

"Show me what it do," Dawk replied as he and DeMarco walked over to the small wooden table inside the kitchen where DeMarco pulled out a knot of twenty dollars bills and placed them in the money counter.

Natalia III and Malik, meanwhile, had walked off from Dawk as the money counter began clicking. The two climbed the stairs, Natalia III following Malik up to the second floor where he pointed out the two bedrooms where the incoming cocaine would be broken down.

Natalia III eyed the rooms, both of which possessed nothing more than a single twin bed, a large wooden table and four chairs. "This'll do," he stated to Malik.

"I think we have else to discuss, right?" Malik asked in a near whisper. "What happened at the McDonald's? I sent my guy Max up there and he was waiting."

"Dawk didn't wanna hit the drive thru," Natalia remarked as he shook his head somberly. "I didn't wanna push the issue and raise suspicion, you know?"

Malik sighed, looked to the floor and said, "We can do it when the first load comes in then."

"That'll work better because we can keep the product," Natalia stated as he patted Malik's shoulder. "We can make it look like some cowboys swooped in and done the job. Only thing is, Dawk ain't tell me the location of the drop off on the first shipment yet."

"I'm over that, homes," Malik answered. "Soon as I find out from Dawk where the drop is we'll be in business. You just make sure your team ready when the time comes."

"My guys is always ready. It'll be a breeze. Dawk trusts me like his father trusted Junior."

"He really put you in charge of security knowing you was in with Junior, homes?" Malik asked seriously. "If Junior would've come to me, the Mexicans and Italians would be running this family right now."

"Can't worry about the past," Natalia III countered. "But didn't I tell you he was gone do that shit?" he smiled slyly. He then dropped his smile and said to Malik, "Just you keep your mouth shut about this thing of ours and we'll be the ones calling the shots in due time."

"Your people in Cherryvale, Kansas," Malik inquired. "Is there any way you can get them to continue to let those loads from Eagle Pass continue on untouched? Tell them the Eagle Pass Cartel is willing to pay for safe passage."

"I dealt with 'em many times before. Used to sell 'em the cocaine I ripped off from other dealers. I'm in good with 'em, and trust me, they have no alliance with Dawk's people. I'll let 'em know what the deal is and work out an agreed upon fee for safe passage across the state of Kansas until we're able to move our distribution point from Minnesota down here to Saint Louis."

"If you can work that out, there will be no stopping us, Natalia."

"You right about that, my friend. We'll get it done soon

enough," Natalia III responded as he and Malik gave each other a pound and then bumped fists before descending the stairs and linking back up with Dawk.

CHAPTER TWENTY-ONE

TOP BILLING

The past ten days had been nerve-wracking for Kimi and Koko. Daytime classes, exams and homework had the twins overwhelmed, not to mention the proposal they had to draw up per their mother's request. The dreaded day of February 9th had arrived and all the two could wonder is if they'd done their jobs correctly.

Under the protection of Dawk and Lee Sato, Kimi and Koko moved about the main suite inside Bay's condo preparing themselves for another all-important meeting with their mother concerning the family's finances. Ever the divas of the family, they took their time dressing, strolling through the walk-in closet in seemingly slow motion and all-out sexiness, wearing nothing but their white silk bras and matching panties with their brown hair pressed and touching the napes of their neck. They moved about the closet, Koko with her sore foot airing out, scanning newly-purchased outfits as they'd just had to go shopping to relieve themselves of the stress they were under in order to look exquisite upon delivering another presentation before their beloved mother.

After walking up and down the closet for a few minutes, Kimi and Koko selected and agreed upon identical egg-shell white, suede all-in-one dresses and black, suede knee-length boots. "Lucky I got a boot that match these shoes," Koko said as she handed her outfit to Kimi and followed her out the closet with the aid of her walking stick.

Kimi laid out her and her sister's outfits before they went and sat on a chaise side by side and began lathering their thick, tan-skinned thighs with a coating of Burberry watermelon lotion. With their first coat of fragrance completed, they reached over and opened identical wooden boxes resting on either side of them and pulled out duplicate sets of pearl necklaces.

Kimi turned away from her sister and Koko gently placed the pearls around her neck and clamped it shut. She then turned and waited for Kimi to secure her pearls. After helping one another to lock in refined oysters worth $4,500 dollars each, Kimi helped Koko to her feet and the two walked over to the tall, oak dresser and placed thick diamond bracelets and platinum Rolex watches onto each of their wrists while staring into one another's brown eyes through the mirror.

"What if momma don't like what we've put together?" Koko asked meekly as she stared at her twin's image and began dabbing new perfume onto the back of her wrists and behind her earlobes.

"Given all we've put into this latest venture, Koko? If momma disagrees, then we've just set the family back eleven million dollars our first time out." Kimi responded as she caught a whiff of her sister's new-fangled eau de toilette. "Girl, what is that you're wearing?" she just had to ask while adorning her ears with $1,200 dollar diamond-drops weighing in at two carats.

"It's called Caron Poivre," Koko responded humbly as she slid the bottle over to her twin. "It's a French perfume with hints of clove."

"Smells like it has pepper or something in there too," Kimi replied as she turned her head to the side to see how the earring she'd placed in her left earlobe looked as it dangled from her ear. "Nah," she said through a frown. "Diamond studs gone work better with this get up," she surmised as she removed the diamond drop and reached for a pair of three karat diamond studs. "Where you get that perfume from though, Koko?"

"Lee bought it for me down in Arizona. There *is* pepper in

the ingredients—black and red pepper and other spices."

"How much it cost if you don't mind me asking?" Kimi asked while placing a diamond stud into her right ear. "There I go," she said in complementation of herself while nodding her head in approval.

"It cost like a thousand dollars an ounce. Try it, Kimi."

Kimi looked over to Koko with wide eyes. "Lee spent a thousand dollars on you already?" she asked surprised. "That, that might be a special gift, Koko. I don't wanna—"

"I already asked Lee and he says it's fine if you wear it, Kimi," Koko interjected. "I wanted you to try it because I knew you'd like it. It's unisex, too. I was thinking of getting you and Udelle a bottle for the dinner party Katrina putting together in Saint Charles."

"Girl, you should've surprised me!" Kimi laughed as she picked up the perfume. "Udelle?" she sniffed the bottle once more, not sure of it being unisex, "I don't know about him wearing this."

"Lee wears it." Koko remarked. "I get turned on inhaling his scent."

"Okay," Kimi nodded, knowing of Lee's resume`. "Lee a man's man. Just when you get it for us? We gone have to let each other know what days we wearing it when we with our men. It'll be weird everybody showing up smelling the same," she remarked as she and Koko shared a quick laugh.

Kimi and Koko went on to finish adorning themselves. They then went and dressed, helping one another to look as professionally-fly as possible. Once done, they walked over and stood before a floor-length mirror and eyed their identical images.

"You think we got it right? The proposal, I mean?" Koko asked Kimi as the two stood side-by-side looking straight ahead at images that could not be deciphered by the outside eye save for the stylish boot Koko wore on her right foot.

Kimi eyed her and her twin's image in the mirror as she reflected on all she and her sister had done to prepare for this day. They'd learned more about international finance, offshore banking and federal tax laws than they'd ever anticipated. Years of training from one of the best to play the money game in Naomi Holland-Dawkins, had been and was still in the process of being rubbed off on the family's middle daughters.

Although ranking as that of sophomores over to the University of Oklahoma, Kimi and Koko had become tops in their Accounting class. So much so, they'd taken on the filing of taxes for several students in their class, and the professor himself as they were able to interpret tax laws that the professor himself hadn't planned on discussing until two semesters down the road.

"I think we got it together," Kimi remarked through a serious gaze as she leaned down and picked up her black suede briefcase. Koko followed suit and together, the money launderers for the Holland family turned and confidently walked out of the room side-by-side.

While walking up the hallway, the twins ran into Udelle, who'd just walked out of the bathroom. He was wearing gym shorts, a white tee and slippers, having just showered. Kimi broke off from Koko and followed her man back into a spare bedroom they were sharing inside Bay's immaculate three-bedroom condo. "How I look, Udelle?" she asked as she gently closed the door and turned back to her man and stuck a pose by placing a hand on her hip and slightly pulling up on her skirt, putting one of her thick, sexy thighs on display.

"As good as you smell, baby." Udelle remarked as he set up an ironing board and laid a pair of burgundy pants down for pressing.

"Don't you have a presentation before your Meteorology class this morning?" Kimi inquired as she went over and scanned a makeshift store rack that held freshly tagged clothes she'd set up for her lover.

"Yeah. Why?" Udelle asked as he leaned down and plugged in the iron.

"Burgundy is not a good color for a presentation, Udelle," Kimi chided. "You should do your demonstration like you were going on live TV, because you will be on live TV in a couple of years at the latest," she added as she pulled a pair of light-tan silk pants from the rack and removed them from the wooden hangar. "Here, baby. This will look much better."

"You think so?" Udelle asked as he took the slacks and placed them against his body.

"Trust me. I know what looks good on you," Kimi remarked while selecting an olive silk shirt and a pair of olive suede shoes for her man. She turned back to Udelle and said, "Those slacks? With these suede Kenneth Cole's I bought you with this tan sports jacket gone set you off, baby. You gone be the fly weatherman."

Udelle smiled over his woman as she went about selecting his clothes. "I feel like a ten year-old," he remarked as he laid the slacks on the ironing board.

Kimi sighed a little. "Aww, come on, Udelle," she remarked in a compassionate tone as she walked over to her love. "Am I going too far, man? I was only trying to help," she pouted as she gazed up into his eyes.

"I know," Udelle smiled as he looked away from Kimi and picked up a teal and white box and placed it on the ironing board. "I'm not talkin' about the clothes, though, when I say I feel like a ten year-old. You may be right about the slacks and all. But you umm, you didn't have to send me a bodyguard, baby," he stated seriously. "Tonto punk ass caught me off guard that night that's all. A pistol 'cross the head would knock most men dizzy. I'm not saying I don't appreciate it, but you didn't have to send Lee down to my dorm room to look after me. I got us from now on," Udelle declared as he pulled the lid off the box to reveal two Tiffany Blue Ruger LCP .380 semi-automatic handguns.

Udelle had responded to what'd gone down the night Spoonie was shot in a way Kimi hadn't anticipated, but by all means was she turned on by his assertiveness over the aftermath. "So you're not mad at me," she declared upon realizing that Udelle had the capacity to understand that the move she'd made was done out of love and not pity. "How you know that's what I was doing when I sent Lee down there, though, Udelle?" she asked as she caressed one of the handguns.

"Because I know how much woo wove me," Udelle answered playfully as he nuzzled his woman's nose with the tip of his nose.

Kimi squealed in delight as she wrapped her arms around her man. "Woo woves you?" he she responded in a good-natured manner while licking her lip-gloss-covered mouth.

"Woo wove me," Udelle answered through light-hearted laughter before kissing his woman deeply and palming one of her butt cheeks.

Passion rose quickly inside Kimi over Udelle's touch as her head drifted off to a place she had no intentions on entering at such an early morning hour. "You gone start something," she cooed.

"I hope so," Udelle whispered as he palmed Kimi's ass cheeks and ran his hands over the back of her thighs.

The area just below Kimi's butt cheeks and the top back of her thighs was her hot spot. What he was doing to her this early Monday morning had coaxed her into an insatiable mood. For the moment, business could wait. She closed her eyes and began planting soft kisses on Udelle's chest and biceps while pulling up her skirt. "Why you doing this to me, baby?" she whispered in a loving tone while easing her legs open slightly.

"I can't be in the same room with you without wanting to make love to you, woman. And what better way to kick off the work week, huh?" Udelle reasoned as his hand slid in between Kimi's thong where he eased a finger inside of her moist slit and kissed her tenderly.

"Imagine that...imagine that..." Kimi sung out in a low, sexy voice as she raised one of her thick thighs and rested her foot on a stack of shoe boxes and ground down onto her lover's finger with a contented smile on her face.

"That I'm stroking your body...imagine that..." Udelle responded, getting in tune with his woman by singing the lyrics

to R Kelly's song *Imagine* in a deep-pitched, raspy voice as he eased Kimi back towards the bed and stepped out of his shorts and silk boxers.

"Strawberries and whip cream...imagine that..." Kimi sung back as she lay down on the edge of the mattress and cocked her legs open to two forty-five. "Come on and get your pussy before I go to work, boy," she commanded as she raised her hands above her head and willfully surrendered everything she had to offer.

Udelle could feel the heat pouring from his woman's wet center as he eased inside, and the room quickly filled with the sounds of lovemaking. Kimi had a vice of a vagina, one that hugged Udelle and sent ripples of pleasure through both lovers' bodies. Her soft skin, the perfume she wore, her beautiful face, and the way she looked into his eyes, as if she was in awe of his skills, melted away what little stamina Udelle could muster up. He rarely lasted long inside, but the feeling was mutual.

Kimi had never known any other lover outside of Udelle. All she knew was that his touch was the right touch, and every time he entered her, she would orgasm over the heat and girth of his manhood. It only took a few strokes most times for both lovers to begin clawing at one another and kissing deeply, sliding their tongues back and forth and savoring one another's taste through sloppy wet kisses so powerful, they would sometimes bump teeth over their hunger for one another.

As Udelle stroked her hard, fast and deep, Kimi couldn't help but to reach out and grab his butt cheeks, her way of urging her man deeper inside while slowly rotating her hips in a circular motion on a thick, hard organ that was hot enough to bore through titanium. "Baby!" she exclaimed as she opened her eyes and stared up at Udelle, completely blown away over the sensations of the hard dick that was impaling her and forcing her legs to tremble. "I love you so fucking much! I love you, Mister Raymond!" she screamed out loud before clasping her hands to her mouth to conceal her squeals of delight while violently thrusting up into Udelle's pelvis and clamping down on her vaginal muscles.

Both lovers had to pause momentarily as Udelle's dick rested deep inside Kimi while throbbing uncontrollably as he ejaculated over and over again. It was as if they both knew. "Boy or a girl, baby?" she asked as she covered her lower face with her hands and looked deep into Udelle's, eyes hoping she didn't upset him with her query as she slowly lowered her trembling legs to the floor.

Udelle leaned down and kissed Kimi's hands in tender fashion before removing them and kissing her deeply while cupping her jaws. "I'm gone love my child no matter what the gender, baby. No matter what. And I hope to God that what we both feeling at this moment last forever. I love the fuck outta you, Kimi. You my life, baby—you my life." he professed as he held her tightly in his arms.

Kimi had no response. All she could do was raise her head from the mattress and kiss her man with a passion so sincere that only God could understand. "You complete me, Udelle Raymond," she confessed. "When I picture my day? It's never a day without you in it. Every day," she declared as she shook her head from to side slowly with a heart thumping sweeter and softer than cotton candy, yet thicker than honey.

"Every day," Udelle responded as he eased off of Kimi and pulled her up to her feet and stared into her gorgeous brown eyes while gripping her tightly.

"I want a repeat of this day when I don't have to work or go to class. Can I get that?"

"Let me know when and I'll give you the weather forecast so we can set the mood early," Udelle responded.

"No matter the season? Our forecast will always be hot and steamy."

"Who you telling? Every day?"

"Every day," Kimi remarked before standing on the tips of her toes and kissing her lover. "Look what you've done to me," she then remarked in mocked aggravation as she pranced before Udelle with her dress still raised above her hips while checking out her shoes. "I look okay?"

Udelle smirked and went over and stood behind the ironing board. "You keep strutting like that and we ain't gone never leave this room today."

"I swear if what was so important could be put off I wouldn't hesitate," Kimi remarked as she pulled her dress back over her hips. "I got you, though," she smiled as she grabbed her purse. "Let me go and get myself together for a second time this morning. I'll see you later on this evening over to Deep Deuce," she added as she exited the bedroom.

Back out in the living room, Lee was all up on Koko as the two sat on the couch. She was laughing uncontrollably as her beau cracked jokes over the gift he'd given her. "Nah, really. You wearing stolen shit, girl. That bottle cost a G stack, but look how small it is. See, I risked my *freedom* for you because I care that much about you."

"Oh," Koko spoke dejectedly. "I'm not worth a thousand dollar bottle of perfume? Lee, I don't, this is not what I want in a man."

Lee sat up on the couch and pulled out his phone. "One thing I'm not is a thief," he remarked as he pulled up his bank account. "And you're worth way more than a thousand dollars. I don't have a receipt, but you can check my bank transactions."

"For real?" Koko asked through a smile, knowing Lee didn't actually steal the perfume, but tickled by his sincerity nonetheless. "Let me see your balance."

Lee thumbed his nose and shut down his phone. "Let's just go with the 'I stole the perfume' story," he remarked as he leaned back on the couch.

"What?" Koko asked as she leaned into over into Lee with a pleasant smile on her face. "You already know what it is with my family. You balling?"

Lee donned a serious look as he scooted up to the edge of the sofa. He picked his phone up, opened the screen once more and handed it to Koko. "Check me out if you want."

With Lee, Koko could just be herself. She hadn't always

been the type of female to like the bad boys, but she'd slowly evolved into that sort of a female the more she branched out and met different members of the opposite sex. Chablis had that bad boy appeal, but he was unable to control his emotions and often grew jealous. He'd become rotten fruit in Koko's eyes. And his treachery had only served to prove her right. "I don't wanna see your balance, Lee," she professed as she took the phone from his hand and threw it onto the sofa cushions. "I'm just glad to be able to joke with you and not have you get offended."

"Well, I am offended because you won't look at it now," Lee remarked as he sat back on the sofa. "I thought if you saw how much money I had I would be in. That's what dudes do now-a-days, right? Brag on how much money they got and how hard they are outside in that world?"

"Not us. I don't want a man like that, Lee. That's not you, right? Because if it is we can just…"

"Koko," Lee spoke in tender fashion as he placed a loose arm around Koko's neck, pulled her close and looked into her eyes. "I was being facetious, baby. You know damn well this ain't about money, how hard I am or what kind of car I drive. I'm just a man taken back by a beautiful soul. You know that's a gift paid for, but we just clowning right now. I wanna see you smile. Nothing more."

Koko had to look away. Lee made her feel right. With him, she was able to be that fun-loving woman that loved to talk gangster talk and carry on as such, but at the same time, not be a part of the street life. Lee also made her feel safe. He lit her soul whenever he neared and she was always ready to engage him in conversation. Despite all the upsides, however, she and Lee were still in the beginning stages of their relationship. Having only slept together two times, both of which were magical moments, the two still had more to learn about one another.

In Koko's mind, she and Lee had to learn one another's habits, likes and dislikes. She'd only known him a short time, but it was time enough for her to see that Lee was a man with a sense of humor, had intellect about his self, and knew how to handle business in the streets. He was much like her father in some aspects.

It was Lee's lifestyle, the danger of it all, that intoxicated Koko. She knew the possible outcome having experienced the loss of her father, but if her mother could love a man more dangerous than Lee in her daddy, then why could not she was her reasoning as she pictured the two of them going through life together.

Koko wanted to be in it for the long haul with Lee. Whether he knew it or not, he'd been chosen, but it all depended on how he would respond to the various situations she had in mind on placing him in over time. She had to know if Lee had that jealous streak in him like Chablis, because if he did, she was prepared to cut him loose the time that one negative quality she abhorred and feared the most in a man reared its ugly head.

"Me and my twin and a few of our friends from my Accounting class having drinks tonight over to Deep Deuce Grill," Koko mentioned to Lee. "I was wondering if you would like to join us?"

"I get to meet the friends and shit?" Lee smiled. "You tryna make me feel special or you just taking pity on my heart?"

Koko laughed just as Kimi walked out from the hall toting her briefcase. "Meet me here around six," she smiled as she handed Lee a card with the address to a place called *Deep Deuce Grill* before she stood and grabbed her briefcase.

Forty-five minutes later, the twins were stepping off the elevator onto the ninth floor of the Kerr-McGee building. The family employed two dozen agents and billing clerks inside the main office and it was never a dull day. Agents inside the real estate division were busy making investment calls and preparing underwritings for various clients looking to sell property. Staff inside the billing department, meanwhile, was processing payments received from the Valley Brook warehouse that'd been modified by Kimi and Koko while the Accounts Payable division filed records and processed billing manifests that would land on the twins' desk shortly after lunch.

Kimi and Koko were making their way over to the main office at the end of hall that was laced with brown tint when an employee ran up to them. "Miss Dawkins," the woman smiled as she held onto a small brochure. "Someone from a Fraser and Company was kind enough to send suite tickets to the Thunders and Trailblazers game this Friday," she remarked as she handed Kimi the tickets.

"Oklahoma Thunder ain't hittin' on nothing, girl," Kimi sulked as she handed the tickets back to the woman.

The woman smiled as she removed her permed hair from her face. "Well, since you're giving them back? Me, me and the billing team was wondering if we could maybe…attend the game after you all close the deal with the British? Naomi said it's fine. You can verify it if you want."

"Nah, go ahead and enjoy yourselves," Kimi conceded. "And whatever y'all order just bill it back to the company. Just don't overdo it," she admonished.

The woman pranced off while clapping her hands as Kimi and Koko turned and continued on to the main office. "Hey, Flacco," they spoke in unison as they walked up to the Mexican and gave him quick hugs.

"Good morning, Senoritas," Flacco replied as he stood before the double-glass doors. He then stepped aside and eased one of the accesses open. Usually, he would hold a conversation for a few minutes with the twins, but he was a little down this morning they both noticed.

"You okay, Flacco?" Kimi asked as she stood in the doorway.

Flacco exhaled and looked down at the outfit he was wearing. It was a purple pair of slacks, white, pointed-toed leather boots and a black, white and purple-patterned shirt. "Today is my wife's mother's birthday," he remarked as if it pained him to admit that fact. "She's flying down to Mexico to celebrate her seventy-fifth birthday. Everybody is to wear purple, black and white—even if they aren't going down to Mexico."

"So, your wife dressed you this morning?" Koko snickered.

"No, but she bought this ugly outfit yesterday and insisted I wear it to take her to the airport. I took pictures with her and my children this morning. She might as well have pulled these ridiculous-looking pants up onto my hips and tightened the belt after tucking in the shirt."

"Aww," Kimi smiled as she reflected on her picking out Udelle's clothes earlier. "Sometimes a woman just wants to see her man look cute."

Flacco eyed Kimi with a stern stare. "Cute is not how I would like to be referred to, Senorita Dawkins."

"Well, you still cute in your little get up," Koko teased as she tugged lightly on Flacco's long sleeve silk shirt.

"Man, you all sour because your wife dressed you?" Kimi laughed. "Just go and change clothes. Your wife hundreds of miles away in another country, man!"

"She swore Naomi to tell if I did change clothes," Flacco responded. He then leaned down and whispered, "After all me and your mother have been through? I still think if I were to change clothes she would really tell my wife—and then I would be in the doghouse when my wife returns so I have no choice today but to wear this stupid—"

"What's stupid?" Naomi asked as she walked past the threshold and eyed her daughters and Flacco standing in a group.

Flacco straightened up and placed his hands before his body without responding.

Naomi looked her beloved friend and bodyguard over one time, her eyes scanning his slim figure as a smile crept across her face. "I know you're not telling Kimi and Koko about how your wife made you wear those clothes this morning, Mister Ramirez," she smirked before taking a sip of her caramel latte.

"We were," Flacco, unable to lie to one of the women he respected most in life, responded as he looked straight ahead.

Naomi laughed aloud as she held onto her morning

beverage. "What honesty," she complimented. "If you want to change clothes go ahead, Flacco. I won't tell your wife."

"But I would know that I did not keep my word, Senorita Dawkins," Flacco responded. "That matters more than how I look."

"Yes," Naomi stated seriously. "You know what that's called, right, Flacco?"

"Not wanting to have the wife get upset?" Flacco guessed.

"No," Naomi smiled as she went and stood before Flacco as Kimi and Koko stepped aside. *"Se llama carácter, que hace una persona cuando otros no están mirando. Es por ello que Doss eligió usted, mi amigo fiel.* (It's called character, what a person does when others aren't looking. That's why Doss chose you, my friend.)

"It is an honor to serve such a beautiful lady, and family," Flacco responded as he smiled down at Naomi and nodded towards Kimi and Koko while holding the door open.

Naomi smiled inwardly. She knew Flacco wanted to be left alone in his clown suit so she let it be. She extended her hand and welcomed her daughters inside the main office. "This is a day I have been looking forward to for the past several weeks," she stated proudly while walking ahead of her daughters. "The schedule is clear for the next couple of hours so we can go over you two's presentation. Who wants to go first?" she asked as the three convened before the family's large circular dark-brown marble conference table in the center of the main office and began opening up briefcases and pulling out folders laced with important documents.

"I'll go," Koko responded as she pulled a manila folder from her briefcase and spread it open. "First, the money we withdrew to pay our investor from Venezuela has been accepted by PNB in Paris. We're in business with the overseas bank withdrawal and deposits."

Naomi pulled out a chair and sat before her daughters with her legs crossed. She was wondering if Kimi and Koko had uncovered everything she knew concerning the cocaine that was being shipped, because if they were going to succeed in washing the dollars, they would need to pull out every financial trick in the book that she'd taught them and then some.

"The trip Ben made to Cayman Island was the easy part," Naomi told Koko. "How will we add to the books from this day forth now that PNB trusts us?"

"Slovak Vineyards has been sold to the Atlantic and Caribbean Produce Company, which is the business we've set up in the Cayman Islands," Koko stated. "Between those two companies, we can add an extra million dollars a month to the books to make it look legit, but we can't go any higher there because we already at the ceiling on that account. PNB will accept all deposits coming in from Atlantic and Caribbean Produce, but we're up against a salary cap of one million from that company."

"On another avenue, we've rigged our billing system to automatically cut the gross weight on each load of produce shipped on our trucks by twelve percent." Kimi quickly followed, all-the-while anticipating the budding problem the family was up against.

"What will that do exactly, Kimi?" Naomi asked as she leaned back in her executive chair.

Koko chimed in by saying, "Cutting the gross weight on the oranges by twelve percent will allow us to add at a minimum, five thousand pounds back to each truck. With fifty of our own trucks running every week out the Valley Brook Warehouse, we'll be able to bill Tropicana for an additional one million pounds of produce we actually ship every month. The government won't know, but Tropicana will figure it out in maybe two years."

"Two years will allow us more than enough time to expand our own agricultural business down in Brazil. We'll be offline with Tropicana before they ever even know what hit them," Naomi replied though an impish smile, ever proud of her daughters' shrewdness. "What else ya' got for me?"

"The New York Stock Exchange rates are fluctuating

between twenty-one and twenty-four dollars a bushel wholesale here in this country," Kimi answered. "With a bushel of oranges weighing in at forty pounds, and an added one million pounds over a month's time, we'll have on average a total of..."

"Twenty-five thousand bushels to sell at wholesale back to Tropicana," Naomi responded as she ran the numbers in her head. "Now," she said as she stood to her feet. "Let's say New York's rate is twenty-two dollars per bushel on average," she added while mentally calculating another round of numbers. "At a rate of twenty-two dollars per bushel on the oranges kept off the books, we're able to free up an additional..."

"Five hundred and fifty thousand dollars a week," Kimi and Koko responded in unison.

"For a total of two-point-two million dollars that we can actually bring into to the legal financial system every month when we factor in profits from Slovak Vineyards." Naomi remarked as she placed her hands on her hips.

"That's gone still leave us with nine and a half million dollars unrinsed," Kimi stated as she and Koko eyed one another, neither speaking a word as they looked down at the table. This was the financial conundrum the twins had seen coming, but weren't prepared to face.

"Is that all?" Naomi asked as she eyed her daughters seriously. "This isn't half of the money coming in from our Venezuelan associates on a gross amount."

"We tried," Kimi admitted somberly. "We looked over every business we own countless times. The only other options left are the nightclub Dawk 'nem opening in Missouri and the entertainment complex back in Ponca City."

"But the amount of money will be so minute we didn't even bother laying out a plan of action." Koko added in defense of her twin.

Naomi eyed Kimi and Koko before looking away briefly. "How much is 'minute' in you two's mind?" she asked lowly as she faced them once more and placed her hands atop the marble table.

"Maybe a quarter of a million dollars a month—and that's stretching it." Kimi answered.

Naomi nodded her head after Kimi had spoken. There was much more her daughters had to learn. She remained silent as she walked over to a large wooden shelf lined with law books and removed a laptop. "Follow me," she calmly stated as she headed for her office that overlooked a portion of downtown Oklahoma City.

Kimi and Koko followed their mother into her decorative office that was more like a studio apartment with its contemporary furniture and lavish bathroom and closed the door behind them. They stood just inside the door eyeing their mother as she opened the laptop, powered it up and walked over to a gold-plated safe planted in the wall to the right of her desk.

While the screen was illuminating, Naomi entered a key code and removed several documents after opening the safe. "You've both done well," she told Kimi and Koko as she walked back behind her desk. "You've managed to hide over three million dollars of profits all on your own, which is right around the amount I'd figure you two would be able to handle. But, there're other ways we can put the money online—legally."

"What way?" Kimi and Koko both asked in puzzled unison.

"We can loan money to the federal government for starters." Naomi answered.

"Federal borrowing?" Kimi asked as she eyed Koko with wide eyes. "Momma, we looked at that!" she added. "The risks involved in loaning money to the federal government would be tremendous given the income's source!"

"Kimi, just hear me out." Naomi comforted. "It can and it will work. The family has seventy-six million dollars in touchable cash and another twenty-five million dollars in cash should we liquidate all of our assets. We have a gross worth of one hundred and one million dollars," she declared as she backed up from her desk. "The United States is running a sixteen trillion dollar deficit and is in a slow recovery. The federal government is giving three points on the dollar for monies loaned from private companies and citizens themselves with a guaranteed return in five years."

"We talking six and half million dollars a month, momma," Koko stated in a confused manner.

"Not every month," Naomi corrected. "We can make a thirteen million dollar deposit every quarter starting next month using our own money," she let it be known as she eyed her daughters. "You two also mentioned that the nightclub and the entertainment complex could wash an additional quarter million dollars every month. Do it." she suggested.

"What would be the benefit?" Koko asked. "I mean, it's more of a hassle than anything."

Naomi walked from behind her desk and leaned on its front edge and folded her arms. Kimi and Koko had good accounting skills and enough talent to figure out that they could loan money to the government, but they were afraid to touch it, let alone mention it. Their understanding of the big picture was somewhat lacking, Naomi quickly surmised.

The way she saw it, her oldest three and their cousin were risking life and limb in a deadly occupation that could make the family wealthy beyond their wildest imagination, but in order for them to succeed, everyone involved, including herself, Kimi and Koko, would have to go above and beyond the call of duty and take equal risks.

Kimi and Koko had answered Naomi's call each time they were needed, but what had gone down in the past with the flexing of cattle numbers and keeping tabs on orange bushels was mere child's play. Naomi was now about take her daughters' white collar crimes to a whole other level by way of coercion and insightful conversation.

"Compared to the chances that many in this family are taking?" she began as she eased up from the desk and walked over to her bay window and scanned downtown Oklahoma City. "The way I see it? And the way it is, is that we owe it to

222

those who are taking chances with their lives and freedom for the benefit of this family. We must give them our very best effort for what they're doing on the streets. Our number one job, ladies," she declared as she turned to face Kimi and Koko, "our number one job is to wash every illegal dollar the family brings in and add it to our own bank account and pay those accordingly. So if that means that we have to ride from here to Wall Street with just a five dollar bill in the glove box to make a deposit in order to keep the books clean that is what we will do."

"We understand, momma. But we're out of resources all on our own. We have nowhere else to place the money." Kimi said matter-of-factly.

"And that's *with* the federal investments you're proposing," Koko added in support of her sister. "I mean, we figured we could place up to fifty-two million dollars inside the system going that route over a year's time, but we can't keep making those high-dollar deposits without the government looking into where we're earning the money to loan."

"And at a minimum, we're talking about adding eighty million dollars to the family's books inside a year's time if everything was to go right. That will exceed our annual revenue by forty-five percent." Kimi remarked in an unsure tone. "This is not easy for us, momma. I'm sorry."

"That's why you have me. I'm here to guide you in what needs to be done exactly from this point forth," Naomi stated seriously as she went and turned the laptop around to face her and her daughters. "We have a law firm and a real estate company at our disposal. We will use them to further our business," she stated as she stepped aside and brought the computer screen into view.

Kimi and Koko leaned in and eyed pictures of shopping malls on the computer screen. The photographs had stores like Neiman Marcus, Macy's and Nordstrom's as anchors and numerous side businesses from Forever 21 to Dolce and Gabbana.

"These are several high-end shopping malls," Naomi spoke,

shaking Kimi and Koko from their hard gazes. "There's one in Las Vegas, another in San Francisco and one down in South Beach. Girls," she smiled. "The deal with Fraser Company went through."

Kimi and Koko eyed one another with apprehension. They knew all about the deal with the Brit, but truth be told, they were against it. Shopping malls weren't cheap, they knew. And their mother had just agreed to enter into a deal to purchase three units in three of the most prosperous cities in America during a recession. Not a good investment in their eyes.

"You do know that seven hundred and twenty-four thousand people forfeited their jobs last month, right, momma?" Koko questioned.

Naomi could sense her daughters' reluctance, but she was top dog and had final say on everything going down in the family. "Ladies," she spoke calmly as she walked behind her desk, sat down and crossed her legs. "It's plain to see that you two have discerned that we're about to make the biggest invest in this family's history with this Fraser deal. It'll be the biggest gamble of our lives, but lord if we should succeed," she couldn't help but to declare as she smiled and scratched her eyebrow while contemplating the upside of the potential deal with Dunkirk Fraser.

"How much money would the family have to put up to join Fraser and Company?" Kimi asked seriously as she and Koko stepped closer to their mother, where they both rested their hands atop the black marble desk and stared her down.

Naomi sat with her legs crossed while twiddling her thumbs and looking down at the final sale price to become part owner of Fraser and Company. Her all-wise eyes scanned the price per square footage on each mall, the annual reports for the past five years on said properties, and the percentages of occupancy on each mall unit. She ignored Kimi's question for the time being and responded by saying, "For the past five years Fraser and Company has sustained on average, a ten percent reduction in annual profits. But last quarter?" she then asked rhetorically as she looked up at her daughters. "Last quarter? Fraser and Company experienced a sixteen percent increase across the board. They're selling early when they should stay in and wait for the continued uptick. The economy's going to improve under the Obama administration if one has the patience."

"How could you be certain, momma?" Kimi asked.

"Right now, the people who voted for Obama are feeling confident in his policies. They believe in his health care bill and the attempts he's making to save the auto industry and feel somewhat safe to free up purse strings."

"I don't see too many people 'round here going shopping no time soon, momma," Kimi retorted while shaking her head in disapproval. "People broke."

Naomi chuckled as she rubbed her chin and eyed her daughters. "You two girls must've forgotten the little shopping spree you both went on down in Cayman Island when we traveled there to hold meetings with Gacha. As I recall, we had a good Christmas last year. Spoonie and Tyke got a new car, jewelry was spread all around. Jane with her new equipment, and that's not to mention the trip to Arizona with Samantha where you two flew into town on a private jet and dropped another twelve thousand dollars just because."

"We have the money to do that, momma." Koko remarked.

"And so does millions of other families here in America, Koko." Naomi replied in a non-threatening, but stern tone of voice. "It's a buyer's market, baby. Everything in this country is up for sale in this recession—if you have the money to buy it," she stated lovingly as her voice slightly raised a few octaves in order to get her point across fully. She then continued by saying, "This here is real a life Monopoly game we're playing—and we got more than enough real money to play the game. Why? Because like millions of other families in this country? Ladies, we're rich. We have not only the power, but the ability and the gumption it takes to do what many in our position are unwilling to do—which is to take major risks and see it through to completion."

Kimi and Koko looked down at the laptop briefly. Both had taken in all that their mother had said and were ready to follow her lead. Their main concern, however, was the amount of money the family would have to put up to become partners with Fraser and Company as they knew it wouldn't be a small amount.

"How much we dumping into this venture with Fraser and Company exactly, momma?" Kimi asked for a second time.

Naomi eyed the bottom line on the proposal she'd sent over her to future British counterparts and said, "Fifty million dollars."

Kimi and Koko both swallowed lumps in their throats. With fifty million invested, and another thirteen being turned over to the government on a loan, the family would have only $7.3 million dollars cash on hand out of their $76 million dollar net worth because $5.7 million had already been turned over to Gacha.

Kimi and Koko, at that moment, had just realized that their mother had nearly emptied the coffers and was placing the family's entire stake into that of cocaine profits, real estate investments and government loans. If played right, it could net a bumper crop of cash, but should it fail, the family stood to lose everything. It was a heavy burden for such young women to bear, but they believed in their mother fully and understood not only the implications, but the potential prosperity that would land in their lap should they execute the plan to a T.

"What's your plan for these shopping malls?" Koko asked as she Kimi got in tune with their mother's plans for the family.

"We'll have to do some remodeling having talked to Fraser, but for fifty million dollars, we can own three shopping malls in three of the fastest growing cities in the country and you two would have complete control. I'll deal with the federal loans and the washing of profits through the trucking company, Slovak Vineyards and the other ventures we have going."

Right away, Kimi and Koko's minds began working. Shopping was their expertise and favorite past time. They knew all the hot stores and were always up on the latest trends in fashion. With so many stores and businesses spread out, it wouldn't be too difficult for them to play around with the numbers. The family could even prop up some stores by running money directly through the businesses, padding the books heavy because the federal government rarely kept tabs on what a shopping mall brought in unless the numbers became too shameful.

"This could be a gold mine, momma," Kimi admitted as Koko nodded her head in agreement. "What's our plan of action?" she then asked as she walked over and began setting up the latte machine, knowing it was going to be a long day.

"We'll have to tour the malls in each city," Naomi replied. "The deal with Fraser and Company isn't to be ratified until we give our approval of the businesses by having our own inspections done. Once that's done, we'll need to hire a renovation crew."

"Don't Dawk have a friend that do that, Koko?" Kimi asked as she filled cups full of latte.

"He do," Koko answered. "He did the club and everything for Dawk 'nem in Saint Charles. I think his name Malik or something like that."

"Malik Gomez won't be getting that contract," Naomi chimed in as she rocked slightly in her chair.

"Why not?" Kimi inquired.

"We're going to give those jobs to black contractors. They get first bid," Naomi stated. "With all these people getting laid off I'm sure there're some of our own who're looking for an honest paycheck."

"That's discrimination. What about a law suit?" Koko asked as she handed her mother a cup of latte.

"Child," Naomi laughed as she eased the latte from Koko's hand and took a sip. "A lawsuit is the least of our worries. While the malls are being renovated, we'll get a marketing campaign going. I know Sharona Benson is somewhat sick, but she's still running her advertising business. I'll give her that job for as long as she can manage it. The parking lots must be filled in order for this thing to work, so let's get to…work," the top financial genius of the family ordered as she and her protégés began mapping out the family's latest venture to launder incoming cocaine profits.

CHAPTER TWENTY-TWO

DESK DUTY

While Naomi and her middle daughters were in the opening phases of instituting the family's biggest money scheme to date, the Valley Brook Warehouse, located just to the southeast of downtown Oklahoma City, was running like a well-oiled machine. It was 9:45 in the morning, break time for the workers working the seven to three p.m. shift. The docks inside the massive cold storage and dry goods warehouse were slowly emptying out as workers shut down for a fifteen minute break in the action. Forklifts were parked in their designated areas and motorized pallet jacks set before dock doors with refrigerated units and dry van trailers waiting to offload.

Martha was standing on the stairwell outside of the building's main office looking over the floor as the workers dispersed. Since she'd arrive four hours earlier, she'd been waiting on one specific truck to touch the docks. From her position, she could see the windows on dock nineteen go dark, letting her know that the truck she'd been waiting on had finally arrived as he was scheduled to arrive at ten 'o' clock.

Deciding to check the security cameras before she approached the driver, Martha turned and prepared to enter the office. Just before she did so, she eyed Irene through the glass pane typing up a document on one of the computers.

From her position, Martha had a clear shot of the screen as Irene sat with her back to her. She didn't appear to be working anything business-related and Martha swore she was looking at a seal belonging to the United States Government displayed on the computer screen. Wondering what Irene was up to, she opened the office door and quickly walked into the office.

Irene jumped and powered down her computer as she began shuffling papers spread out on the desk into a single pile. "Martha, how long you been, you scared me barging in the office like that, girl." she stated in a startled tone of voice.

Martha licked her lips as she eyed Twiggy. With the Laredo load was coming in, she was now suspicious of everyone not involved in the business, including Twiggy. "What you working on?" she asked Irene as she went and powered up the computer.

Irene went to shut the computer off once more, but the look in Martha's eyes told her it would be best if she remained frozen in her tracks. The arrival of one hundred kilograms of cocaine had her on the verge of paranoia. She knew of Naomi's plan to dump nearly every dollar the family possessed into new ventures. To lose on the first run would be devastating. The family would still have a few millions, but much of that would have to be spent on lawyers trying to keep everyone involved out of jail. Not to mention the family could be hit with the RICO statute and have all of their assets seized by the federal government.

Irene knew the reasons why Martha was acting so paranoid this day. She'd been asked to secure the best driver to make a run from Oklahoma City to Laredo and back. The driver was scheduled to arrive at ten a.m. and she'd seen the truck backing into dock nineteen while working on her computer. She knew from jump that she'd been the one responsible for providing the driver that would deliver cocaine to the Valley Brook Warehouse, but she didn't bitch up under Martha's scrutiny.

"Now it's me you don't trust?" Irene asked Martha in disbelief as she watched the computer screen light up.

Martha took on an entirely new demeanor when she eyed the computer screen. "The Gift of Hope," she said aloud as she read the banner of an organ donor's website. She looked over to Irene and asked, "What's this about? You dying, Twiggy?"

Irene laughed half-heartedly. "Martha, I'm fine," she declared. "I was placing Sharona's name on a donor's list. She's dying of kidney failure. I was only trying to help her out."

"Why you being so secretive about that, Twiggy?" Martha asked concerned.

"Because, Mar," Irene sighed as she rolled her chair back and stood to her feet. "What I look like helping the woman who slept with my man? I kept it secret because I feel like a fool, but I have my reasons on why I'm doing this bullshit."

Martha sat down in the high back chair at her desk across from Twiggy's desk and looked to the floor in shame. "I'm the one who feel like a fool, Irene. And what you dong ain't no bullshit," she spoke somberly as she kicked herself internally for having ever doubt her friend's loyalty. "I been so involved in what's been going on I never even sat and talked to you about that thing with Sharona and DeeDee. How's it going?"

"Me and Sharona are friends now," Irene remarked seriously as she walked back over to her desk and pulled up her search history. "You think I'm a spy. Go on and search," she demanded.

"Twiggy, I was only—"

"Protecting the family's interests," Irene interrupted. "Well, so am I, Martha. You have your mission, and so do I. Doss the third is why I do what I'm doing. He needs his mother. I just want to give him every chance possible to keep his mother in his life because I don't know if I can raise that boy on my own."

"You raised Peter Paul and Simon, Twiggy. You know how to be a mother. Don't even be that hard on yourself."

"I was never a mother." Irene retorted as she turned her back to Martha and shifted her weight while placing her hands on her hips. "Simon and Peter Paul may have looked to me as a mother, but the truth of the matter is that I took my brothers down a path that led to destruction. I got Peter Paul, Simon *and* Sandy killed. I condoned everything they did on the streets and was only sorry after the fact. I'm no good to no one. Not even my damn self," the torn woman fretted.

Martha rose up from the chair and went and stood behind Twiggy and placed a hand onto her shoulder and gently nudged her around. "Sister," she said as she looked deep into her friend's eyes. "I feel what you sayin' and all, but, look where you at now. We been here before with the guilt you feel. Let it go, girl," she said as she briefly looked back over the things she and Irene experienced while growing up in Ghost Town.

"I'm scared for Sharona and Li'l Doss, Mar!" Irene exclaimed as she stared back at Martha as her eyes watered. "And then, then this shit here with you thinking I'm some kind of a snitch? Ever since I got outta jail I been tryin' to the do the right thing by God, by myself, and by this family! But bullshit just keep get putting in front of me! It's like the world wanna see me destroy everything in my way or get devoured by everything in my way—all because I done found a real purpose in life!"

"It's not either or, Twiggy," Martha stated. "You just overwhelmed, sister."

Martha had an epiphany at that moment. It'd been nearly nine years since she and Twiggy had touched down in Oklahoma City. During that time, they'd taken a few trips down to Oklahoma City and went out on the town, but the moments were few and far between. "You stagnant, Twiggy," she smiled. "As your boss? I'm ordering you away from here come next week."

"You laying me off, Martha?"

"I'm sending you on a trip up to Montana with Francine, Tak, Regina and my great nieces and nephew next week. Tak gone need somebody to help make that drive anyway. And Regina and Francine definitely gone need help with Tacoma, Malaysia and Malara," Martha replied.

"Mendoza and Francine's spot," Irene smiled through a nod of appreciation. "I bet it's beautiful this time of year. I'd like that, Martha."

"Let me set it up then," Martha replied as she walked up to Irene and hugged her. "I'll never play you like that again. I know you solid," she confessed as she held onto her friend for several lingering seconds before pulling back.

"Forgive me, Martha," Irene remarked somberly. "I'm past you, but I can't say how I'll truly feel until after this trip is over. But, I do feel better just knowing I'm going somewhere far from here. I need to get away. Thank you."

"I should be thanking you," Martha replied as she hugged Twiggy once more and apologized a second time.

****

Meanwhile, over to OU Medical Center, Bay and T-top were visiting with Spoonie. The second-to-youngest in the family was still confined to a bed and recovering in an inpatient suite. Spoonie had lost nearly sixty percent of her strength in her left leg and had over two feet of her small intestine removed. The family had wanted to bring her home to recover, but doctors, namely Doctor Duchene, had ruled it against it, stating that Spoonie's wounds were too severe and she'd prefer to keep the seventeen year-old under close, guarded condition rather than transfer her to a healthcare provider in Ponca City.

Naomi was the one to sign off on the suggestion, knowing Spoonie would be better off in Oklahoma City. Bay, T-top, Kimi and Koko were in town more than they were back to Ponderosa, and Walee and his crew was only a short drive away back in Stillwater. Spoonie would be laid up for nearly three months during her recovery, but each and every day she had visitors from home. Mary and Regina were regulars, as well as DeeDee and Francine.

No visit, however, meant more to Spoonie than having her oldest sisters in her presence. Although weakened, she still managed to hold conversation with her Bay and T-top. "Softball season starts in just days," she stated in a dejected manner as she lay back in a stack of soft pillows. "I wish I could swing the bat."

"You be back next year to knock it out the park," Tiva stated as she twirled around in a swivel chair. She and Bay were having the times of their lives whizzing back and forth in the swivel chairs as ESPN ran on the wall-mounted TV. "Now, what you gone have to worry about is if they make the playoffs without you this year. That mean you ain't important," Tiva joked.

Spoonie laughed and said, "With Tyke on the team? We're practically guaranteed a spot in the playoffs. But even if we don't make it to the post season, I just wish I could play. I'm gone miss a whole year of sports and I have to be here until April," the recovering youngster sighed.

Bay eyed her disappointed sister and her heart went out to Spoonie as she placed an order on several Papa John pizzas with her cell phone. She knew how much Spoonie was looking forward to playing for one of the most prestigious softball teams in the nation, but there was a greater picture to appreciate in Bay's eyes. "Look at it this way," she stated as she pressed her heels to the floor and propelled her swivel chair over to the bedside while ordering the pizzas, "you can sit back and watch how things get done in the game. Be like a coach for yourself. It's not always a bad thing to have to sit on the sidelines," she added as she reflected on how she and Tiva were placed out of the action over in Saint Louis until things blew over with a federal agent by the name of Laddy Norcross.

"Be a coach for myself," Spoonie repeated. "I can be a coach for the whole team too, Bay, and maybe coach the team for real someday. And, and when my career over in college I can maybe become a sports broadcaster if not a coach."

"I thought you and Tyke were going to be Veterinary Pathologists." Tiva remarked just as the cell phone she had tucked inside the back pocket of her 7 For All Mankind jeans vibrated. "Ayeee! Got a text! This might be my li'l boo-in-the-making Terrence writing me," she quipped as she stood up and pulled out her phone.

"Bet he wanna leave early again," Bay chided. She then turned to Spoonie and asked, "You changing careers, girl?"

"I love animals, Bay," Spoonie responded. "But I been laying here thinking. I wanna be around people and make an impact on society that way. I mean, I'll always love the animals, and we can still set up the research lab because I'm not changing majors. But missing this season of softball makes me not want to leave the sport ever. I just wanna be around the game for as long as possible."

"Speaking of game," Tiva remarked as she eyed a text from Martha that read...*we live*. "Yo, Bay, we live, sister." she let it be known.

"I just ordered the pizzas for the staff," Bay remarked just as Tyke and three members of Oklahoma State's softball team walked into the suite dressed in their orange softball uniforms.

"How she doing, y'all?" Tyke asked in a near whisper as she removed her Oklahoma State snap back.

"She fine," Tiva responded as she looked over to Bay and nodded towards the door. "That thing waiting on us," she stated in reference to the Laredo load.

"Y'all leaving, man?" Tyke asked as she and the three girls with her surrounded Spoonie's bed.

"Yeah. We already running behind," Bay remarked as she and Tiva walked over and gave Spoonie kisses on her cheeks.

"We gone stay with her until grandpa and Mary get here. They be in around two," Tyke remarked as she hugged her oldest sisters goodbye.

Bay and T-top left the suite soon after in order to tend to their task at hand, 'desk duty' they called it, which was the mixing, repackaging, and shipping of one hundred kilograms of cocaine from the Valley Brook Warehouse over to a location in East Saint Louis.

****

An hour later, Bay and T-top had made their way over to the 100,000 square foot Valley Book warehouse. Each was toting a stack of pizza boxes for the morning shift. One thing about the women who ran the Valley Brook warehouse was the fact that they kept it real and were down-to-earth.

Martha, Irene, Bay and Tiva were highly accessible at all

times. They weren't the type of bosses that stayed locked up in their office and only handed down orders. To the contrary, they were hands on with their workers. They often bought lunch for all shifts, and often times, one or more could be found on the floor pulling orders or kicking it with the employees during lunch and breaks. It was a family atmosphere they'd created, but everyone knew how far to go and who ran what when it came to the job.

A few of the dock workers walked up and freed Bay and T-top's hands free of the pizza boxes they were toting. One was a twenty-three year-old man by the name of Terrence Mays. Terrence was originally hired as a CDL driver, but a DUI had forced Irene to place him inside the warehouse as a forklift operator. The young man was still in his ninety-day probation period and the chances of him holding on to his job weren't looking all that promising.

After a couple of the guys he was walking with took the pizzas, Terrence, purposely making sure he didn't grab any boxes himself, lagged behind. "Miss Holland, can I talk to you for a minute?" he asked, directing his question towards Bay.

Bay rolled her eyes. "You're not leaving early again if that's what you're about to ask," she sternly declared as she walked off while shaking her head in disbelief.

Tiva eyed Terrence through curled lips and was prepared to walk off herself.

"So, you just gone leave me hanging without allowing me to give an explanation, twin?" Terrence asked with a hint of frustration as he extended his arms.

Tiva paused and eyed Terrence for a few seconds as he stood before her in a black work uniform and leather, wheat Timberland boots. The tall, brown-skinned, physically fit brother with the tapered Afro and thick beard had that certain bad boy appeal that Tiva liked in a man. He was edgy and could be assertive at times, but he was mainly a man of reservation. Grumpy could best describe Terrence Mays' demeanor, and it was a behavior that left Tiva intrigued.

Bay had washed her hands with Terrence and his countless

excuses for having to leave or not showing to work at all.

Tiva, however, had stayed behind. "What you gotta say for yourself, Terrence?" Tiva asked.

"Your sister don't like me all that much, huh?" Terrence asked Tiva.

"Because you keep puttin' yourself in a bad position." Tiva reasoned. "What's your problem?" she asked as she tilted her head to the side and eyed Terrence in a guarded manner.

Terrence shook his head as his dark eyes stared into Tiva's eyes. "My baby mama be trippin'," he answered in frustration. "She done laid up there and took the child support payments I'm making for daycare and shit and blew the check. Now the daycare calling saying I have ta' come and pick up my daughter because we a whole month behind."

"Where she at?" Tiva asked as she reared back with her hands on her hips, the pitch in her voice going up a few octaves.

"At home sitting on her ass talkin' 'bout the shit my problem to deal with!" Terrence remarked through gritted teeth. "I do everything right by my daughter, but her bullshit ass momma stay tryna sabotage a brother."

"That's why you asked to leave early three weeks in a row?" Tiva asked a little concerned. She was growing incensed over the situation, but for all she knew, Terrence could only be telling one side of the story and trying to play her just to get off early and be with his baby momma.

"The first time? She told me my daughter Tara was sick. So I rushed over to her house, ya' feel me? She answer the door naked talkin' 'bout 'can I handle that'."

"You fucked?" Tiva asked with a smirk.

"Nah!" Terrence snapped as he mean-mugged Tiva. "I just walked off. The second week, it was the excuse that she needed a ride to the pediatrician because Tara was throwing up blood. I rushed over there that morning and she served me with court papers for an increase in child support when she learned I got a better-paying job here. Today I got a call from her on my way to work this mornin' and she told me I need to pay the daycare bill unless Tara gone have to be picked up early. I hung up on her. I ain't believe what she was saying—but right before break I got a call from the daycare. Candace really didn't pay the daycare bill. I gotta go pick my daughter up."

Tiva had no words for Terrence's plight as she was dismayed over the entire scenario. Baby momma drama was never an issue within her family or the click she ran with. This was all new territory—foolishness Tiva had often heard about and knew existed, but had never encountered until now. She couldn't judge, though; because she herself was involved in an occupation that could very well remove her from her own daughters' lives forever and render them parentless for the remainder of their years. That in itself could label her a bad parent, and when coupled with what she'd allowed to happen to Junior, she could be deemed one of the worst mothers of all times.

Indirectly, Terrence's plight, had led Tiva to examine her own parenting briefly. She quickly caught herself, though; because this wasn't about her and how she raised her kids. It was about a woman she'd never met, but had deemed trifling nonetheless in the way she handled her child and disrespected that child's father.

Tiva knew firsthand that she'd just judged the woman Candace, but none of that mattered. She liked Terrence, they guy was a good and hard worker and had strong character—a team player with potential. If he was telling the truth, she would try her best to help him, if only to see his wretched baby mother come out on the losing end. "Go on and take care of your daughter," she told Terrence.

"You sure?" Terrence asked surprised.

"Yeah," Tiva nodded through a smile. "But you gone have to make up the hours this weekend. We got a rail car coming in that needs unloading."

"Twin!" Terrence exclaimed in an appreciative manner as he raised a leg and pumped a fist. "I get to make the hours up so I don't get behind on my payments? I appreciate it! I be in

Saturday no doubt."

"We'll see. Remember, you still on probation," Tiva remarked. "This our deal. If you don't uphold your end of the bargain? Don't even worry about coming in next Monday," she let it be known before walking off.

As she climbed the metal stairs leading to the main office, Tiva caught a glimpse of Terrence swiping his badge to clock out. She hoped the guy got whatever problem he was facing resolved because she would truly hate to have to cut him loose. It would be fair to say to that Tiva had a thing for Terrence, a man she believed was trying to the do the right thing, but was just getting a few bad streaks in his life. She would give him a break this time around, but what comes of the two, if anything at all, remains to be seen was her thinking as she walked into the main office.

Martha and Bay were staring down at the security screen while the driver in door nineteen pulled away from the Tropicana trailer he'd just released when Tiva walked into the office. She stepped behind the two and eyed the driver pulling off. "That's the Laredo load?" she asked while eyeing the screen.

"Yeah," Bay remarked as she scanned the main floor down below. "While everybody having lunch we can go on and offload that and put it in the big freezer and break it down and have it ready to move before first shift end."

"I called Dawk and let 'em know what was up, but he didn't answer so I left him a message," Martha remarked. "In the meantime, I got an empty trailer in the door eighteen billed to Saint Louis."

"Let's get to work," Bay remarked as she and T-top grabbed sets of forklift keys.

By the end of the first shift, Bay and T-top had repackaged the family's first load of cocaine using the Levamisole formula and had it loaded onto a trailer bound for East Saint Louis. They then notified Dawk, who in turn, put Natalia III on alert.

CHAPTER TWENTY-THREE

A PERFECT MATCH

Later that evening, after the first shipment had been sent off to Saint Louis, Lee had just entered The Deep Deuce Grill and sought out Koko. It was nearing six p.m. and the dimly-lit place with tables galore and a bar sporting countless liquors and beers was beginning to fill with corporate types who worked in the downtown area. "Over here, Lee!" a voice called out, capturing his ear.

Lee walked over to a table and knelt down and kissed Koko's cheek and then spoke to Kimi and Udelle. He then eyed their three friends, two females, one white, the other black, and a burly black/Hispanic guy with a bald head and a thick beard. The guy hovered over the table as he nursed a mug of beer. He looked up at Lee without smiling and nodded. "You want a beer, homie?" he asked in a deep-pitched, slow drawl.

"Yeah, man," Lee responded. "Let me order drinks for everybody since I see the ladies don't have nothing to sip on."

"I already got 'em covered," the guy laughed. "Them and Udelle ordered them mixed joints so it take a minute to make. I'm Devin," he added as he gave Lee a fist pound.

Lee grabbed a chair from a nearby table and sat beside Koko. "Everybody ordered dinner already?"

"Still waiting on our drinks," Koko responded. "So what y'all think about the Accounting professor and his dissertation

241

on auditing a multi-corporation?" she asked her friends.

The white female, named Katie, leaned forward and slapped her hands to her forehead. "You mean the part I stayed awake for? That guy lulled me right to sleep. Right to sleep! I mean, I like, I literally could not stay woke two minutes into the dissertation!" she stated as everybody at the table outside of Lee laughed lowly.

Kimi sat up straight and said, "The professor was reading too much into the federal guidelines for the current tax year. The IRS changes the corporate tax laws every year and if you can understand the new laws outside of comprehending the established laws that they roll over into following year from the previous year there will still be legal loopholes that you can use to explain any discrepancy in a company's finances."

"But an audit is different," the black female, named Affinity, contradicted as she removed her eyeglasses and polished them with a silk cloth before placing them back onto her face. "We may be granted the privilege of following the previous year's tax laws, but we still would have to adhere to the tax laws on record for whatever year a company under audit is being assessed, right?"

"True," Kimi declared. "But you can file a form eleven-twenty if it's within the allotted time of the filing period to avoid a penalty,"

"You can spend weeks and months trying to correct indecorously-prepared taxes and cost a company thousands, maybe even millions of dollars in fines if you don't meet the deadline handed down by the Internal Revenue Service." Katie complained.

"The only time that could happen is if a company is knowingly hiding profits," Affinity countered. "Even then, it'll be hard to detect if the CPAs laundering money are up to par."

Kimi and Koko smirked at one another on the slick over Affinity's last statement because they both knew she was spot on. Neither would elaborate any further, however, because as far as their peers knew, they were just interns for their mother and that's exactly how they wanted to present themselves to the public.

Lee, meanwhile, was totally lost in what was to him a bunch of gobbledygook, but he was intrigued nonetheless. Koko and Kimi's friends were interesting to him. "What does indecorously-prepared taxes mean?" he couldn't help but to ask.

"From the sound of things it means the people counting the dollars done fucked up," Devin answered through a smirk just as a waitress approached the table with a tray of drinks. No one outside of Lee and Devin were old enough to drink, but like many a college student, Kimi and Koko and company all had fake IDs.

"Just to let everybody know," Udelle chimed in as a S'mores cocktail was slid before him. "I received the highest grade in the class on my weather report this afternoon. Professor looking at setting me up with an internship down at the NBC affiliate."

Kimi reached out and tapped Udelle's arm. "It was the slacks wasn't it?" she smiled.

"It was the skills," Udelle chuckled as everyone at the table outside of Lee fanned him off. "But, but," he added as he raised his hands in protest. "The professor did say I had the look of a meteorologist that was 'prepared and smoothly-textured', is what he said."

"See?" Devin chimed in as he leaned back in his seat, "I was there for that. This dude here talked more about sports than he did the weather, but the analogies he put together made it entertaining. I wish I had done a presentation like that one."

Lee looked over to Devin surprised and asked, "You a weatherman, dude? I thought you played ball."

Devin smoothened out his beard and leaned forward, resting his elbows on the table. "I play football, Lee—offensive lineman—but they asked me what I was interested in when I accepted the scholarship. I shrugged, hell, growing up here in Oklahoma? I done seen so many tornadoes, ice the size of softballs falling from the sky and lightening that turn night into day. I was like, how that happen?" he remarked as he leaned back and downed his beer. "Shit, I told 'em I'm interested in weather. Next thing I know I'm enrolled in the geography and meteorology class. That's how I met this bum," he added as he pointed over to Udelle.

"I kind of understand weather," Lee remarked.

"You do?" Udelle asked curiously. "How?"

"Not on the level you and Devin on, man," Lee laughed. "But my parents, my father at least, he paints the Golden Gate Bridge. That's his job. Every day, he climbs up on that bridge and paints it. It takes a whole year, and when he's done, he and those guys start over again. They say it's because of the saltwater in the air. They have to keep painting it to prevent it from rusting."

"Interesting," Devin remarked as the waitress slid the last drink across the table. "Waitress," he then called out, "bring my man here a beer. What's your preference, homie?"

"I'll just have a Heineken," Lee answered casually as he scanned the menu. "And could you bring us three hot wing appetizers and two orders of lobster rolls, please?" he added.

"Lee, I love those!" Katie guffawed as she raised her hands even with her shoulders. "Koko, your man friend is on point!"

"So, Lee, you still live out in San Francisco?" Affinity asked as she sipped her Texas tornado.

"I'm down in Arizona. Work over to a detail shop there fixing up high end cars."

"He fix up rides like Xzhibit used to do in Pimp My Ride only way better," Udelle chimed in.

"That's hot, bro!" Devin remarked. "I just got a sixty-three Impala. I bought it from this old lady who husband died last year. You think you can pimp it out?"

"I ain't got no tools or nothing, man." Lee answered.

"Just check it out, baby," Koko chimed in. "You might be able to do something with it."

Lee rubbed his chin and said, "I'll look at it, man. I might be able to tell you what could be done and give you a quote on it so you'll know around how much to pay."

"Shiiddd," Devin laughed. "Boosters paying for that shit, Lee!"

"Devin, even if that was true you shouldn't be saying that out loud! You on scholarship and that is prohibited! You can get kicked off the football team, man!" Affinity snapped.

"What? I say that too loud?" Devin asked as he looked around, pretending to scan the bar for eavesdroppers. He then looked over to Lee and said, "It's legit, man. I paid like two thousand of my own money." he admitted as he leaned into Affinity and laughed. "That old lady gave that thing away because she didn't know what a classic she had. I drive it up to campus err'day. Meet me over to Udelle dorm tomorrow around three and I'll show it to you."

Lee nodded just as his beer was placed before him, and the group went on to enjoy their outing. He'd learned that Devin and Affinity was an item and Katie was merely dating. They were a cool bunch that knew how to hold conversation, tell a joke and possessed a great deal of intellect. It was refreshing for Lee to sit back and not be the center of attention. By night's end, he'd grown fonder of Koko and the family in general.

CHAPTER TWENTY-FOUR

UNEXPECTED GUESTS

The Saint Claire Avenue warehouses, old buildings that were once used by Carmella Lapiente` to hold meetings with her organization, and the same warehouses where a body had been found the night Pepper and her crew were fleeing the law, were once again being used to conduct illegal activity several hours after Koko and Kimi's outing with Lee.

The backside of the three-story building that faced Interstate-55 on the front side held two SUVs situated in between an abandoned rail spur that held three rusted box cars whose doors were sealed shut with the exception of the box car in the middle. Four flat cars loaded down with rusted steel were also connected to the boxcars, and the SUVs were parked beside the warehouse's crumbling concrete dock as the rising sun peaked over the horizon to the east.

Natalia III climbed from behind the wheel of his Expedition and walked over to Malik's Benz jeep. The window eased down and the two bumped fists. "You talked to Dawk this morning, homes? He coming today, right?" Malik asked from the passenger seat with an AR-15 resting in his lap.

"He should be here any minute now. He called from Saint Louis and said he was on his way. You and your crew ready to do this thing this morning?" Natalia III asked while checking the chamber on a chrome .45 caliber handgun.

Malik looked down at the rifle in his lap and thought briefly.

For nearly five years he'd been a loyal ally to the family. Never had he thought of double-crossing Dawk, but pomp and circumstance was now guiding his judgement.

When the Holland family went into a two year hiatus after Doss Dawkins' demise, Malik's focus had shifted. While aiding the family in their plan to take down Toodie Perez, he saw weakness within the organization where he was a ranking Enforcer. An opportunity had risen that would allow him to build his own family with the aid of a crew of Mexicans he knew from back in the day that was operating out of San Antonio.

With Natalia III agreeing to go along with the coup, Malik was now in position to take down the top man inside the Holland family. Dawk Holland would have to go in order for there to be a shift in power and Malik was prepared to do the honors. The plan was to make it look like a crew of cowboys swooped in during the deal. Gunplay would ensue, and during that time, Malik would pretend to lead Dawk to safety. During that time, he would take his friend and boss out and contribute his death to his being shot by one of the raiders, men Natalia III had hidden inside the abandoned warehouse.

Malik answered Natalia III's question by racking his AR-15. "Let Dawk come near my Benz before you give your men the signal," he told the Italian as he mentally prepared himself to execute one of his coldest moves ever. "I'll take care of things from there. Have them shoot over the roof of my Benz. Tell them not to hit it, my homeboy Max here, or me especially," he ordered.

Natalia III slapped the side of the door as he walked back over to his Expedition and climbed back behind the wheel. "What the deal?" one of his henchmen asked as he turned the volume down on the stereo.

"We waitin' on Dawk to show. Malik's really gonna go through with it," Natalia III remarked seriously as he rubbed his neatly-trimmed black beard while looking out the windshield at Malik's Benz. "Remember the plan once Dawk arrives."

"I know how to play it," the young Italian remarked as he sat up and scanned the area from his passenger seat and noticed a pair of headlights illuminating the side of the building just behind Malik's Benz. Several seconds later, a semi turned onto the gravel road.

The truck came to a halt beside Malik's Benz and the driver's side door opened on the tractor and a short and stout man hopped out. His boots landed in the snow and they remained firm as he went into his jean trench coat pocket and pulled out a small plastic bag. He reached down and grabbed what looked like chocolate covered raisins and popped a few into his mouth as he began walking towards the Benz.

Malik let the passenger side window down on his Benz jeep and eyed the man approaching in wonderment. "Senor," the man spoke in a raspy voice, "would you like a chocolate covered grasshopper? They're like vitamins that give you energy for the day, no?"

"I don't eat that shit, homes." Malik remarked disgustedly. "Where's Dawk? And who are you?"

"I'm just the driver, Senor. I wait like you wait, okay? You need me I'll be in the truck where it's warm. Until then don't bother me," the man ended as he eyed Malik and his driver with contempt before walking off.

"Who that, Malik?" Max asked from behind the wheel of Malik's Benz.

"I never seen him before. He's just the driver, I guess," Malik answered as he sat up and scanned the area. While looking around, he spotted Dawk jumping out of the middle boxcar that had its door slightly ajar. "The fuck Dawk doing?" he asked puzzled as he watched Dawk walk in between the boxcars and head away from him on the backside of the flatcars.

Malik was expecting Dawk to ride up on him in either Bay's Lincoln, or the bulletproof Escalade he sometimes rode in, but here he was walking by his self along the railroad tracks. He looked over to the warehouse where Natalia's men were hiding and could see that they couldn't get a clear shot because the

249

steel atop the flatcars was shielding Dawk from the line of fire. The driver of the semi also had him on edge.

The plan wasn't going as expected, but Malik had an ace-in-the-hole with Natalia III. He sat patiently, waiting for his moment to strike.

Dawk, meanwhile, continued walking along the railroad tracks until he was across from Natalia III's Expedition. He emerged from behind the flatcars and made his way over to the Italian's SUV.

Natalia III stepped out and greeted Dawk with a firm handshake at the front of his SUV. "I see everybody ready to go," Dawk remarked as he leaned down and looked inside the car. Noticing that two of Natalia's men were missing, he asked, "Where the rest of your boys?"

"They at home sleep. Figured we didn't need 'em," Natalia III responded casually as he scanned the area cautiously.

"Who over there with Malik?"

"Just that boy Max. That Hollywood guy you told me about over there in the truck."

"I'm a walk over there and hollar at my dog Malik before we start unloading." Dawk remarked.

"Yeah, you do that," Natalia III remarked nonchalantly as he spat into the snow and went and grabbed his .45 caliber off the seat. He emerged from the SUV and watched Dawk walking away from him out in the open.

Malik sat inside his Benz jeep waiting for the bullets to start flying as Dawk walked towards him. "When they start shooting," he told Max. "When they start shooting, you jump out and run to the back of the jeep. When the driver shows himself, you kill him. I'll take care of Dawk at the same time." he stated as he eased the door open on his ride and greeted Dawk by giving him a quick hug. "You ready for this morning, boss?" he asked as he scanned the docks where Natalia III's men were waiting.

"About as ready as I'm gone get, Malik." Dawk replied as he checked the backseat of the Benz to make sure there were no other soldiers laying in wait.

Natalia III, meanwhile, was standing beside his Expedition with his .45 caliber. He and Malik were looking directly at one another from across the way when a rumbling sound was heard. Dawk turned around at that moment and saw the tail lights of a flatbed truck backing down the opposite side of the building with its flashers blaring.

At the same time, Jay-D's Navigator pulled up behind the semi loaded down with the family's cocaine. He and Dooney jumped out with AK-47s and walked in between the semi and Malik's Benz, approaching Dawk and Malik as they causally looked the scene over.

"Homes," Malik smiled as he reached out and gave a pound to Jay-D. "I didn't know you was coming this morning."

"It's all good, fam," Jay-D remarked seriously. "We need all hands on deck to off this product, ya' feel?"

"No doubt, no doubt." Malik agreed. "Yo, Dawk? Who that with the flatbed truck?"

Before Dawk could answer, a medium-built average height black male jumped out the passenger side of the flatbed and walked up to Natalia dressed in a thick, hooded leather jacket that covered his head. The two talked briefly before they made their way over to Dawk.

The guy with Natalia face was hidden, but when he neared Dawk, Malik, Jay-D and Dooney recognized the short, stocky black male right away. It was NonStop—the famed rapper that came up with Ben Holland and was now one of the top rappers in the country on the Dirty Deeds record label—a label run by Big Derrick and Torre`, childhood friends of Ben.

"Aye yo!" Dooney laughed as he stepped forth. "Fuck you doing here, boy?" he asked NonStop as he gave him a quick hug.

"Shiddd, nigga!" NonStop stated casually as he flipped off his hood. "Me and my people part of the team now, ya' dig? I come for my people twenty bricks off top. We want our work fresh off the pallet! What up, Dawk?"

"Chillin', fam. Glad y'all made it. Let's offload so we can stab out from 'round here before the sun come up good."

Malik eyed Natalia III as the group split up and climbed up onto the docks. The bullets he was waiting on had never flown and his plan had been thwarted by several unexpected guests. He had no choice but to go along with the flow of things and abort the mission.

After thirty minutes had gone by, the entire shipment had been offloaded. NonStop took his twenty kilograms and placed them inside the trunk of a junked-out car that was strapped to the flatbed he and his goon had ridden up in. The rest were split up amongst Jay-D, Natalia III and Malik to transport back to their respective safe houses for distribution.

In under an hour's time, the Saint Charles Avenue warehouse was clear and all parties had separated. Malik now had forty bricks to off for the Holland family. He had no choice but to play along for the time being, but he undoubtedly had some questions for Natalia III that warranted answering. He would be sure to call him once he made it back over to Fox Park.

CHAPTER TWENTY-FIVE

LET ME FIND OUT

Natalia III was busy working out back over to his two-story brick condo located over in Soulard, a historic French neighborhood located south of downtown Saint Louis that was tucked in between interstates forty-four and fifty-five to the north and west, and the Mississippi River to the east. It was several hours after the meeting with Dawk over in East Saint Louis and the morning sun had risen.

The leader of the Italian faction of the Holland family had several deals set up for the sixty kilograms of cocaine he had stashed inside a storage unit just two miles away from where he was camping out. His first deal was with a dealer from Kansas City, Kansas by the name of Delilah Mobley. Delilah was looking to score thirty bricks. Natalia III's cut of that deal would be twenty percent on each brick sold wholesale at a cost of $36,000 dollars. With thirty kilograms being offed at once to Delilah, his first transaction would net him $216,000 dollars.

Natalia's remaining deals on the thirty kilograms he had left over after Delilah copped her thirty birds wasn't as easy. Besides having to have the cocaine shipped up to Chicago, he had to ride around to five different sets in the city, dropping off four kilograms there, three here, seven there.

Natalia and his crew of three had a rep up in Chicago for ripping off other drug dealers from out of town. From his point of view, there was no telling if either of the clicks he dealt with in Chicago had taken, or would take on a contract for his life. There were too many sets for him to watch in Chi-town, unlike in Kansas City, where he was able to off over half his stash in one deal with Delilah.

Without the go ahead to move in on Minneapolis, however, Natalia had no choice but to roll deep into hostile territory and deal with people he didn't really trust. The upside was that he stood to make just over $21,600 on each deal at a minimum. The pay was good for several minutes of work, but Natalia knew it was ten times less pay with ten times the risk compared to how he handled things with Delilah over in Kansas City.

The Italian knew of the open market in Minneapolis, Minnesota and he was fiending to get his feet wet in the game. If he could get his hands on the clientele left behind after the Somalis' demise, he would be able to off his remaining thirty kilograms to a game warden in the Minneapolis suburb of Twin City who had ties to a right wing militia group by the name of CESRA that sold illegal firearms in the cities of Philadelphia and New York.

Natalia III could not care less about the guns being put on the streets outside of where he was operating. His only objective was to off the cocaine the Holland family was supplying him in the quickest fashion possible in order to reap his $512,000 dollar payout for offing all sixty kilograms when rounded off. Thoughts of the market he was going to gain once everything went down with Malik and Dawk ran through his mind as he busied himself with an extensive workout that had him bench pressing three hundred pound weights.

While in the midst of an upstroke, Natalia's phone rang. He racked the weights atop the bench supports and reached into his sweat shorts and grabbed his cell. "Yo?" he asked through heavy gasps once he'd answered as he lay flat on his back atop the workbench.

"What the fuck happened out there this morning? Your boys inside the warehouse didn't shoot when Dawk was out in the open!" Malik snapped as the paced the floor inside his diner.

"You seen how many men Dawk had out there? I waved my

guys off." Natalia III countered nearly out of breath as he sat upright on the workbench and wiped his face with a large towel. "Jay-D and Dooney and those other mutherfuckas from Atlanta?" he panted as he ran the towel over his large, tatted-up biceps. "And who the fuck was that driving the rig? What you wanted was a bloodbath, something I didn't agree to. Dawk is who we're after in this here deal."

"He'll be harder to get to now," Malik countered. "He put in place on how he wants the product moved and he won't be around for any more deliveries for a while now. We won't be able to touch him until after the club opens next month at the earliest."

"Let him be for now," Natalia III suggested. "That entire deal over to the warehouse could've made him suspicious anyhow the way we were all moving."

"Dawk has to go down before summer's end, Natalia. My people are ready to move in on the Saint Louis market. If we're going to really do this, we have to move fast." Malik let it be known.

"We'll get him. Don't worry about it, my friend," Natalia III assured as he tucked the phone in the crevice of his neck and picked up a twenty-five pound dumbbell and began flexing it up and down.

"How will we get to Dawk now that he's fallen back?"

Natalia sat the phone down on his wooden floor and placed it on speaker before picking up a second twenty-five pound dumbbell. "Dawk coming up to Cicero sometime after he marries in April to visit the old neighborhood," he stated while pumping the iron. "When he comes there? I'll let you know and we'll take him down in the deli I run. My grandfather owns a car crusher over to Gary. We can make him disappear altogether if we set up a meeting on my own turf."

"If he were to disappear, that would keep the heat off of us." Malik stated as he nodded in appreciation of the plan Natalia III had just put together.

"You damn right it'll keep the heat off us. And it's better

than shooting all over the place like some Hollywood movie set let me tell ya'." Natalia III stated as he exhaled heavily while steady lifting the dumbbells.

"Okay, homes," Malik remarked. "In the meantime, I'll just continue moving the work to keep things on the up and up with the family."

"Yeah, you do that," Natalia III remarked nonchalantly as he ended the call and resumed his workout.

****

"That's all of it?" Kree asked Jay-D as he knelt down in a closet and closed the door on a five-foot tall cavernous steel safe.

"Yeah, that's the last of 'em," Jay-D answered as he stood and closed the closet doors in Kree's third bedroom. "Remember what I told you, don't let nobody know what's in here. Let Jessie or whoever use the other bedroom if they have to spend the night."

"This is New Riley's room. No one never goes in there," Kree responded as she followed Jay-D out of the room and closed the door.

"Let me show how to use this alarm since it's brand new," Jay-D remarked as he headed up the hall towards the living room.

"Jason," Kree laughed. "I know how to operate the alarm."

"I just had it put in two days ago. You sure?"

"Trust me," Kree smiled as she walked up and gently nudged Jay-D back towards her dining room table and pulled out a chair for him. "Now, sit," she playfully commanded.

Jay-D let out a smirk as he eased down into the wooden chair. He then donned a serious look as he stared up at Kree. "You know what you involved in now, right?" he asked as he rested his elbows on the table.

Kree planted her hands on the table and looked down into Jay-D's eyes. "If this is what it takes for me to show you how much you mean to me, then so be it. But to answer your question? I know what you and I are involved in. I'm actually flattered that you trust me on that level."

"My niece Nancy say you more trustworthy than any female I ever dealt with. She ain't lying." Jay-D remarked.

Kree was one to focus in on words when it came to Jay-D. The way he referenced her as that of being female meant the world. If he could just see how much she cared for him, loved him, maybe they would have a chance. The hopefulness of having him someday be her man was the driving force behind her agreeing to allow Jason David Cotton to stash eighty kilograms of cocaine inside her home, if only to keep him near.

For a week's work, Kree was going to make $32,000 dollars for stashing Jay-D's cocaine. The product was going to be offed in the cities of Cape Girardeau, Nashville and Indianapolis. The dealers from Cape Girardeau and Indianapolis were affiliated with the Germans was the word, while the boys from Nashville ran a small record label while getting their hands dirty.

"Can I touch you?" Kree asked as her eyes subconsciously fixated in on Jay-D's handsome face, her words shaking him from thoughts of the task that lay ahead.

Jay-D leaned back in the chair and patted his hands up against his silk slacks before spreading his arms. "Don't molest me," he joked.

Kree laughed as she ran her hands over Jason's shoulder in a sensual manner. He was firm and warm to the touch was her quick assessment. She placed her right knee on the edge of an empty chair, growing close enough to inhale Jay-D's cologne as she gave a light squeeze of his arm. When Jason didn't protest, she went a step further by moving her hand up to the back of his neck where she massaged him gently.

The things Jason was allowing her to do had excited Kree to arousal and brought about a slight embarrassment as she was shame to become stimulated before her crush. Satisfied for the moment, she drew her hand back and said, "See, that wasn't so bad now was it, Jason?"

Jay-D shrugged. "It was just a touch," he stated nonchalantly.

"For you maybe," Kree responded through a coy smile as she bit her bottom lip and fantasized all what she would do to Jason if ever given the chance.

"I take it you done molesting me." Jay-D chuckled.

The mood was broken at that moment for Kree. She had one more thing she wanted to do to Jay-D, but his remark left her not wanting to ruin the moment as she'd already gone further than she'd expected in her request to touch the man she loved in a sensual manner. It was at that moment that she then remembered the surprise she had in store for her crush and his family. "Jay!" she exclaimed as she backed up from the table.

"What's wrong with you, girl?" Jay-D asked perplexed.

The smell of steamed broccoli filled Kree's nostrils before she could answer. She darted off to her kitchen and pulled the lid off a small pot and poured a waiting cup off water onto the fresh vegetables and turned the fire down low. She then checked the meatloaf in the oven, making sure it was baking evenly before prancing into her second bedroom and grabbing her laptop.

"I have to set the mood for this," Kree stated as she emerged from the hall and set the laptop before Jay-D. She then ran over to her wall-mounted stereo and pulled up a playlist on her cell phone after linking it up to her Wi-Fi.

As the O'Jay's song *Family Reunion* began playing inside the living room, Kree powered up her laptop. Several seconds later a profile to Linkedin came up. Jay-D eyed the head shot of a brown-skinned female with curly black hair smiling back at him. "Katrina McMillan?" he asked as he eyed the young woman, who had a resemblance to his niece Nancy, save for her being older and more thick in the face. "We looking for a Katrina Sanders, not a Katrina McMillan."

"I know," Kree remarked as she scrolled down through Katrina McMillan's Linkedin biography. The cursor stopped on a paragraph and Kree clicked onto a link titled *The New*

Orleans Café. The screen opened to a news article that had the heading *Local University Grad Opens New Orleans Themed Restaurant.*

Jay-D scanned the article's opening paragraph which read, *"When eighteen year-old Katrina Sanders accepted a full academic scholarship to Arizona State University, the New Orleans native had no idea that her joy of cooking on weekends inside her Tempe apartment would lead to her becoming an entrepreneur that would usher in a new cuisine that many in the greater Phoenix area were aware of, but had never been able to sample the real thing—until now."*

"Wow," Jay-D smiled as he rubbed his thin, neatly-trimmed beard and leaned back in the chair. "They got a New Orleans Café opening up across from the...you found...you telling me...Katrina..." he was at a loss for words over the prospect of Kree having found his sister as he eyed the photos that accompanied the article.

One picture in particular caught Jay-D's eye. It was a picture of the young woman Katrina with a dude he'd seen before. He'd met him once on the runway at the airport in Saint Louis with Malik and Pepper. The guy he knew as Ben Holland was the one who'd handed over $150,000 for the crew to split up just a few days before Christmas of 2008.

"Is that her?" Kree asked caringly as she stepped closer to Jay-D.

"I believe so," Jay-D responded as he hugged Kree around the waist and pulled her close while eyeing the images.

Given the circumstances, that of Jay-D's happiness over finding his sister and the good rapport they had going before the revelation was even made known, Kree threw caution aside and took a chance on love by leaning down and kissing Jay-D on the lips. When she felt him pulling her close while allowing their tongues to freely touch, she knew she'd made the right move.

Jay-D had finally come to terms with his self over the way he felt for Kree. Her loyalty and trustworthiness spoke volumes for a man of his caliber and the business he was involved in.

On top of that, she was passable. Unless you pulled her panties down, you'd never know she was born male. Jay-D saw no maleness in Kree, however, as she brought out every male instinct in him. The need to protect her and keep her safe was emotions his heart couldn't deny no matter how hard he tried. To add to the budding passion, she was willing to stash bricks for him, eighty kilograms to be exact, without giving it a second thought and holding it secret.

"Yes, baby," Kree exhaled as she planted herself in Jay-D's lap and faced him head on. "Are you sure this is what you want?" she asked while staring deep into his eyes and running her hands over his braids.

"Let me call Dawk before we go any further and check something out about Katrina," Jay-D remarked as he picked up his cell phone and dialed Dawk's number. "We got dinner, but umm, what you gone make us for breakfast?" he asked over the ringing phone.

Kree eased up from Jay-D with a smile on her face while biting her bottom lip. "We'll figure it out when we wake up in the morning," she smiled as she let her love tend to his business. "I'll go and check dinner," she ended.

CHAPTER TWENTY-SIX

THREE BROS AND A NIECE

"So, you saying Katrina got three brothers and a niece back in Saint Louis and you know who they are," Lee stated to me as he wrapped the last brick of cocaine that we'd cut with Levamisole.

"That's what Dawk told me on the phone last night, fam," I remarked.

"That's that boy Jay-D, right?" Victor asked me as he dragged a wooden pallet over to the table and kicked it into place.

"Yeah, brer. Jay and Dooney and Eddie is supposed to be her brothers and she got a niece, too."

"I don't know the niece or Dooney, but I remember Jay-D," Lee remarked as he set the last brick down and removed a surgical mask. "I remember meeting that guy before we left for the Cayman Islands that day. And Eddie was the one who killed Q-man up in Rockville, right?"

"Right," I remarked as I slid off my latex gloves and tossed them aside.

"Katrina got some gangsters in her family." Victor said.

"She been a gangster herself. Guess it run in the family," I stated. "Look here, though, don't say nothing to Katrina about this here. When the club open she gone open her café the same night. The family got something special lined up for her and I don't wanna ruin the surprise."

"Gotcha," Lee and Vic remarked at the same time.

Me and my dogs was about ten miles north of the town of Flagstaff, Arizona where Slovak Vineyards lay. Dawk had gotten his load of two hundred bricks yesterday morning and had distributed the product to his team, and now we were on the clock. The truck driver had arrived three hours earlier from Laredo, Texas with what he believed was a simple load of oranges, but mixed in with those bags of fruit was a pallet of Levamisole and two hundred bricks.

I'm not sure how long this deal with Gacha gone last, but as of now, the Colombian floating that work in something major. We'd offloaded the pallets of oranges and reloaded the driver with a trailer load of grapes bound for Napa Valley. He'd been off the set for two hours now and me and my boys had just turned two hundred kilograms into four hundred bricks using the Levamisole formula. We had stacks of kilograms laid out on a long wooden table inside the cold storage warehouse and had just begun palletizing the work when my cell buzzed. I answered and heard Grover Kobayashi's voice.

"What up, fam?"

"We about twenty minutes out, my man. Be on the lookout for two black semis pulling chrome reefer units. We right behind 'em in a brown Jaguar."

"Gate open, dog. Roll on through and follow the road to the brown wooden warehouse at the end."

I stepped out on the concrete dock a few minutes later and saw the Asians rolling my way. They climbed out their ride and walked up the stairs in their silk suits and greeted me with handshakes. "Ben, my father says you've met the leader of the Germans. Are they on the up and up?" Phillip Tran asked me.

"As far as I can tell. Can't say the same about Gacha, though," I remarked as we headed back inside the warehouse.

"My godfather told us about it," Grover stated as he eyed the work we had laid out. "Impressive," he remarked. "Me and Phil thought you'd need our help mixing the product."

"That's a skill you don't forget, fam," I stated. "This deal with Gacha might not last long," I then added. "The family looking into some things in South America to shore up our production."

"Anything we can do to help?" Phillip asked.

"Nah," I remarked as I grabbed a pallet and threw it down onto the cold floor. "I gotta couple of hits lined up in New York and Florida for right now. We just gone keep focusing on moving this product until after Asa Spade trial. Then y'all can go ahead and take care of Tammy Moto. We talk again on opening night back over in Saint Charles next month when you drop off the payment and re-up money."

"Understood," Grover answered as we began palletizing the remaining bricks for shipment to Vegas and San Francisco, the two cities the Asians now distributed to on the west coast.

For the next few weeks, things should remain low key and quiet for me and the family. We were in the opening phases of offing six hundred kilograms and everybody knew to keep a low profile. Quiet is how we wanted these bricks to move. The dealers were in place, everything was cut and packaged, now all we had to do was make money and kick back and wait on the next shipment.

CHAPTER TWENTY-SEVEN

TIME TO GO TO TRIAL

Temperatures were in the mid-sixties over to Denver, Colorado on this sunny day in March, five weeks after the family had received their first load of cocaine. Dante` O'Malley and his three-man team of aides climbed from the back of a black stretched BMW limousine with mirror-tinted windows that had just pulled up in front of the Denver Federal Courthouse. There were no reporters around on this day, just your normal everyday citizens looking to have traffic tickets expunged, fines paid, or the receiving of probation for some misdemeanor they'd managed to collect in some fracas or other minor infraction over a wild weekend. The case dockets were minimal for the most part on this sunny, late winter morning, but there was one case that was of the utmost importance to the Holland family.

"I want you guys to remain silent and look like you've come prepared to kick ass, alright?" Dante` O'Malley asked his three interns, who were nothing more than props that had been filled in on the case a month earlier.

"This is all a stage show," one of the men remarked nonchalantly. "But it would've been a pleasure for us to battle a federal prosecutor."

"We would eat her ass alive," another aide fresh out of law school said in assuredness of himself as the men climbed the stairs.

Dante` thumbed his nose and chuckled while casually lumbering up the stairs. He turned around and faced the wanna-be defense attorneys while holding onto a thick, caramel-colored leather satchel that matched his $5,000 dollar silk suit and said, "A federal prosecutor the caliber of one Lisa Vanguard would have you three not for breakfast, but a midnight snack because she'd know each one your angles before you ever set foot inside a courtroom. You young men have no idea what's about to happen here, so stop your Ivy League bullshit bravado talk and pay attention to the procedure."

The three young men, all in their late twenties, looked at Dante` perplexed, one chewing on a Fiber One bar as his one-size-too-big wool suit with sleeves too big drooped down below his wrist.

Dante` stared at his interns with a hint of disdain. They were a rag-tag, undisciplined trio in way over their heads in his mind's eyed. "This is the best Harvard has to offer me on an internship?" he sighed. "If either of you want to earn a position at O'Malley and O'Malley, you must come far greater than what I have seen the past several days. I gave you free reign the week we were here in Denver and all I've seen is an extensive tab run up on each of the suites you've been given and all you've managed to show me is a video where you've partied with strippers here in town. Where're the prepared opening statements if my ass had to be rushed into the hospital on some emergency? Neither of you three has ever so much as hinted to me that you had a prepared opening statement should you be asked for one by the judge or the prosecution. If I wasn't able to make it today, what would be the course of action for the defense?" Dante` asked as he stood several steps above his interns.

The three aides looked around at one another perplexed until one of them, twenty-nine year-old Quinton Namely, a stout, short-in-stature red-haired, geeky-looking young man of Irish descent blurted out, "A continuance!"

"The prosecution could recommend that the trial proceed given the lead lawyer's aides, whom she knows are fully aware of the mitigating details surrounding the trial and are present here in court," Dante` countered. "What then?"

Quinton swallowed the remnants of the fiber bar he was chewing on and said, "We make it up as we go based on what we know. Lie our asses off and see if the prosecution can rebut anything we say. Court is nothing more than an intellectual argument is what the great Dante` O'Malley told me my first day as an intern."

Dante` heaved through heavy laughter with his lips closed. He reached out and squeezed Namely's shoulder. "An intellectual argument? You remembered that, Quinton?"

"Just as the sure as the day is long, Mister O'Malley," Namely responded seriously as he opened his briefcase and handed Dante` a prepared dossier on Lisa Vanguard, Tammy Moto and Laddy Norcross. "I may love me some hookers, but that by no means is a reflection on my legal prowess. I'm faster than most," the young lawyer stated as he cut eyes at what he knew to be his less-savvy colleagues.

Dante` flipped through the documents briefly, but he'd brushed what he viewed as Namely's 'extra credit report' aside as he knew all he needed to know concerning Lisa Vanguard and her team. The shrewd and experienced lawyer had recently instituted an internship program in conjunction with Harvard University and had agreed to take on three lawyers every two years that'd completed the college's school of law for an internship. Upon completion of the program, Dante` would award one intern a spot inside his firm.

The three aides before him were Sesame Street characters to Dante` in the beginning and throughout the duration leading up to Asa Spade and his crew's trial. He'd given them little chance, but Quinton Namely had struck a chord with him outside the courtroom on this day. His mind had been made up given the young man's reply and course of action. Win by all costs was Dante`s creed, and Quinton Namely fit the description well. The rest of the proceedings with his interns would be a mere formality as he was planning to cut ties with the other two holds upon his return to Boston, Massachusetts.

"Let's convene to the courtroom and prepare for trial, gentlemen," was all Dante` said as he turned and began trotting up the stairs with his interns following close behind.

****

Back inside the courtroom's holding facilities, thirty-eight year-old Asa Spade, along with thirty-two year-olds Xiang Nyguen and Francesca Aranello, and thirty-one year-old Douglas 'Dougie' Hunt, were all preparing to have their day in court. The four were placed into two separate cells and handed new clothes by the bailiffs to change out before the impending trial. This was a day over two years in the making. Last time Asa and his crew had seen daylight was back in October of 2006 on the day Doss Dawkins was killed over in Saint Charles, Missouri.

Per, Dante`, who'd taken over the case back in October of 2008, it was understood that no contact should be made with the free world until after the trial. The only person to not adhere to that advice was Francesca Aranello, but hers was of a different circumstance in her eyes, however; she'd written home to her family in Palermo, Italy and had gotten them to set her up with a ticket for a flight to Rome, Italy if she were to be set free. The black/Italian had had about all she could take from the life, but only for a little while as she was planning on returning to America after she'd spent time with her family back in her homeland.

Asa Spade, meanwhile, was pondering what he was going to do with his life should he beat the charges. "Nevada and Colorado don't want us," he told Dougie as he pulled a pair of off-white silk slacks up to his waist and sat down on a steel bench inside the holding cell he and Dougie were sharing. "We might get off, but we gone be dead broke time we walk out this courthouse."

"What about Samantha, fam?" Dougie asked as he stood facing away from Asa Spade while looking down at his chest and tying his silk tie.

Asa leaned down and placed a fresh pair of black wing tips on his feet and exhaled when he righted himself. "This thing with Samantha," he said as he leaned forward and rested his elbows on his knees. "Dante` never spoke on that the few times we met so I can't say, Dee."

Dougie turned around and faced Asa as he stood in his olive green silk suit and black wing tips and said, "With Samantha around we might have somewhere to stay for a while until we figure shit out. Right?"

"Maybe so, Dee," Asa pondered as he rubbed his hands together while staring at the floor beneath his feet. "But baby girl, I just don't wanna get her caught up in whatever may come out all this shit, you know?"

"I understand that, Ace. But we gone have to do something, man, because if we beat the rap we ain't got nowhere to go."

****

Meanwhile, in a holding cell across the way from Asa and Dougie, Xiang and Francesca were taking turns applying mascara to one another's faces. "I wish I were able to travel to Rome with you, Francesca," Xiang remarked through a smile as she dabbed nude powder onto her friend's cheeks and forehead.

"You're not leaving Asa Spade's side," Francesca chuckled. Xiang's entire demeanor changed after Francesca's remark. The 5'11' black/Italian with short, curly, jet-black hair and dark eyes noticed her friend's apprehension and looked down into the short and petite Asian's green eyes. "What's going on with you? What's on your mind, girl?" she asked concerned.

"I would like to be married, Francesca—married to Montoya," Xiang remarked in a downtrodden spirit. "That is a conversation we've never had in life. I've been Asa's whore, his side kick and his business partner. I've been everything he's needed and wanted me to be, but the one thing I want most from him? I don't think I will ever have it."

Francesca licked her ample lips and nodded her head in agreement. "I don't know what Ace got planned for his life when he get out, Xiang, but I'd be missing something if his plans didn't include you."

269

Xiang scratched the back of her head through her cropped, shiny black hair in wonderment. It was the thought of the day, the possibility of the crew being free again that had her filled with anxiety. Afraid could best describe her feelings at this moment. She was afraid of losing Asa if they were to enter the free world once more, but she also knew deep down that she would follow the man to the ends of the Earth, married or not. That prospect was the very thing that worried her, however, because just like Asa Spade, she knew if the crew was to be released ever, they would eventually return to their old ways. The game was their life and she knew it all-too-well—perhaps better than anyone else inside this faction of the family could ever understand.

In Xiang's eyes, work still had to be done. Going off nothing but hunches, if she had to tell it, there was still unfinished business with Phillip Tran and Grover Kobayashi. And if she was right, something lay ahead—something potentially dangerous and deadly. Through it all, the loving woman had made up her mind that she would remain loyal to Ace and the crew. Her only problem, which couldn't be taken lightly from her perspective, was the unresolved issue as to whether Asa Spade would marry her, or would she forever remain his loyal companion who lay down with him at the end of the day.

****

There were scant pedestrians outside of the Denver courtroom as Lisa Vanguard and her entourage rode up in front of the courtroom in a series of three black H-1 Hummers in a single file line and being escorted in by a half dozen Colorado Highway State Patrol, three in the front and three in the back of her entourage. To say Lisa Vanguard was laying it on thick would be an understatement. There was no need for such extensive security at this point given she was planning on throwing the trial in order to have Asa Spade back on the streets so she could finish what she'd started with the Maruyama Clan, but the woman wasn't about to take any chances with her life.

Reason being was because just before Christmas 2008, Tammy Moto had sold two hundred and thirty kilograms of cocaine that she and Lisa had removed from evidence back in Seattle after they'd won the Maruyama trial, to a woman by the name of Brenda Marshall back over in Philadelphia, Pennsylvania.

In order to keep their exceptional record with the Justice Department intact, Lisa and Tammy had set up a sting on Brenda. In the process of making the deal, with Tammy posing as the supplier, Lisa Vanguard raided a Philadelphia shipyard with a team of federal agents where the deal was unfolding and apprehended Brenda Marshall, a woman by the name of Vivian King, and several other members of a Bronx-based organization. The bust had all arrested now facing anywhere from thirty years to life.

During the processing of the arrestees in Philadelphia, namely one Brenda Marshall, Lisa had uncovered a small picture of the woman with a young child and a man she recognized as being that of a man by the name of Ricky Gross that was inside the glove compartment of Brenda's Range Rover. The perceptive federal agent remembered having killed Ricky Gross inside a hotel room over to Pittsburgh, Pennsylvania in June of 1990, nearly nineteen years prior, and through that photo, she'd made the connection between Brenda and Ricky Gross. Lisa dug deeper, probing the background of Vivian King and learned that the woman had been charged with assault and simple robbery alongside a current Senator by the name of Willameena Slack back in April of 1985.

Records stated that Vivian King had a sister by the name of Zelda King. She'd uncovered the fact that the King Sisters had done time together at Saint Gabrielle's Prison for Women down in Louisiana and were released on good behavior in June of 1990, the same day she'd killed Ricky Gross.

Lisa then probed into Senator Slack's background and learned that she was born in Davenport, Iowa and had been friends with a woman by the name of Tanya Weinberger in her youth. Tanya's last address was listed as being down in New Orleans on Saint Louis Street inside the French Quarters in the year 2005, but she'd practically dropped off the map shortly after Hurricane Katrina stuck the city.

Tax records showed that Tanya Weinberger had donated to Willameena Slack's campaign for State Representative in 1990 and 1992 respectively back down in New Orleans. Slack had loss her first bid in 1990, but she won by a landslide two years later and was now a Senator sitting on the Foreign Relations Subcommittee after the seat had been vacated by long-serving Senator Mabel Sougherbraun-Mobley from Patterson, Iowa— Sheriff Corey Mobley's widow.

In Lisa's eyes, the coincidences were too hard to ignore. It seemed as if Senator Slack was being propped up by drug dealers that had ties to Iowa, a place where one of her most secretive and infamously-manipulated crimes to date had unfolded. She began to wonder, given the close proximity of the circumstances over to Patterson, and the unresolved death of Sheriff Corey Mobley, if her nemesis Faye Bender played a role in all she'd uncovered in what was only a bust meant to do nothing but pad her and Tammy's resumes`.

The evidence uncovered lended no such disclosure to Lisa, however; and on top of that, it would be hard for her to connect the dots without exposing her own hand as regards to Senator Slack, Brenda Marshall, Tanya Weinberger and Vivian King— especially given the fact that Senator Slack sat on the Foreign Relations Committee. The politician would be able to conduct her own investigation and probe into Lisa's background.

With so many skeletons in her closet that she had no intentions of allowing to come to light, the federal agent/prosecutor deemed it best to not subpoena Senator Slack over her past life if only to prevent her own past crimes from possibly coming to light. With that aside, Lisa Vanguard knew full-well that the bust she and Tammy made back in Philadelphia could have devastating repercussions play out on the streets given the perceived power she believed the woman Brenda Marshall had backing her in Tanya Weinberger, a German woman, and her natural enemy by race, along with that of a powerful African American Senator in Willameena Slack, who was by all accounts, a sleeping giant she did not want to awaken. And it would be because of those facts, that Lisa Vanguard was now taking no chances. Security wherever she traveled was a must.

While Lisa and her staff were exiting their vehicles, Special Agent Laddy Norcross rode up to the scene in an inconspicuous blue Nova. He climbed from behind the wheel and looked around at all of the extra security as he made his way over to Lisa and Tammy and met the women at the edge of the courtroom stairs. "You can't possibly need all of this security," he stated to Lisa as he eyed the cars.

Lisa looked at Laddy and said, "This trial isn't to be taken lightly, Laddy. For all I know, Asa Spade may have a team ready to bust him out should he lose this morning. How's your case against Naomi Holland progressing?" she asked as the trio began making their way up the stairs with numerous aides and armed State Troopers bringing up the rear.

"This guy Doss Dawkins was killed back in October of two thousand six. His daughter was injured in that attack. Her name is Bena Holland."

Lisa looked over to Dante` with a serious gaze. "Is she—"

"She's Naomi Holland-Dawkins' daughter. Bena also has a twin named Tiva Holland." Laddy remarked as he hurried up the stairs beside Lisa.

"What's your future course of action?" Lisa inquired as a couple of aides ran ahead and held the door open for her, Tammy and Laddy.

"I still have more probing to do. I'm unable to pin anything on the Holland twins just yet, but they're believed to have done away with one Kathryn 'Toodie' Perez. I got that from an informant by the name of Bahdoon LuQman."

"Have you gotten back to LuQman in reference to Bena and Tiva Holland being the ones who killed Toodie Perez?" Lisa asked as she led the way through a metal detector.

"LuQman was murdered inside Stateville Prison January past. No further evidence can be gained from that angle, but I've set up a small unit back in Saint Louis. I believe that city to be a hub for a drug organization in which Bena and Tiva Holland is a part of."

"Or maybe at the head of," Tammy followed.

"Perhaps," Laddy replied as the legal team approached the courtroom.

Upon entering, Lisa immediately laid eyes on Dante` O'Malley and his legal team along with Montoya Spencer and his crew. "Counselor," she remarked as she strode past Dante`.

Dante` merely smirked as he eyed Lisa over the top of his specks. The man was prepared for whatever the woman threw at him given he knew all of her angles. Everyone rose when the middle-aged white-haired judge entered the courtroom and all were sworn in.

"Okay," Federal Judge Gregory Bernstein remarked as he opened the docket, "the court is prepared to hear opening statements in the case of the United States of America versus Francesca Aranello, Douglas Hunt, Xiang Nyguen and Montoya Spencer. Miss Vanguard, you now have the floor."

Lisa rose and said, "The prosecution is prepared to offer the defendants ten years in a federal prison to be determined if they plead guilty to conspiracy to run a criminal enterprise. On eighty-five percent of time served they'll be out in eight and half years."

Asa Spade leaned into Dante` at that moment. "Eight and a half compared to thirty ain't bad," he mumbled.

"It only sounds good, Montoya," O'Malley countered. "She has nothing but receipts." Asa Spade was about to speak again until Dante` stood and said, "My clients have declined the offer and are opting to go before the court and have the judge decide their fate, your Honor."

"In that case? Miss Vanguard, proceed with your opening statements."

"The prosecution would like to defer opening statements to rebut the defense's presentation, your Honor."

Dante` buttoned his silk suit jacket and walked before the judge, who would also render the verdict as he'd opted to not allow a jury decide his clients' destiny. "My clients are innocent of the charges of racketeering and running a criminal enterprise, your Honor. Asa Spade and those charged alongside him were mere workers inside of a club owned by a man whom Lisa Vanguard had already prosecuted in one JunJie Maruyama. The man is serving a fifty-plus year sentence for the same charges my clients now find themselves facing. This is a mere extension of an investigation that no longer has legs as the real culprit is now behind bars."

"Your Honor?" Lisa interjected.

Judge Bernstein nodded towards Lisa, who was now standing behind her desk. "Asa Spade and his defendants knew all that JunJie was involved in. They not only ran a club for Mister Maruyama, they distributed cocaine on his orders and were the main conspirators in a racket where money was being laundered through the now defunct Royal Flush Night Club. And as the defense knows, ignorance is no excuse for the law," she added as she cut her eyes over to Dante`. "Money was brought into the Royal Flush by Xiang Nyguen and Francesca Aranello, transferred to Montoya Spencer, and then placed onto the books of said establishment for rinsing clean," she remarked as Tammy handed a folder to one of the bailiffs.

Judge Bernstein opened the folder after receiving the documents and read an outline Lisa had prepared that chronicled money being moved. "A paper trail was left," she told the court as she walked from behind her desk. "Douglas Hunt was the middle man in Shorter Arms Apartments. From there, Xiang Nyguen and Francesca Aranello would make the pick-up and drop off back over to the Royal Flush."

"And the prosecution knows this how?" Judge Bernstein asked while peering over his glasses. Lisa deferred further comment by looking back at Laddy.

Laddy stood at that moment. "Special Agent Laddy Norcross, your Honor," he spoke as he stepped from behind the desk. "In August of two thousand five, I tailed a Tahoe SUV owned by Francesca Aranello from Shorter Arms back to an airport in Fort Collins. I was able to witness the defendant Xiang Nyguen hand a satchel over to JunJie Maruyama, who was the head of this organization. It is believed that a drop off was witnessed on that day."

"Request for a rebuttal, your Honor," Dante` interjected.

"Proceed, Counselor," the judge remarked as he grabbed a ceramic picture and poured himself a glass of water.

"What Agent Norcross just described could be anything. Has either of us here in the court never passed a bag to another individual? Agent Norcross's testimony proves nothing against my clients. Now, unless the prosecutorial team has solid proof that either one of the defendants actually passed along profits stemming from some drug organization run by JunJie Maruyama, this entire case should be dismissed on the grounds of lack of evidence."

"The evidence lies with GPS tracking of that Tahoe and a dead man by the name of Finland Xavier, your Honor." Laddy countered.

Asa Spade let loose with an inward smile at that moment. His belief that Finland had been killed was confirmed at that moment and his heart grew ever fonder of Doss's family. Dante` noticed Asa's glee and nudged his side while shaking his head. The jubilant spirit the lawyer was sensing from Ace then quickly dissipated. "Quinton, you may speak, sir," he then stated.

Quinton Namely rose from his seated position at that moment. "The defense would like to see the prosecution's warrant to track the SUV in question," he remarked while jotting down a few notes in his legal pad.

Lisa and Tammy began searching through their files at that moment. "Give us, give us one minute, your Honor," Tammy nervously requested as she pulled hair from the side of her face. "Do you have the warrant?" she was heard asking Lisa.

"I, I'm sure I had it somewhere," Lisa fretted as she picked up a briefcase and pulled out stacks of folders and began thumbing through them at a frantic pace.

Laddy's eyes widened in disbelief at that moment because he knew his entire discourse was now running the risk of being aborted. "Where're the warrants? Did, did you even *get* the warrants to track the GPS?" he asked angrily as he walked back over to the prosecution's table.

"That was your responsibility, Agent Norcross." Lisa hissed under her breath. "The Tahoe recordings and warrants of said proceedings was your duty to oversee and secure."

"How could I oversee the securing of the warrant when you sent me off to Chicago on some solo mission to track down a witness whose whereabouts are still unknown," Laddy whispered.

"They're not here. We haven't the warrants," Tammy whispered to Lisa as she threw her hands up in defeat.

"Your Honor," Namely remarked in mocked exasperation while extending his arms out towards Lisa's table.

"Where're the warrants?" Judge Bernstein asked curiously while looking over to the prosecutorial team as he grabbed his gavel, preparing to hold Lisa and her team in contempt.

"We have no warrants on file." Lisa blurted out as she threw several folders aside.

Namely raised a hand at that moment, but the judge knew what was to come. "Have a seat, Counselor," he stated through closed eyes while nodding his head. He then turned his attention to the prosecution. "The bench will strike Agent Norcross's entire presentation from the record regarding Douglas Hunt, Francesca Aranello, Xiang Nyguen and the Tahoe's movements per GPS. Agent Norcross, is there more to your argument? Can you, other than the evidence you've presented, evidence that has been stricken from record mind you, can you corroborate what you're accusing the defendants of being involved with as it pertains to the charges of racketeering and conspiracy to run a criminal enterprise without warrant?"

"I have no further warrants, Judge," was all Laddy could manage to say as he stood with a dumbfounded look displayed upon his face. The agent began wondering what it was exactly Lisa Vanguard was up to at that moment as it was obvious she'd sent him before the court and had made him look like a complete and utter ill-prepared fool before the bench.

Dante` said nothing as he sat back in his chair with his legs crossed while picking at the frayed leather armrests bordering his chair while in deep thought. He knew Lisa was going to throw the trial, but the way she'd just played Laddy was a move unexpected. Reading the man's face, he could tell he had no idea what Lisa and Tammy had planned for this particular trial. In his mind, it wasn't a coincidence that the warrants needed to track Francesca's Tahoe had been unable to be presented during trial. He was expecting Lisa to withhold evidence, but it wasn't a guarantee given the woman's erratic behavior inside a courtroom. His hunch had been spot on, however; he now he knew for certain that Lisa Vanguard was going to come off as ill-prepared via unfiled paperwork in order to purposely lose the case. The witnesses no longer mattered. One was dead, and the other was God knows where, and Lisa had no intentions on tracking the guy down to have him testify.

As unethical as Dante` could be in court, Lisa, in his eyes, was going above and beyond. She was making it way too easy for him to win this trial and he began to wonder just how safe Asa and his crew would be once they were set free. Not knowing all of the gradations Ben, Grover and Phil had going on with Lisa and Tammy didn't sit right with Dante`. His gut was telling him that things with Lisa extended far beyond the courtroom. In his mind's eye, Ben and his team were battling Lisa not from a measure of legality, but from a more deadly aspect, like that of a gang of desperadoes that were holding court in the streets. Ben he could understand having to come to know the man, but what the hell was Lisa up to was the question that gnawed at Dante` as he'd never expected to find himself in the middle of a possible war between the feds and a criminal organization he gave counsel to.

With that aside, as Lisa and her team searched for answers as to why warrants needed to further their case had not been filed, Dante` stood and requested to take the floor. "You Honor," he began as he walked before the judge's bench, "and I mean this in no disrespect, but this is the most unprofessional court proceeding I have ever been involved in. If the prosecution cannot produce any warrants, I ask that we move ahead with the proceedings while asking for an outright dismissal on the grounds of faulty prosecution."

Judge Bernstein looked over to Lisa Vanguard, who was steadily bickering with Laddy. He picked up his gavel and rapped it. "Miss Vanguard, do you have anything further to present by way of evidence?"

"No, your Honor. On behalf of the United States government, I'd like to ask for a continuance to gather further information due to lack of witnesses and unfiled court documents."

Bernstein leaned back in his seat and looked over to Lisa with disdain. "This is what we spend our tax dollars on?" he questioned in frustration. "For the past two years there has been nothing but requests for continuances. And where *are* the witnesses, Miss Vanguard?"

Lisa wanted to blurt out that the witnesses were dead, but she kept it as professional as she could. "O'Malley is the one who can answer that question," she stated while looking over to Dante`.

Dante` had just been thrown an underhanded softball. He could've shredded Lisa's ass in under sixty seconds. The lob was such a beauty, he decided to pass it on to his chosen protégé. He looked over to Quinton. "Here's your time to shine," he told the young lawyer. "Make me proud."

"Is all I know how to do," Quinton Namely replied as he stood, faced the judge and said, "Your Honor? It is not the defense's job to secure witnesses for the prosecution and the prosecution is aware of that fact. All we have today is our clients. Clients who've willingly come before the court to plead not guilty to the charges they face and to have their day in court after being held for over two years while awaiting trial. I ask that the prosecution's motion for a continuance be denied, and my clients be released without supervision. I'm asking for a dismissal of the charges."

Dante` tugged on Namely's silk suit jacket and the young counselor leaned down. A few words were whispered into his ear, and he turned back to the judge. "I'd like to add another stipulation, your Honor."

"The court is listening," Judge Bernstein replied.

"Should the prosecution obtain any further evidence, the defense requests an entirely new trial that would allow for further appeals and continuances while my clients remain free on bond. The trial should be an entirely new one and not a continuation. A new beginning, as if this travesty that has unfolded today never even occurred—with all due respect, your Honor."

"Given the lack of preparation on the part of the prosecution, I second the motion," Judge Bernstein answered as he looked over to Lisa's team, who was still in a state of flux.

"Where're the wire taps on Douglas Hunt?" Laddy whispered as he looked down at Lisa and Tammy.

"The taps were garbled, Laddy," Lisa whispered back. "Forensic technicians in Quantico couldn't decipher the codes being used in time for us to enter it into evidence and we had no more continuances to file."

"You should've admitted the taps and played them and laid out what we believed transpired. We had Hunt talking to Montoya Spencer about making a pickup."

"It was speculation," Lisa countered lowly. "We have nothing. Without the GPS we have *nothing*, Laddy. Let it go!" she remarked in an annoyed manner as she began closing folders.

"Everything we discussed? You two cannot, and are not that incomp—" Laddy caught himself before he went any further. At that moment, he was hit with a moment of clarity. Lisa and Tammy were not on the-up-and-up in his eyes. He had his investigation going back in Saint Louis with Sandra Cordova, so in his eyes, this is where he and Lisa would begin to part ways. She may have been his superior, but for how long was the question Laddy began to wonder.

"Are you ready to rule, your Honor?" Dante` asked as he ushered his four defendants to their feet. They all remained silent with their hands before them as the judge leaned forward.

"It pains my heart to have to make this decision knowing that the federal government is ninety-plus percent victorious in their cases, but this proceeding leaves me to wonder if all avenues have been exhausted by the prosecution."

"Amen!" Laddy blurted out.

"Quiet!" Judge Bernstein sternly admonished. "In the case of the United States versus Francesca Aranello, Douglas Hunt, Xiang Nyguen and Montoya Spencer, all charges have been dropped until further evidence can be presented whereby a new trial will begin."

Asa Spade and company erupted into laughter while high-fiving one another as Judge Bernstein rapped his gavel once more. "It is, it is the court's order that neither of the defendants call Colorado home!" he yelled aloud as he stood to his feet. "You all may be free, but the state of Colorado has no welcome mat for the likes of you four! Unless you all are to be retried here you're not welcome. If you are caught here on so much as a speeding ticket, you will have to answer to me for violating the terms of this release and will thereby be ordered to serve a five year mandatory sentence for violating the terms of this verdict. You four now have seventy-two hours to leave my state. Case dismissed!" Judge Bernstein ended angrily as he rapped his gavel for a final time and marched off his bench in total disgust.

CHAPTER TWENTY-EIGHT

ON LEADERSHIP

Dante` led his clients out of the courtroom in a hurry. He cared not to engage Lisa in after-trial theatrics like they normally did as he was now on an entirely different level. Things were only beginning in his mind as he and his interns trailed several of their newly-freed clients on another successful case, albeit a sham.

Asa Spade was lingering to the back of the group. "You a master magician in the courtroom," he stated as he walked up to Dante` with his hand extended.

Dante` shook Asa's hand in return. "Do you have a place to go, son?" he asked concerned.

Asa smiled to hide his uncertainty while looking off in the distance. "Nevada has been my home for as long I can remember, man. But I can't go back there, and I damn sure ain't wanted here in Colorado. Not that I would stay anyway. With those two places off the table, my only option is the city of my birth, Oakland, California."

"I'm sure your mother will be glad to see you, Montoya."

"My mother's dead, Dante`. Oakland's my hometown and it's where my mother's buried."

"I'm sorry to learn of that, Montoya. Forgive me. Do you have any family left?"

"I'm looking at them right now," Asa Spade remarked as he

looked over to his crew. "As far as my mother, it might be for the better because I don't know if I could look her in the eyes after all I done the past few years," he remarked somberly as he reflected briefly on the night he'd killed his own brother, Alvin Spencer, over to the Asians' mansion in Paradise, Nevada. "I have people to look after and right now, I can't do jack shit for 'em," he added dejectedly.

"You're a free man and are in good health, Montoya," Dante` remarked as he opened his briefcase and handed Ace four packets.

"What's this?" Asa asked while looking over what he knew to be airline tickets.

"Four first class tickets to Phoenix, Arizona on a flight that leaves out at seven fifteen tomorrow morning."

"I wonder who's behind this here." Asa chuckled as he patted the tickets in his hands.

"I think you know, young man. She wanted to meet you here, but I denied the request. When you get to Phoenix, head over to the Hilton. Four rooms will be ready for you in your name. Your people will be out of town for a few days and they ask that you all remain inside the hotel. Relax and run up a tab with room service until they return."

"I don't know whether to be thankful or suspicious."

"You can be both, you know?" Dante` remarked. He then donned a serious look and leaned into Asa Spade and whispered, "Be thankful for your friends in Arizona, and be suspicious of Lisa Vanguard."

"Why would I have to worry about that prosecutor?"

"Because it was not my court prowess that got you off, Montoya."

Asa looked up to Dante` puzzled. "You sayin' she blew the trial on purpose? Why?"

"She wants you on the streets. You can fill in the rest yourself. Lisa had every chance to put you away, but she didn't."

"I guess she got plans for me and my family," Asa remarked as he looked over to Dougie, Xiang and Francesca and pondered the fate of him and his crew.

"You're in an unforgiving business, Montoya, but you haven't been hung out to dry, son. Make the flight—you and your crew."

"I plan on doing that," Asa responded while looking Dante` square in the eyes. "I just wonder what this world is coming to when those sworn to uphold the law is just as ruthless as the ones living outside of the law."

"I'm sure you'll be enlightened in due time. Now," Dante` said as he smiled proudly with a firm hand on Asa's shoulder, "your team is back, young man. We'll have brunch and go over a few things before I drop you all off at your own suites to enjoy the evening before your flight tomorrow."

****

"I can't believe what I've just witnessed here," Laddy complained as he neatly-placed documents back into his briefcase. "Had the necessary warrants been filed and presented, Montoya and his crew could've all been sent away until twenty-forty! What are we doing if we're not sending the men and women who sit at the head of some of the most violent criminal organizations in the United States to prison where they belong?"

"It's not like this thing with Asa Spade is over, Laddy," Lisa countered. "Me and Tammy will handle the guy, you just continue your probing into Naomi Holland and let us deal with it."

"Oh, I will," Laddy scoffed as he gripped his briefcase. "And just to let you know? I want no further dealings in this investigation into Montoya Spencer. As far as I'm concerned, it's a waste of time."

"You're going out on your own?" Lisa asked matter-of-factly. "I'm still your superior, Norcross. Any investigation that you conduct must cross my desk. Your budget, field officers, requests for wire taps and search warrants?

Everything you do must be verified and sanctioned by Lisa Vanguard. On your own you're powerless, but if this is what you want? I'll grant you that right, and wish you all the best," she ended as she began to exit the courtroom with Tammy on her heels.

"You're cutting me loose? Just like that?" Laddy asked as his voice echoed through the empty chamber.

Lisa turned to face Laddy. "I've given you all the knowledge I could possibly give, Agent," she remarked sternly. "You've grown up now, Laddy. Why should I clip your wings if you're ready to fly?"

"Go on and leave the nest," Tammy Moto chuckled as she flapped her arms.

Laddy eyed Tammy, slightly-bewildered as she stood beside Lisa flailing her arms like a bird taking flight. He could only shake his head over his being denigrated by the two agents who were once his partners in what he viewed as that of doing a virtuous work in the eyes of the law. They were hiding something, he knew, only he hadn't an idea as to what or why. He came to the realization at that very moment that Lisa Vanguard had just replaced him with Tammy Moto, an agent who seemed to be dancing to Lisa's tune no matter the melody.

With his own investigation now underway back in Saint Louis, Laddy accepted his being removed from Lisa's team in order to pursue his own investigation. He'd just lost a lot of power separating himself from the woman, but it was worth it to the man, if only to allow him to conduct legal affairs with a clear conscious because it seemed as if Lisa and Tammy were just as dirty as the criminals he now found himself investigating on the streets.

Laddy had angles to play, however; one was what State Trooper Sandra Cordova disclosed to him concerning an incident with Lisa that had occurred thirty years prior. Lisa was now on Laddy's radar, and should he uncover any dirt on the woman, he would surely expose it, if only to knock her down a notch or several.

The only problem for Laddy, which was no small affair, was

that he now had no budget. He kicked himself silently, realizing he should've held his tongue so as to remain a part of Lisa's team in order to keep the money train rolling full steam. He'd been here before, though; and he remembered the processes Lisa had taken to earn her own budget when she went before the Senate Appropriations Committee when she was in the process of taking down JunJie Maruyama. The cunning and knowledgeable agent would began to use the same tactics to gain his own budget, but in order to do that, he needed more proof to fuel his investigation. And that meant returning to Saint Louis to link up with Sandra Cordova in order to land a bust.

"See you around," was all Laddy said as he left the courtroom.

Lisa and Tammy soon left the courtroom themselves. They were walking behind their aides as they left building. "Do you have any idea what Laddy is looking into?" Tammy asked Lisa as the two walked down the stairs towards an awaiting H-1 Hummer that had its back door open and an armed aide standing outside.

"I really don't care." Lisa replied causally. "Laddy hasn't the sagaciousness to conduct his own investigation. He's a rookie at this game. He exposes his hand before it's time. I wouldn't be surprised if Naomi Holland already knows he's in Saint Louis sticking his nose into her business. My best guess is he'll end up back in Quantico filing paperwork. He's no longer on our team, and that's a blessing in itself given what we have going on over to the east coast."

"Which reminds me," Tammy followed. "Raiden and Arata will be stateside come June. The poppy field on our land in Yokohama will soon be harvested and processed."

Lisa paused on the stairs and looked over to Tammy seriously. "Well now," she stated through a stern gaze, "it's time to put the next phase of our plan into action."

"How will we get the women in Philadelphia to flip and give up their boss, or bosses?"

"Brenda Marshall is the key. She already feels she's been

left to hang in Philly by her crew," Lisa replied as she and Tammy resumed walking. "I have a plan to get her to flip, if it works, Raiden and Arata will take down her bosses upon their arrival and Brenda will be left holding the bag on a thirty year sentence."

Tammy silently nodded her head in agreement as she and Lisa climbed into the back of the SUV. These two were a dangerous duo, no one more than Lisa Vanguard. Instead of keeping the people she'd locked up behind bars, she'd rather set them free and murder them outright. Hers was a demented mind that sought the complete annihilation of her competition.

The stakes are now higher than ever with the moves being made by these two renegade federal agents. Lisa had in mind to take down Asa Spade, Brenda Marshall and Vivian King. All were major players in the cocaine and heroin industries and posed a threat in some form or fashion; their status, however, had called about the need to bring in some heavy hitters from the Asian Pacific in Tammy Moto's brothers, Raiden and Arata Moto, who were members of the Yakuza, the Japanese version of the mafia.

The conspiratorial agent had no idea, however, but her decision to knock off three ranking members inside of two of America's most violent criminal organizations would set off a wave of violence that would span the entire American continent from coast to coast and propel this flourishing battle amongst power players across that of international waters.

CHAPTER TWENTY-NINE

FINALLY FREE

Several hours later, over dusk skies, Asa Spade and company had just exited the elevator onto the sixteenth floor of The Four Seasons Denver. The crew had spent most of the day with Dante` and his staff. They'd enjoyed a brunch at a premier diner near the defunct Royal Flush Club and then took up shopping, all on Dante`s dime, before adjourning to separate Presidential Suites inside the Four Seasons after being dropped off by the attorney.

Toting numerous shopping and garment bags holding new shoes, suits, dresses and lingerie and many other accessories, Asa and his team made their way to their respective suites inside the luxurious hotel. Dougie entered his suite solo and looked around at what he knew to be over two-thousand square feet of immaculateness that consisted of a large living section with seating for six and a brick fireplace. There was a gourmet kitchen with sterling silver faucets, and island counter with granite countertops near a window that had one of the most gorgeous views of downtown Denver he'd ever witnessed.

After laying his clothes on the circular sofa inside the living area, Dougie pulled out a CD he'd picked up while shopping. He found the dock to the surround system and popped in Spice 1's Greatest Hits disc and selected a song titled *Welcome To The Ghetto*. As the music thumped throughout the suite, he headed for the bathroom while stripping out of his clothes. Dougie was the last survivor of Asa's team down in Vegas outside of Xiang. In his time, he'd loss a best friend in Wayne Miller and California Louis, and also a cousin in Percy Hunt, not to mention a down ass chick named Ponita Felton. The game was Dougie's life, though. He knew about the tickets to Saint Louis and in spite of his losses, fatalities that would cause any sane person to rethink their entire lifestyle, Dougie couldn't wait to meet Samantha's people to get back in the game as the game was the only life he'd ever known. He walked through the suite butt naked and tatted up as he grabbed a bottle of champagne from the mini bar and popped it open as he headed for the shower to wash off two years of penitentiary stench with Spice 1's lyrics coating his ears with that funky west coast style of rap.

Francesca's room, meanwhile, was a bright spectacle of tranquility. The sun's rays from the southwest lit her room up in a soft glow of light orange that soothed her soul. She looked to the southeast without blinking as she let her shopping bags slide from her hands. Home was in that direction, across many miles of land and water deep. Her eyes welled up as she went and stood before the bay window and fell to her knees and gave thanks to God for giving her another chance at freedom. Drugs were out for Francesca, but the criminal within her knew that this was only the beginning of a new phase of her criminal career—one that didn't involve drugs, but was illegal nonetheless. The black/Italian had basically plea-bargained with God—no drugs—but asking for forgiveness for whatever she may do with the rest of her life.

Although having her own suite, Xiang followed Asa Spade into his Presidential suite. They'd been touching and hugging ever since they left the courtroom; now, finally, they were alone, which was exactly where the two had been wanting to be for over two years now. Nothing was said as Asa slammed the door shut and looked around for the stereo system's port. He eyed it situated on the mantle of the marble fireplace off to his right and walked in that direction. Asa was old school to the core. He popped in Keith Sweat's Make It Last Forever CD and selected the song *How Deep Is Your Love* before turning back to his woman.

Xiang was standing across the way inside a large suite

staring with loving, longing eyes as the song's soft violins spread out over the room before its deep, sensual bass took over. Unable to resist, she ran into Asa's arms and kissed him deeply. She was soon moaning into his mouth and was forced to let out a gasp as he picked her up and carried her over to the plush, white suede sofa.

Wrapping her legs around her man's waist, Xiang used one hand to pull down on the buttons lining the front of her sweater dress and had raised her silk bra to free her breasts while gripping the back of Asa's neck with her other hand. The two wobbled into the living room and slid down onto the soft carpet before a c-sectional sofa. Asa pressed his muscular body atop of Xiang as she spread her legs and assisted him with the removal of her silk panties as Keith Sweat's voice filled the room…*"Spend all day thinking…all night wondering…why love has to change…"*

"I need you! Fuck me, Montoya!" Xiang panted as she wrestled with Asa's belt.

"Yeah, baby?" Asa questioned as he unzipped his silk slacks and shoved them down to his knees. "You want this dick?" he asked as he placed the tip of his rock hard shaft to Xiang's opening.

"God!" Xiang exclaimed as Asa eased forward and slowly penetrated her moist slit.

Legs went up into the air and arms were wrapped around necks and backs as the two lay on the carpet kissing deeply while in the opening phases of a freedom fuck that both had been dreaming of for months on end. The two sexed one another like frenzied rabbits on the floor while gripping one another tightly, Xiang's pussy making those sloppy, wet slushing sounds as her man took her to where she needed to be as Keith Sweat sung on… *"Are we living a lie, baby…is that magic gone…"*

Every time was like the first time for Xiang when with Asa Spade. What she'd done in times past with other men was business. She never got into the act no matter how good the sex. With Ace, however, it was real and from the heart each and every time for Xiang as he was the only man she'd ever loved in life. It was fair to say that she loved Ace more than she loved herself at times given all she'd done to see the man come out on top back in the day. She was moaning uncontrollably as Asa raised up with his hands planted on either side her waist and began driving deep inside, his balls slapping against her asshole.

Xiang's pussy quivered and she creamed as her body tensed. Asa, knowing he'd taken his woman over the edge, pulled out and spoke in a raspy tone to Xiang. "I want all of you, baby," he stated over the music as he stood over Xiang and began to remove all of his attire while staring deep into her slender, alluring eyes.

The Japanese/Vietnamese removed her dress while sprawled out on the floor and crawled up on her knees and took Asa into her mouth. She tasted her own sex on her man's pole as her lips massaged his organ. The gentle hand on the back of her head running through her lengthy black hair only added to her willingness to please. Being so close to Asa in the most intimate way imaginable was the ultimate for Xiang. The ability to do as she pleased after being caged up for so long was a turn on incomparable. She made love to Asa with her mouth, allowing him to stroke her face the same as he'd done her slickened vagina many times before in the past until she came all over herself, only with less thunder.

Xiang's mouth was sauna hot to Ace, and her sucking and licking was toe-curling. He stood in the center of the room with the setting sun at his back in a slightly-leaned back position as he stroked Xiang's face while nearing the end game of male sexuality. Her oral skills were beautiful, but he'd released many a time behind bars to the hand method, and in his mind, spilling forth down his woman's throat, as dirty and sexy as it was, would leave him unfulfilled, so he stepped back and pulled Xiang up to her feet.

Without a word being spoken, Xiang knew. She stood on her tippy toes and kissed Ace deeply before turning around and pressing her back to his. His course hands palmed her breasts and her nipples were thumbed and pinched as she leaned forward and reached back and spread her cheeks.

Xiang's vagina throbbed. She could feel the heat from Asa's dick nearing her opening. In want, she bent forward more to allow a perfectly unguided, hands-free entrance into her womb while in the standing position.

Asa gripped Xiang in the pit of her elbows as he began stroking her from behind. Both lovers' knees were bent, the back of Xiang's thighs resting atop Asa's lap as if she was sitting in a padded chair with a hard dick poking up into her spine.

Ace placed his right hand to Xiang's shoulder and used the other hand to slap her left ass cheek as he dug off into his woman. After several stings, Xiang leaned back, tilted her head and extended her tongue. "I love you, Montoya," she panted as she raised her right hand and palmed the back of Asa's head while kissing him deeply.

If the level of passion had the ability to become a chemical fuse, all one had to do was spark a lighter and the entire suite that held Asa and Xiang would've gone up in flames. Down and dirty they were. Not ready to come, Asa pushed Xiang forward gently, guiding her over to the c-sectional sofa were he placed her on her knees and knelt behind her and began tonguing her pussy while using two fingers to spread her lips as his tongue rapidly flicked back and forth over her throbbing clitoris.

"Baby," Xiang panted as she planted her face into one of the suede pillows to suppress her delight. She then tilted her head to the side, no longer willing to hide her pleasure once she remembered she was now a free woman. The nights where she'd fingered herself thinking of Asa was now a reality.

Through unspoken words, Asa sensed Xiang's pleasure increasing. He sucked harder on her clitoris while running his hands over her butt cheeks and inner thighs. He smacked on the pussy that was sweet to his palate until that warm liquid coated his tongue. He then rose at that moment, much to Xiang's protest, but her complaint was vanquished in a matter of seconds when Asa's hard dick slid into her once more. She pushed back as she bit her bottom lip, this time determined to bring her man home. "Fuck it!" she pleaded as she slammed back onto Asa's pole.

"Give me this mutherfuckin pussy!" Asa groaned as he drove deep into Xiang while gripping her waist tightly.

"Take me, Montoya! Take me!" Xiang blurted out, pleading in fact, as she continued rocking back and forth on her man's love stick.

Requests for pleasure quickly vacated both lovers' vocabularies and were replaced with 'hmms' 'ooohs' and other incoherent sounds as Asa took Xiang from behind as she knelt on her knees atop the suede couch.

One could've written a drum line to the 'plop, plop, plop, plop' sounds of flesh against flesh exploding inside the suite.

"Fuck!" Asa growled as he drove deep into Xiang,

At the same time, Xiang thrust back and clamped down on her vaginal muscles. She felt her belly warm slightly the moment her lover's seed spilled off into her insides. His convulsions set her off for a second time, forcing fluid to trickle down her inner thighs as he relaxed and lay atop the couch's suede pillows spent.

CHAPTER THIRTY

ALL HUNDREDS

"Money, hoes, cars and clothes...that's how all my niggas roll...blowing dro... twenty-fo's...that's how all my niggas roll... Money, hoes, cars and clothes...that's how all my niggas roll...blowing dro...twenty-fo's...that's how all my niggas roll..." The mean strings and hardcore bassline to T.I.'s song *24's* blared out over the packed streets as patrons dressed in their finest attire stood on either side of a roped-off red-carpeted runway leading up to the double doors.

The night of the grand opening to Club Indigo had finally arrived. The corners of Lindenwood Avenue and Elm Street were lit up with heavy vehicle traffic and countless pedestrians that were walking on both sides of the street leading up to the club. Women ranging in ages from their early twenties to late thirties, some decked out in tight-fitting outfits and knee-length boots with shades covering their eyes, while others sported maxi-dresses and stilettoes, raised the roof and vibed to the music coming from packed club while the males, mostly dope boys and players from various parts of the city, stood around in groups boasting street status and running eps while waiting to get them and their shorties and homeboys in on V.I.P., which was hitting for $5,000 a pop for a crew of four.

Fresh whips, from old school box Chevys on big boy rims, to the latest luxury ride ranging from Ashton Martin to Rolls Royce, all the way down to rare classic cars such as the 1966 Soviet-made Zaporozhet was on display. Cameras flashed as men and women whose names were unknown, climbed from cars most had never seen in their lives and carried names they couldn't even pronounce.

There was a banner lineup of musicians on hand as well, including a rap act from Nashville Jay-D had brought in, along with Narshea, the Grand Diva herself, who was scheduled to perform a new track she and NonStop had recorded inside the studio on the first floor of Club Indigo. The Jane Dow Band was scheduled to debut and close out the night with what would surely become a classic performance, and the entire night was being hosted by The Fantastic Four, who were on hand doing a live nationwide remote from inside the club's DeeJay booth.

Men and women from all races were pouring off into the club, but all heads turned when a black, four door 2008 Bentley Continental Flying Spur with black mirror tint cruised up to the front of the club. Some of the spectators watched as a slender, pale-skinned woman with a nappy, tan afro climbed out of the driver side. She flipped the collar on her mid-quarter-length leather coat and eyed the crowd with a blank expression and rounded the front of the $465,000 dollar whip as her counterpart, a red-haired, tall and full-figured woman was helped from the car by an attendee, who just so happen to be Natalia III.

Together, Helen Weinberger and Maggie McPherson were escorted into the crowded club and led through a private walkway that ran behind the bar. The group climbed the stairs and headed for the third floor where the V.I.P. section lay. Natalia guided the women to their glass-enclosed booth, which had a bottle of *Dom Perignon vintage 1995 white gold Jeroboam* being chilled in a diamond crusted ice bucket laced with four stems that had crushed diamond specks lining the outsides of the glasses. A platter of boiled shrimp that was still steaming, their aroma lighting up the enclosed booth with a hint of spice and lemon, rested on a silver platter.

"Compliments of the New Orleans Café` from across the street," Natalia III spoke in a respectful tone as he helped Maggie into her seat. "As you can see, the Holland family has taken upon itself to extend the first olive branch."

"Tell the Holland family that my family accepts the offer and is willing to make the peace, but we will not back down or apologize for what has happened in the past."

"Neither do we," Natalia III responded just as casually. "As far as I'm concerned, it's water under the bridge. Loopy might not feel the same way, though, understand?"

Helen stood and removed her coat. "I will tell this Loopy to her face that she is lucky to be alive and that she should thank me if nothing else. At least she can put flowers on Pepper's grave now," she ended as she took her seat once more and extended her hands, silently requesting that Natalia III pour her and Maggie a glass of champagne.

"I wish like the fuck I would," the Italian laughed as he backed away from the table and tucked his hands into his silk slacks.

Helen looked over to Maggie before reaching for the bottle of champagne. "It has been a long drive from Cherryvale," she sighed while crossing her legs. "The least you could do is have a drink with us for old time's sake. We did do business in the past and are still doing business together with your people from San Antonio, remember? I'll pour."

"I have to watch the floor." Natalia III countered as he turned and headed for the door.

"*Questa non è una richiesta.*" (This is not a request.) Maggie chimed in as she picked up a corkscrew and eyed Natalia III from her seated position.

"*E vogliamo farvi mangiare alcuni dei gamberetti con noi, troppo. Vieni ora.*" (And we want you to eat some of the shrimp with us, too. Come now.) Helen chimed in as she slid the tray of shrimp to the opposite side of the table.

Natalia III turned around and faced Maggie and Helen. In all his time of knowing the Germans, he'd never known either of them to speak Italian. He eyed the women in wonderment over their lack of trust and said, "*Pensi di essere invitati qui per essere avvelenato? Questo è un gioco da ragazzi per noi. Si dovrebbe dare voi stessi molto più credito anche se si pensa che la famiglia è lo stupido. La famiglia ritiene altamente della vostra organizzazione come fare I. Questo non è un gioco che viene giocato. La famiglia Holland non è il tuo problema. Essere preoccupati per i messicani."* (You think you've been invited here to be poisoned? That's child's play for us. You should give yourselves much more credit even if you think the family is that stupid. The family thinks highly of your organization as do I. This isn't a game being played. The Holland family is not your problem. Be worried about the Mexicans.)

"Do you have any advice for us when we meet with your people?" Helen asked as she stuffed the corkscrew into the chilled champagne and twisted downwards.

"Yeah, I do," Natalia III answered as he walked back over to the table and picked up a stem glass and waited for Helen to pop the bottle. The cork popped and the bubbly fizzed, but didn't spill over the bottle top.

Maggie grabbed a glass for herself and she and Natalia III waited as Helen poured herself a glass, then poured for her and the Italian. *"Qual è il vostro consiglio, bello italiano?"* (What is your advice, handsome Italian?) Maggie asked as she held onto her glass.

Before the bubbles could settle, Natalia downed his drink and licked his lips. He then grabbed a fork and poked a steaming hot boiled shrimp and dipped it into the cocktail sauce and took a bite. "My advice to you both is to set that German pride aside and apologize. Apologize and mean it because it's the right thing to do for a unification of both families," he stated upon swallowing the seafood.

"But an apology isn't a guarantee that all will be forgiven." Helen countered before she took a sip of her champagne and picked up a fork.

"Apologies carry a lot of weight with the Mexicans." Natalia III retorted. "And we need them on our side in order to see the deal go through."

"We will listen to what your people have to say," Helen

replied as she dipped the shrimp into the cocktail sauce and took a bite and quickly swallowed. She wiped her mouth and said, "But if we don't agree with what your people have to say, there will be no apology. To be truthful, I have never been sorry for what we did to Pepper, Simone or Donatella. The same as the Holland family are not sorry for killing my brother RJ in Naptown."

Natalia III realized that he was on the verge of negotiating for the family, which was a definite no-no. He downed the remainder of his drink, set his glass down and said, "I've given you two all the advice I can give going in. After tonight? We'll either see one another again as business partners, or that of enemies."

"Heads or tails?" Maggie asked nonchalantly as she leaned back in her seat and sipped her champagne.

"Your call," Natalia III ended seriously as he left the two women to be alone inside their V.I.P. suite to enjoy their shrimp and champagne as he walked a ways down the corridor and trotted up a wide, black marble staircase leading up to the main office that overlooked the entire club. He entered the black-carpeted room that was bordered in black ivory and had walls painted in a light shade of blue and closed the leather-padded double doors.

Malik Gomez, Jay-D, Grover Kobayashi and Phillip Tran all stood around a medium-sized black ivory table with Dawk standing at the helm. A .45 Glock was tucked into a holster and clearly visible over his white button-up silk shirt and black, burgundy and white paisley tie. Each of the men present with him was also decked out in lavish suits as they stood waiting his arrival.

"The Germans are comfortable for now with their champagne and shrimp," he remarked as he walked up to the table while rubbing his fists together. "It's a go on the meeting," he added as he eyed Malik briefly.

"That's what it is then. This here deal been almost three years in the making," Dawk spoke while eyeing the family as he held onto a bottle of *Shipwrecked 1907 Heidsieck,* a rare bottle of wine that went for about $275,000 dollars. "We all come together on this night to toast the family's next venture and set the tone on how we gone break bread from here on," he added as he left the head of the table and began pouring wine into each of his comrades' glasses. "But before we toast, we need to tally up," he added as he resumed his position at the head of the table. "What the money count be like?"

Phil and Grover leaned down briefly and came up with four slender briefcases and laid them flat on the table. They opened the cases simultaneously and turned them towards Dawk. "This is the family's share—eleven and a half million dollars on four hundred kilograms wholesale and rounded off. All hundreds," Grover stated.

Dawk eyed the money and nodded his approval. "Everybody eating on the west coast?" he asked.

"No problems on our end. Vegas and San Francisco is a well-oiled machine, my friend." Phillip responded in a serious tone. He then looked over to Jay-D in silence.

Jay-D leaned down and placed two briefcases on the table. "I can't compete with that shit there," he stated seriously, respecting the Asians' hustle game. "This here is two point nine million dollars rounded off, fam—all hundreds," he stated. "Nashville, Naptown, and Cape Girardeau done fell in line with what we puttin' down. Two point nine is what it is every rip unless my hundred bricks get upped. Them boys from Atlanta copped twenty off top, too—all that's included."

"We gone keep you at the level you at for right now to keep a even flow with those clicks," Dawk remarked as he looked over to Malik.

"It's nothing, homes," Malik stated as he threw a dingy duffle bag onto the table. "One million, four hundred and forty thousand dollars—rounded off."

Dawk reached out and unzipped Malik's payment and eyed a jumbled mass of hundred dollar bills. "This how you bringin' money in, fam?" he asked as he flipped the bag shut and stared Malik down.

"The money counters was all broken," Malik countered. "Me and Max counted everything out and just threw it in the bag because we didn't have time to band everything."

"You should band as you go even without the money counters," Grover retorted in a harsh tone, having become annoyed over the lack of respect being shown by Malik. "That is sloppy work and you know it! What the hell is wrong with you, guy?"

"He's upset about the Germans being here." Natalia III laughed lightly as he placed a briefcase on the table, opened them and turned it around to face Dawk. "One point seven million dollars rounded off—all hundreds."

Dawk ran the numbers briefly as he'd been tallying the count along the way and saw that his money team was dead on with the count. After re-upping with Gacha for $5.7 million dollars, the family's take for a month's worth of work would be $11.7 million dollars, $1.3 million dollars less than projected the projected $13 million dollars, but within the margins of error given the weight being moved as the family was allowing for a ten percent shortage at maximum. Whether the individual crews taxed dealers to earn extra or sold at a lower price to off the product more quickly, it didn't matter to the Holland family so long as each of the factions were within their allotted boundaries when tallying up.

Dawk also knew that Kimi and Koko were freeing up HDE's books with $2.2 million dollars, a move that would leave a total of $9.5 million dollars that would have to be rinsed over time. The remainder of the profits earned on the first shipment would be taken to a safe location in Cutbank, Montana via Francine Cernigliaro until Kimi and Koko could clear the books and send for more money.

After toasting to their future endeavors, the top money makers inside the family's respective factions all savored the flavorful wine and set about enjoying the remainder of the club's opening night. Dawk, however, still had business to conduct. Top priority was for him, Natalia III and Malik to hold a meeting with the women sent on the Germans' behalf. The three exited the office after Jay-D, Phil and Grover had left and broke off from the group and made their way over to where their guests were parlaying.

The silk curtains that shielded the V.I.P. room from any spectators was pulled back and Dawk, Natalia III and Malik could see the two women sitting inside their booth sipping on the champagne they'd sponsored. Natalia III walked up and entered a key code and pulled back on the sliding door leading to the booth.

"Boss? This is Maggie McPherson and Helen Weinberger. Everybody calls her Boogie," Natalia III stated while pointing to Helen. He then ran down the names of the men standing behind him to the Germans.

Dawk stepped forth, looked over to the woman nicknamed Boogie and said, "Your family was bold enough to take down one of our lieutenants and two of our soldiers last January. That there ain't sittin' well with my people."

Boogie set her stem glass down as she and Maggie stood from their seated positions. The women waited several seconds, allowing Natalia III to close the sliding door completely before dialogue began.

"Peppi Vargas was part of a contract handed down by Jada Murdella," Boogie defended as she eyed Dawk and Malik. "Forgive me and my family for not warning our marks that a contract had been placed on their lives," she sarcastically remarked. "We're not the feds, only the feds would do such a detestable thing in this business. My family fulfills contracts once money exchanges hands with no questions asked."

Dawk nodded and said, "RJ will be considered as compensation for taking down Pepper's crew, but you owe it to Loopy to apologize. We done talked about the matter with her and she still undecided. If she decides to go after those responsible, including the women I'm staring at tonight? I'm not gone stop her."

Helen looked over to Maggie with curled lips and then turned back and faced Dawk. "You would want to do all that you can to avoid this conflict, Dawk Holland," she let it be known. "I will offer an apology as Natalia suggested to me earlier, but if this Loopy character decides to come for me or my family? I can guarantee that the three men standing before me and Maggie will all have to answer for it."

"What's to stop us from killing you two now, huh?" Natalia III asked. His face wrinkled as he placed his hands on his hips, subtly pulling back on his suit jacket to reveal a holstered .45 Glock.

Boogie eyed the gun on Natalia III's side unfazed and calmly stated, "When me and Maggie walk out of this club, like I know fuckin' well right we will, we better not so much as get an angry stare unless we become offended and give a bad report to our mothers and plunge us all into a world of shit."

Dawk stepped forth at that moment. "I think the question here is whether the apology is accepted by Malik on behalf of Loopy, right?" he asked as he looked back at Malik.

Malik eyed Boogie and Maggie in silence for several seconds before nodding his head in disagreement. "There is no apology that could ever make me agree to make peace with these people," he stated while staring at Boogie and Maggie.

Boogie raised her hands to her sides. "Without an agreement," she declared, "without an agreement we will leave here as enemies. No one will be safe. You boys might as well kill us now. Because if we leave without a peace deal, we will be forced to go on the offense."

Malik grimaced over to Boogie and said, "*No importa qué acción tomar! ¿Matar a tres de mis propios y quieren que de acuerdo a la? No se hacerlo! Va a obtener el extremo sucio de la vara!*" (I don't care what action you take! You kill three of my own and want me to agree to that? No way will I do that! I will be getting the dirty end of the stick!)

"Calm your guy, Dawk!" Maggie snapped. "Me and Boogie agreed to come here because we were assured that all scores would be settled. Any remaining animosity was to be forgiven and both our organizations will enter new deals with a clean slate. Why is Malik so hostile knowing why me and Helen have come here?"

Dawk patted Malik on the shoulder and said, "You have to understand my family, Maggie. Pepper was his own project. He had dreams and aspirations for the teenager," he let it be known as he eyed his Enforcer with compassion. "Malik," he then said, "I know how you feel about this deal, but I need you to understand that we have to make the peace. Remember the last war over what Junior pulled?"

"Si, homes."

"This one here would be ten times worst. The bosses will be warring. We got the feds lurking in the middle of us moving six hundred bricks and we don't need to heat up the streets. You gotta decide what's more important—business—or settling an old score that would lead to more murder and take us all down. We beyond revenge. It's all about the money now. Make the deal."

"We can talk," Malik responded. "But like you said, if Loopy disagrees, all this will mean nothing. I owe her at least that much."

"I know you gone make the right decision. Don't worry about Loopy, we'll get her on board," Dawk remarked. He then turned to Natalia III and said, "I have something to be apart of over to New Orleans Café`. I'm gone leave you with Malik to negotiate on my behalf with Boogie and Maggie. You already know to call me if shit go sour."

"No doubt, boss. Give my congrats to Katrina while ya' at."

"Done," Dawk remarked before extending a kind hand to Boogie and Maggie before stepping out of the V.I.P. suite.

Once the door was closed, Natalia III, Malik, Boogie and Helen all eyed one another briefly. Within seconds, smirks appeared on their faces. "I thought he would never fuckin' leave!" Natalia III sighed while shaking his head in frustration.

Boogie and Maggie eased back down into their seats and looked over to Malik. "Dawk bought your reluctance looks like," Boogie remarked. "Me and my family are glad you've decided to join us. With your own cocaine network, and our muscle? We'll push the Holland family clean off the map and they won't even see us coming."

Malik nodded somewhat somberly. "Dawk has been my friend for years now," he admitted. "It won't be easy doing what I have to do to him."

"Forget about it," Natalia III countered as he stood beside Malik. "I'm gone be there with you every step of the way. And don't you dare go feeling sorry for Dawk. He willing to make a deal with the same people responsible for killing your protégé in Pepper. You came to me and asked what I thought of the deal and I told you it was fucked up from the beginning. I never told you to kill Dawk, I told you it would be best to work it out for family's sake. You wasn't with it so this is where we are. The Chicago faction has been muscle for as long as I been in this thing, it's time we call the shots—right alongside our German counterparts."

"Natalia's right," Boogie chimed in. "If you want real revenge for Pepper—because Dawk obviously is putting money over her life—join us."

Malik rubbed his face and said, "I want a fair deal on the tax your family will charge for allowing my crew to pass through your state untouched next month. Once Dawk is out of the picture, I'll have it routed back here to Missouri."

"State troopers in southern Kansas patrol a hundred mile radius, and they have contacts with other units all the way up to Kansas City," Maggie stated. "The highway leading from the Oklahoma border to our town is rarely patrolled, though. It's what's north of Cherryvale that should be of your concern. When your people make it up to Cherryvale, we'll provide them with the Kansas Highway Patrol's stakeout locations, roadblocks and sweeps further north. The cost for that information is twenty-five thousand a load, no matter how much weight you move."

"Si," Malik responded while nodding his head.

"And to make good on it, I'll put up the payoff for the first load," Natalia III remarked, much to Malik's surprise and appreciation.

"Do we have a deal, Mister Gomez?" Boogie asked.

Malik extended his hand while Natalia III nodded his approval while staring at the two Germans. With all in agreement, Dawk Holland's fate had just been placed into the hands of all involved in one of the most treacherous acts to ever unfold inside of the organization, and Malik Gomez was the main driving force behind the betrayal.

CHAPTER THIRTY-ONE

A LONG TIME AGO

"Dooney, hurry up, boy! Faye and Miss Joyce waiting on us to walk them down to the other corner!" Nancy yelled out as she trotted down the stairs inside the Cottonwood home, never bothering to wait for her uncle's reply.

After verifying with Dawk and Ben that the woman Kree had showed him the night over to her home was indeed the Katrina Sanders he, Nancy and Dooney been looking for, Jay-D caught a flight to Chicago the day after Valentine's Day and visited his father and brother in Rockville Prison where he obtained Miss Joyce's address down in Joliet. He traveled there and the woman was already waiting, having been contacted by Big Eddie.

Jay-D got to meet Faye Sanders for the first time in Illinois and ran down what he knew about Katrina Sanders. The woman was more than eager to see her daughter, but Jay-D wanted to do something special. He told Faye and Miss Joyce of Club Indigo's grand opening night and suggested they fly into town and surprise Katrina and both women agreed. They'd made it into town the afternoon before and had been inside the Cottonwood home ever since, patiently waiting for the moment to arrive as they dealt with bouts of anxiety.

Nancy jumped down the stairs and pranced into the living room where Miss Joyce and Faye were; both women were casually dressed in business pantsuits and heels. Nancy eyed the women and asked, "Y'all ready? Soon as—Dooney come on, man!" she complained as she stomped in her heels.

"I'm coming, shit!" Dooney scoffed as he wobbled down the stairs in a tuxedo with a short jacket and wing tips.

Just then, the doorbell rang. Nancy trotted over the wooden floors and answered, only to see Kree standing on the porch. "Nancy," she smiled. "All Ben family down there and they know what's up! Katrina getting ready to present her menu and take their orders!"

Dooney saw Kree and shook his head. "The fuck you doing, man?" he complained as he stepped onto the first floor.

"We not gone have this tonight, Donnell!" Nancy barked. "If it wasn't for Kree we woulda never found Katrina! Give her that much, bruh!"

"It's okay, Nancy," Kree spoke in a humble tone. "Jay-D sent me to let y'all know while he keep an eye on Katrina. I'll, I'll see y'all later. Me and the crew from Bangin' Heads going inside the club."

As much as Dooney despised Kree, he couldn't help but to keep it real at this moment. "Kareem," he called out as he stood in the foyer. Kree turned and eyed Dooney, prepared for another scathing rant while remaining silent. "Not tonight," Dooney stated seriously as he walked over to the door and stood beside Nancy. "We all about family around here," he let it be known. "We might not never see eye-to-eye on how you live your life or the way you feel about my brother, but through all that I'm not too proud enough to say thank you. Just thank you for finding my sister."

Kree, forever optimistic that Dooney would someday accept her, couldn't help but to let loose with an, "Awww," as she stepped towards him with her arms spread.

"Nancy, get ya' man!" Dooney snapped as he threw up his hands and walked off, denying Kree the hug she was going for.

Nancy and Kree laughed to themselves as Dooney walked back into the house. "Your ass is a trip!" Nancy mocked.

"It was worth a shot," Kree responded. It wasn't a big deal

for her, though, as she was already working her way into the family. She and Jay-D had made love for hours the night Katrina was found and the images were still fresh in her mind as she patiently awaited the next time they shared the same bed again. "See y'all later, Nancy," she smiled as she turned and trotted back down the stairs.

"Bye, girl! Come on, y'all! It's about that time!" Nancy called out, signaling for Miss Joyce and Faye.

Back inside the New Orleans Café, Katrina was a nervous wreck. The entire Holland family, minus Flacco, Francine, DeeDee, Bay and T-top and the babies, was on hand inside the café. Bay and T-top were still remaining off the scene being the feds were probing their activities and Francine and DeeDee cared not to deal with the young crowd they knew were going to be present on Elm Street.

A great portion of the seats inside the restaurant were dominated by family members as they went over the menu. Mardi Gras music from speakers posted in the corners of the restaurant that sat directly across from Club Indigo created the perfect ambiance. Katrina had her designers decorate the establishment with a New Orleans theme under dim lighting. Carnival beads resting inside the mouths of authentic alligator heads hung from the walls along with smiling and frowning Mardi Gras masks. Pictures of the swampland surrounding the Crescent City ran throughout and each table sported a small billboard that told a story pertaining to the history of New Orleans.

Katrina hadn't gotten the chance to make it back to the ranch to present her menu as she was way too busy setting things up in Saint Charles. She'd been in town off and on for nearly two months with her staff preparing items for this special night. She was now in the massive kitchen decked out in a white chef's uniform and hat going from pot to pot, assisting JoAnne, Dana and Alicia by stirring the gumbo and checking to make sure the stuffed crabs was baking evenly. The island counter was lined with sterling silver plates being decorated by a team of assistant chefs dressed in white tops and hats with light grey pants.

"Okay, everybody!" Katrina called out to her staff as she clapped her hands together briefly. The dozen or so crew paused their activities and turned to face their boss as she stood in between six waitresses and waiters decked out in black suits and dresses with neat haircuts and styled hair with nets covering their heads. "We're ready to make our grand entrance. Umm, the last of the entrees while be done in a couple of minutes so, so let's, let's umm, God I'm so nervous!" the twenty-eight year-old laughed as she removed hair from her forehead.

"Come on nah, sister! We done been here before!" JoAnne remarked as everyone nodded and began clapping, giving Katrina a boost of confidence.

Katrina managed to smile and thank her staff before turning to face the double doors. She checked her appearance against the reflective steel and was satisfied with her appearance. After taking a deep sigh, she eased the door open and stepped out onto the main floor. Immediately her ears were coated with the sounds of carnival music and an array of voices and laughter.

When the family saw Katrina emerged from behind the double doors, Ben stood up and said, "Here's the woman of the hour! That's my wife right there, ya' heard me?"

The family all stood and clapped as Katrina walked up the aisle thanking them and giving hugs along the way. She went and stood in the center of the room and said, "I would like to thank you all for coming out to the New Orleans Café tonight to celebrate the grand opening. It is my every intent to deliver nothing but the best in New Orleans cuisine to my very best ability."

"We hope so," Naomi, who was sitting next to Katrina, remarked jokingly as she read her menu. "'Cause if it ain't we gone be asking for some go plates and the bill."

"We don't have any go plates because our food is too good to take home, Auntie," Katrina laughed as she tapped Naomi's shoulder lightly. "Okay, everybody! My wait staff is prepared to take your orders! We have a fine selection of wine and a host of domestic and imported beers for your pleasure along with daiquiris, mixed drinks and sodas, both Coke and Pepsi products! Shall we began?"

"Let me get a spicy gumbo appetizer for starters," Naomi said aloud. "This here what I been waiting on, shoot!" she added as she closed the menu and crossed her legs.

"Make that four spicy gumbo appetizers," Kimi quickly followed. "Me, Koko and Udelle wanna see what that's about. We'll order our entrees when you get back."

"I will personally prepare your orders," Katrina smiled. She then noticed a set of empty chairs behind Naomi and company's table. "Is anyone seated there?" she asked.

Naomi looked around and said, "I don't think so."

"Well, I know there're some customers waiting to get in. I'll have the maître d call for four."

"Umm, I think some people were sitting there. They got up to use the bathroom." Koko remarked as she shook her head at her mother.

"Mea culpa," Naomi silently mouthed.

"Okay. I'll have someone grab their orders when they return," Katrina replied as she turned and walked back into the kitchen shaking in her heels.

Naomi was the one person Katrina wanted to please with her recipes. Her hands were shaking as she grabbed a ceramic bowl and ladle, preparing to scoop. Several minutes later, she emerged with a silver tray holding four bowls of steamy gumbo over rice that was laced with a thick, brown roux and smothered in blacken shrimp and andouille sausage. She walked past several of her wait staff taking orders from Dawk, Oneika, Samantha, Amber, Lee and Victor and returned to Naomi, Kimi, Koko and Udelle's table. Ben was now standing with his back to her talking to a lady seated at the table behind Naomi.

Katrina made it over to Naomi's table and set bowls of gumbo before everyone and stepped back. She watched anxiously as Naomi slowly pulled a silver spoon from her rolled cloth napkin and held it up to the light and checked it for spots. "Was the silverware steamed at the proper temperature?" she asked while witnessing her reflection in the eating utensil.

"Momma, stop playing!" Kimi laughed as she wiped her spoon and began mixing the gumbo.

"She got a hundred and five on the inspection, but I know my word carry weight." Naomi chuckled. "Okay, let me stop messing with you, Katrina baby." It seemed as if everything was playing out in slow motion as Naomi's spoon slid into Katrina's gumbo. She came up with a scoop and blew it to cool it before sliding her lipstick-coated lips over the helping of seafood delight. "Oh my God," Naomi sighed through closed eyes as she savored the spicy concoction.

"You like it, Naomi?" Katrina coyly asked.

Naomi kept chewing and gave a thumbs up and said, "Send us your best bottle of red wine and an entire round of spicy gumbo entrees, baby," she added as Koko, Kimi and Udelle, all of whom had tasted the meal nodded in agreement while giving thumbs up and stuffing more food into their mouths.

"Be right back!" Katrina stated proudly.

"Baby?" Ben called out.

"Yeah?" Katrina responded as she turned to face Ben.

"This here lady wanna place an order."

"I'll send a waiter right over," Katrina remarked as she went up and hugged Ben. "Naomi liked the gumbo!"

"Let me see what that gumbo taste like, Katrina, don't leave me hanging!" the woman stated out loud.

Like a baby amongst a room filled with hundreds of mothers, Katrina recognized that single voice. She wondered if her mind was playing tricks on her, or was she actually hearing what her ears were reporting to her brain correctly. Easing around Ben, her eyes focused in on the woman seated at the table and began to water as the image of Faye Sanders came into view.

All of a sudden, Katrina's life flashed before her eyes. From her earliest memories of being spoon fed by Faye when she was a toddler, to nights spent in smoke-filled rooms sleeping on bare mattresses listening to her mother moan and walking amongst filth when she was seven and eight years old. The day she burnt her hands trying to feed herself and how she'd lost her virginity. How Manny and Ben protected her in her vulnerable time. Katrina's memory of her mother consisted of nothing but heartache and pain. There was very little to smile about having been raised the daughter of a junky, but there was a part of Katrina where she blamed herself for thirteen years of disconnect with Faye: the day her mother returned and visited her at Ben's dope house on Piety Street back in 1996.

That day could've been the day she and her mother began to make amends, but Katrina was too hurt and angry to forgive. Having grown in years and wisdom, however, twenty-eight year Katrina Holland had become a different woman. She was no longer the angry, promiscuous teenager of her youth; instead, she was a grown woman with the capacity to forgive those who'd transgressed against her in times past.

With a face full of tears, Katrina walked over to Faye, who sat with trembling lips and a heart pounding and begging for forgiveness from within as tears dripped out of her eyes. She knelt down at her mother's side as everyone inside the restaurant grew quiet, and whispered, "I never thought I'd see you again, Faye."

"I always knew I would see you again, Katrina. If only to be able to say that I'm sorry for not being a good mother to you. I let you down. That's all I ever wanted to say. I let you down and I'm sorry."

"You did let me down," Katrina admitted through her tears. "But I see you're willing to never give up on your daughter. You want me to forgive you? Well, I do, momma. I forgave you a long time ago," the emotional woman cried as she leaned in and wrapped her arms around her mother. "A long time ago," she softly confessed.

Faye gripped Katrina and cried aloud, "My daughter! This is my daughter, everybody!"

Ben stood beside Katrina and Faye and smiled along with

everybody else as they all watched mother and daughter embrace. The family was wondering how Katrina would react to seeing her mother for the first time in over a decade, and by all accounts, it'd been a reunion that was having a positive beginning.

"I didn't come by myself," Faye said as she leaned back and smiled at Katrina.

"Who came with you, Faye?" Katrina asked in wonderment.

"I know Manny would be smiling from ear to ear seeing you and your mother reunite," a woman stated.

Without a second thought, Katrina stood and ran towards the voice. "Momma Joyce!" she screamed through wide, stunned eyes. The two embraced in the center of the restaurant and it was there that Katrina had broken down completely. It was easy for all to discern that the woman named Joyce had more of an impact on Katrina than her biological mother, but both meetings were touching to the heart nonetheless.

Miss Joyce held onto Katrina and said, "Me and Faye, we, we found your father, baby."

"My father? Where is he?" Katrina asked as she looked around the restaurant for an unfamiliar face.

"He's not here, but he sent his sons on his behalf."

"His sons?" Katrina asked as she eyed a slender, dark-skinned male with dreadlocks hanging just below his shoulders and another yellow-skinned overweight young man in a tuxedo, who was being followed by a slender teenage female, walking her way. "I have a daddy and brothers?"

Miss Joyce kissed Katrina's forehead and said, "This is your brother Jason David Cottonwood, your brother Donnell Cottonwood, and your niece Nancy Cottonwood, she's your oldest brother Eddie's daughter."

Katrina had a hard time taking it all in. She took in her brothers' appearance, seeing images of herself in their faces. She had Jay-D's cheekbones and skin tone, Donnell's eyes and Nancy was the spitting image of her when she was younger. It was love at first sight. A family. Relatives. A bloodline. It was as if the outside world no longer existed as Katrina walked amongst her family. "Hey," was all she could manage to say as she stood in reverential awe of the people with whom she shared the same bloodline.

A booth in the back of the restaurant was cleared out as Ben walked up and whispered into Katrina's ear, "Let's go sit down and have dinner with your family, baby. JoAnne 'nem got the kitchen."

"No," Katrina protested. "I, I wanna serve my family. Everything! Tonight? This is a dream come true for me! I've, I always wanted this!" Katrina let go as she reached out and hugged Dooney, whom she felt an instant connection to for some unknown reason.

"Show us you can burn some pots, sis." Dooney laughed as he held onto Katrina. "It was hard not being able to come down here, ya' feel?"

"Y'all knew?"

"Been knew since last month," Jay-D remarked as he reached out and hugged Katrina. "We been looking forward to this day. I wanna know everything there's to know, fam."

"Sis, we didn't know how you was gone act being hit all at once but we chanced it anyway!" Nancy stated as she herself hugged Katrina.

"That's your sister, I mean that's your niece, girl!" Dooney quipped.

"I know, but she feel like a big sister and shit already. Let me have my moment, man." Nancy retorted as she held onto Katrina and smiled through closed eyes. For Nancy, this was all she ever wanted. She'd always dreamed of having an older sister. Katrina may have been her aunt, but she would always be big sister in her eyes.

Katrina laughed and backed away from Nancy. "Faye, Momma Joyce?" she smiled proudly as she reached out her hands. "Let me seat y'all. Come on," she ended as she guided her family to a large booth at the back of the restaurant.

CHAPTER THIRTY-TWO

POOL BLUNTS AND COGNAC

I gotta say that Club Indigo's opening night had been a tremendous success for the family. They'd cleared $125,000 dollars on V.I.P. suites alone. Liquor sales were through the roof, and meals being sold inside the club were nearly as much as Katrina's take inside The New Orleans Café. In total, the family had cleared over four hundred thousand dollars their opening night. It would be fair to say that Club Indigo and its accompanying restaurant was now the hottest club in the Greater Saint Louis vicinity. After parlaying all day Sunday, it was now time for everybody to head back to their respective homes and get back down to business as a couple of prearranged dates and deals had come out of the club's opening night.

In a few days, I was flying back down to Grand Cayman Island to score another three hundred bricks, but before I did, I had a couple of things to take care of back in Arizona. Everyone involved in Katrina's reunion last night had exchanged addresses and numbers. Katrina and her people were now making plans to visit Big Eddie and Eddie Junior in Rockville Prison in a few weeks and she was expecting a call from her father in a few days.

The Jane Dow Band had performed a Fleetwood Mac song and had impressed Jay-D with their performance. Jane was now in the opening phases of securing a record deal to begin recording an album that would be distributed through Dirty

Deeds. A lot of good had come out that grand opening and it was a night I'm sure everyone who'd witnessed it all would never forget it.

The family was pouring out of suites inside the Ritz Carlton in downtown Saint Louis preparing to catch flights back to their hometowns. Naomi was leading the way with me and the rest of the family following close behind. Light conversation abounded as we made our way towards the elevators, but I knew off top that one person hadn't much to be happy about: my sister.

Samantha knew Asa Spade had gone to trial and had won his case as she'd called the day after his scheduled court date and had learned the verdict. All night she kept asking me was Ace in town, was he coming to the club. I told her I wasn't sure every time she asked me and left it that, but I knew she was hoping to have her own reunion like Katrina.

By night's end, Asa hadn't made his appearance and Samantha's hopes were dashed when the lights went on inside of Club Indigo after The Jane Dow Band's performance. Asa was nowhere to be found and his not being present had crushed her soul and shattered her dreams of ever seeing dude again. She told me, as we walked up the hall, that she was glad she didn't have to fly back to Arizona as her heart was just not in it on this late evening.

I watched Samantha wheel her suitcase onto one of the elevators amid the jovial laughs of some of the family and followed her on board. "Samantha, you all right, sugar?" I heard Naomi asking her as the doors closed.

"I'm fine, Auntie. Just…just ready to get home and lay down in my bed. If it's all right, me and Amber will fly back into Ponca City in a couple of days with Tre` to pick up Gabby and Tabby."

"Them kittens is walking all over the place and having full conversations with Malaysia and Malara. Gabby and Tabby learning the ways of the world from those two," Naomi laughed.

"We'll be there tomorrow with the quickness then,"

Samantha chided as she leaned into her aunt. "Something I wanted to happen last night didn't happen last night," she then stated softly as she laid her head on Naomi's shoulder.

"Aww," Naomi comforted as she pulled Samantha close and rubbed her shoulder. "Sometimes there's a reason why, baby. But all wishes within reason are realized at the appropriate time God has set for us." Naomi remarked as she eyed me while shaking her head somberly.

"Why God make us wait so long for what we want?"

"Because we may not be ready. It may not be the proper time. Or it may not be in our best interest," I heard Naomi reason as the elevator bell rung, signaling out arrival to the lobby.

"Whatever," Samantha sighed as she led the way off the elevator and began heading for the family's six waiting limousines.

We exited the hotel and spread out under the hotel canopy as chauffeurs began pulling doors open on stretched, white Cadillac Avalanche limousines with mirror-tinted windows while taking our luggage.

Samantha was going for the third Avalanche when Tre` called out to her. "Baby, we over here with Amber!"

"What difference does it make, Tre`? We all going to the same airport, damn!" Samantha screamed as she slammed the door on the one ride, stomped over to Tre`s limousine and jumped into the backseat.

"Ben," Naomi called out to me as I was just about to climb in behind Tre` with Lee and Victor.

"What up, Auntie?"

"Take care of my niece when you get back to Arizona. I hated to see her grow sadder as time ticked down last night."

"It's already done, Auntie," I replied before me and my boys climbed into the limousine.

****

The flight home was a smooth one. Samantha had slept the whole flight with her head on my shoulder. When we touched down, Henrietta was there to greet us and take Katrina and JoAnne 'nem home. Amber had her car in parking and me, Victor and Lee was gone drop Tre' and Samantha off in the H-1 Hummer I'd left in parking.

Wheeling out of the airport, I looked over to Samantha and said, "Sis, we need ta' stop over to the shop before we drop you off."

Samantha curled her lips and sighed as she placed a hand to her forehead said, "That's totally out the way, Ben. Just…look, man, I just wanna go home, alright? I'm tired, I'm frustrated and just wanna be left alone. Y'all men go and take care of whatever y'all need to do without me."

"Nah, we right there," I playfully countered as I jumped onto I-10 and headed west.

"Everybody gets what the fuck they want except me!" Samantha snapped as she began shaking her legs, bumping the insides of her knees together.

Tre', Lee and Victor was silent in the backseats as we rode. The entire time, I had to listen to Samantha rant about how all she wanted was for one thing to happen last night. "I'm happy for Katrina," she stated as she wiped subtle tears from her eyes. "I was hoping, man, hoping that I could…" her voice then trailed off as she went silent. I looked over and saw that her eyes were squint and I could tell she was biting the insides of her cheeks to prevent her from going completely ballistic. I was damn glad when I made it over to the shop to get her out my ear. We usually closed on Sundays, but I had the remainder of my team working on a special project and I was there to see how they was coming along with it.

Lee and Vic hopped out and walked inside the lone open garage door while me, Tre' and Samantha stayed behind.

"You want something to eat from the wing shack up the street, baby?" Tre' asked Samantha from the backseat, breaking the silence.

320

"No, thank you, baby," Samantha answered. She then looked back at Tre` and said, "I'm sorry for how I acted since the lights came on at the club last night. Me and, me and Amber had in mind to try and do that threesome again but I was so pissed that I—"

"Yooo," I interrupted as I opened the door and stepped out of the ride. "What I told you about talkin' like that 'round me, girl?"

Samantha and Tre` both laughed while looking away from me. "Ben, I forgot you was even in the ride," Samantha blushed. "I, I didn't mean to put that out there."

"Too late for that. Y'all some sick individuals," I clapped back as I walked off. "Talkin' about threesomes and shit! Buncha freaks! All three y'all!"

"Don't act like you all innocent, Dirty Red!" Samantha sassed at me from the passenger seat as I rounded the front of the SUV and stepped onto the sidewalk.

"Watch ya' mouth!" I stated while pointing back at my sister before stepping off into the garage.

I went in and checked on the project my boys was working on and listened to a few messages inside my office. I had three new clients lined up for the week and a couple of wire transfers on some jobs my team had completed the week before. I'd just transferred $35,000 dollars to my personal bank account when Lee walked in and said, "We all set up in the lounge, boss."

"For sho'. Let me go and get Samantha so she can calm her friggin' nerves for good this evening."

I walked back outside and saw Tre` and Samantha walking up the sidewalk sharing a wing dinner from the chicken shack down the street. "Thought you ain't want nothing to eat, Samantha," I said to her as I stood in place bumping my fists together with a smirk on my face.

"All the time you took my stomach started pinching my back. With Gabby and Tabby still in Oklahoma I don't have to cook dinner tonight now. I can just hop in my bed and relax."

"Alright, then," I coolly responded. "Before you do that,

though, I gotta handle another piece of business on the inside. Come on chill in the lounge while I handle that there."

"Come on, Ben, I'm ready to go, man!" Samantha complained as she followed me and Tre` back inside the shop.

We made our way through the detail shop where a black on black 2009 Maserati Ghibi sitting on black chrome rims was having tint placed on it. "Looking good, fellas. Make sure that tint come out even for me. This here ride rolling out tonight," I remarked as we walked past the car and entered the showroom where Elton John's opening piano solo to the song *Your Song* was playing over the speakers.

"Ohhh," I heard Samantha say. I looked back and saw her smiling as she bobbed her head up and down. She still was in the blind about what was about to go down. With all the delays, me avoiding of her questions last night and what I knew to be one of her favorite songs playing, she still didn't put the pieces together. She woulda let met walk right through the double doors leading to the lounge had I not stopped and checked the heel of my shoe for a staple that wasn't there.

Samantha walked ahead of me and Tre` and pushed the door open with her elbow as she bit into a chicken wing section. I was staring at her from behind, watching as she froze in place. Slowly, her arms lowered. The bowl of chicken she was holding onto slid from hand along with the wing she'd been snacking on and her hands raised up to her shoulders as she balled up her fists.

I stood with my hands in my suit pants as Samantha slowly turned and said, "You didn't forget about me, brother! You didn't forget!"

I could tell Samantha wanted to run up and hug me, but she was so eager to get to the man sitting at my bar that I just had to propel her. "He waiting on you, yeah? Thank me later if need be. Go on, sis."

Samantha turned and ran into the lounge, leaving me and her husband behind. Tre` walked up and held the door open for me and I got to see my sister and Asa Spade embrace for the first time in eight years, nearly to the day she and Trudy Tucker had joined the Navy on March, 9 2002 when she was only eighteen years-old. She held onto Asa Spade with her head planted in the crevice of his neck and all I could see was her black, curly mane and the back of her knee-length skirt as her body heaved uncontrollably.

"I thought I was never going to see you again! I thought you just went away from me after you got out of jail, daddy!" I heard her cry out. "I missed you so much! I missed everybody! All y'all!"

"As long as I'm breathing, and if it's ever a way possible, I'll always be a part of your life, Samantha," I heard Asa Spade say. The man who'd been a father to my sister eyes watered as he looked over to me while I walked up to him.

"Ben, I can't repay you for what you done for me and my people, man. Samantha like the daughter I never had and one of the most precious things in my life." Asa Spade remarked over the music.

I shook Asa Spade's freehand and nodded understandingly. "My sister was at the weakest point of her life," I said to him. "Being the man you were back then? Her entire life could've been totally different, brer. But because of the man you were back then, she was able to fly if you get my point."

"I understand the metaphor," Asa said in a serious tone as he kept a firm grip on my hand. "Thanks for all you've done for us, brother."

"I'm the one that's thankful." I humbly countered.

I found myself getting emotional over this here reunion. I ain't had a clue that I even had a sister back in the day because of my repressed memories. While I was down in New Orleans doing my thing, my baby sister was up in Kansas City fending for herself while living with the sociopath who'd killed our parents. Vegas could've been the end of the road for Samantha had not Asa Spade showed up the night she was about to be raped in that alley. From there, dude could've turned her out, had her selling herself on the streets and crushing her dreams in the process. Ace let her live, though. He took my sister to her dreams and made sure she became something in life despite his lifestyle. I'm forever indebted to him, whether he know it or not.

Samantha's sobs broke me from my thoughts as I wiped my watery eyes and coughed. "Let's have a drink," I remarked as I walked behind the bar.

"I swear I thought you gave up on me, dad," I heard Samantha remark as I placed a corkscrew into a bottle of champagne and popped the top.

I looked up to see Samantha's friends Xiang, the dude Dougie and the black/Italian chick, Francesca, surround her. They all hugged in a circle, kinda like the day me and Henrietta had found Samantha when she returned stateside after losing Trudy. I'm happy for my sister. She'd been reunited with the survivors of the first real family she'd ever known and was deserving of every moment of happiness bestowed upon her on this day.

"To deny or forget about you would invalidate my existence," I heard Asa remark as I poured up glasses. "You gave me real purpose, baby girl," he added as he looked into her eyes. "I never stopped being proud of you. I knew you were going to make it. I knew it!" he stated through a proud smile.

"I made it because of you, daddy. Because of you. What are you going to do now?"

"I don't know what I'm gone do, baby girl," Asa remarked. "This here wasn't of my doing, but I'm loving every second that passes by. Me and everyone else with me have nowhere else to go. We skated on the trial you knew about, but we not in the clear. We got the feds all over our ass, and I'd rather never see you again in life than to give you the kind of reunion you was hoping for in Saint Charles if only to save your life and have you not get involved in my shit."

Samantha looked up into Asa's eyes and just stared as tears dripped from her chin. "I have plenty of room, daddy. Tre`? Would you mind if we open our home?"

"What?" Tre` laughed lightly. "The man who allowed me to

marry the greatest woman I've ever met in life got a place to lay his head."

"I'm sorry," Samantha meekly stated. "Daddy? This is my husband, Tre` Mitchell. We have twin daughters named Gabriella and Tabitha. Tre` runs this business with my brother, and his friends Lee and Victor over there."

"You taking care of my daughter?" Asa chided as he shook Tre`s hand.

"Me and Ben both." Tre` affirmed.

"Alright, y'all," I said as I downed my drink. "Let's make this here official." I held up my glass and toasted everyone. "To family," I remarked as I extended my stem glass.

"And to freedom!" Asa added as we all touched rims and sunk back into a family atmosphere.

****

After everything had calmed down with Samantha, and while she was preoccupied with catching up on old times with Xiang, Francesca and Dougie, me, Lee, Victor and Asa Spade had dipped off into my office for a game of pool, blunts and cognac. I broke the game open as Asa stood beside the table toking on bubble gum Kush. He choked off of that potent and shook his head.

"I ain't had nothing like that in a while, Ben," he coughed.

"I know, fam. We got what's good all the way around, ya' feel?" I smirked as I called low ball on the table. I lined my cue up and knocked a ball in and said, "Dawk had in mind to give you a job overseeing the club in Saint Louis, but as you know, feds lurking out there. We doing good with the drops over that water in East Saint Louis and think its best you and your crew not hit the scene in Saint Charles just yet."

"What we supposed to do in the meantime?" Asa asked me.

"Just live, brother. Take a breather until the streets clear up."

"Taking a breather wasn't my plan," Asa countered.

"But it sounds good, baby," I heard Xiang tell Ace. "We've

earned it."

"We did. I'd like to take a trip to see my family in Italy," Francesca said. "I feel I earned that."

"Y'all earned y'all keep around here," I remarked as Lee put four hundred thousand dollars on display. "That's a hundred racks for each of y'all. There gone be more where that come from, but the family asking that y'all lay low for now. We gone get y'all back in the action in due time."

"I can live for a minute off this, dude," Dougie said to me as he picked up a stack of money. "I'm probably gone get a couple of outfits and hit the club scene down here, ya' know? I'm gone need some wheels, too."

"Got y'all covered, fam. That Maserati we was looking at in the garage while we was heading over to this here office? That's for y'all." I replied as I threw the keys onto the table. "We keep cars available, so it ain't a thang. We inviting y'all to lay up on our dime. Take it."

Xiang picked up the keys and twirled them in her hands. She looked over to me like she was surprised that I would offer such a gift. I was nothing big in my eyes, and I'm sure she was used to being in the realm of luxury, but I could tell she now understood that I had my shit together and was only looking out for our crew and willing to help them get back on their feet.

"This means much," Xiang said to me as she raised her glass and nodded.

I raised my glass from across the table and pointed at Xiang. "It's a family thang," I let it be known before taking a quick sip to be cordial in return.

"How's JunJie doing, Ben?" Asa Spade asked me as he grabbed a cue stick.

"JunJie is doing as good as a man could be that's locked up. He know y'all beat the rap, too. He told me over the phone to tell y'all to stay outta trouble." I sneered as I took another shot and missed.

"Is that right?" Asa laughed as he chalked up his cue stick. "Advice warranted from the wise man. I can take his advice for now, but the streets is how we survive, my brother. Tell JunJie that next time you talk to him," he said to me as he missed a shot. "Let me ask you something, Ben," he then remarked as he sipped his drink. "You really gone let Phil and Grover do that thing with the feds?"

"They be heading to the east coast soon to take down Tammy Moto. I gave 'em every chance to back out, but it done got way too personal between them and the feds."

"You think they gone pull it off?" Asa asked me as I lined up my final shot.

"To be honest, I don't know, fam, but they earned that right. It's not gone be on our hands no matter the outcome, but if I was a betting man? I'd put my money on the Asians. They just sick enough to pull that shit off." I replied as I sunk the eight ball.

"If they do, it'll be one of the coldest moves any organization ever attempted. Guess we'll see," Asa replied. "Rerack. Turn the music up and fire up that smoke, man! Shit! Asa Spade home, baby!" he laughed as he began throwing balls back onto the table.

CHAPTER THIRTY-THREE

THE UGLY TRUTH

It was month after Asa Spade's release. Mid-April 2009. The weather was warm down in Ponca City as the family all geared up for Spoonie's return, but there was another event to be shared on this day as well: that of Dawk and Oneika's marriage.

Ponderosa was swirling with activity as the family prepared meals, went over renditions while setting up the patio area for the upcoming event. Everybody was on hand contributing to the Cause and the atmosphere was radiant. The past four months had been some of the most trying times for many in the family and a day like today was not only welcomed, it was needed. And while most, such as Irene and Sharona, were turning over new leaves and getting past their animosities, some in the family were bothered by some of the things that'd gone down over the past four months. One person, who was particularly bothered and had unanswered questions, was Dimples.

As she, Tak and Tacoma rode onto the property this early morning hour in their new Range Rover with Tak behind the wheel, Dimples looked down at the set of keys she'd found a few days earlier that was resting under her dresser. The day she and Tak had returned from Oklahoma City with Francine's RV, Dimples noticed that Bianca's things had been cleared out of the room she'd been sleeping in. She'd called her sister phone and when it rang, Dimples heard it coming from the

329

shelf inside her dining room. She went and retrieved the phone, expecting Bianca to return later on in the day, but she never did.

Later that night, Dimples drove over to her mother's home and asked if Mary had seen or heard from Bianca and Mary replied that she hadn't.

"But all her stuff is gone, momma," Dimples complained. *"You think she left? If she did, why didn't she let me know she was leaving like that?"*

"I don't know, Regina. Maybe she felt it wasn't a need to inform you. And if she left this morning she may not have made it back to Vegas yet. I'm sure she'll call once she settles back into her home."

"How can she when she left her phone behind?" Dimples wondered out loud.

"Those things sometimes happen," Mary comforted. *"Just mail it back to her when she calls."*

"I guess you're right," Dimples replied somewhat unsure. *"I have a charger that matches Bianca's phone. I'll keep it powered up until she calls."*

That call never came for Dimples, however; now four months removed from her sister's sudden disappearance, she was left with more questions than answers. Riding onto the ranch no longer had the same excitement it'd been carrying for years on end now in Dimples' eyes. The hundreds of acres of land was becoming a place of mystery to her as two people she cared about in life had visited, been rejected by the family outright, and then mysteriously dropped off the face of the earth. Horses galloped and cows grazed on this seemingly tranquil land that was becoming a place of dread for Dimples as she knew the capabilities of some inside the family. To her, it wasn't a coincidence that her father and sister had vanished, and her finding Bianca's set of keys only added to the mystery that'd been thrust into her lap.

Tak pulled the family's SUV around the backside of the home and Dimples was out of the ride before he could place it into park. She ran up the stairs and entered the home through a set of French doors. "Momma!" she called out, forcing the activity to cease.

"Dimples, are you okay?" Francine inquired as she dried her hands on an apron.

"Where's my mother?" Dimples fretted as she held onto Bianca's keys.

"What's the matter?" Francine asked as she held onto Dimples arms to calm her.

"I found Bianca's keys while I was cleaning my bedroom the other day! Since January I been waiting on her to call but she never did! I just assumed that she forgot about me!"

"Maybe she has!" Francine countered. "People do move on you know?"

"How could she move on without her house keys?" Dimples retorted as she dangled the metal key chain before Francine. "Something's going on here and I want to know where and what happened to my sister and my daddy!"

"Momma coming with Spoonie, everybody!" Walee was then heard yelling from the front of the home as he, Tyke and Kahlil trotted down the grand staircase.

Mary ran into the kitchen at that moment, having heard Dimples call out for her. "What's going on?" she asked as she hurried over to Dimples' side.

"Spoonie's arrived." Francine smiled, trying to divert the tension. "Come on, Dimples."

"No, Francine!" Dimples snapped as she pulled away from the woman.

Francine threw her hands up and turned to Mary. "She's all up in arms over Bianca leaving without giving notice," she told Mary, subtly giving her a heads up on what was to be expected.

Mary eyed her daughter without saying a word as she reflected briefly on all that'd gone down over the past nine months or so. Like Francine, she knew everything. She knew what'd become of Reynard, and she also knew what Siloam had done to Bianca. "Francine? Everybody? Go on and welcome Spoonie home. I'll talk to Regina. Come on, baby."

Back in the day, Mary was never the one who would even consider condoning the violence the family perpetrated against others. It'd taken her nearly being murdered to understand that what Naomi had done, was for not only the betterment, but for the preservation of life on the ranch. Reynard was going to kill her she understood. And Bianca may have very well sought to finish the job had Siloam not killed her instead. For Mary, the things she were about to reveal wasn't about keeping the affair Siloam and Takoda engaged in hidden from Regina, it was all about exposing the ugly truths her father and sister were plotting against the two of them.

Leading Dimples down the hall, Mary guided her daughter to the theatre room where the two sat alone under the dim lights on the front row. Side by side the two sat in total silence as the joyous sounds of Spoonie being welcomed back into the home echoed up and down the pristine hall that lay behind the closed doors.

"I don't know how you're going to take this, Regina," Mary finally stated once the celebration outside began to die down. "And I hope to God it doesn't place you at odds with the family," she added as she crossed her legs and rested her forehead in the palm of her right hand.

"Take what?" Dimples asked as she looked over to Mary.

Silent tears began to form in Mary's eyes. "The night Spoonie was shot," she began. "We were in town to look for a new mansion on Naomi's behalf, remember?"

"Yeah, I remember."

"A couple of days before that, your father flew into town unannounced. He and Siloam, he and Siloam were going to come into the guest home, take me over to the barn and have me open the safe to where the veterinarian medications are stored. They were going to make it, they were going to make it look as if some drug addicts had stolen the drugs and killed me in the process."

"I don't believe you," Dimples seethed as she as she leaned away from her mother.

"I wasn't expecting you to, Regina. Truth can be stranger than fiction sometimes, but I'd rather be veracious with you rather than make up some fantasy that everything is okay with Reynard and Bianca because it's not. It's just not, baby."

Dimples looked the floor downtrodden. "Will I ever see them again?" she asked as tears filled her eyes while deep down inside, already knowing the answer to her question.

"No." Mary stated as she licked the corners of her mouth, absorbing her salty tears as she looked Dimples square in the eyes. "They've, they've been removed."

"Removed?" Dimples gasped as she stood to her feet. "What the fuck does that mean? Removed?"

"You watch your mouth with me! And you know very well what I'm referring to, Regina!" Mary snapped as she jumped from her seat.

"Who did it? Who inside the family killed them?"

"What difference does it make? They were going to kill *me*! Why can't you understand that, Regina?" Mary asked whille standing before her daughter.

"I don't care about that! I wanna know who killed my father and sister!"

Mary's jaw dropped as she eyed her daughter in dismay. And right away, Dimples had just realized what she'd said. "Momma, I'm sorry. I didn't mean it that way I promise!"

"You would stand there and defend people you barely knew instead of siding with your family? People who wanted to kill me? Take me away from you, my grandson and everybody else in the family?"

"They're my blood, momma! Why shouldn't I care?"

"You're not supposed to care about outsiders! You only shared Reynard and Bianca's DNA!" Mary boomed with tears pouring down her face. "Your real sister was killed in Ghost Town and you never had a father in life!" she declared. "Those people weren't your blood! They were bloodsuckers! Parasites who were only concerned about the almighty dollar who didn't give a damn about you or anybody else in this family!" she ended as she turned away from Regina.

Dimples covered her face as she cried aloud. "I knew! Deep down I knew it wasn't real! But I wanted to believe! A father? And another sister? That was real to me! To *me*!" she emphasized as she patted her chest while looking at her mother. "And no one had a right to take that away!"

Mary had her back to Dimples and was intently listening as her daughter expressed her pain. She understood what her child was going through as theirs wasn't a normal upbringing. Mary was basically a child herself when she entered Ghost Town, her and Martha both. She, Martha, Dimples and Ne`Ne` had all grown up together in a poverty-stricken, violent environment that offered little hope for a better life. Yet they'd survived. By the grace of God they survived. Had held on just long enough for the big sister they always knew existed had found them and rescued them from a life of despair.

Mary was on the verge of committing suicide when Naomi rode into their neighborhood in her rig. She thought she'd never see Martha again in life and was only hoping for the best for Dimples once she was gone. When she reached Ponca City, however, the dreadful emotions and self-pity she carried, had dissipated. For a long time, Mary had been secretly ashamed of herself for wanting to give up on life, and more importantly, for having contemplated going through with a selfish act that would've ruined her only surviving daughter for all times. She was once Dimples. That one person in the family who questioned why those who lived outside of the law did the things they did and lived the way they lived.

Doss' death had opened Mary's eyes to the truth. No longer was she that naïve woman living a utopian dream. Hers was a family of gangsters that refused to allow anyone against them to gain the upper hand. Reynard and Bianca Jacobs were two people who'd tried to gain an advantage over the family and they'd come up short. Naomi and Siloam had saved her life, an act that left her indebted, grateful, and now loyal. The problem she now faced was that of getting Dimples to see and understand what she now knew and respected about the family in its entirety.

"You're right, Regina," Mary stated as she turned and faced her daughter. "No one had a *right* to take way something you held dear."

"But?" Dimples said as she picked herself up from the floor.

"But it was a necessary evil and I think you know that already. How would you feel if something would have happened to me? If the family had to carry my casket to Ne'Ne's Hill? How would that make you feel? Because that's what was in store for me had Reynard and then Bianca had gone unchecked."

"Why Siloam? What did she have to do with everything that happened?"

Mary coughed as she stared Regina in the eyes. "I want you to listen to me," she spoke calmly. "Whatever way you feel about this, I want you to just look at the alternative, which is me getting killed."

"What're you tryin' to say, momma?"

Mary stepped closer to Regina, placed a hand on her shoulder and said, "Takoda and Siloam, well, they slept together once."

Regina stood stunned. Her jaw dropped and she backed away from her mother, turned around and placed her hands on her hips. "This, this is what this is all about? This is why they were killed?"

"They were killed because they were trying to kill me, Regina. They had insurance policies on my life. Reynard caught the two of them in the act and started extorting Siloam for sex, and was bribing Takoda to keep quiet. He was only buying time until he could find a way to do it. Siloam uncovered the plan. Had she not had that affair, Reynard would've gotten away with killing me."

"I don't believe you," Dimples seethed as she turned and faced her mother. "Where's Siloam?" she then questioned as she headed towards the theater room stairs.

Mary held Regina back. "No!" she protested. "You're not going to ruin Dawk and Oneika's wedding. You wanted the truth and now you have it!"

"You think I care about a wedding?" Dimples cried. "I want Siloam's ass!" she reiterated as she tried to brush past Mary.

"Sit down!" Mary yelled as she pushed Dimples down into one of the leather chairs on the front row. "You're not leaving this room until you promise not to ruin your cousin's wedding!"

Dimples leaned back in surprise as she eyed her mother standing over her in her tight-fitting sequins dress and three inch heels. The look on her mother's face told her she'd better get it together, but she couldn't find a way to do so just yet so she remained seated with her arms folded like that of a spoiled child being told she couldn't go outside to play. "I'm not believing nothing," she told her mother. "For all I know, this could just be one big lie to get me to side with the family for doing what they did."

Mary bothered not responding as she sat beside Dimples. "I understand how you feel, Regina. But, you're wrong on this," she ended as the two sat in silence inside the dimly-lit room.

Mary didn't know, but as soon as Dimples saw an opportunity, she was going to confront Siloam first chance she got—wedding or no wedding.

****

Back over to the north side of town, Siloam and Montenegro and four more ranch hands were just emerging from Oneika's parents' pristine brick, one story home being followed by Oneika, her parents and a large portion of Oneika's family, most of whom now lived in Dodge City, Kansas and had driven into town to be in attendance of their most beloved family member's special day.

Dressed in a white sequins dress and three-inch heels, Siloam reached back and helped guide Oneika down the stairs. She was seven months pregnant now and fully showing through her dress. "You look beautiful, girl!" Siloam exclaimed happily as she held onto Oneika's arm.

"Thank you, Siloam," Oneika replied as she raised the lower portion of her white bride's gown to prevent the train from dragging along the ground.

Siloam took in Oneika's appearance as she walked beside her. The Caucasian/Creek Indian woman's mane of brown hair was cut just below her neck and curled. She wore little makeup save for a nude foundation. Her brown eyes were full of joy on this warm, cloudless spring morning. Siloam's take was that Oneika would make a perfect wife for Dawk. She was homegrown. A boss's wife. Not one to dabble into Dawk's affairs, yet knowing all along the man he was while remaining loyal.

Bay and T-top, meanwhile, were sitting in one the family's Suburbans along with AquaNna, Kimi, Koko and Tyke and Oneika's niece, who was to be the second flower girl alongside a wheel chair-bound Spoonie. The females were all going to caravan back over to Ponderosa and meet the bridegrooms. They all sat and watched as the bride was escorted up the sidewalk towards Naomi's white on white bulletproof Phantom with a dozen or so members of her family behind her. She was helped into the back seat of the car and Siloam climbed into the front seat with Montenegro behind the wheel.

"Is the lovely bride all set?" Montenegro asked through a side smile while peering over the back seat.

"She sure is," Oneika smiled. "God, I can't believe it!" she happily stated as she looked back at her family climbing into their cars.

"Okay, let's get you home," Montenegro stated as he placed the car in drive.

"They leaving us!" Tyke yelled from the Suburban she sat in with her sisters. One of the family's ranch hands had just placed the car in drive when one of Oneika's relatives backed out of the driveway. The rented Dodge Murango was placed in drive, but the SUV had stalled out, blocking the road for a moment.

The ranch hand climbed out and trotted over to the vehicle. "What's the matter," the muscular, young Mexican, who was dressed in a white tuxedo asked.

"It won't start," Oneika's aunt replied as she turned the car over repeatedly.

"We have room," the ranch hand stated. "We'll push this car aside and you can all ride with a few of us. We'll come back tomorrow and look at the car, but we have to move it out of the way because it's blocking everyone else," he stated as he whistled for several more ranch hands to help push the car back into the driveway.

Back inside the Phantom, Siloam, Montenegro and Oneika were nearing the subdivision's exit. Montenegro had just flipped on the right turn signal when three Kay County Sheriff patrol cars swung in off the main road and surrounded the pristine ride. Five men hopped out with shotguns pointed at the ride as they crouched down behind their cars.

Oneika instinctively covered her swollen belly and crouched down in the backseat as Montenegro and Siloam both grabbed their Tech-9 semiautomatic pistols.

"What they want?" Siloam asked as her adrenaline began to flow.

"It's that Nimitz guy," Montenegro scowled as he kept his eyes focused on Nimitz, who'd just walked past his guys and was now nearing the Phantom. The Mexican kept his hand on his weapon as Nimitz approached and tapped on the window. "What?" he asked while eyeing the Sherriff of Ponca City.

Nimitz couldn't hear Montenegro through what he now realized was bulletproof glass. He reached over and grabbed his shoulder-mounted radio and clicked. "Hold your fire, guys. They're a packing. Bullets just gonna bounce off, too. Let me incapacitate the driver and clear you all's line of fire." Nimitz stated just before making a winding motion with his hand to signify to Montenegro that he needed to roll down the driver's side window.

Montenegro raised his hand towards the button to lower the

window. Siloam, however, reached out and stopped him by pulling his hand away from the controls. "No, Montenegro!"

"What's the matter, Siloam?"

"We don't know what this guy wants. Why is he stopping us? Why're his men holding shotguns on us?"

"Let it down!" Sheriff Nimitz commanded while repeatedly tapping on the window. "Just wanna ask Oneika Brackens back there some questions!"

Just then, the entire caravan, five cars of family members that'd been held back in front of Oneika's parents' home, rounded the corner. Oneika's father was in the lead car. When he saw Naomi's Phantom, the car he knew to be carrying his only daughter, surrounded by Sheriff's deputies with shotguns aimed at its windows, he slammed his Cadillac LTS into park and jumped out of the car in his tuxedo and held his arms up high. "I'm unarmed!" he yelled aloud as he slowly walked over to Sheriff Nimitz. "What's going on here?"

Nimitz had no intention on exposing his hand, neither that of his actual intent, so he shifted direction. "Got word through the town paper that a wedding was taking place today, Mister Brackens," he smiled. "Thought we'd tag along and give the bride a full escort as it is our duty!"

August Brackens, a forty-eight year-old Creek Indian, and former city council member therein Ponca City, eyed the Sheriff he'd known for some years now with a hint of suspicion. "Nimitz, you and I both know that this is all unnecessary. You're making a scene and you're frightening my daughter. Tell your men to put their guns away!"

"It was for our safety, August! Do you know who you're daughter's marrying today?" Nimitz asked as he backed away from the Phantom.

"Do you?" August asked as his face wrinkled.

"Ya' damn right I do! And I wouldn't risk putting my men in harm's way. Hell, I'm doing your ass a favor! You and ya' daughter both! You were once a good man, August. What ever happened to you, man?"

"I'm still the same man I was some years ago, Nimitz. Can you say the same?" August asked as several members of his family, along with that of Bay and T-top climbed from their rides and walked up on the group.

Bay walked up and stood alongside August and eyed the Sheriff in her white Tuxedo as she kept her hands raised to her sides. "We have a wedding to attend and you're blocking our way, man." she told Nimitz.

Nimitz eyed the group of people before him and chuckled in response as he turned and began walking off. He waved over towards the men with him and said, "Day's shot, guys! Our services aren't warranted. You people have a safe time at it," he ended as he turned and eyed Bay seriously. He then looked over to the Phantom and then eyed August for several seconds before walking off while twirling a single finger in the air. "Wrap it up, men! Time for some lunch! Let the good people be for now!"

As the family dispersed, Bay and August remained standing side by side. Both couldn't help but to wonder why Nimitz had ridden down on the family with such a show of force. "Think this has something to with Tonto?" August asked Bay.

"I can't say right now, Mister Brackens. All I know is that we have to protect Oneika until we find out what's going on exactly because Sheriff Nimitz isn't to be trusted. There's security around the clock on the ranch. She'll be safe there inside the home Dawk built for her and your grandchild," she ended as she turned and walked back towards the Suburban with her head bowed in deep thought.

Meanwhile, back on the ranch, as the caravan began rolling once again, Regina, now with calmed nerves, exited the theatre room with Mary following close behind. She'd promised her mother that she wasn't going to make a scene, but she'd had her fingers crossed at the time, a superstitious way of asking God for forgiveness of the lie she'd told and what she'd actually planned on doing the time she laid eyes on Siloam.

As she walked up the marble-floored corridor leading out into the open area of the first floor inside Ponderosa, she could see countless family members moving about. Their joyful, spirited voices echoed in her ears as her dark-brown eyes scanned the people, searching for one person in particular to no avail.

"Seats, everybody! Seats now!" Francine could be heard yelling aloud as Regina neared the end of the wide hall. Faces were all against her in seemingly loathing protests it seems, but in all actuality, the family was merely preparing to welcome the arriving bride and were unaware of the contempt Regina was carrying in her heart.

When she cleared the hall, Regina caught a glimpse of Martha, Ben, Lee Sato and Victor Felix walking out onto the patio in their white attire. *Did they know? Were they involved?* was the questions she silently asked herself.

"Regina, help us with these flowers, please? We only have a few minutes before Oneika arrives," a voice called out. "Regina? Regina, you hear me?" the voice called again, shaking Regina from her trance. She looked to her left and saw Naomi and Sharona Benson clipping the ends of white tulips and placing them into some white silk bags resting in Spoonie's lap.

None of the beauty unfolding on this day mattered to thirty-two year-old Regina Holland-Kitori. She was aiming to have a confrontation on this day. Siloam was wrong for sleeping with her man was her reasoning as she walked over and grabbed a handful of white tulips.

Naomi watched as her niece picked up a pair of scissors and aggressively clipped the ends of the tulips. "You okay, child?" she asked.

"Umm, hmm," Dimples nonchalantly answered as she grabbed the last set of tulips and clipped the ends. She then threw the flowers into Spoonie's lap and abruptly walked off.

"What's wrong with her, Naomi?" Sharona asked as she gathered the flowers and helped Spoonie place them inside the silk clothes.

"Nothing I can't handle," Naomi replied as she eyed

Dimples walking off with the scissors.

Just then, Walee, Kahlil and Jordan Whispers walked through the front door. "Bay 'nem on the main road about to turn in, momma," Walee remarked.

"Okay. You all wheel Spoonie out and get her to the edge of the patio stairs so she can be ready when they pull up," Naomi replied as she saw the group off.

Dimples was ahead of Spoonie and company. She emerged onto the patio and encountered row after row of white chairs facing the patio's entrance with the scissors hidden behind her back and sat quietly on the front row to her right.

Back out on the road leading to the ranch, Siloam and Montenegro led the way inside Naomi's Phantom. Siloam was looking over the backseat to make sure nothing happened to the caravan. She felt the car turning to the left and sat back down in her seat as the cars all cruised onto the property. "This wedding is going to be awesome!" she stated in jubilance as the cars traveled over the land, the front side of Ponderosa now coming into view.

The large, extravagant patio on the back side of the mansion, meanwhile, was filled to near capacity. Dozens of family and friends sat facing the back of the mansion as Spoonie was wheeled out of the middle set of French doors and positioned at the edge of the stairs. Some in the crowd had stood and taken pictures while others like Henrietta Jenkins and Rolanda Jones, filmed the entire event.

Dimples remained seated, facing the left set of patio doors when she eyed Naomi walking out of the middle set of doors in her tight-fitting, white sequins dress and white stilettoes with her black hair straight-pressed and wearing a pair of dark-tinted shades while holding onto a manila folder.

Naomi eyed Dimples through her lens for a few seconds before walking over and handing her the folder. She then leaned down and said, "This is your last chance to get your act together. Don't you ever feel sorry for the people who were out to kill your mother no matter what Siloam did. Had not she fucked your husband, my sister would be dead. Read this, because something good did come out of Takoda's betrayal. And just so you know? Siloam is not your problem. Your man is. You deal with him, but not here, not now, and not today. Understand?" she ended as she walked away without waiting for a response from her niece.

Dimples pouted and grabbed the folder from Naomi's hands just as Dawk walked out onto the patio in his white tuxedo. He looked over to Dimples through his clear lens with a stern look on his face that said, *"Don't' fuck my day up."*

Dimples then looked over to Naomi just as her aunt had taken her seat beside Francine on the opposite front row. Off in the distance over Naomi and Francine's shoulder, and clearly visible, was Moses' pen—the last living creature to ever touch the flesh of her blood kin without Dimples ever knowing.

Obeying Naomi's orders, Dimples opened the folder as the tops of the Suburbans came into view over the side of the patio and to her back as she began reading over what she could clearly see was that of a life insurance policy…

Company: Prudential Life Insurance of Las Vegas.

Policy Holder: Mary Holland.

Beneficiary: Reynard Jacobs.

Payout: $500,000

Agent: Bianca Jacobs.

Dimples flipped the page and read over a second policy…

Company: Prudential Life Insurance of Vegas.

Policy Holder: Reynard Jacobs.

Beneficiary: Bianca Jacobs.

Payout: $250,000

Agent: Bianca Jacobs.

It was now clear to Regina that the things her mother had told her earlier were true all along. She was now left with no further recourse, save for the anger she harbored over her husband's betrayal. But could she really be mad under the conditions was a question she was left to ponder as Oneika was helped from Naomi's Phantom by Siloam. Besides documented copies, Dimples found herself staring at photocopies of Bianca's employment badge, her employee number and her actual home address located down in Dallas, Texas. Bianca had stood to gain $250,000 had she been able to prove that her father was actually dead. It was now plain to see for Dimples that her sister really was looking for a payday.

The entire group sitting on patio stood and faced the rear as Oneika's preteen niece took her position behind Spoonie's wheelchair where the two began throwing flowers as the bridesmaids and bridegrooms joined hands and fell into place.

Dimples looked over to Naomi at that moment as tears flowed down her cheeks. She got up and walked over to her aunt and handed her the scissors while nodding a silent nod of approval before walking back over to her seat where she stood and turned to face the bride. Only then did Naomi stand, and from that moment forth, the wedding would unfold unhinged as Dimples had decided on not stabbing Siloam out of rage, but to deal with her husband behind closed doors once everything had settle down.

CHAPTER THIRTY-FOUR

STRIKE UP THE BAND

"Iiayad Sheinheimer is crooked as your friend Ben Holland said," Willameena 'Willie' Slack told Tanya Weinberger as the two sat with their feet inside the warm water of Willie's heated indoor pool inside her two-story brick mansion located west of Washington D.C. in Falls Church, Virginia. "Iiayad is over marketing inside Tropicana Produce, but there's more to his story," Willie added as she tied up her slightly-greying brown hair.

Fifty-six year-old Willameena Slack was a second term Junior Senator from New Orleans, Louisiana, having won her first bid back in 2002. She'd been a state representative for ten years prior to earning her senate seat and her entire career was partly owed to Tanya Weinberger, who'd pumped millions of dollars into each of her campaigns over her fourteen year political career.

Willie had a checkered past, to say the least. She was once a woman of the night, selling sex for dollars alongside the King Sisters in her late teens and early twenties until she made a switch to politics at Tanya's request. She was the Germans' information source being she sat on the Foreign Relations Subcommittee, a committee that investigated international crime and illicit drugs. Willie knew of ongoing investigations, or investigations getting underway as all budget requests for investigations crossed her desk for approval. She was one of the most, if not thee most powerful member within the German organization and was just as dirty as the outlaws inside the family who pushed drugs and killed people for money.

It was now late April, a couple of weeks after Dawk and Oneika's wedding and Tanya was preparing to fulfill the contract Ben Holland had put before her. Willie had just confirmed what Ben had told her at Cincinnati Municipal Lunken Airport back in February and she was now ready to move forward with the Sheinheimer job and the New York hit on the Jamaicans.

"What else is there to Sheinheimer?" Tanya asked Willie as she swayed her feet to and fro inside the warm water.

"Back in ninety-two, when Alfredo was killed? DEA was looking into Iiayad for being affiliated with a man by the name of Rafael Gacha from Bogota, Colombia," Willie began as she sat beside Tanya waving her feet to and fro inside the pool's warm water. "DEA had this program called CENTAC where they were able to listen in on phone calls being made by known men belonging to the Medellin cartel without using a wire. It was fuckin' ingenious," she laughed in admiration of the federal government's prowess. "Pablo had no idea how he was being tracked, Gacha either, but the DEA was noticing a split inside the Cartel and the names Sheinheimer and Gacha kept coming up."

"You mean they could've prevented Alfredo from getting blown to pieces?" Tanya inquired as she grabbed a bottle of baby oil out of a wicker basket situated beside the swimming pool.

"No, babe," Willie assured. "The DEA was able to track those calls using a plane that circled over Bogota. After a few weeks, Gacha and Sheinheimer dropped off the radar. Informants later told the DEA that Sheinheimer was the man behind the shipments Pablo was sending into the United States by rail. Tropicana was and still is just a front for him. He's heavily involved in the cartel business."

"How's he still free? How's he still alive after all this time?"

346

Tanya asked as she shook the bottle of baby oil in order to loosen its contents.

"Killing Pablo was the wrong move," Willie answered as she splashed water up into her face and placed a pair of clear goggles over her brown eyes. "DEA should've brought Escobar in alive and got some intel. Sheinheimer slipped through the cracks and the investigation against him lost its legs when Pablo went down."

"How the government know Iiayad was behind the hit on Alfredo and the Darvish men down in Caracas?" Tanya asked as she squirted baby oil onto her pale skin and began spreading it over her slender arms and legs. "Here," she added as she handed the baby oil to Willie.

Willie took the bottle of baby oil from Tanya, shook it rapidly and flipped the top open. "Our American government has no proof that Sheinheimer was involved in Alfredo and the Darvish men's death 'til this day," she stated as she spread baby oil over skin. "With that being said, it wasn't a coincidence Iiayad's passport was stamped two days before the bombing in Caracas back in ninety-two. Rumor had it that Sheinheimer sat in on a meeting with Gacha and Hugo Chavez the night of the bombing. It has never been confirmed, though, and no one has ever bothered to reopen the Sheinheimer investigation," she let it be known.

"Chavez is the President of Venezuela now. What kind of repercussions would that bring back on us once we kill Sheinheimer?" Tanya asked as her hand flipped through a second wicker basket containing numerous brands of goggles.

"None," Willie replied as she eased into the pool and pushed off from the wall and began treading in twelve-foot deep water. "Chavez takes payment from this guy Gacha, but that's about all. Rumor circulating around the capitol is that Chavez is in failing health. By all accounts he won't be a problem at all."

"What about the Jamaicans in New York?" Tanya asked as she selected a pair of Nike goggles and placed them over her eyes. She then picked up her mimosa and took a sip while looking down at Willie as Willie waded in the clear blue water.

"I couldn't find anything significant on a Jaffrey and Theron Fischer from Kingston." Willie replied as she reached out and grabbed the edge the pool and planted her feet against the wall. "Jaffrey and Theron Fischer aren't under investigation and have no priors. I did uncover that they have a sister named Bridgette Fischer if that helps. You sure you wanna do this, girl?"

"As sure as I sit with one of the most beloved Senators in D.C. at this time," Tanya cooed as she took another sip of her mimosa. She then sat her glass down and said, "I never heard of a Bridgette Fischer. I had Zelda and her girls in the Bronx track down Jaffrey and Theron. They been on those two for the past month. I think now is a good time to send Sascha and Boogie up to the Bronx. Before that happens, I need to know if we have the green light on the Jew. We do have the green light, right?"

Willie nodded while looking up at Tanya. "I would say so. How're you gonna get at 'em, though?"

"I'll figure it out when we get there," Tanya replied as she placed her goggles over her eyes and eased down into the water.

"Let me fill your basket so you can head to the checkout counter with the quickness," Willie stated as she pressed her feet to the edge of the pool and took on a racing stance. "Sheinheimer likes to play tennis in between the hours of nine and eleven in the morning over to an athletics club. It's the only athletics club in Boca Raton and the yard is almost always empty is what my son Popeye tells me after doing surveillance on the guy."

"Good job by Popeye," Tanya replied. "If we play it right, we'll get both jobs done the same night or within a day apart. You ready?" she asked Willie as she pressed her feet to the wall inside the pool, preparing to push off.

"On three," Willie remarked, "but before we do this? You must know while Sheinheimer plays his tennis match alone? He likes to wear these loose, high ass shorts and is a known exhibitionist. Popeye observed him making advances on several women and they left with him in his, his flashy little Mercedes. He likes the athletic, raunchy types that're willing to play his game, if you get my drift."

"I'm drifting with ya', sister," Tanya replied in a cool demeanor as she pushed off from the wall and began freestyling up the middle of the medium-sized pool alongside Willie.

Tanya didn't win the race, but she did go on to enjoy the remainder of the day with her lifelong friend before catching an early flight back down to Cincinnati the following morning where she put everyone involved up on the fact that the crew was now in opening phases of executing their hits.

****

"*...with Gilligaaannn...the skipper, too...a millionaire...and his wife...a movie star...the professor and Mary Ann...here on Gilligan's Isle...*"

"Okay, this is my ninth time watching this dumb show," fifty-six year-old Sascha Merkendorf complained in her heavy German accent as she sat in the backseat of a 2009 black on black Dodge Charger belonging to the Cherryvale Deputy Sheriff's department back over to Kansas as the midnight hour approached. "They have to, they just *have* to make it off that godforsaken island and make it back to civilization," she added as she sat watching Gilligan's Island on a portable DVD player.

Maggie McPherson, who was sitting behind the steering wheel of the souped-up, dark-tinted Charger, looked over to forty-five year-old Cikala Dunbar and shook her head in disgust. "How many times do I have to tell you that they never get off the fuckin' island, Sascha!" she complained.

Sascha mumbled incoherently as the quirky theme song came to an end. "I'm waiting on the part where they kill the guy Gilligan, then. He has to soon go because he's messing it all up for everybody else on the Gilligan's Island!"

"It's called Gilligan's Island for a reason, Sascha, girl!" Cikala Dunbar, a heavy-set, light-skinned Lakota Indian with dyed black hair laughed from the front passenger seat.

"That fat Captain who wears the same shirt everyday should be the one to do it!" Sascha suggested, ignoring her girls' remarks. "He has to do it because he's the only one that can get close enough to Gilligan! Or the woman Mary Ann. She can offer Gilligan some pussy and slit his throat, but she looks like the scary type. The fat Captain may have to kill her after she kills Gilligan to cover his tracks. Someone has to kill Gilligan to get off the island."

Cikala was laughing in silence, her body heaving as she covered her mouth to suppress her delight. Sascha Merkendorf hadn't really caught up to the times, she knew. The six-foot-one, green-eyed giant-of-a-woman spent most of her time watching old TV shows on a portable DVD player she'd gotten for Christmas.

Maggie regretted the day she'd bought Sascha that DVD player because all she ever did was watch old shows, shows Maggie already knew the ending to, while trying to decipher the plot, and for Sascha, just about everybody, in nearly every show she watched warranted being killed to resolve the issue no matter how large or small the infraction. And no matter how many times Maggie told Sascha how plots to shows like Happy Days, Good Times, Laverne and Shirley, and Cheers went, she always ignored her and drew her own conclusions and always ended up engaging her in pointless rhetoric.

"They got seven mutherfuckas on that island," Maggie declared, somewhat frustrated. "If the Skipper kill Gilligan and Mary Ann, how the professor, the millionaire and his wife not gone put that shit together?"

"The fat Captain can blame it on the movie star. Ginger! She looks like she would do it. And she's persuasive enough to convince everybody that it was the right thing to do. That's how the story is going to go!"

"This broad here," Maggie sighed as she placed a hand to her temple. "Look! They never getting off the fuckin' island, alright? They ass, they asses is stuck there forever!"

"Well, how did the camera people get on the island? They

can just leave with them, then."

"This bitch!" Maggie snapped in frustration.

"She's fuckin' impossible," Cikala stated as she laughed while rubbing her watery eyes. "And you sitting there arguing with her!"

"Maggie falls for it every time," Sascha smirked just as another Dodge Charger pulled up alongside the ride the women were sitting in.

The window rolled down and fifty-one year-old Faye Bender and forty-nine year-old Bonita Bender came into view. Bonita leaned over her sister and said, "Our lookouts spotted the RV rolling into town from the south! We meeting up with Delilah over to the Biscuitville on the north side let's roll!"

Cherryvale was a still, dark and quiet town after sunset, but it was the time when the Germans were most active. Travelers did well to steer clear of the lawless town after dark because just one's mere passing through could be a fatal mistake if some were out for mere sport.

Business had to be conducted at the present time, however, so all games were shunned aside as the two Dodge Chargers left the main intersection therein in town and headed north into the night for about five miles and made their way over to a Biscuitville that was owned by Maggie. The crew pulled into the parking lot of the yellow and brown structure and parked before the empty building that held one female waitress and one female cook who were on the German's payroll and involved in the business.

Cherryvale belonged to the Bender sisters and their crew, night or day, but night time was the right time for the unexpected. A time where shady deals were made and real life plots were hatched.

After parking, Bonita, Maggie, Sascha and Cikala climbed from their rides in their black Cherryvale Deputy Sheriff's uniforms and were leaning up against their cars when a black on black Lincoln Town Car with dark tint pulled in and parked alongside them.

The crew remained relaxed as twenty-eight year-old Delilah Mobley climbed from behind the steering wheel. Delilah was a pale-skinned, brown-eyed, petite and short woman of German descent with a long mane of brown hair that she let flow freely. She was a throwback to the eighties. A hippy of sorts. The granddaughter of the now deceased Senator Mabel Sougherbraun-Mobley and daughter to Iowa Governor, Mary Beth Mobley. Delilah, along with Faye and Bonita Bender, Maggie McPherson and Sascha Merkendorf, were the central force behind the Germans who controlled the Kansas underworld.

"Where are they?" Delilah asked as she walked up and hugged her crew at random.

Just then, a pair of headlights illuminated the dark, two-lane road from the south. "Here they come now," Cikala replied just as an RV painted in the San Antonio Spurs' color scheme of black, white and silver slowed and cruised past the Biscuitville before backing into the parking lot with its flashers blinking.

"Okay, ladies," Faye remarked as she pulled down on her sheriff's hat. "Let's make the boys from Eagle Pass feel at home this early morning hour."

"Wonder if they got a bathroom on there," Bonita wondered out loud as she clinched her thighs together.

"Use the one in the restaurant," Delilah suggested as Faye went into her patrol car and pulled out a folder.

"It's been broken for the past two days." Sascha remarked.

"And no one bothered to tell me the crapper in my restaurant is broken?" Maggie asked as she looked around. "What about my customers?"

"It's your hut. You should be keeping tracks of things like that." Sascha admonished.

"You don't need a S on tracks." Maggie snapped.

"But, if I had to take an S I would have tracks in my panties because if I was dining inside the Biscuitville I would not be able to shitsss…" Sascha stated as Maggie cut her eyes over to her. "What?" she then asked. "Are you offended? Just fix the crapper already because it is health code violation!"

The door on the lavish RV, which resembled many a rock star's traveling carriage, slowly opened and a lone, medium-built Mexican in his mid-twenties emerged dressed in a jean outfit and a pair of black Jordan's.

The Germans stood in a semi-circle in their black sheriff's deputy uniforms and gun belts cautiously eyeing the man as he walked past them. "Is there a bathroom inside I can use?" he asked, breaking the ice as he strode past the women.

"We was just talking about that," Bonita replied though a smile. "It's broken. Can I use yours instead?"

"So you want to go inside our RV?" the Mexican asked in an unsure tone.

Bonita looked her crew over, then back at the Mexican. She spread her arms and asked, "Where else am I going to pinch a loaf, guy?" she laughed.

"What are you ordering?" Faye abruptly asked just as two more Mexicans stepped off the RV.

"Four BLT biscuits. And you are ordering?" the Mexican asked, waiting for the woman to reveal her code in return.

"Grilled chicken club." Faye remarked while walking over to the man.

"That's all?" the man asked in a serious tone.

"On English muffin," Faye added as she paused before the man and stared into his eyes.

"Okay," the Mexican stated as he let go of a sly smile. "Let's talk inside. I'm Malik Gomez," he added as he and Faye shook hands briefly.

Bonita, meanwhile, had trotted over to the RV where Malik's men were standing. "Hey, guys," she playfully stated over some thumping bass as she held her hands on her crotch. "I need to take a...can I use the toilet? The one inside the restaurant is broken."

"Max, let her on!" Malik yelled back just before he and Faye walked into the Biscuitville.

Max led Bonita up the stairs to the RV and she scanned the layout. The driver of the bus was a middle-aged Mexican. He sat in the driver's seat with one leg leaning outwards as he held onto a mini-Uzi inside the darkened interior. "I'm just going to use the toilet. The one in the diner's broken," she said to the obviously suspicious man. "Malik said it's okay," she added over the music.

"Leave your gun...officer," the man replied with a snarly attitude.

"Just tryna relieve some pressure on my stomach, guy. I ain't no trouble," Bonita replied she handed the man her gun and walked deeper inside the RV.

Up ahead was a bar area that had glasses hanging from leather racks on both sides that had mirrors for backdrops. A single door led into an open area that held two square tables and benches where three more Mexicans sat, and there were four beds situated behind the tables and benches. *"I'm counting eight. They only ordered four BLTs, though,"* Bonita thought to herself as she nodded her head to what she knew to the instrumental to Tupac's song Hail Mary. *"Come with me with me...Hail Mary...run quick see...what do we have here now..."* she sang aloud as she swayed from side to side.

"What you know about Tupac?" Max asked as he walked up behind a gyrating Bonita.

"My niece Maggie plays his music sometimes. I like him." Bonita answered as she smiled back over her shoulder while moving in place.

"I love Tupac," twenty year-old Maximillian 'Max' Zamora stated while smiling up into Bonita's green eyes in a lustful state. The 5'8" one hundred and eighty-five pound Mexican was taken aback by the older woman's beauty and by how she seemed willing to engage him in courtship. "Me and my boy DeMarco rap to Tupac all the time," he remarked in an attempt to impress the woman before him. "What's your name, mami?"

Bonita blushed. "I've, I've never had a man half my age take interest in me," she playfully stated as she turned and faced Max. "I'm Bonita."

"Bonita, Bonita my senorita...my name is Max and it's nice to meet ya'..." Max rapped over Hail Mary's instrumental. "So, you like them young thugs, huh?" he asked as he licked his lips and took in the alluring, pale-skinned older woman's appearance as her wide hips rocked to and fro in her black sheriff's uniform.

"Enough of playing with you," Bonita sassed as she turned away from Max. "As sexy as you are, you won't think I'm so tempting when I come out that stall."

"I bet you smell like roses, Bonita!"

"Don't count on it!"

"Maybe next time while my people ordering biscuits we can do our own thing."

"I wouldn't rule that out," Bonita remarked through a smirk. "Check and see if I smell like roses when I'm done, will ya'?" she joked as she made her way to the back of RV and entered the bathroom, locking the door behind her.

Back inside the diner, as a grill full of bacon and a mesquite chicken breast began to sizzle, Faye and Malik sat and discussed business. "The price for safe passage is twenty-five thousand dollars, but our friend Natalia the third has paid the tax already," Faye said as she slid the folder she'd been carrying over to Malik. "Can I ask you something?" she quickly followed.

"Go ahead," Malik responded as he flipped the folder open and eyed a map with a route outlined in red.

"Why are you willing to do business with the same people who killed your protégé Peppi Vargas?"

Malik nodded and said, "Dawk 'nem never asked me how I felt about the whole deal. I'm just supposed to go along with it and be the humble sheep? Why should they make the deal? If anything, I deserve this deal after all the losses me and my crew has taken. I'm the one that has been on the frontlines, it is my crew that has taken the most casualties and I have the most muscle. The Holland family has grown weak, been weak ever since Doss Dawkins got killed."

"Can't argue with you there," Faye replied as she stirred her coffee and crossed her legs. "I never expected to see you, though. Why take the risk, Malik? You have, what? One hundred kilograms moving north into Minneapolis?"

"Eighty to be exact," Malik responded. "Twice as much as what I'm moving for the Holland family right now. And all of the profit goes to me and my family."

"You and Natalia will make perfect allies for us. I know about the trip to Chicago that Dawk is making soon. I want to be there to help you take down Dawk Holland. It'll be my way of showing you that this pact we form is legit."

"That way we can send a message to the rest of the family that we aren't to be fucked with and they no longer have the power."

"The Italians have been trying to take down the Holland family ever since Junior. Do you know Junior?"

"Junior was a good man, Faye. During this takeover I've learned from his mistakes. He failed to cover his tracks."

"Because he had sloppy people backing him. We aren't Toodie." Faye responded. "And you are by no means Junior, Malik," she added as she reached out and placed a hand atop of his. "Just so you know, there's no turning back from this day forth. We will kill Dawk Holland first chance we get and we're prepared for the fallout. Can you and your family say the same?"

"On my own? No," Malik responded. "But with Natalia on our side, they won't be able to stand up to us."

"That I know," Faye smiled. "Now," she quickly followed, "what you have is a map marking the locations of road checks all the way up to Kansas City. As you can see, this month is a busy month. There're three road checks that are ongoing along the road leading north out of here, and several along interstate thirty-five so that route is no good. I've routed you back west to the town of Neodesha. From there, you head north on highway seventy-five until you reach Topeka. Cross over interstate seventy and take highway four to the town of Nortonville. There, you will take highway fifty-nine north to Atchison, cross over the Missouri River and head further north to Saint Joseph, Missouri. Take highway thirty-six east out of Saint Joseph and it will run into interstate thirty-five. From there? Your family will be free to ride straight north into Minneapolis-Saint Paul."

"I thank you for this," Malik stated as he got up to use the bathroom.

Faye remained seated at the counter and watched as Malik headed for the john. He emerged seconds later holding his nose. "Did you think we were lying about the toilet?" she laughed. "It's always broken."

Malik coughed and fanned his nostrils. "I won't be on any other run," he let it be known. "I learned from the Holland family that you have to get your hands dirty with your crew when you're the boss—"

"To show them that you aren't in it for yourself," Faye responded, finishing Malik's thought.

"Order up!" the cook spoke aloud as she rung the bell with her spatula.

"Well, now," Faye smiled as she grabbed two bags of biscuits off the counter, "let's get you guys back on the road, Malik. If you run into any trouble out there? As long as you're in Kansas, call me, okay? I'll vouch for you all the way up to Missouri. From there, the ball is in your court."

The two were walking out the restaurant just as Bonita ran off the RV laughing like crazy with Max on her heels spraying Lysol back into the vehicle's interior. "*¿Qué carajo comiste? Hueles como te cagas un caballo muerto!* (What the fuck did you eat? You smell like you shit out a dead horse!)

"You actually did that? You went in after me and smelled my shit?" Bonita laughed as she rejoined her group and turned to face an anguished Max. "Okay, okay," she relented as she held back further laughs. "Next time I won't be so offensive. I got you next time, young man. Forgive me, but I really had to go."

"Malik," Faye remarked as she walked alongside the leader of the Mexican group, "Forgive my sister, but you've seen for yourself that our bathroom is on the brink. Her shameless act is not indicative of how we conduct business," she added as she extended her hand out towards her crew and the Dodge Chargers. "We own this town. And we have the connections you need. We want the Holland family removed for what they did to us in Indianapolis. From there? We do further business. I will give you the state of Kansas as it pertains to cocaine if you help us do this job."

"Consider it done," Malik responded seriously as he shook Faye's hand to seal the deal. The German stepped back and smiled a nod of approval as she watched Malik climb back onto the RV.

When the door closed and the RV began moving, Faye turned to Bonita. "You could've ruined this deal, sister."

"You didn't see what I saw on that RV," Bonita laughed. "It's nothing. They're on board with everything, trust me."

"Okay," Faye responded as she eyed her crew. "Let's keep things the way they are until we reach Chicago and finish the job with the Holland family. Sascha? You're up, chick. Get ready to meet up with Boogie day after tomorrow in New York. I'll be heading down to Boca Raton with Tanya to take care of Sheinheimer at the same time. While I'm away, Bonita has the reins here in Cherryvale. We all know ours jobs from this point on so let's do it like we know how and make it back in one piece," she ended before walking back into the dinner to enjoy her grilled chicken club sandwich on English muffin.

CHAPTER THIRTY-FIVE

ZELDAVILLE

"Now where I'm from we say whoaday, whoaday...and where I'm from we say shawty, shawty...ATL and New Orleans...that's how we do it when we do it, shawty...U-wayyyy!"

Atlanta rap duo Young Bloodz' song U-Way remix thumped from the interior of a blood red Cadillac Escalade resting on thirty-inch chrome wheels with red back-paneling as it cruised up I-95 with five women in tow. A vibrating text on her phone caught forty-four year old Zelda King's attention and she checked the phone that was resting in the palm of her hand. *"B in here wiggin out I'm thinking about copping to fifteen."*

"We gone get y'all out. Tell B take it to trial." Zelda shot back.

"She pissed at y'all for leaving her stuck out!"

Zelda sucked her teeth and began texting at a furious pace. *"V tell that bitch shut the fuck up and take a seat! We got this shit!"*

"Gotta hide the phone freeman coming." Zelda's fraternal twin, Vivian King, shot back, ending the conversation.

Zelda sat in the passenger seat of her ride having just picked up Sascha Merkendorf and Boogie from Newark/New Jersey International thinking hard about her fraternal twin and lifelong friend, Brenda Marshall, both of whom were locked up down in Philadelphia. She was the last leader of the black portion of the German outfit out on the streets, having avoided being arrested the day Brenda and her sister Vivian King were busted down in Philadelphia trying to score two hundred and thirty kilograms of cocaine from a woman she now knew to be a federal agent in Tammy Moto.

After Hurricane Katrina had struck New Orleans, Zelda, Brenda and Vivian had moved to Cincinnati, Ohio where Tanya had set up new operations. The three had helped Tanya and Boogie remove three rival heroin clicks inside of a year's time before moving up to Philadelphia where they'd set up shop and began supplying heroin to south Philly. Competition was fierce in the city of Brotherly Love and Zelda, Brenda and Vivian soon found themselves involved in a war with two rival gangs who'd clicked up and had made the decision to rid the city of three black women whose background they really didn't know.

Sascha Merkendorf, Cikala Dunbar and Bonita Bender were sent by Faye to 'resolve' the issue back in 2008, and in their wake, they'd left eleven men dead in south Philly. What became known as the Philly War had left the heroin market devastated in Philadelphia and the Germans decided to move up to New York with thirteen kilograms of cocaine they'd ripped from a dealer back in Cincinnati right around the time the war was drawing to a close.

Things were good for a while up in the Bronx, but Zelda, Brenda and Vivian had trouble keeping a steady supply of cocaine until Brenda caught wind of an Asian woman looking to sell two hundred and thirty kilograms of cocaine for three million dollars. The street value, given the way Brenda was planning to move it at wholesale cost, would've netted over thirteen million dollars. Faye and Tanya were against it, but Brenda kept pushing the issue. Willing to trust their partner, Faye and Tanya put up the buy money—which proved to be a big mistake as Brenda had gotten involved with the feds and they'd taken her and Vivian down.

Zelda was ordered to fall back on Tanya's orders, and lucky

for her she did, or else she would've been locked up with Brenda and her twin as well.

"This a fly ride, Zel," Boogie remarked from the backseat, shaking Zelda from her thoughts.

"I know, chica. Thanks. We been making some major loot over in the South Bronx in Hunts Point off one fifty six street, ya' heard me?" Zelda remarked as she reached over and turned down the stereo.

"You heard me?" Zelda's associate, a twenty-three year-old Puerto Rican with a short-bald fade named Nadia, mimicked as she cruised up I-95 under the clear night sky. She looked through the rearview mirror at her younger sister, another Puerto Rican, twenty-one year-old Eva, who sported long, black braids, and the two burst into laughter.

"Y'all hoes got jokes early in the morning," Zelda chuckled as she deleted the messages and threw her phone up onto the dash. "These two bitches riding with us like to make fun of my New Orleans dialect, yeh, Boogie? You from down there, tell 'em this how we talk down in that boot."

"Nadia and Eva been on our dialect. How long you been knowing them now, Zelda?" Boogie asked from the backseat.

"Shiiddd," Zelda sighed as she rubbed her chin. "About what, three years now? Brenda and Vivian know 'em. They was helping us move that cocaine until B and Viv got popped."

"I remember that. I remember them," Boogie remarked casually. "So, with that cocaine out the picture, what y'all been doing? This ride smell brand the fuck new."

"It is," Zelda remarked as she clapped her hands together once. "When B and Viv went down we had already had a deal set up with some white boys down in Manhattan to score some pills, ya' dig? It was just something to fuck around with, but Boogie?" she said seriously as she looked over the backseat. "We making over a hundred large a week off that shit!"

"What y'all pushing? X?" Boogie asked, referring to ecstasy pills.

"No X," Zelda remarked as Nadia and Eva shook their heads

while chuckling.

"No one uses X like talking about it in Manhattan," Nadia remarked.

"Island girl right. We moving Percocet, Boogie. Pain pills," Zelda followed. "The guys that sold us the pills turned us on to Wall Street. Them stockbrokers buy our shit before work, during lunch and we rack up after they get off. We be all up through lower Manhattan in all the clubs. We get in on V.I.P. and shit for free all the time! We done partied with some major stars, too! And we know people! That's why it was easy to track down those Jamaicans Jafrrey and Theron."

"You know where they hang?" Sascha asked as she sat beside Boogie.

"Where they hang? We know where they live! They be throwing these fancy parties for some of the brokers on Wall Street on the Upper West Side and be having us pass through there sometimes because not everybody want that heroin they be selling. I mean, people ain't tryna fuck up they life and shit snorting and shooting, ya' know? So they kick back, down a few 'Cets with they expensive ass champagne and mellow the fuck out."

"You have to get me over to Manhattan," Sascha schemed.

"Ahh, see? You thinking, you thinking like I'm thinking. We on the same page," Zelda chirped as she looked back at Sascha while flicking two fingers back and forth between her and Sascha's eyes as the Escalade wheeled up the freeway and slowed as traffic began to thicken. "We just went there the other night. They usually call us like every three days or so? So we gone just fall back and wait on that call. That'll give Tanya and Faye time to get at that Jew mutherfucka down in Boca Raton," she let it be known as she sat back down in the front seat just as Nadia pulled up to the toll booth on the George Washington Bridge's upper deck.

"Two in the morning and there's traffic?" Sascha asked as she looked up at the stories-tall buildings that lined the freeway. It's like we're in a canyon or something. A city canyon."

"You in the city that never sleeps, chica." Zelda laughed. "Y'all hungry? They got this li'l Chinese spot that stay open twenty-four hours and they have the bomb chicken plates!"

"I'd prefer a Russian meal." Sascha objected.

"You talkin' about having us ride down to Sheepshead Bay in Brooklyn and I ain't tryna ride that far out this time of night," Zelda snapped. "And ain't your ass German? The fuck you want Russian food for? Y'all don't even get along in life!"

"Neither do blacks and Puerto Ricans are supposed to be getting along, but I said nothing about you being friends with Nadia and Eva," Sascha countered.

"They ain't Puerto Rican, they black! Ain't that right, homegirls?" Zelda laughed as she high-fived a like-minded Nadia. "For real, we ain't going to Brooklyn. Your ass tryna sightsee. You'll have time for that tomorrow night because we heading to South Bronx right now. Nadia, hit up Beck Street off east one fitty-six." she ended as Nadia cruised through the EZ Pass lane and crossed the G.W. Bridge.

****

It was nearing three in the morning when Zelda and company reached the South Bronx. Boogie had just awakened from a brief nap she'd taken during the ride since crossing over the G.W. Bridge. She looked out the back window and could see not much had changed since she'd last visited South Bronx a year or so earlier. Brownstones with cars, some foreign and flashy, lined the block and a handful of stoops had groups of hustlers of both sexes hanging out, either sitting on the stairs or standing on the sidewalks blowing smoke into the air while sipping out of red cups.

"This our backyard, peoples! Zeldaville!" Zelda stated proudly as Nadia wheeled her Escalade onto Beck Street and pulled over to the curb before a bodega that had a yellow and red neon sign on the front that read BS Take Out.

"We eating BS," Sascha remarked as she chuckled.

"I know, man!" Zelda snapped as she pushed the door open and stepped out in her tight-fitting jean outfit and ankle-length leather boots. "I keep telling them Chinese mutherfuckas in there they need to get rid of that BS sign and just spell out Beck Street. I got my island girls. Come on, Helen, and the other one," she added as she led Sascha and Boogie inside while Nadia and Eva remained behind in the Escalade.

"Don't forget the eggrolls and the soy sauce and shit!" Eva called out right before Zelda entered the bodega.

Once inside, Zelda trotted up to the counter. At forty-four, she was a fine woman that still sported an Afro. She had wide hips and large mounds that still sat naturally high. She was known throughout Hunts Point as the Percocet Princess and was known to party with many a young hustler. And although in her forties, Zelda looked ten years younger and carried a youthful disposition. She talked the lingo, knew all the dances and stayed up on fashion. She saw herself as 'gettin' down', but it was an attribute she did well to rid herself of because whenever she was in the Bronx, she tended to get a little off base as it was her comfort zone. A place that reminded her of the Saint Bernard projects to a degree, but she was failing to keep in mind that the Saint Bernard was no more, and the Bronx was a totally different arena.

"Me and Viv got a big house over in Long Island, but most of my time spent here in the Bronx with Nadia and Eva," Zelda told Boogie as she escorted her and Sascha up to the counter. "We got a spot further down one fifty-sixth on the other side of Bruckner Expressway where we chill and do our thang, ya' know? We gone go there after we order. Yo, Chinaman? Five chicken plates! And make sure you fry the chicken in the same grease you fry the fish and everything else, son!"

"That has to be some sort of a health code violation." Sascha stated as she walked back over to the door and looked out towards the block to make sure Nadia and Eva were still present and accounted for. "This place is all bad. BS is just what the sign says. You move wrong here in Bronx, Zelda."

"It's not 'in Bronx', it's the Bronx! And how the fuck you know how I move back here?" Zelda barked as she turned away from the counter. "Them people out there is my people! I been 'round them for a while now and everybody know me!

They don't fuck with me in the Bronx! Nobody don't fuck me and my girls, period!"

"It was just an observation. Didn't mean to strike a nerve," Sascha calmly remarked as she pushed the door open. "I'll wait outside in Zeldaville. Thank you for the BS meal," she ended as she walked out of the door.

"Yo, that bitch there?" Zelda remarked as she shook her head while eyeing a smirking Boogie. "I hope Tanya 'nem be ready early because me and that hoe right there gone end up engaging in some passionate fisticuffs before it's all said and done!"

"She's a cynical person at times. How you have passionate fisticuffs, though?" Boogie chuckled.

"You know what I'm saying!"

"She might have a point, though, Zel."

"That bitch ain't got a point about shit! She need some dick in her life is what she need! And that's *my point*! Let's get our food and get the fuck outta here and go home! When we get up I'm calling Tanya to see where her and Faye at with it because Sascha gotta get the hell up out of New York in a New York fuckin' minute!" she added as she pulled out a knot of money and paid for everybody's order.

A few minutes later, Zelda and Boogie emerged from the bodega and saw Sascha surrounded by three black males in their late teen and early twenties. They'd been having a conversation with their newfound friend for a few minutes, asking her name, how old she was and what she was doing in the neighborhood with Zelda and her crew.

Sascha remained quiet for a while, but she soon began to speak a language the young men hadn't a clue as to its origin. It was fun for a minute, but Sascha had become annoyed as she came to realize she was being mocked by one of the men and he had no interest in who she was actually, which was perhaps to him and friends' benefit.

"Bet she can dunk. Tall ass!" one of the men remarked as he laughed.

"Ich mag das Spiel der Basketball. Kobe Bryant und Timothy Duncan sind meine Favoriten." (I like the game of basketball. Kobe Bryant and Timothy Duncan are my favorites.)

"Okay," I heard her say something about basketball and Tim Duncan. "She understand us, bruh!" a second young man remarked as he laughed. "What language is that, though?"

"I think it's Swedish," the first male who'd spoken answered.

"Es ist nicht Schwedisch es ist Deutsch spreche ich Ihnen Attrappe." (It is not Swedish it is German I am speaking you dummy.) Sascha replied to the young man who started the mocking. *"Sie würde ich im Schlaf zu töten."* (You I would kill in your sleep.) she truthfully added.

"Nah, Swedish not that harsh, fam. That sound like Russian or German. They have that hard dialiect and shit," the oldest guy in the trio remarked. "Am I right, ma?"

"Yes, you are right about one, young man. It is German," Sascha politely stated as she managed to smile just slightly. *"Sie Ich mag, junger Mann. Sie sind aufmerksam. Ich kann so weit gehen, wie Sex mit dir haben. Ich bin ein Puma."* (You I like, young man. You're observant. I may go so far as to have sex with you. I am a cougar.)

"What Krause from Benson saying?" the first youngster asked, his voice forcing Sascha to drop her smile as she believed he'd just insulted her by calling her a kraut.

"Ich bin nicht Kraut von Benson! Es gibt nicht einmal ein Benson nirgendwo in Deutschland! Ich habe Ihnen keine Namen genannt! Warum muss ich ein Kraut sein? Ich würde dich tagelang quälen und du mich rufen Gott, bevor ich die Kehle herausreißen!" (I am not kraut from Benson! There isn't even a Benson nowhere in Germany! I haven't called you any names! Why do I have to be a kraut? I would torture you for days and make you call me god before I rip out your throat!)

"Yo, son, you done upset her!" the young man who Sascha favored, told his friend as he laughed while clapping his hands.

"I think you should, you should maybe quit talking to her before she fucks you up," he nodded just as Zelda and Boogie emerged from the building holding onto four plastic bags. "Yo, let me help y'all with that, Zelda," he then said as he eased past Sascha and took the bags from Zelda and Boogie's hands.

Sascha climbed into the backseat complaining in her German tongue the entire time.

"Yo, Boogie? What's wrong with Godzilla?" Zelda mocked.

"He called me a kraut back there the young one!" Sascha complained.

Boogie laughed and said, "All them old ass shows you watch and you never saw Benson? There's a German on that show named Krause. He was calling you Krause not kraut, because like the lady on the show, you a German."

"And you look like that, bitch, too!" Zelda added. "Come on, Nadia. Take us home so we can finish making fun of Krause ass back there," she added.

"I stand corrected," Sascha remarked. "The Benson Show," she then said aloud as Nadia wheeled off the block. "I have to see The Benson Show to find out if I do look like the woman Krause."

CHAPTER THIRTY SIX

WE DONE HERE

"Ayeee! You said you were going to go easy! I'm new to this game, girl!" Tanya laughed after missing a serve from Faye, who was on the opposite side of the regulation tennis court the two were playing on down in Boca Raton, Florida, the morning after Boogie and Sacha had linked up with Zelda up in the Bronx.

The two were dressed in shorter than normal white tennis skirts and white sneakers, both looking the part of wealthy northern vacationers who were out enjoying the Florida sun, but there was much more going on with the two if one paid closer attention; like the man on the court beside the two frisky gals.

On a court right beside Tanya and Faye, an older man in his early seventies ran around the court in his white shorts, white polo shirt and Ralph Lauren tennis chasing balls served by a portable launcher.

Faye and Tanya had waited inside a rented Toyota Rav 4 that they'd rode down in from Cincinnati for nearly an hour until seventy-one year-old Iiayad Sheinheimer arrived over to the paradisiac athletics club that was filled with lush green grass and palm trees in his 2009 white on white convertible Mercedes Kompressor.

The women sat patiently as Sheinheimer set up the portable server and walked to the opposite end of the court under the warm Florida sun and begun his routine before they climbed from their ride, grabbed their tennis gear and flung it over their shoulders. Light talk about much of nothing was made and the two giggled like teenage girls as they walked onto the court, knowing their outfits and good looks had caught the elderly man's attention.

While setting up, Faye and Tanya kept bending over near the green, chain-link fence that separated the courts, purposely giving Sheinheimer eyeful shots of bare ass cheeks and pink pussy lips in the process. The man had begun sweating, and had even missed a couple of serves he was so absorbed in the black-haired, well-toned eye candy that'd paraded onto the court just off to his right.

Like most members of the male species do when encountering a member of the opposite sex, Sheinheimer, the white-haired, knock-kneed, wrinkly old man with numerous skin blotches on his arms and legs, began moving around the court like a vigorous silver back guerilla. On occasion, he would look over at the two women who'd been giving him flesh shots to see if they were watching, and they were, much to his delight, so he picked up the pace while acting as if it was just a regular day for him out on the tennis court.

Faye and Tanya were laying it on thick in return as they slid into their manipulative game of cat and mouse with their latest mark. Faye was on the end of the court nearest Sheinheimer when she and Tanya began their game. She held onto her tennis racket with her back to Sheinheimer as she bounced a tennis ball up and down, preparing to serve. Had other members of the athletic club been out during this time, someone may have surely notified the main office and point out the fact that there were two sluts out playing tennis and flirting with an old man as Faye's stance would've made it obvious.

Sheinheimer watched, chuckling to himself as the black-haired woman stood bouncing the ball while bent over further than necessary. It was a stance that'd forced her skirt halfway up over her ass he noticed as he eyed the shadowy mound while admiring the woman's long, curvy, tan legs. When she went to serve the ball, the Jewish man watched amazed as the woman jumped into the air and hit the ball as hard as she could in seemingly slow motion.

Faye's skirt flew up over her waist completely and everything had been put on display for Iiayad. She could barely contain her laughter as her feet touched the ground and her dress settled back into position.

Tanya, meanwhile, although knowing what was at stake, really was into the tennis match. For her, it was all about beating Faye before she killed Sheinheimer, but she had no clue as to what she was doing on the court, or how the game of tennis was actually played. She went for the ball Faye had hit by running to her left and taking a swat at it, but she'd missed it entirely.

"Love!" Faye laughed out from across the court as she grabbed another ball and began bouncing it up and down, making sure to bend over more than necessary to keep Sheinheimer off base.

"I love you, too, sister!" Tanya shot back as she readied herself for the next serve.

Faye stopped bouncing the ball and stared at Tanya with a blank expression. "No! That's the score, Jezebel!" she yelled aloud.

"Wait! What? How you score like that and I ain't even hit the ball back over there?" Tanya questioned as she walked towards the net.

"That's the object of the game!"

"Hey, you ain't, you ain't say all that! Let me serve if the shit's that easy then!"

"It's not how the game is supposed to be played, but if that's how you wanna do fine!" Faye relented as she went to grab more tennis balls. When she turned back towards the tennis court, she saw Tanya crossing over the net to her side of the court. "What, just what are you doing?" she asked dismayed.

"It's my turn to serve so I came on this side to serve."

"Have you ever watched a tennis match?" Faye asked as she chuckled. "You can serve from your side, yeah?"

"I can? Look, tennis isn't my game, okay? I'm just tryna win something here," Tanya replied as she met up with Faye on the opposite side of the court.

"Like you did in Willie's pool?" Faye smirked.

"Why not? It's a competition!"

"Are you serious, girl?" Faye asked lowly. "You takin' this game serious?"

"Fuckin' right I am! I'm not gettin' beat by two old mutherfuckas inside a month!"

"You know," Faye smirked as she licked her lips and stared into Tanya's brown eyes. "At first, I thought it was because of your age when you were younger? But as you've gotten older it's plain to see that you just can't help being a goofy ass woman sometimes," she laughed as she placed a loving hand on her friend's shoulder and squeezed lightly.

"This is the strong side. I need to be on the strong side to serve it right." Tanya remarked as she walked around the court while checking her racket and tennis shoe heels.

Faye was left speechless; she stared at Tanya for several more seconds while laughing. "Fine! If you think it'll help? Have at the 'strong side'!" she quoted before walking off towards the opposite end of the court.

Sheinheimer had witnessed the entire scenario while wheeling a cart around his tennis court picking up the served balls before making his way to the opposite end of the courtyard to reload the automatic server. "Never seen you two here before," he stated to the woman who'd served minutes earlier as she made her way back onto the court. "Look like you and your, uhh, your sister or what have you get along well."

"We do," Faye remarked as she dropped her tennis racket before bending over and pulling up on her socks, giving Sheinheimer another clear shot of her privates.

"That's a beautiful sight," Sheinheimer remarked as he began loading his automatic server.

"Excuse me?" Faye sassed as she rose, turned, and faced her mark with her hands on her hips.

"You and your sister. The way you two get along is a beautiful thing. Me and my sister hated one another for years and years. She passed away last year and we never resolved our differences. I regret not making amends with her."

"Sorry to hear that," Faye placated. "Thought you were talkin' about the other thing."

"What other thing?"

"Come on, man!" Faye laughed as she left her and Tanya's court and walked over to Sheinheimer. "We all but put our asses in your hand, guy! What? Your wife is around or something?"

"Yeah. I mean, no! I'm not married. And it wasn't like I didn't notice the show. I was just trying to keep it cordial and share a moment."

"How about we share something else instead of reminiscing about some woman I don't even know." Faye spoke lowly as she reached out and touched Sheinheimer's hip.

"You don't know me either," the man replied, yet never bothering to step back from the woman who was all up in his private space.

"Yeah," Faye spoke in a seductive voice as she stepped close enough to Sheinheimer to inhale his scent. He smelled good to her surprise as she was expecting an odor comparable to old clothes and stale piss given his age and she'd told him so.

"I may be old, but I take care of myself very well…and all my parts still work, darling." Sheinheimer let it be known as his eyes dropped down to his midsection.

Faye looked down and saw the pink head of a semi-hard dick sticking out from under Sheinheimer's tennis shorts. "You're not the only one who's an exhibitionist around here," the elderly man stated as he flexed his organ muscle, making it throb against his grey-haired thigh.

Faye took her fingertips and ran them along the bottom side of Sheinheimer's dick. She could feel the man stiffen as his precum coated the tips of her fingers as his organ grew longer and longer the steadier she coaxed it. *"Damn,"* she said to herself as thoughts of Brenda's old man, Ricky Gross Senior, and the dick length he sported came flooding back into her psyche as she reflected on the night Ricky had blown her back out up in Cincinnati during the Kazuki and Cho Moto job back in January of 1984.

Faye's pussy moistened and her knees wobbled a bit as it'd been a while, nearly a year, since she'd been fucked. "You got a place?" she asked as she gripped Sheinheimer's dick tighter.

"Your place is over on the court so I can serve, cow!" Tanya boomed, breaking the trance and startling both Faye and Sheinheimer. She looked down in time to see Faye remove her hand away from Sheinheimer's dick.

"Damn!" Tanya said to herself as she'd never seen a dick that big in her life.

Sheinheimer laughed as he tucked his rod back into his shorts as best he could. "Glad it was you and not some stuck up cunt looking to report me to the main office," he unapologetically stated. "Your sister and I were just making plans on blowing," he paused at that moment and eyed the woman who'd been stroking his pole before looking back over to her 'sister'. "Your sister and I were about to blow this joint, right?" he asked as he placed an arm around Faye's neck.

Faye looked over to Tanya as she lay her head on Sheinheimer's shoulder. "Can we, Tanya?" she asked coyly.

"Really, bitch? I mean, really, Faye?" Tanya asked through a blank stare. In the same manner in which Faye had called Tanya goofy, Tanya could see that Faye was actually getting into Sheinheimer.

"Can we, sister? Please? Just one time before we head back north to Connecticut tomorrow afternoon?" Faye cooed like a child not wanting to be depraved of its favorite toy while rubbing the front of Sheinheimer's bulging shorts.

"Looks as if I got me a pair of snowbirds looking to wade in uncharted waters!" Sheinheimer laughed. "Hey, let's do the formalities. My name is Iiayad Sheinheimer."

"I'm Faye and this is my sister Tanya," Faye remarked as she tickled Iiayad's neck with the tip of her pointed nose. "Are we gonna stay on this court or are you going to take us somewhere and show me and my sister the time of our lives before we go home to our boring, executive husbands?"

Sheinheimer's grey eyes lit up at the prospect of having a married woman and fucking her royally before sending her on her way. It would be one amongst many conquests he'd experienced in Boca Raton as he'd been with many a married woman who'd traveled from the north down south to live out their wildest fantasies in animosity, but never in a potential duo.

"I don't know about all this," Tanya protested with a reluctant look on her face. "If my husband was to find out about this I would lose everything. I mean, Faye, you said it would be possible, but I never believed it. I just went along," she added, getting into the act.

"That means you just have to trust me more now doesn't it, sister?" Faye mocked as she smiled over to Sheinheimer. "We'll follow your lead."

"All my balls have been picked up with the exception of two that needs draining," Sheinheimer laughed. "You girls gather your stuff and I'll meet you in the parking lot."

"Okay now," Faye smiled like a champion as Sheinheimer whizzed off like the cat that had just captured the elusive mouse in his paws' grip. "You left DNA from your pussy on the net when you crossed it, yeah?" she then whispered to Tanya.

"That's why I'm taking the net with me," Tanya retorted. "You might wanna check the ground where you were standing because you might've left some moisture on the ground."

"It only reached my thigh if you wanna know the truth. You

didn't plant your ass on none of the benches, right?" Faye countered as she and Tanya gathered their items.

"No. I farted once. If they can trace that shit then I guess we'll be camping out in Florida."

"You know what they say about Florida," Faye remarked as she threw her duffle bag onto her shoulder.

"Where you come on vacation and leave on probation." Tanya chuckled as she and Faye walked to the center of the tennis court and pulled the net down from both ends and rolled it up into a single ball before carrying it off to the parking lot.

"What's with the net?" Sheinheimer asked as he eyed the two women walking his way.

"Souvenir," Tanya remarked as she threw the net into the backseat of the Rav 4 along with her and Faye's tennis equipment. She slammed the door, sniffed her armpits and said, "I'm ripe, man! Could use a shower."

"I have a four head shower over to my three story condo and it's stocked out with wine and has a grill pit out back before a hot tub," Sheinheimer bragged as he stood beside his convertible Mercedes. "Who's riding with daddy?" he asked as he looked over to Faye.

"Me! Me! Me!" Faye thumped like an excited little girl.

"Tanya? Follow me and your sister to paradise!" Sheinheimer laughed as he climbed behind the wheel of his Mercedes.

Faye eased into the passenger seat of the Benz and immediately eyed a bottle of Viagra in the console. She said nothing as Iiayad reached down and grabbed the bottle and pushed it down in between the seats.

"It's okay," Faye stated in comforting manner. "My husband is on the pill."

"You make it sound like it's birth control or something," Sheinheimer replied as he pulled the Viagra up from in between the seats and threw it up in his hand one time. "I haven't taken any today, Faye," he admitted as he looked over to what was to him, one of the most beautiful women he'd ever laid eyes on. "You nearly made me ejaculate in my shorts just by your touch today. I was aroused naturally the first time I laid eyes on you. How often do you come down to Boca Raton?" he asked through heartfelt conviction as he started the engine on his Mercedes while looking into Faye's fascinating green eyes.

"Not often, Mister Sheinheimer," Faye replied as she faced Iiayad and rested a hand against her cheek, once again putting her bare pussy on display. "I take it you want to see more of me?"

"I would love to, Faye." Sheinheimer smiled as he put his Benz in reverse and backed out of his parking spot. "I can give you the world, if that's what you want."

"I have a husband that gives me the world, Iiayad. What can you offer me that's so different?" Faye asked as the car lurched forward. "And don't say money or good dick because that's not what excites me at this point and time in my life because I have it already."

"Just a good time," Iiayad remarked as he made his way to the exit with Tanya following his lead. "You wouldn't be doing this if you weren't happy at home am I right, Faye?"

"True," Faye smiled as the noon time sun beat down on her skin. "It's hot now, man. Can you raise the roof on this thing?"

Sheinheimer reached down and pressed a button and the roof began to rise on his Kompressor as he waited for the light to change. Not bothering to wait for a green light, he made a right turn when the flow of traffic cleared and merged onto a four lane boulevard filled with cars just as his top latched. "One of the things I hate about this time of year is the tourists. They clog up the roads," he complained.

Faye merely smiled over to Sheinheimer, who'd immediately realized the distinction he'd just made. "I didn't mean it that way. Where we play tennis is high dollar. Most of the people here in Boca Raton ride down in RVs and take up space in the Walmart parking lot and the beaches and crowd the restaurants around here. It gets annoying sometimes."

"I understand," Faye soothed as she reached out and rubbed Sheinheimer's thigh. "I'll tell my husband about the meat market I went to while I was down here. Let him know how accommodating the people in Boca Raton are and I want him to buy me a vacation home here. How's that sound?"

"Without even sampling the goods?" Sheinheimer asked as he smiled over to Faye as his dick began throb over her soft hands.

"A woman knows when she's working with the real thing," Faye remarked as she leaned over and took Iiayad's dick into her moist mouth. She'd been wanting to do it all along in spite of the job needed doing, which was the reason why she'd asked him to raise the top on his Mercedes.

"Jesus!" Iiayad groaned as he unbuttoned his shorts, freed his member and palmed the back of Faye's head as he drove down the boulevard headed towards his subdivision.

Sheinheimer's hand on the back of her head let Faye know she was pleasing the man as her lips slid back and forth over his rod. A few minutes into it, she felt his dick veins flexing over her lips and she quickly rose and began stroking him hard and fast. "Feels like a pussy don't it? You fuck my pussy I just may kill you with it because you can't even take my mouth and hand can you?" she groaned as she continued stroking Iiayad. "Feel good?" Faye asked as she leaned over and flicked her tongue across the right side of the man's jaw while blowing her hot breath onto his neck.

Sheinheimer panted like an embarrassed little boy as he gripped the steering wheel and tilted his head back. "Faye!" he cried out. "Oh, sweet Jesus, Mother of Mary!" he exclaimed as he neared the turn leading into his neighborhood.

While in the throes of an intense ejaculation, Sheinheimer was turning off into his subdivision, making a wider turn than necessary before correcting the Benz and pulling over to the right side of the road before a home that was under construction, but void of workers as they were all out to lunch.

Tanya swerved in right behind Faye and Sheinheimer, pulled up alongside the two and let the passenger side window down.

While looking over towards the Benz, she saw her phone lighting up and recognized Zelda's phone number. "Hold on a sec!" she spoke into the throwaway phone after answering while watching the driver's side window on the Kompressor descend. "You two all right?" she asked out of concern, as things seemed to be going off kilter.

"It's kosher," Faye laughed as she wiped her hands clean with a napkin. "What's up?" she asked, noticing Tanya was taking a call. "You okay, baby?" she then whispered into Sheinheimer's ear.

"I'm smoked, baby."

"You need me to drive?" Faye asked as she stroked the back of Iiayad's neck.

"Would ya', please? It's about a mile down the road." Sheinheimer replied with his head laid back in his leather headrest.

"Who this?" Tanya asked as she watched Faye ease out of the passenger seat and walk around the front side of Sheinheimer's Benz.

"Bitch! Y'all need ta' gone let Godzilla do what the fuck she need ta' do quick-like so she can raise up outta the Bronx ya' heard?" Zelda boomed into Tanya's ear. "I done called your ass like five times since ten this morning over the past two hours and you just now answering? How long before y'all done down there?"

"Hold up right quick," Tanya replied as Faye stepped in between the passenger side window of the RAV 4 and the driver's side of Sheinheimer's Benz.

"Who that?" Faye silently mouthed.

"Zelda! We ready?" Tanya mouthed back.

When Faye nodded to say yes, Tanya reached down into her duffle bag, pulled out a .22 semi-automatic and eased from behind the steering wheel of the Rav 4. "We ready right now," Tanya then told Zelda.

"You for true?" Zelda asked as Tanya walked around the

rear of the Rav 4 and came up along the driver's side of Sheinheimer's Benz.

"You know we don't play about this shit. It's going down right now," Tanya replied as she watched Faye helping Sheinheimer to slide over into the passenger seat of his own ride.

After crossing over the console, Iiayad rubbed his legs and looked over to Faye as she knelt down outside of the driver's side door in her tennis outfit with her bare pussy on display for the countless time to keep the man entranced.

"That was some workout," Iiayad smiled as he flicked his limp dick up out from the bottom of his shorts to play along with Faye. "I say after another pill and an hour in the hot tub we'll be ready for a second round and maybe a third if the old ticker's up to it," he joked as he patted the shirt covering his heart with his free hand.

Faye smiled back over to Sheinheimer. "In some other life I could see us. Maybe," she stated in a serious tone of voice while diddling her clitoris. "If only revenge were age discriminate," she abruptly ended as she rose and walked away from the Benz.

Sheinheimer was left in a baffled state after hearing his 'friend' speak in such a cold-hearted manner. He was preparing to open the passenger side door and question what he believed was that of a new acquaintance when he heard what sounded like two firecrackers erupting from inside his pristine ride. His entire left leg went numb and he was forced back down into the passenger seat as sharp pains that felt like that of hot needles aggravated his left hip and left thigh.

"Good to meet you, Mister Sheinheimer," Tanya stated as she pulled the driver's side door shut, placed the car in drive and made a quick U-turn out of the subdivision and merged back into the west bound traffic.

"What is, what is this? You two aren't like some Aileen Wuornos copycat serial killers are you?" Sheinheimer panted as he ran his hands over his wounds while leaning up against the passenger side window.

"Aileen ain't got shit on us, Iiayad! She ain't got shit on *me*, you mutherfucka you!" Tanya scoffed as she held her gun on Sheinheimer while wheeling his Mercedes down the busy boulevard. "I'm not out for money! I'm not out here about to murder your ass because I was molested by men when I was a child! I'm here to avenge the death of my husband Alfredo Lowes down in Caracas!"

"Rafael Gacha asked, he asked me to give him some C-4! Tropicana was clearing land for a railyard in Venezuela at the time and I did him that favor! I thought he was clearing land for a new runway down there!"

"I ain't tryna hear that shit! And if I can ever get to Rafael I will!" Tanya seethed as she pressed the gun to Sheinheimer's left side. "But just killing you right now is good enough for me because if it wasn't for you my husband would still be alive!" she let it be known as she came up on a red-light that forced her to bring the Mercedes to a halt in the middle lane of the busy road.

Sheinheimer saw his chance to alert surrounding people to his plight and made an attempt to pound on the windshield. Tanya was expecting that move, however; before Sheinheimer could utter a cry for help, she pulled him back into his seat, pressed the barrel of her .22 semiautomatic to his left side and pumped three slugs into the left side of his rib cage.

The seventy-one year-old Jewish man died with his eyes wide open and his mouth agape while looking up into the roof of his pristine Mercedes at a busy intersection down in Boca Raton, Florida after suffering five gunshots, three of which had penetrated his heart and left lung, wounds that had left the fronyt side of his white polo drenched in a hellish, reddish hue.

Faye had witnessed the moment Tanya shot Sheinheimer through the small tinted window on the back of his Benz. When the light turned green, she trailed her friend down the boulevard lined with numerous strip malls and fast food restaurants and was now left wondering how she and Tanya were going to cover their tracks as Tanya drove though the retirement community with a dead body in the passenger seat.

After crossing under I-95, Tanya drove west out of Boca Raton for twenty miles or so until she came up on a swampy area that had an abandoned bait and tackle shop situated on a gravel lot. She pulled around to the backside of the dilapidated wooden structure and purposely drove the Mercedes into a pool of black water dotted with cypress trees and sunk the nose of the car into the swamp water. She then lowered the roof before she climbed over the back seat and jumped out of the car without getting her feet wet.

When Faye pulled up to the backside of the bait and tackle shop, Tanya ran to the back of the Rav 4 and grabbed a two gallon plastic jug of gasoline and trotted back over to the Benz where she climbed back onto the car and poured the liquid all over the interior, making sure to coat Sheinheimer's body and the steering wheel before she stepped back onto the trunk and put a lighter to a napkin and tossed it into a deceased Sheinheimer's lap.

The interior of the Benz sparked up with a loud whooshing sound as it became engulfed in flames. Tanya admired her handy work as she jumped down from the trunk of the car and trotted back over to the Rav 4 where she grabbed the tennis net she'd taken from the athletic club. She balled the net up tight and ran up to the blazing Mercedes and threw it into the flames that were now dancing off Sheinheimer's corpse and the interior of the Benz altogether. The wax-coated net quickly crumbled under the blazing heat, leaving Tanya satisfied and under the belief that no DNA would be left behind once Sheinheimer's body was discovered.

With another job done, Tanya went and climbed into the passenger seat of the Rav 4. Faye pulled away without saying a word as Tanya sent a text back to Zelda that read, *"We done here do your thing."*

"Just so you know, Faye? I'm docking you some cool points." Tanya then spoke casually.

"For what?" Faye asked in wonderment.

"For suckin' that dirty old man's dick earlier. I saw what you did inside that car." Tanya remarked nonchalantly as Faye shoved her playfully and continued driving further west with the smoke from Sheinheimer's rising up in her rearview mirror.

CHAPTER THIRTY-SEVEN

ONE CAME BACK

"Do you have The Benson Show on DVD here?" Sascha Merkendorf asked a salesperson a few hours after Tanya had killed Iiayad Sheinheimer down in Boca Raton. She was inside a Best Buy on Fifth Avenue in Midtown Manhattan perusing the store with Zelda making a few purchases before the two of them headed over to the Upper West Side with Zelda, Nadia and Eva to see the Jamaicans.

"The Benson Show?" the young sales clerk pondered as she eyed the DVDs. "Never heard of that. Is it new?"

"It's an old show they told me. It has a German woman named Krause on there," Sascha remarked as she towered over the young woman.

"Ohhh, I know that show! My grandmother used to watch that when I was younger. It's just Benson, not The Benson Show. We have seasons one and two. I'll get it for you," the salesclerk remarked as she moved about the DVD aisle scanning the shelves.

"Good. And I'll need a portable DVD player so I can watch on my flight home after I complete my task here." Sascha responded as she followed the young woman.

"You're in town on business?"

"I don't call it business, more like a sport."

"Let me guess…you're an attorney," the salesclerk

presumed as she knelt down on one knee.

"No." Sascha remarked dryly. "I'm into deconstruction. I destroy things for a living," she added as Zelda stood behind her shaking her head in disbelief.

"Sounds dangerous," the young woman replied, never bothering to make eye contact with the customer as she was busy searching for the DVD and merely making idle chat while doing so.

"It can be for those things that are on the list to be destroyed, but I do it quick most times." Sascha boasted.

"Cool," the young woman replied as she scooted along the floor. "Found your items. It was on the bottom shelf. Guess it's not too popular, but I think you'll enjoy it. The DVD players are over in portable electronics. Good luck on your job," she ended as she stood to her feet and handed her customer the DVDs and walked off.

"Why you didn't just go one step further and tell her you were in town to kill two people you told her damn near everything else," Zelda complained in one breath as she followed Sascha over to where the portable electronics lay.

"She wasn't listening to me although hearing. I could've told I her I was here to do anything and she would not have cared. It is called small talk, Zelda," Sascha replied as she walked into the electronics department.

"Yeah, whatever. I bet you the only person in this city buying a portable DVD player," Zelda smirked. "If your ass ain't old school and throwback," she added.

"These are creature comforts," Sascha remarked as she picked up a portable DVD player and tucked it underneath her arm. "I will need some entertainment while I wait for the right time to strike," she said as she headed for the checkout counters.

Zelda followed, picking up a magazine to read while she and Sascha waited in line. The items were rung up and the cashier smiled and said, "That'll be one hundred and thirty-one dollars and fourteen cents. Debit or credit?"

"No debit or credit. Cash. And my friend here is paying for it." Sascha remarked as she threw a thumb back at Zelda.

"I wish like the hell I would!" Zelda boomed as threw the magazine back onto the rack. "That's your stuff!"

"But I have no debit or credit or cash right now," Sascha declared as she patted the pockets on her cashmere coat.

"Then what in the hell you doing up in here then?" Zelda questioned in a disgusted manner.

"I am here in town doing deconstruction work. My job is to —"

"I got it! I got it!" Zelda hissed as she shoved Sascha from in front the cashier and pulled out her knot. "You did this on purpose you ole oversized cow! Can't wait to you leave!" she said under her breath.

Sascha remained quiet with a smirk on her face as the cashier bagged her items. She and Zelda left the store and made their way back to Zelda's Escalade where Boogie and the Puerto Ricans were waiting and the five were off to the Upper West Side. "It's going to take us a while to get to Eighty-Eighth Street," Nadia remarked as she wheeled out of the parking garage. "It's five in the evening now."

"That's good, when we get there the sun should be going down and people will be settling in." Sascha remarked as she set her bags down and settled in for a nap.

Two and a half hours later, Nadia was turning off Columbus Avenue onto Eighty-Eight Street as the sun began to set behind the manmade canyons of New York City. The street was lined with stories-tall buildings on either side in an artsy part of Manhattan.

Nadia wheeled into the parking area of a condominium complex directly across from Central Park, backed into a parking spot and climbed from behind the wheel with Zelda and Sascha following soon after. The three walked east and made it to the corners of Eighty-Eighth Street and Central Park West and walked along the busy street with the twenty-story tall condominium complex on their left.

Sascha was taking the scene in as she walked up the crowded sidewalk trailing Nadia and Zelda. There was a bus stop with several benches on the opposite side of Central Park West with a dozen or so people waiting in front of stalled traffic she noticed. "Is this area always so crowded, Zelda?" she asked as she eyed an Indian man and woman selling fruit beside the bus stop from behind a wooden vendor's stand.

"It usually clear up around midnight on Central Park West. If you gone catch 'em you gone wanna do it on Eighty-Eighth Street, though because it's less foot traffic," Zelda replied as the trio approached the entrance to the condominiums. "If they ask about you, you're an investor new in town we met on Wall Street looking to party," she added as she swiped a card, entered a key code and pulled one of the double doors open and entered the condominiums' lobby area.

****

"I'll see you...when you get there...if you ever get there... see you when you get there... I'll see you...when you get there...if you ever get there...see you when you get there..."

"Come dung! Sidung!" (Come sit! Sit down!) twenty-nine year-old Jaffrey Fischer said to a Caucasian woman in her early-thirties who was dancing by her lonesome to the instrumental to Coolio's song *I'll C U When You Get There* while twirling her auburn hair in the middle of Jaffrey and his brother Theron's seven million dollar condominium located on the seventh floor.

A party was under way on the second floor of the immaculate, three level, spacious suite that had a partial view of Central Park. This was a high-end, private party consisting of wealthy clientele the Fischer brothers was hosting this weekday evening. Men and women in stylish suits, the rich business types who handled millions of dollars a day for wealthy citizens across America and beyond moved about in a quirky manner, tilting their heads back and kicking their legs out doing an odd, tango-like dance by themselves as they paraded over marble floors and underneath crystal chandeliers. It was their way of winding down from the excessive demands of working Wall Street, but in reality, they were merely high-class junkies able to hide their habit through their opalescent wealth and pompous dialogue.

The group of thirteen, including the Fischer brothers, had just gotten into the swing of things by doing a couple of lines of cocaine and were now awaiting their pill connect as Jaffrey had called Zelda earlier in the day and requested she drop by.

Jaffrey smiled as the woman fell back beside him on a leather chaise in a dream-like state while still twirling her hair. *"Wa a gwaan? Look on mi bling? Dat wicked, nuh?"* (What's going on? See my chain? That's cool, huh?) he said to the woman as he held out a platinum chain with a diamond-crusted crucified Jesus that sported ruby eyes.

The woman merely smiled as she reached out and rubbed Jaffrey's vanilla thighs through his silk pants. "Do you have the pills? I want pills," she said in a raspy voice while nuzzling up against his neck as she held onto an empty stem glass.

"Naa worry bout it, they soon come," Jaffrey responded as he picked up a bottle of champagne and topped off the woman's glass. "We have us some fun later, aright?" he rhetorically asked as he began kissing the woman's shoulders and chin.

Meanwhile, down on the first floor of the condominium, thirty-one year-old Theron Fischer was on a cell phone wrapping up a call with his sister. *"Ya and Jaffrey stay tallowah! My ironbird leaves in an hour and ah go back to Margarita! I see over yah package and it be in Satday."* (Stay strong and sturdy. My flight leaves in an hour and I go back to Margarita. Your package will be in Saturday.) the woman stated in reference to a new shipment of heroin that was coming in.

"Dat cris! Yah a don gorgon!" (That is cool. You is a master of situations!)

"And Mi lub yu kyaan done." (My love for you can't end.)

Theron laughed and said, "Say tuh your husband big up!" before tucking his phone inside his suit jacket. He was headed upstairs to join the party when the doorbell chimed.

Theron walked over, peered through the peephole and saw Zelda's tan-skinned face and puffy Afro and pulled the door open. *"Zelda King, Wa'ppun?"* (What's happening?)

"Hey, bad bwoy!" Zelda smiled as she hugged Theron and turned to introduce her new friend. "You know Nadia, aright? This here is my friend Krause," she said, introducing Sascha.

"Where yah meet the ooman, Zelda? She's a bit long in the teet!" Theron laughed.

"We all old except for Nadia," Zelda remarked as she stepped aside so Theron could lock the door.

"Coo yah, we have a coil upstairs but it is lickle for Chewsday. Only seven tousand." (We have a roll of money upstairs but it is little for Tuesday. Only seven thousand.) the Jamaican stated as he extended his hands outwards towards the spiral staircase.

"Jaffrey told me. Krause came to sample the goods. She has friends that love to party," Zelda boasted through raised eyebrows.

"We'll see about dat," Theron stated as he led the trio up the stairs to the second floor.

Zelda and Nadia were making small talk with Theron as Sascha tailed them in silence. She was scanning the place for weakness but could find none on the inside as she eased up the clear, glass stairs. Before she'd made it to the second floor, Sascha understood that she would have to catch the Fischer brothers on the outside. From that point on, she had no interest in being in the presence of her marks nor that of their company.

Jaffrey saw the group walking up the stairs and smiled over the music. *"Zelda! Nadia! Nah Wi gwaan hab a bashment time."* (Now we are going to have a great time.) he said as he eased up from the chaise and went and greeted his friends and their guest.

The Fischer brothers, although being ruthless, were the type of men who loved to party whenever the opportunity arose. They were hard for their sister to control when they had heroin to sell, let alone when they were awaiting a shipment, as they were on this day.

"You damn right we gwaan bash!" Zelda laughed as she hugged Jaffrey and walked with him over to a large, circular table. She went into the small satchel she was carrying and spread out hundreds of tablets of Percocet pills. "Have at it! Theron, where my coil?" she yelled aloud.

"And the champagne?" Nadia followed as she began clapping her hands above her head to The Fugees' song *Killing Me Softly* while sliding across the marble floor.

"Yuh no dance, Krause? Yuh no toke or snort?" Jaffrey asked his new guest as he handed her a flute of champagne.

"Me no toke or snort," Sascha replied as she took the glass from Jaffrey and smiled.

"*A weh ya baan?*" (Where were you born?)

"I'm from that way. London." Sascha lied as she pointed east.

"Yuh undastan mi!"

Sascha smirked over Jaffrey's remark as his surprise reminded her of the night before when she encountered three of Zelda's associates over in Brooklyn. Only those who knew her closely understood just how dangerous a woman she really was at her core.

All of the Germans had a certain touch of goofiness to them to a degree as they were fun-loving, but they were the type that would smile in your face while sticking a knife in your gut at the same time. Jaffrey and Theron had no clue as to who they'd just let into their home, and in the end, it would cost them dearly as Sascha Merkendorf was a killer of international sorts with dreadfully cunning tactics and had the patience of Job.

"Let me tell you why I come here," Sascha said to Jaffrey as she sipped her champagne and eyed Central Park. "Me and my banker friends come here often, but I have been coming to America since my youth. My friends, all female, and years younger than I, asked me to find them a place to party and they are willing to spend up to twenty-five thousand dollars every time they bash. For that, I will take a solid twenty percent off the top every time if you allow them to party here. The rest they will spend on the party stuff you and your brother have to offer. The cocaine, the heroin and or the pills. Whatever they fancy on any given day."

"Here we bash all the time. If yuh frens have the gwop dey can play with us."

"I will have the money next time you bash. Let Zelda know and she will alert me and I will tell my friends. It is only three of them."

"Small group! Small group! Yuh brang the twenty-five and take yuh twenty percent cut and if dey will spend the rest on any toot or smoke of spliff or wuteva we have deal." Jaffrey remarked as smiled up at Sascha.

"Can I have more champagne?" Sascha requested.

"Follow mi!" Jaffrey cheered. "Enjoy yuh self, fren!"

Sascha had her glass refilled and set it aside as she took a seat at a bar counter and began people watching. She'd had one drink and that was enough as she had to remain focused. The Fischer brothers ran a loose ship in her eyes. She'd seen far better and deadlier in past jobs.

Like the job she'd done overseas back in 2006 in the Netherlands where she murdered two of Amsterdam's top heroin dealers in order to make way for Tanya and Faye to begin shipping their own manufactured poppy seeds back to America via a port in Savannah, Georgia. It'd taken three months to get the men to trust her and let down their guard, but Jaffrey and Theron had welcomed her in on the strength of Zelda in a matter of hours.

While others partied, Sascha texted Boogie, who was waiting with Eva inside Zelda's SUV, and had her and Eva go and purchase a tan wool coat, size forty denim jeans and a brown extra-large turtle neck sweater, a medium-sized kennel, three pairs of shoestrings, and two pairs of dark grey mittens. She also requested a blonde wig, scissors, a dark grey skull cap, black shoe polish, a can opener, four large cotton towels, three wool blankets, duct tape and an empty shopping cart before heading back to Eighty-Eight Street—things she would need to complete her job the following morning. From that point forth, she remained in the background, pretending to drink and pop pills while Zelda and Nadia kept Theron and Jaffrey preoccupied while she laid out her plan.

****

After hanging with the Fischer brothers for nearly four hours, Sascha and company left the condominium. Boogie and Eva had gone out to fulfill Sascha's scavenger list and had returned just as the women walked back into the parking lot.

"How'd it go, Sascha?" Boogie asked from the front passenger seat of Zelda's Escalade.

"It looks good. The Fischer brothers will be no more come mid-morning. I will catch them at that time," Sascha remarked as she removed her pristine cashmere coat and donned the cheap tan wool coat. She then grabbed hold of the kennel, gathered her DVD player and DVDs and backed away from the car. "Did you get the empty basket like I asked, Boogie?"

"Yeah. It's in the back. What you doing?" Boogie asked puzzled as she watched Sascha open the kennel and rip open the roll of duct tape.

"I will stay on this side of town tonight." Sascha replied. "Zelda and Nadia, could you remove the empty basket from the back of the car for me, please? Boogie, open the hood for me so I can get my things."

Boogie pooped the hood and Sascha went and removed two black .380 semi-automatic handguns and stuck them inside the kennel and secured them to its roof with the duct tape. She then meticulously placed the wool blankets, her DVD player and DVDs, can opener and shoe polish inside the basket before donning the blonde wig. "They're all clean, but they look as if they belong to someone homeless, right, girls?" she asked as she slowly walked around the basket.

"If you say so." Eva quipped as she eyed Sascha's costume.

"From a distance yeah," Boogie nodded, now fully-understanding Sascha's murder scheme.

"All that's fine and dandy, but where you sleeping at?" Zelda asked. "And what's with the kennel? You can just hide the guns in the blanket."

"You would do that and get arrested," Sascha responded as she checked to make sure her DVD player was fully-charged. "Now, I need three hundred dollars and you ladies can be on your way."

Zelda curled her lips and looked over to Boogie. "Your turn, chick!" she adamantly stated. "I donated earlier today at Best Buy."

Nadia looked over to Zelda and said, "But we just got like almost seven thousand dollars from Jaf—"

"Eh…eh…eh…" Zelda interrupted while clapping her hands and stomping in her heels. "We done rode around with pistols and Percocet pills all day helping Godzilla get her shit together. If it was me I woulda ran in there and shot everybody until I got to Jaffrey and Theron—but this big-enough-to-dunk-one done laid out some diabolical shit and wants to be on her own! Let her have it!" she dragged as she threw up her hands.

"What's with the money?" Boogie asked, trying to learn a new angle as she pulled out her knot and handed Sascha fifteen $20 dollar bills.

"I need more homeless people props, Boogie. There's a bus stop with a bench across the street and they can't see from there from no point inside their home because I looked while I was inside. I will be fine. Just call me every two hours. If I answer, I am fine. If I don't answer something is wrong and you should come," Sascha remarked over blank stares. "I have to do it this way. Trust me," she ended as she gripped the handle on her basket and began wheeling it back towards Central Park.

Now alone, Sascha was free to fulfill her latest contract in the manner in which she felt the most comfortable. She walked back onto Central Park West and headed south, walking for six blocks until she found a market that sold fruit and can goods.

She went into the market and bought four cans of tuna, a pound of peaches, three gallons of water and a bag of ice and began making her way back to Eighty-Eighth Street.

By two a.m. Sascha was sitting on the bench beside the bus stop just outside of Central Park in her tan wool coat. She'd used some of the shoe polish to dirty her face and the coat itself, and had ripped the tips off one of the pairs of mittens. She placed the full set of mittens over her hands and slid the second pair over the top of the first pair before pulling out a can of tuna and using the can opener to cut the top off.

Late-night strollers walked past what they viewed as that of an innocuous homeless woman camping out for the night on a park bench and paid her no mind as she toyed around with a kennel while mumbling incoherently. Amid tossed cigarettes and derisive stares, Sascha eased up from the bench, growling in the process to add luster to her rouse as she leaned down in her blonde wig and picked up the kennel and walked a few paces behind the bench.

In the darkness that was only feet away from light foot traffic, Sascha knelt down amongst the shrubs behind the bench and tied a shoestring to the cage's opening. She then dumped the contents of the can of tuna inside and returned to her seat while holding onto the shoestring. She'd thought about asking passersby for change for extra-added effect, but she felt that would've been laying it on too thick, so she opted for complacency.

Making herself at home, Sascha pulled her basket close, pulled out her DVD player, opened season one of Benson, and put the first DVD in. Right away, the eccentric orchestra of music caught her attention as she watched a black man being patted down by a security guard and then being chased by Doberman pinchers in front of what looked like to her, the White House. "*I see no humor in that. Where's the woman Krause?*" she wondered to herself as the music settled down and the show began.

Not even two minutes in, Sascha was left intrigued by the characters on the show, especially the black man who' been chased inside the white mansion. With her heart content, she settled back and opened her bag of peaches, poured up a cup of water over ice and began watching Benson for the first time ever. The show was everything to her. She didn't agree that she looked like the woman Krause, but she appreciated the woman's Bavarian accent.

While laughing away and eating her peaches, Sascha felt the shoestring she had tied to her coat flex a little. She turned the volume down on her DVD player, peered over the top of the bench and saw half of a cat's body creeping inside the cage. She turned to the side in her seat just as the cat's tail disappeared inside the kennel. She was prepared to pull her hand back to pull the cage door shut until the sound of, "Whoop! Whoop!" and flashing lights startled her, causing her to jump and pull the kennel over onto its side as she turned around and found herself staring at a NYPD patrol car.

"What the hell are you doing over there?" a heavy-set Caucasian asked in a New York accent as he sat in the passenger seat.

"Look what you've done just now!" Sascha complained as she rose from the bench just as the cat she'd been trying to ensnare darted out into the street.

"You're a cat lover?" the police officer laughed as he looked over to his partner. "Funny how nearly every homeless person wants a pet when they have no shelter for themselves. Not that I'm knocking it, though. It's a good deed, I guess. You wouldn't be tampering with that fruit stand beside ya' now would ya'?" he asked as his stubby, dark-blue jacket-covered right arm hung out the passenger side window.

Sascha pointed to her bag of peaches and said, "I have my own eats. The cats are entertainment. Maybe dinner."

"Dinner? Well," the officer laughed as he took in Sascha's appearance. "I have your description now. I best not get a call about you fitting the description or we'll come back through here and run ya' down to precinct."

"The only way I'll fit a description is if you say I fit a description and come back and try to harass me because you say I fit a description." Sascha countered while staring at the officer.

"You tryna be a smart ass this morning?" the officer asked as he moved to open his door.

"Chill out! You'll make detective soon enough, but this ain't way!" the officer's partner suggested as he held him back.

"These homeless broads, man I tell ya'. You better behave now, young lady. And nothing better not happen to that fruit stand over there!" the first officer said as he pointed to the unknown woman. "I never forget a face."

"Neither do I," Sascha stated.

The officer eyed the homeless woman for several lingering seconds. "I got my eye on you, blonde. Be careful!"

"Likewise," Sascha replied with her head bowed as the patrol car eased on up Central Park West headed north.

Once the police unit had moved on, Sascha went on and set up her kennel for a second time before resuming her seat on the bench with her DVD player, fruit and ice water. From her vantage point, she could see the lights from the Fischer brothers' condominium, and had keen sight on the entrance, clearly able to see all who came and went as the three 'o' clock hour approached. The three-story loft on the seventh floor of the building was dark in its entirety, letting her know that the Fischer brothers had turned in for the night.

Unless she'd missed a face, Sascha had witnessed ten of the people inside the condominium leave the premises inside of an hour, neither of which was that of the Fischer brothers. That meant that there were three people left inside the condominium —Theron and Jaffrey, and that of a white female—if she was correct in her observation. Sascha also couldn't rule out late night arrivals, but the job would be adjusted accordingly because come dawn, she had in mind to fulfill her contract and move on to her next assignment.

****

"Yuh ready tuh be taken tuh work, mi gal?" Jaffrey asked the brunette woman he'd spent the night with as he stood in the threshold decked out in an off-white silk suit and dark tan leather shoes while watching her place eyeliner onto her eyelids.

"One moment, Jaffrey," the woman politely replied. "My husband is going to question my actions. What ever shall I tell him?" she asked in a prim manner.

"Ooman naa like bait." (Women don't like punks.) "Yuh here because it's wuh yuh gwaan be."

"I do want to be here," the woman replied as she backed away from the bathroom counter and took in her appearance. "Doesn't answer my question, though."

"Yuh husband's chi chi! Forget him!"

"He's not gay. He's just…"

"A Half eediat! (stupid person) Make haste! Mi and Theron gwine adoor! (are going outside.)

"You're of no help to this relationship!" the woman complained as she grabbed her purse off the marble sink and walked behind Jaffrey at a hurried pace.

****

"In case things go right? You need to be on the east corner of Eighty-Eight Street within an hour." Sascha stated to Boogie over the phone.

"We leaving the Bronx now," Boogie stated from the back passenger seat as she rode with Zelda, Nadia and Eva.

After ending the call, Sascha set out to begin her day. The constant 'meows' from two cats she'd captured hours earlier coated her ears as she poured up a cup of water and pulled a toothbrush from her basket and coated it with toothpaste. Foam lined the corners of her mouth as she eyed the people at the bus stop, who were staring at her in repugnance. She went about her routine, rinsing her mouth and washing her face with a towel as people did their best to avoid her for fear she would ask for a handout or engage them in conversation.

Like the working class at the bus stop, Sascha was happy when the bus pulled up and picked up the riders. She thanked God silently as she sought out breakfast by easing up from the bench and walking over to the fruit stand.

"Four peaches, please," Sascha requested to the Indian man as he opened the lid on his fruit stand. It was nearing eight 'o' clock and time was ticking down. Central Park West was lined with traffic from pedestrians, to the trademark Yellow Cabs, as the morning rush got underway.

"I git dem fresh from South Carolina every morning at a warehouse in Jers-see!" the man stated proudly as he bagged the fruit. "Four dollars."

"I paid three dollars for a whole pound last night." Sascha reasoned.

"From the store six blocks south of here I know," the man replied. "But you are not six blocks south of here this morning."

"That's your tactic? To belittle your customers?" Sascha asked as she sat her kennel. containing two captured cats, down on the ground and pulled out a twenty-dollar bill while eyeing the entrance to the condominium.

"I don't have to do that because it is the truth," the owner of the fruit stand retorted. "I've just opened and already my business has many customers besides yourself. Do you have anything smaller than a twenty? If not, you'll have to wait for my regulars who bring me ones every morning."

The cats inside the kennel began fighting with one another at that moment. When Sascha turned and looked down at the squabbling felines, she caught a glimpse of a man in a bright suit walking with another man and woman. "Today is your lucky day," she said as handed the man a $20 dollar bill and placed the kennel inside her basket. "Keep the change."

"Gracias! Gracias!" the fruit stand owner smiled as he held onto the twenty-dollar bill.

"For me it's Danke," Sascha stated in a nonchalant manner as she sat her fruit inside her basket and began pulling it towards the intersection.

When the walk signal turned white, Sascha began wheeling her basket across the intersection. She kept in mind to give off a decrepit appeal while timing things just right as she wanted to cross and began pushing her cart behind the Fischer brothers and their lone acquaintance.

Halfway across the boulevard, Sascha could see that she was getting ahead of herself and her marks, so she inconspicuously slowed her pace on the southbound side of Central Park West as she passed in front of a row of cars waiting for the light to change from red to green. She kept her head bowed, but her eyes upward, as she scanned Eighty-Eight Street, which ran along the side of the condominium and held its parking lot.

The morning foot traffic was the thing bothering Sascha. People were everywhere. Standing on all of the corners bundled up in groups holding onto cups of coffee, purses and briefcases, and nearly everyone had a cell phone pressed to his or her ear and was enthralled in their own personal conversation. Sirens off in the distance could be heard as America's most famed city, set against the symphonic sounds and movements of everyday life, became New York's lead Conductor.

Sascha made it to the opposite side of the street just as the light turned green. Cars darted out into the intersection right before she stepped onto the curb and fell in behind Jaffrey, Theron, and their female acquaintance.

Eighty-Eight Street wasn't as hectic as Central Park West, Sascha noticed, just as Zelda had stated to her the night before, as she wheeled her shopping cart. Here, most people walked alone while absorbed in their daily weekday routine. Cars parked up and down the street shielded her from pedestrians on the opposite side of the street as she pushed her cart behind her marks. Halfway down the block, she clicked on her DVD player, picked up its remote and hit the pause button just before the DVD began to play. She then set her kennel on top the three blankets, getting it level with the top of the basket as she continued tailing the unsuspecting trio.

Jaffrey and Theron, meanwhile, had rounded the backside of the building and walked amongst the many lavish cars until they reached their burnt orange four door 2009 S-Class Mercedes.

Just outside of the parking lot, Sascha Merkendorf heard an alarm chirp once and decided to make her move by wheeling her cart into the parking lot. She peeered out from behind the rear end of a parked SUV and could see the Fischer brothers up ahead to her left. At that moment, she used her remote to click on her DVD player while pulling the door open on her kennel. The theme song to Benson began playing as the two feral cats she'd captured the night before leapt from the cage.

"Ohh, noooo! Oh, mi feline! Mi feline!" Sascha feigned.

The commotion was enough to get Jaffrey and Theron to look over their shoulders where they eyed a homeless, blonde-haired woman in a dirty tan coat pushing a grocery cart and crying over cats that were running away from her.

"*Wa a gwaan?*" (What's going on?) Theron asked suspiciously as he reached inside his suit jacket and placed his hand on his Colt .45 semi-automatic.

"*Naa worry bout it.*" (Don't worry about it). "Just a poor Caucasian and her cats." Jaffrey answered as he pulled the driver's side door open on the Mercedes.

Seeing the brothers were at ease, Sascha purposely knocked her kennel onto the ground before pushing the cart forward in order to give it momentum. She then knelt down before the kennel and reached inside and loosened the duct tape that held her two .380 silencer-tipped semi-automatics while steadily crying out for her runaway cats.

Jaffrey, meanwhile, had just helped his mistress into the backseat of the Mercedes. He and Theron were climbing into the front seat of their ride when the back window on the Mercedes shattered.

"Bloodclot! She be ah bumboclot assassin! Assassin!" Theron screamed aloud as a bullet lodged into the back of his shoulder, forcing him up against the dash and leaving him in agonizing pain and unable to react.

Jaffrey jumped from behind the steering wheel and pointed a .40 Glock in the homeless woman's direction. He was aiming to shoot, but all he saw was the morning air and an abandoned shopping cart filled with blankets and a portable DVD player rolling in his direction. He kept his gun aimed on the basket trying to locate the assassin, but he was quickly distracted by a cat that'd run from underneath his car. He looked down briefly, pointed his gun and let off a round that'd ricocheted off the asphalt.

"Bumboclot, show yuh self!" Jaffrey demanded as he raised the gun a second time as the shopping cart rolled up and bumped the rear of his Benz. "*Yu wanna romp wit me?*" (Do you want to mess with me?) "*Yu waan tess mi?*" (Do you want to test me?)

"I have tested you and you have failed the test," Sascha countered as she came up behind Jaffrey from the front side of the Mercedes and pumped two slugs into the base of his neck from her muzzled .380 semi-automatic.

Theron could only watch his brother dropped from sight as the blonde homeless woman's face came into view. "Yuh was in mi crib last night!" he said through wide, terrified eyes the time the woman pulled the driver's side door open. "*Mi always inna crosses.*" (I always have bad luck.) "*Naa Badda mi.*" (Don't bother me!) he pleaded as he lay up against the dash of the Mercedes bleeding profusely from his right shoulder.

"Bad luck you have today, but to not be bothered today is just a wish unfulfilled today," Sascha casually responded as she placed the muffled barrel of one her guns into the interior of the Mercedes and squeezed the trigger at her leisure while looking over the car's roof to see if anyone was watching the hit unfold.

The morning hustle and bustle was unwittingly cooperating to the fullest extent possible as Sascha fired off a final round. She leaned down and saw that she'd shot Theron four additional times, the bullets landing in the left side of his face and neck in a checkered pattern as flesh lay splattered on the dash and in lower corner of the inside windshield.

Not one to forget, Sascha peered over into the backseat and eyed the Caucasian woman balled up on the floorboard whimpering. She stepped back, gently closed the driver's side door and casually pumped two more rounds into Jaffrey's skull as she crept over his body and pulled the back door open on the Mercedes.

The woman pleaded for her life by screaming aloud, "Please! I'm, I'm a married woman! I'll never say nothing! Just let me go!" She'd surrendered by raising her hands as she lay on the back floorboard of the Mercedes.

"It's nothing personal between you and I. Just the company you keep," Sascha stated in a nonchalant manner as she leaned down into the car and let off three rounds that sliced through the woman's heart. She then pulled back from the car's interior and eased the door shut on the Benz and returned to her cart without raising suspicion.

As she made her way out of the parking lot, Sascha called Boogie. "I am done here. Where're you at now?" she asked once Helen had answered.

"We on the Henry Hudson about twenty minutes away. Walk west to Columbus Avenue and head north to Ninety-Sixth Street. We'll pick you up there."

"Okay," Sascha responded in a calm manner as she picked up her kennel and closed the cage. As she was placing the coop back into the basket, one of the cats she'd freed ran up to her and began purring while brishong up against her legs. "One of you came back I see," she stated happily as she picked the cat up, sat it on the piles of blankets and began pushing the cart out of the parking lot while opening a can of tuna, retuning the role of an innocuous homeless woman who simply loved cats as she made her way over to 96th Street.

CHAPTER THIRTY-EIGHT

SIX GOOD APPLES

Me, Phillip Tran, and Grover Kobayashi left our cars behind and walked along Pier 80's railyard in San Francisco as I eyed the two freighters the Asians' owned that were undergoing repairs as they prepared for a trip to Philadelphia. From Saint Louis to the San Francisco Bay Area, product was being moved under the radar and things were quiet on all fronts, but it was only a false sense of security, I knew, as the entire organization, Germans included, had heat on the horizon.

We looking at two weeks since Sascha had killed the Fischer brothers up in New York and the Germans were putting pressure on the family to fulfill the contract on Tammy Moto being they'd offed three men free-of-charge before Tammy had even been touched. Knowing what was on the line, I went on and gave the go ahead for Phil and Grover to go on and take care of Tammy and square things up with the Germans before our alliance broke down.

Since Club Indigo's opening night, I'd had flown to the Cayman Island two more times to re-up and the family was in the last stages of offing another six hundred kilograms. My plan was to wait for Phil and Grover to handle Tammy before setting up another deal with Swan. The family had moved over seventeen hundred kilos in three month's time and had netted a total of thirty-four million dollars off the cocaine, and a grand total of fifty-five million dollars when coupled with our legitimate businesses.

We pulling in nearly twenty million dollars a month, but this money coming with a heavy price tag that's forcing us to make adjustments accordingly. My main concern is Gacha. Dude been quiet lately. Swan ain't have no news for me the last two times we met and nobody ain't answer for the Fischer brothers or the Sheinheimer job down in Boca Raton yet. We can't be getting away murder this easy. Instincts telling me something up with it all, but I can't crack the code. Faye assured me that everything was copasetic according to the Senator on their payroll, but I can't help but to think that we overlooking something in all that's going down.

Maybe it's just a case of paranoia over what's about to go down with Phil and Grover on my part, but I can't ignore it. I wanted all bases covered while they away so I'm gone keep an eye on things here in San Francisco with Samantha and Lee at my side until they get back. Naomi gone be in town with Walee, Kimi and Koko to look over the mall we just bought so that'll give me time to kick it with the family and learn some new business in the process. My order as it stands is to not move anything, neither a brick, a gram or a single line of coke while me and my people in town and Phil and Grover away. When they done, I'll be headed back to the Cayman Island to re-up on our next shipment, but to be honest, I'm not sure if I'm gone make it back alive or not, but I keep that to myself because I don't wanna upset the family because it's my burden to bear in silence.

"How long before those freighters be ready to move?" I asked Phil as I took in the massive orange, brown and white cargo ships that had a score or more men hanging off the sides of either ship welding steel plates while others worked on the top sides of the decks.

"Two months, Ben," Phil said to me. "You know, with this move, we'll be moving into the heroin distribution market, right? From what you've told me, the Devereaux family has the capacity to move five hundred kilograms a month. Can the Germans handle that much supply? And what will be our port of entry?"

"It's this Navy town Samantha told me about down in

Florida where she trained called Pensacola. It got a port that's able to handle a ship that size," I told Phil as I nudged my chin over to the freighters off in the distance. "Totally off the radar, fam. What we gone do is lease about a hundred containers and load 'em down with the Devereaux family coffee and mix that boy and that girl in with it, ya' dig? Bury it inside legitimate freight. The first loads out gone have our merchandise on those trailers and we can route 'em anywhere from there."

"I know of Pensacola, Florida," Grover stated. "It has this big World War II Museum my father took me, Phillip and Xiang to as children. It was the place where Ted Bundy was caught and sent to death row. There's a saying down in Florida, Ben…you go there on vacation and—"

"Leave on probation," I stated, finishing up Grover's statement as I'd heard that Florida slogan myself a time or two from way back in the day. "But we have a Senator on our side," I told him as I paused under the setting sun and looked down into his eyes with my hands tucked into my slacks. "From Pensacola we only five hours away from Atlanta, and ten a hours' drive from Cincinnati and Charlotte, North Carolina. The drivers can run that legal."

"What about Saint Louis?" Phillip asked.

"Saint Louis still gone be in play, but we have to learn more about those feds Jay-D uncovered. In the meantime, we expanding operations further east to keep the feds off our tail. All that's gone be left is the club, my wife restaurant and the recording studio Jay-D just opened up for a while. We working on going legit in Missouri. It's all part of the plan to move away from drugs entirely."

"What about our business here on the west coast?" Grover asked.

"You have two freighters," I said to Grover. "We'll send both to South America, but only one will go to Florida. The other one—"

"We'll dock right here," Phil stated, finishing my thought as he nodded with understanding. "It'll be just like how we operated in Seattle when my father was in control of the organization."

"You and Grover are our biggest earners, Phil," I remarked. "After all the hits the west coast faction of this family done sustained? Y'all deserve it. Earned it, to be real with ya'. I'm giving you and Grover control of the west coast faction when you come off this Tammy Moto hit. Run it as you see fit on a sixty-forty split our way. Whenever the day comes that the Holland family close shop on this drug game? You and Grover gone get the keys to the car tax free. Until then? We do things our way. The Holland way."

Phil looked over to Grover at that moment and I could tell they both respected the arrangement. The thing behind my reasoning is the fact that taking down a federal agent was basically a suicide mission. Last year alone, in 2009, forty-eight federal agents were killed in the line of duty and every single assailant was captured or killed. I looked the shit up before signing off on it and I'd given Phil and Grover more than one chance to back out, but they'd refused. And with the Germans having killed three people whose name I'd dropped on them, we'd come to a point to where there was no backing out on Tammy Moto. Somebody in the family had to get at her, and Phil and Grover had been chomping at the bit to get at either her or Lisa. It wasn't my intent to play the Asians, though. Should they complete the job and make it out alive, they would've earned the right to run their own family and I was willing to concede to it, because it was the right thing to do for business sake.

"We accept your offer on a preliminary, Ben," Phil stated to me as Grover nodded in silent agreement. "But my counter is on the sixty-forty split. Give us the sixty percent, that way, me and my god brother will use that money to pay our soldiers."

"Fifty percent," I countered, anticipating the counteroffer. True enough the Asians had the ships, but we had the product, and without product, they'd be moving nothing more than coffee beans, oranges and cheap fabric twice a month.

"Fifty percent is fair," Phil told me as he extended his hand. "Tomorrow morning we leave for Philadelphia. It may take some time."

"Take all the time you need, fam. You make it back you got a fifty-fifty split with the family on the product."

Phil nodded his approval before looking over to the ship. "Let's do a tour and make sure everything is to the family's liking for this next phase we enter. Our plane lands at five thirty in the evening. Have someone meet us out there to supply us with the guns for the job," he asked of me.

While walking, I dialed up Faye to put her up on game, letting her know my people would be in Philly the following night and they needed guns to complete the job.

"Someone will meet with them at Wharton Square Playground in Point Breeze the time they land," she let it be known before ending the call.

****

"Son-of-a-bitch took off running!" Lisa Vanguard radioed through her portable CB as she threw on her FBI jacket, climbed out of her red '64 Mustang, and crept along the worn brick wall of an abandoned warehouse.

It was now three weeks after Sascha Merkendorf had killed the Fischer brothers up in New York, and a week after Phil and Grover had met up with Ben over in San Francisco, early May of 2009. Lisa Vanguard was down in Allegheny West, a rundown neighborhood in north Philadelphia, conducting field operations. For the past couple of months, she and Tammy Moto had been operating undercover, working a case against a man in his early thirties who they believed was the main source of heroin flooding the streets of north Philadelphia.

Today was to be the day the agents were going to make their bust and gain the upper hand; but the guy they had suspected of dealing large amounts of heroin had grown suspicious and fled the scene, disappearing into the darkness with seven kilograms of heroin tucked inside a duffle bag when Lisa pulled up into the dirt-covered parking lot in her red Mustang. She radioed Tammy and now the two agents were in pursuit of their suspect under the Philly night sky.

"Do you have a visual?" Tammy radioed back to Lisa as she

rode past her partner's Mustang and drove along the front side of the warehouse.

"Negative," Lisa whispered back through her handheld CB radio as she neared the end of the wall and removed her Glock .40 from her shoulder holster. She waited several seconds before emerging from behind the building with her weapon aimed. On the opposite side of the building, she could see the man running along a set of railroad tracks with the duffle bag draped over his shoulder. "He's headed east towards Twenty-Eighth Street," she radioed to Tammy as she took off after the bag of heroin.

"Headed that way. I'll cut 'em off," Tammy shot back as she sped up in her black on black Ferrari.

Lisa was running full speed in her denim jeans and sneakers with her gun out and her FBI jacket flapping in the wind as she kept the man in her line of sight. "Drop that bag!" she screamed aloud.

"Fuck you, one time!" the man yelled back as he jumped a fence and landed inside a small trucking company that sat across from a line of boarded-up row houses. He was preparing to run up 28th Street and lose himself inside the neighborhood, but he was halted in his tracks when a black Ferrari with a blue light blaring in the dash pulled up in front of the trucking company's entrance.

Tammy jumped from her car with her Glock .40. "Walk this way with your hands above your shoulders!" she commanded.

The man smirked at Tammy before turning around and taking off back in the direction in which he'd previously run. He was hopping back over the fence the same time Lisa was climbing over from the opposite side.

"Shit!" Lisa barked. Her feet touched the ground for not even a second before she jumped back up on the fence and climbed back over, this time, being joined by Tammy. Together, the two agents chased the suspect through litter-filled alleys lined with overflowing dumpsters and discarded furniture while scanning the ground to make sure he hadn't dropped the bag of heroin they so-badly wanted to seize.

They'd both seen the man turn in between a set of row houses and head back towards the railroad tracks, but when they entered the alley behind him, the man was nowhere to be found. Gunshots from above sent them both ducking for cover behind a dumpster as bullets rained down from a fire escape and ricocheted off the metal container and surrounding concrete walls.

When the gunfire hit a lull, Lisa and Tammy rose up from the overflowing, foul smelling steel bin at the same time and unloaded on the fire escape, but their suspect had vacated the balcony and was climbing up towards the roof. "I'll go up here behind him! You run around to the other side and climb up from the other side of the building," Lisa told Tammy as she moved from behind the dumpster and slid another clip into her Glock .40 while running towards the fire escape ladder.

Up on the rooftop, the guy grew anxious as he watched the agent climb the stairs approaching the ledge. He'd run out of bullets in his .44 magnum revolver and had no choice but to keep running. He ran across the asphalt towards the second fire escape and was preparing to climb down when a black plastic Glock was stuck in his face.

"Going somewhere?" Tammy asked matter-of-factly as she stepped up on to the roof. "Drop the bag and your weapon." The man remained frozen in place as he held the bag with one hand and his gun in the other. "Put your gun on the fuckin' ground before I kill you tonight!" Tammy yelled just as Lisa ran up with her gun aimed at the man's head.

"It's over, man," Lisa said while gasping for air. "Do, do like my partner says and set your gun down with the bag and get on your knees."

"I know, I know what, what you really want," the man scoffed through heavy breathing as he eyed Lisa with the Philadelphia night skyline at his back. "This ain't a bust it's a fuckin' jack move. You been setting me up for a sting the whole time."

"That's what you think?" Lisa smirked. "I'm not after you. You're small time."

"Not moving seven kilograms," the man retorted.

"Are you really that stupid?" Tammy scowled as she held her gun on the man. "You just confessed, you dummy!"

"Fuck difference does it make? Y'all running me in, right? I'm caught red-handed, right?"

"Perhaps, but maybe not," Lisa responded. "Drop that gun for me, then we'll talk." The man eyed Lisa as he let the gun fall from his hand. "Good," she said as she stepped closer to the man with her gun still aimed at his head. "What I want to know is who are you working for?"

The man remained quiet as he eyed the women with their guns on him. "She dance real good," he laughed. "Yeah, she dance real good."

"What the fuck does that mean? No riddles! Who's your supplier?" Tammy growled.

"Fuck that! I want my lawyer!" the man stated.

"That's not how this shit works!" Lisa boomed as she tightened the grip on her Glock. "We ask questions and you answer! Correctly! Who're you scoring from? Are they from Philadelphia? Out of town? Who is your supplier? What does she dance good mean?"

"If I tell you, what's that gone do for me, huh? I mean, you, y'all gone let me walk? Or offer me ten years maybe? With my record? That shit ain't gone fly. And the people I fucks with would kill me and my whole fuckin' family if I was to talk. You wanna know where I get my shit from? Do like you been doing and investigate because I ain't got nothin' to tell ya' funky asses."

Lisa eyed the man with disdain as he stood in his baggy black jeans, white hooded sweater and white Jordan's. "This how you wanna play it?" she asked seriously. "Okay, then. Drop the bag."

The man laughed and said, "So you can go in there and take six good apples and leave me stuck with the rotten one and sink me for thirty flat? You want this shit? Go and fetch it!" he exclaimed as he flung the bag off the side of the building before either Lisa or Tammy had a chance to react.

"Fuck!" Tammy fretted as she looked over the side of the building.

Lisa kept her eyes on the man as she crept around his back and peered over the side of the building where she looked down and saw the bag laying in the darkness with its contents still intact. She moved over to the man and held her gun on him as she reached for one of his hands while removing a pair of handcuffs from her waistband. "You're under arrest for conspiracy to distribute heroin in the presence of a federal agent," she stated calmly as she latched the metal to the man's right wrist.

"You serious?" the man asked dismayed as he looked back at Lisa. "I know you want the dope! Go get the shit and leave me the fuck alone!"

Lisa clamped the handcuffs to the man's left wrist, securing him completely before turning him around to face her. "We can make things a lot easier if you just tell me who supplies you."

"We going back to that? I told you I'm not talking!" the man grimaced as he stared down at Lisa with his hands cuffed behind his back.

Lisa pressed her lips together and nodded matter-of-factly. "Okay," she relented. "You wanna play it all the way through to the end I see. Well, let's get started on the paperwork, big man. But first, you have to go and get that bag of heroin you just threw off the roof," she added as she pushed the man over the ledge as he faced her head on. "Be right down!" she yelled aloud over the man's horrifying screams as he plummeted three stories to his death. "Let's go and hide that bag before we radio city patrol," she then said to a stunned Tammy as she moved towards the fire escape and began her descent.

CHAPTER THIRTY-NINE

OVER THE BUBBLY YELPS OF NIMROD

Flashing lights blared from a dozen or more Philadelphia City Police patrol cars and detective units blocking the street as numerous cops, narcotics agents and paramedics walked in and out of an alley where yellow tape surrounded the body of a Caucasian male in his mid-thirties. According to preliminary reports, the man had fallen from the roof of a three story building while trying to elude two federal agents who were operating undercover. A few feet away from the body lay a burst open package of heroin encased in white chalk, and an empty .44 magnum was found on his person.

"Anybody knows this guy's name?" Lisa asked as she walked around the crime scene wearing a pair of thin-framed sunshades and latex gloves.

"Yeah, I know 'em without having to fingerprint 'em," a narcotics detective remarked. "His name is Jesse James Glen."

"The clichéd three first name bad guy," Lisa smirked.

"Right, like Charles Lee Ray, Wayne Lee Gacy and James Earl Jones," the detective responded.

Lisa eyed the detective bedazzled. "I don't think James Earl —"

"Nah, I'm just fuckin' with ya', agent. Who doesn't like the voice of Darth Vader?" the detective laughed. He then jumped serious and said, "I arrested Glen five years ago for cocaine possession and sent him upstate. Guess he changed his marketing strategy."

"I arrested Glen eight years before that for manslaughter and sent his ass away," a patrol officer followed. "He grew up in Strawberry Hill and got a rap sheet longer than interstate ninety-five. I'm not surprised it came to this. Guy's been in and out of trouble since his early teens. Surprised he lasted this long."

"I really would've like to had brought him in," Lisa stated as she looked down at the broken corpse. "Any idea who this guy's supplier is? Does the narcotics unit have anything to help further the federal investigation?"

"I got nothing. I'm Daniels by the way. Detective Daniels," the narcotics detective responded as he sipped his coffee and shook Lisa's hand briefly. "To be honest with ya', I never knew Glen was back in the business. Good work, Agent Vanguard. I know it's the not the outcome you were expecting, but it's one more notch for the good guys. You need help with future investigations be sure and let us know."

"I will hold you to that, Detective Daniels," Lisa smiled. "If I'm of no more use here I'll be excusing myself and let you guys handle things. My report will be filed and turned in tonight before I sign off."

"You and Agent Moto take all the time you need, Agent Vanguard. It's not like Glen has somewhere to be," Detective Daniels joked as the patrol officer beside him chuckled.

Lisa smirked and patted Daniels' shoulder as she strode past him and walked out of the alley over to her red '64 Mustang and climbed inside. She eased through the enclave of government cars with the blue light on her dash flickering and her hand out the window with her FBI badge on display. Upon clearing the guarded crime scene, she pulled up alongside Tammy's Ferrari and the driver's side window eased down.

"They brought it hook, line and sinker," she smiled over to Tammy. "Is the merchandise secure?"

Tammy raised her hand and put the duffle bag on display

briefly before tossing it into the passenger seat of her ride. "What now?" she asked in a dry tone.

"You all right?" Lisa asked in suspicious manner.

"You pushed that guy. He could've been taken in alive." Tammy stated as she eyed Lisa.

"Like the woman you killed in Salem, Oregon in '08?"

"That was different. She had a shotgun," Tammy retorted.

"And Glen shot at us, Tammy. We could've both been killed tonight had he not missed us, ya' know?" When Tammy had no recant, Lisa removed her sunshades and went further. "Didn't look at it from that aspect, huh? What the fuck are you feeling sorry for a dirt bag like Glen for? We still do good police work, Tammy. Tonight was good police work. Another bad guy off the streets!"

"I guess you're, you're right," Tammy finally relented and agreed. "Things could have gone much worse. What's our next move?"

"Good. You're back on the winning team," Lisa smirked as she placed her sunshades back over eyes and pulled a cell phone from her FBI jacket. "We need to keep with the formalities for now. I'm headed downtown to file a report. In the meantime," she said as she held the phone up and threw it over to Tammy, "in the meantime you head on over to Jersey and look through Glen's phone and trace the numbers. Maybe he made contact with his connect. Check emails, texts, that Facebook website, MySpace, everything. Gut that son-of-a-bitch. If something's there? It's your job to uncover it. I'll handle the paperwork for us and meet up with you when I'm done."

"Gotcha," Tammy responded as she tucked the phone into her FBI jacket. "I'm hungry."

"Cook us something while you work," Lisa smiled as she placed her Mustang in drive. "I'll bring the wine," she ended as she crept forward.

Tammy fell in behind Lisa and tailed her downtown where the two split off, Lisa keeping south on Highway 611 while

Tammy headed east on I-676, crossing the Delaware River and entering into the state of New Jersey with six kilograms and a cell phone belonging to Jesse James Glen in the passenger seat of her Ferrari.

****

While Tammy Moto made her way over to Haddonfield, six hundred miles away, over to Cincinnati, Ohio, Helen 'Boogie' Weinberger was on the second floor of 2300 Mulberry Street in her ballerina studio. Ever the eclectic, Boogie was one to keep odd hours. Dancing was her anxiety relief. Like Ben, yet totally unaware of the man's own apprehensions, she, too, was wondering when the hammer would drop. Sheinheimer, by all accounts, was a case closed, but the Fischer brothers were another story, as it was just too quiet for her comfort.

Symbols and high hats dominated the soundproof room as Boogie pranced over the wooden floor in floor in her five-inch heels, black fishnet stockings and ballerina suit while flailing her arms to and fro, bending at the waist on occasion and slowly raising back up while gyrating her hips to her favorite song. Before long, she was in a full ballerina rendition, vibing to Heatwave's song Boogie Nights.

"*...boogie night...get that groove...let it take you higher(boogie night)...make it move...set this place on fire... dance with the boogie get down(dance with the boogie get down)...'cause boogie nights are always the best in town...got to keep on dancing...keep on dancing...*"

All worries were vanquished for Boogie as she stood in one place while snapping her fingers and rocking her shapely hips in the middle of her dancefloor while twirling her nappy, tan afro. Had she not had her cell phones tucked into her ballerina outfit, she would've never felt one of them vibrate against her hip. She paused momentarily, grabbing a towel off a wooden stool as she walked over to the turntable and removed the needle from the groove. "Yeah? What's up, Daniels?" she asked while smiling and breathing heavily.

"They killed 'em," Philadelphia narcotics Detective Daniels told Boogie. "Your guy Glen's been taken out by the feds."

"What?" Boogie asked stupefied. "You said nothing about the feds being in town! What are we paying you for to allow this to happen?"

"Cut me some fuckin' slack will ya'?" Daniels defended. "The investigation was conducted without narcotics being notified, but I have the agents' names to counteract what's been done. It's all I can do for now. I'm sorry, Boogie. They slipped right under my fuckin' nose. I'm, I'm fuckin' sorry, I swear ta' god."

"Who are the agents?"

"Their names are Lisa Vanguard and Tammy Moto. I haven't run any checks on them yet because I'm still on the scene with Glen, but I'll let you know what I can find out the moment I learn anything." Detective Daniels remarked as he stood with his back to the crime scene.

"Nein! Nein! Nein! Fick mich!" (No! No! No! Fuck me!) Boogie exclaimed as she stomped in her heels. "We did our part and this is what we get in return?"

"I can tell you're upset," Daniels stated over loud static as he listened to Boogie repeatedly slamming her phone up against God knows what.

"Upset is an understatement!" Boogie scoffed. She then thought about telling Daniels about the upcoming hit on Tammy Moto, but she'd opted not to do so for the fact that Senator Slack's son, Popeye, had dropped off two .45 caliber semi-automatics and a twelve gauge semi-automatic to some Asians in Philadelphia a week prior and he was now back in Philly.

Tammy's killers were in town, Boogie knew, but having lost her only dealer that allowed for a foothold on the east coast, she was now left wondering what would come of the situation and couldn't help but to think that the Holland family had played her and her family short. Erring on the side of caution, which was a painful decision, Boogie opted to give the Holland family one more day for business sake as she couldn't, or was unwilling to believe that such a thorough family was actually playing mind fuck games that could lead to an all-out war.

"Do nothing, Daniels," Boogie decided after briefly weighing the risks.

"You sure?"

"It is my order. Bother not contacting my mother on this. Let's give it one more day. If I hear nothing, I'll call you back tomorrow night with our next move. Until then? Do nothing."

"You got it," Daniels replied as he looked down at his wristwatch. "It's two in the morning. Talk to you twenty-four hours from now. I'm going home to the wife and kids now, all six of 'em," he sighed before ending the call.

"Come on, Holland family," Boogie said aloud to herself as she rested her hands on the wooden stool she'd been dancing before as she bowed her head in wonderment and digested the reality of it all. "A war between us is not what we need," she ended as she contemplated the ramifications should the hit on Tammy Moto fall by the wayside as she pondered the Asian woman's whereabouts.

****

Just off Highway 70 in the state of New Jersey, lay the town of Haddonfield, the second wealthiest suburb of Philadelphia where homes had an average price tag of $450,000 dollars. Tammy Moto came from wealth. When her parents, Kazuki and Cho Moto, were killed down in Cincinnati back in 1983, she and her two brothers, Arata and Raiden, had split a four million dollar inheritance. At the tender age of fifteen, she had a net worth of $1.3 million dollars from monies that was turned over to her when she turned eighteen.

Lisa had helped Tammy every step of the way. The mansion her parents owned in Indian Hills, just outside of Cincinnati, was sold four $290,000 dollars, good money for the times during the early eighties. She'd paid her way through college, earning a degree in Criminal Law from Temple University alongside Lisa Vanguard. The experience had endeared her to the city of brotherly love and she'd originally purchased a home in Berwyn, Pennsylvania. The home was sold three years ago, back in '07 just before the housing market collapsed, for $700,000 thousand dollars. As of date, Tammy Moto had net worth of $6.5 million dollars, earning on average, somewhere around two hundred thousand dollars a year from her job in law enforcement and other 'outside ventures'.

As she rode up Kings Highway, Tammy received a call from overseas, never noticing the set of headlights tailing her Ferrari. Recognizing the number, she answered. "Raiden," she stated happily. "How are you, brother? How're things in Yokohama?"

"It is two in the afternoon here on the other side of the world, surprised you're up over there. Our beloved oldest brother, Arata, has good news that he wanted me to share with you. Can I speak openly?" Tammy's youngest brother, thirty-five year-old Raiden Moto, asked in a serious tone of voice.

"Yeah, this is a secure line," Tammy replied as she wheeled her Ferrari through the presumably vacant streets of Haddonfield.

"Okay," Raiden stated as he stood atop a blend of elephant and rhinoceros ivory that laced the floors of he and Arata's pristine, high-rise business office while gazing down upon cargo ships that were being loaded down with containers inside a harbor lining Tokyo Bay. "The poppy seeds have been processed and our Yakuza associates gave us a command—a delay is unacceptable. We have to ship right away."

"We haven't the dealers lined up yet," Tammy countered.

"But you have the cities," Raiden reasoned. "Seattle, Salem and Philadelphia is what you have, and there's room for expansion down in San Francisco from what we know. The dealers will come once we establish the market."

"Seattle and Salem are a go, but Philadelphia is a mess right now. And we don't know who's the supplier in San Francisco. That will be a reestablishing, Raiden."

"Comes with the territory," Raiden admitted. "We will ship our product tomorrow morning. It'll take two weeks to cross the Pacific where it will dock in Seattle. Someone, preferably you, must be there."

"What about Philadelphia and San Francisco? You can't just

move into new territory like that!" Tammy objected.

"We can and we will," Raiden firmly countered. "This isn't a negotiation, dear sister. This is what will be. We're coming… we're coming to America with two hundred kilograms of heroin to put out on the market for starters. Like the movie with Murphy Eddie," Raiden arbitrarily joked. He dropped his smile and said, "Warn those if you must, arrest them if you have to, because if not? We will kill them all the time our feet touch the shore."

"I have no one to warn or arrest, Raiden," Tammy sighed.

"All that signifies to me is that we will have to bring more artillery and soldiers than previously planned upon," Raiden stated seriously. "Let me work on that. I'll call you back with the ship's arrival date later this morning. I'm awaiting an official manifest and departure time as we speak," he added before the call abruptly ended.

"People," Tammy sighed as she placed fingertips to her temples and leaned her head back briefly as she turned onto Chews Landings Road, a side street that was bordered on either side by lavish two and three story homes with that of palatial, colonial or contemporary designs. A short, winding drive led to her spacious, contemporary two-story home where she parked in front of her door underneath the semi-circle cobblestone driveway.

Tammy nearly fell onto her lacquered wooden floors the time she closed one of the double doors leading into her home. The day had been a long, drama-filled one that had culminated in the murder of a perp, and the news that her brothers were in the process of shipping two hundred kilograms of cocaine to American shores.

Believing she was getting back in focus, Tammy carried the bag of heroin up to her second floor office and threw it onto her wooden desk along with Glen's cell phone before leaning down to unlock her safe. A ruffling sound was heard out in the hall as she pulled the safe open, so she eased from behind her desk while removing her Glock .40 from her shoulder holster.

"Lisa, is that you? Who's there?" Tammy hesitantly asked as

she aimed her gun at her office's entrance. A few seconds later, Nimrod, her Bull Mastiff puppy wobbled into the room wrestling with a rubber toy bone. "You found your toy," she smiled as she set her gun aside and moved from behind her desk and knelt down to greet her pet. "You're my therapy," she admitted to the playful mammal.

At that exact moment, while in a state of innocence and contentment as she rubbed Nimrod's jowls in a happy state-of-being, Tammy's entire journey through the course of life had slipped into its final stages. Over the bubbly yelps of Nimrod, her slender, green eyes made contact with a pair of black wing-tipped shoes that'd eased up into the threshold. She looked up and saw a face she recognized from the Maruyama trial back in Seattle in '08 and her heart sunk into the pit of her stomach.

Refusing to engage in dialogue, Tammy leapt behind her desk, grabbed her Glock .40 and racked it. She came up blasting from behind her desk within milliseconds, the gun in her left hand as she guarded her face with her right hand while moving side-to-side. Tears of regret flowed from her eyes as she knew this was a battle she could not win, let alone survive.

The man who was in the threshold ducked down inside the room. Tammy shot at him, but the bullets missed, landing just above his hunched over torso. Another Asian crept in low and let loose with a chrome twelve-gauge semi-automatic, catching Tammy by surprise. Buckshot penetrated the agent's chest and torso and she fell back against the paned, bay window that was cut into the wall behind her desk. The glass cracked slightly, a spider pattern appearing in the pane as the gun slipped from her hands over the re-racking of the shotgun. A few seconds later, Tammy's entire body was blown completely out of the window by a powerful shotgun blast.

Grover Kobayashi lowered the barrel on the smoking twelve-gauge as he crept over to the window and peered down on his victim. He could see Tammy laying face up on her stone balcony surrounded by broken shards of glass. One piece had cut through her carotid artery and another had pierced her back and was now poking out through the side of her stomach as she lay dead with her eyes open.

When he turned to leave, Grover was met by Phillip, who was standing behind Tammy's desk. "She left the safe unlocked." Phillip remarked.

"Just like she did the front door," Grover calmly stated.

"Looks like, maybe forty thousand dollars in here," Phillip stated as he knelt down and picked up a banded stack of hundred dollar bills.

"We can't get on the plane with that much money. We should leave it." Grover suggested.

"We must take it to make this look like a robbery," Phil countered as he stuffed the money into his suit jacket.

"What about this?" Grover asked as he held up the opened bag of heroin. "Six kilograms."

"We'll give it to our contact when we drop the guns off. He can have the money as well," Phillip remarked as he grabbed an encased CD and read the lettering. "Insurance?" he questioned. "Wonder what's on here," he pondered out loud as he tossed the CD to Grover. "We'll check it later."

"Fine. We're done here?"

"Yeah," Phillip answered as he stood up and stepped past his god brother. The two men left the room with six kilograms of heroin and forty-thousand dollars in cash, but neither was more valuable than the CD labeled 'Insurance' as they would eventually come to learn.

After leaving Tammy's residence undetected, Phillip and Grover made their way back to Philadelphia where they met up with William 'Popeye' Slack, their contact on behalf of the Germans throughout the Moto job. The two parked their burgundy Dodge Ram station wagon at the end of Race Street Pier down in Old City alongside a black Excursion just before four in the morning as water from the Delaware River lapped at the shoreline.

The window rolled down and Popeye, a yellow-skinned Black/Lakota Indian with neatly-braided hair, came into view as he let the passenger side window down on the SUV.

"You boys took care of business, I take it," Popeye stated calmly as he looked down at the Asians.

"Everything is done," Grover stated from the passenger seat. "We learned some things after the hit," he added.

"Such as?"

"Do you have a laptop?" Grover asked as he held up a disc.

Popeye reached over into the backseat, grabbed a computer and took the CD from Grover. A minute or so went by before the audio system kicked in. The names mentioned and the voices heard therein sent a chill up and down Popeye's spine. "And you got this from Tammy house?" he asked Grover in wonderment.

"That we did. Along with something else," Grover responded as Phillip exited the car with a bag in his hands.

Popeye was handed a bag containing six kilograms of heroin and a stack of hundred dollar bills. "What you want done with this?"

"We can't take it with us," Phillip remarked.

"Not the drugs, but I can get you two some traveler's checks before the flight back to San Fran. I got some people down in DC that can move this product wholesale for four hundred racks. I'm taking fifteen percent of that there for my services and my people in Ohio gone get the rest back to y'all next month some time."

"We don't care about any of that," Grover remarked. "What we want is on that disc."

"I'm gone turn this over to my mother," Popeye remarked. "Just give us some time, alright? Ain't no need in jumping the gun on this here thing because if we play it right, it'll work in our favor big time. Just let us do what we gotta do to set everything up."

"Being patient is not what we do best. Especially in light of the newly-discovered circumstances," Phillip remarked.

Popeye stared Phillip in the eyes with a serious gaze. "The job you did was an agreed upon contract," he stated. "If you wanna go off on some wild vigilante campaign then knock yourself out, brer. But you need to understand, if you don't already, that you and your man right there just murked a federal agent. And now you wanna run off and do another one? Already my people can come under scrutiny for what done went down tonight so we need to be thinking things through clearly before we make a move."

"He's right, Phillip," Grover concurred while nodding his head. "Let the politics play out."

"My man," Popeye smiled over to Grover. "Come on and get in, y'all," he added as one of his goons climbed from the back of the Excursion. "My man right there gone get rid of that Dodge. I got y'all set up on a straight through flight outta Baltimore back to the west coast at eight thirty. I need ta' make a stop and turn this cash into checks beforehand so we need ta' get moving."

****

"Tammy! I got us some wine, girlfriend!" Lisa called out as she used the spare key to enter Tammy's home. "Did you find anything on Glen's cell phone?"

While Grover and Phillip prepared for their flight back to San Francisco, Lisa had just arrived over to Tammy's home just after five in the morning. She was up for a celebration having taken down a rival heroin dealer and getting away with his murder. On top of that, she and her partner now had six more kilograms of heroin to move which could net another four hundred thousand dollars easily when sold wholesale.

Unaffected by the quiet inside the home, Lisa moved towards Tammy's kitchen while removing her FBI jacket and flinging it onto a bar stool before the island counter. "No dinner?" she complained out loud while pulling the refrigerator door open. "You have ground beef thawing! Maybe we can whip up a quick pan of lasagna to go with the wine since you have plenty of mozzarella and cheddar cheese on hand?"

With the wine in her hand and holding on to two bags of cheese, Lisa turned to face the counter and had an epiphany: she'd been talking to herself the entire time. She set the groceries down, pulled her Glock .40 from her shoulder holster and began creeping through the home in silence. The entire first floor had been checked before she made her way over to the staircase and entered into a slow ascent while scanning the floor above. As she neared the top of the stairs, a whimpering sound encompassed her ears.

Lisa peered around the edge of the wall and saw Tammy's office just down the hall with Nimrod sitting before the doorway scratching his ears. With her gun cocked, she crept over the marble floor, stepped into the room and immediately laid eyes on the shattered bay window. The rogue agent grew stoic in the face as she made her way over to Tammy's desk and saw her partner and lifelong friend laying face up on her balcony. The opened safe and missing heroin would lead a less experienced detective to believe that Tammy was the victim of a home invasion.

Lisa knew better, however; she and Tammy had done so much wrong in times past that there was not a single doubt left in her mind that this was nothing short of an orchestrated hit. The who was unknown for certain, but Lisa's first guess would be that of JunJie Maruyama's clan as only they had enough crazy in them to take down a federal agent. Either way, this was a bad scenario for Lisa; but she'd been left with a way out. The opened safe would lead any detective worth his or her salt to conclude that a robbery had gone bad and Tammy Moto had come out on the losing end of a gun battle.

With the crime scene speaking for itself, Lisa opted to remove herself entirely and not bother notifying authorities and let things play out on their own. Once Tammy's body was discovered, New Jersey law officials would be overseeing the investigation alongside the federal bureau of investigations and it would be a while before she would be contacted to assist in the investigation. She was preparing to leave the home when a cell phone ringing on Tammy's corpse chimed.

Lisa refused to touch Tammy's body with her bare hands. She donned a pair of latex gloves and went to retrieve the phone, but it'd stopped ringing. She eased the phone from the inside pocket of Tammy's suit jacket and read a missed call whose number she didn't recognize right away. She was preparing to set the phone back in place, but was alerted by a notification signaling an incoming message. She placed the phone on speaker and listened in on the message while kneeling over Tammy's body. *"Tammy, Arata here. You went to sleep on me? Our ship, the Red Dragon, will dock in Seattle on May twenty-ninth at three in the afternoon. Me and Raiden will be on board and look forward to seeing you when we arrive. Talk to you soon."*

Two weeks or so would be enough time for Lisa to give her statement regarding Tammy's murder while deciding on how she would explain things to her brothers once they arrive. She knew of their plan to traffic heroin into America and she wanted to keep that line up and running. Tammy may have been out of commission, but she was still very well much part of the action.

On top of that, with Arata and Raiden coming to American shores, she would have the muscle needed to go after the people she believed responsible for her partner's death without getting her own hands dirty as the Asians would surely want to exact revenge. Lisa tucked the phone in her pants pocket, gathered all the items she'd brought into the home and left the scene to await a phone call from investigating officers.

CHAPTER FORTY
CHECK MY RESUME`

"Everybody that has spoken in commemoration of our fallen comrade has been spectacular," a Deputy FBI Director spoke into a microphone before scores of fellow law enforcement officers from around the country inside of Arlington National Cemetery. "Tammy Moto's unexpected departure serves as a reminder to all of us inside of law enforcement to keep in mind how dangerous the profession we've chosen for ourselves truly is in the big scheme of things. Every day we place our lives on the line. Every day we encounter situations that would frighten ordinary citizens, but it is what we have been trained to do. With that being said, no one knows a fellow law official as well as one's partner, and it is my honor to introduce Miss Lisa Vanguard, Agent Moto's partner for the past two years now."

The crowd clapped in reverence as Lisa Vanguard took to the podium under the bright morning sun a week after Tammy's body had been discovered. She looked over the crowd through her tinted sunshades wondering how long the rouse she'd been carrying would last. The past week she'd come under heavy scrutiny as to her whereabouts the night Tammy Moto was killed. Lucky for her, detective Daniels and his men were able to confirm that she was at Philadelphia Police Headquarters filing a report on the Jesse James Glen case. Her alibi didn't prevent suspicions from rising amongst some inside the FBI, however, and rumors were now swirling around Lisa Vanguard that she and Tammy had been conducting rogue investigations. Lisa was aware of the distrust, but as long as the Deputy Director had her back, she was practically untouchable.

She opened a folder and bowed her head briefly before looking back up at the crowd and opening with, "Many are not here to cry for my friend because they can't. Instead, they cry for a fallen officer, which makes the sentiment all the more heartwarming because it lets me know that I am on the side of righteous conscience and stand with many others who believe and respect the law of the land. Like the Deputy Director said, every day we as law enforcement officers face perils that are of nightmares for the average citizen. Me and Agent Moto have had years of friendship. I remember the day she graduated Temple University. I was there to—"

Lisa's voice trailed off when she eyed Senator Slack sitting off to her left on the front row beside a slender, yellow-skinned young man who was nearly identical to the woman. Of all the people she'd eyed while eulogizing Tammy, including that of Laddy Norcross and his new sidekick, Sandra Cordova, no one unnerved Lisa more than the Senator for the simple fact that she had a connection with the woman going back decades through the death of Ricky Gross and the recent arrest of Brenda Marshall.

"When my friend graduated from Temple," Lisa resumed, "when she graduated, she told me she couldn't wait to take the oath of the FBI because it had been her life's dream. I was there with her in Quantico on that day of personal achievement. An achievement that launched one of the most fascinating careers of any agent I've ever known and had the pleasure to meet and work with. Let me tell you a little about this great woman who left us way too soon. I met Tammy at a boarding school in Pennsylvania coming off the death of her parents, who were dear friends of mine from Cincinnati, Ohio when she was only thirteen years old. So, she was more than just my partner, she was my best friend."

The crowd listened reverentially as Lisa paid homage to her friend and partner for twenty minutes or so by highlighting her teen years, the adversity she had faced after losing her parents at such an early age, her determination to gain the best education possible, and her many world travels. By the time she was done, many had gained appreciation for Tammy Moto and concluded that the country had truly lost a good soul.

"That was an awesome eulogy," Laddy told Lisa just as she walked off from a group of Washington reporters who were doing a feature on Tammy and looking to get a few direct quotes.

"Thank you, Laddy," Lisa responded in a somber tone. "Life won't be the same without Tammy. It all seems so surreal. How are you?" she then said as she shook Sandra Cordova's hand.

"Any idea on who was behind her murder?" Laddy asked as he and Lisa resumed walking while Sandra tailed the two in her Missouri State Highway Patrol uniform.

"You know I'm not allowed to discuss an ongoing investigation, Laddy."

"That means they have nothing. Absolutely nothing."

"I'll leave you to draw your own conclusions," Lisa replied as she and Laddy walked alongside the lush green grass and white crosses of Arlington National Cemetery that marked the graves of countless fallen veterans. "How's your investigation going over in Missouri?"

"I'm at a standstill. I can confirm that Doss Dawkins' daughter was shot alongside him the day he was killed, and she has a twin, but I have nothing more to go on. Drugs are coming in, but I can't pinpoint who's behind it all. Bena and her twin haven't been seen in the Saint Louis area since I've been in town."

"You've been fingered," Lisa advised.

"How so?"

"You told me over the phone a while back that you staked out a block in Saint Charles, the location where Doss was killed. If Bena and her twin had people on that block watching? They made you the time you set foot on their turf. That's why you haven't seen those two. They're avoiding you, Laddy."

"This task is harder than I anticipated."

"You're having regrets leaving the team?"

"Not really. Me and Sandra are working things. I've been trying to connect the dots on homicides committed via the long shot since the Onishi hit up in Seattle."

"Seattle is not where you should look," Lisa responded as the trio neared her Mustang.

"That I know," Laddy replied. "I'm backtracking. The last hit via long shot was on a guy named Ricky Gross Junior over in Indianapolis. If I can figure out how that job ties in to the Onishi brothers' murders, or even the Abbadando hit in Denver, I can gain serious ground. You familiar with any of those killings?"

"Sorry, Laddy. We've parted ways. I gave you what advice I could based upon my past experiences in dealing with a criminal organization and that is the best I can do. Besides, I have my own issues to deal with," Lisa stated in a nonchalant tone as she eyed Senator Slack walking her way. "Excuse me, please," she added as she broke away from her former partner and met up with the Senator at the front of her Mustang.

"Agent Vanguard," Willie stated through stern eyes as she greeted Lisa with a head nod as she stood before her in her white, five-inch heels with her hands tucked behind her silk, teal-colored pantsuit.

"Senator," Lisa remarked with a pleasant smile. "Besides the death of my partner, what brings you here to Arlington National?"

Willie tilted her head and chuckled at Lisa. "You're a slick one," she admitted. "I don't know what all you're up to, but I'm here to advise you on watching your step."

"Watching my step?" Lisa repeated. "In what way?"

"I'm not going into details, just know that I know you're not on the up and up."

"Neither are you, Senator."

"Well," Willie smiled. "I guess we'll have to see who can

cause a bigger tsunami here in DC. A crooked federal agent?"

"Or a dirty Senator?" Lisa countered.

Willie leaned into Lisa and whispered. "I can ruin you. Whatever dirt you have on me has already been laid bare. You better check my resume` more thoroughly, agent. I've ran and won on corruption down in Louisiana. Where I'm from? Lies keep the people loyal, money wins votes and violence runs off the competition. I come from sex, money and violence. Tell my story if you think it'll knock me out of position, but if you do, I promise to you that I will haul your ass before a Senate committee and have all your sins exposed for all the world to see. I'll make sure that you spend the rest of your puny life behind bars before I decide not to run for a third Senate term and return to my life of sex, money and violence with a full pension paid for on the backs of your kind. I will survive this —can you say the same?"

"What is it that you want from me?" Lisa asked as she eyed the Senator with a disdainful, yet forced measure of respect.

"I want for you to leave. Leave the east coast and never return. Do your business elsewhere."

"My office is here on the east coast. I operate of Philadelph —"

"You used to operate out of Philadelphia." Willie corrected. "Your home in Baltimore? The Jonas Club you own in Highlandtown? No more, Lisa. Pack your shit and move on before I crush you out of existence."

"You haven't the authority."

"You want to find out how much authority I have?" Willie rhetorically asked. "You better think about what I told you. I know where you live. I know the business you own. How much else do I know about you, Lisa?"

"What all do you know about—"

"Enough!" Willie scoffed under her breath through gritted teeth. "Take heed, Lisa! Leave the east coast! End of discussion!"

Lisa stood motionless with a look of wonderment on her face as she watched Senator Slack walking off from her just as calm as the day was long. This was the sleeping giant she had no intentions on rousing during the Asa Spade trial over in Denver, Colorado, but it'd been awakened nonetheless, and deep down inside, she knew she couldn't go up against Senator Slack as the woman was way too powerful. She would agree to leave the east coast, but there was an angle to be played by Lisa before she vacated the area. She smiled slyly as she walked back to the driver's side of her Mustang where she climbed behind the wheel and set her GPS for the Philadelphia House of Corrections.

If Lisa Vanguard had any good sense about herself, she would've taken heed to Willie's words, jumped onto I-70 and headed due west this very day. Pride, however, would not allow her to concede to Senator Slack, even if she knew the woman carried more weight inside the beltway than she could ever muster up from a legal aspect.

From Lisa's point of view, Senator Slack may have been in a position to win a legal battle, but the streets were hers was not only how she felt, but what she believed to be true. And before she left the east coast under duress, she was determined to fuck the game up for Senator Slack and shit in the woman's face before she moved on to Seattle and link up with Raiden and Arata Moto and press on with her criminal endeavors.

Lisa Vanguard, sad to say, couldn't see it, nor did she suspect it, but the truth was that she was in a downward spiral and had crossed the point of no return the time Senator Slack was handed a copied disc that her son Popeye had obtained from Grover Kobayashi and Phillip Tran the morning after they'd killed Tammy Moto. The decorated federal agent had no idea that the move she was about to make out of spite would become the catalyst that would lead to her inevitable demise before everything was all said and done.

CHAPTER FORTY-ONE

THE FEEBLE ONE

"Marshall! You got a visitor!" a corrections officer called out over the speaker inside the pod where Brenda Marshall was holed up with thirty-one other women inside Philadelphia House of Corrections awaiting trial. It was the day after Tammy Moto had been buried down in Arlington, Virginia and Brenda had just received an unexpected visitor's call.

"You think that's Zelda or Tanya 'nem?" forty-four year-old Vivian asked as she sat across from Brenda, the two of them playing a game of spades with two other inmates in order to pass time during the monotonous afternoon hours of confinement.

"I don't know, girl," forty-six year-old Brenda Marshall sighed as she threw her cards onto the table and stood up from the iron bench.

"The agent working our case got knocked off last week! That might be our people tellin' us the charges being dropped, B!" Vivian happily reasoned.

"Yeah?" Brenda asked nonchalantly. "We been in here for over a year, going on two years and never got a visit from a fuckin' lawyer, and not no one out the crew. They left us, behind Vivian!"

"You know they can't come here and run the risk of getting fingered. B, you trippin'! These federal trials take time. You should be glad we not going to court! The longer we wait the better it is for us! Somebody doing something because we still got a chance at freedom!"

"As long as massa 'nem keep fightin' for us, right?" Brenda facetiously asked. "You keep hope alive, sister, but I see this shit for what it really is…all the blacks in the family is locked up while the white mutherfuckas just keep raking in the dough," she ended before walking over the door leading off the tier.

Although approaching fifty, Brenda Marshall still had a youthful appeal. Her brown skin was still smooth and her trademark afro was still full of luster without a single strand of grey to blemish her black hair. Thick in all the right places, the short, voluptuous outlaw had a figure that forced many women to ponder taking up membership at some gym and look for beauty tips.

Gates clanged and keys jangled as Brenda was escorted off the tier towards the visiting room. For nearly two years, she and Vivian had been locked down on a distribution charge awaiting trial. Vivian was upbeat over the situation. She believed Tanya and company would not leave her and Brenda out in the cold to take a fall without putting up a fight, even if they'd gone against all advice given and went ahead with a deal that had gotten them busted and having to face thirty years behind bars.

Brenda Marshall, on the other hand, was distrustful of her crew for validated reasons in her own mind's eye. She and Vivian hadn't received counsel from a lawyer and weren't allowed to call neither Tanya, Willie nor Faye. Zelda was their only contact with the outside world, and her visits were few and far in between, although Vivian called her on the regular with a smuggle-in cell phone.

"Right this way, Marshall," the corrections officer remarked, shaking Brenda from her thoughts. She entered the visitor's room and looked around the area. Kids were hugging inmates and kisses were being exchanged between some. "There in the back," the corrections officer remarked. "Must be your lawyer," she smiled as she walked off from Brenda.

The woman sitting at the table was a lawyer, Brenda knew, but not her lawyer. She walked over and sat before the red-haired, slender woman stone-faced and silent.

"You're probably wondering why I'm here," Lisa stated.

"Damn right," Brenda responded as she leaned back and crossed her legs.

"My partner set up the entire sting against you back in '08. She was buried yesterday after getting killed in New Jersey last week." Lisa paused for a reply, but Brenda merely stared at her with her lips curled. "You don't care about any of that shit," she resumed after a brief chuckle. "But you may care about your son RJ?"

Brenda rose up in her seat at that moment. "What about my son?"

"Back up a second," Lisa spoke calmly, knowing she'd struck a chord with a vulnerable Brenda. "With Tammy off the case? I can get you out."

"You bullshitting me," Brenda whispered.

"I wouldn't come here to bullshit you. I offer you a deal instead."

"What kind of a deal?"

"Join me," Lisa requested.

"Join you?" Brenda laughed. "You tryna get me dead like your partner? The people I deal with don't fuck around like that. They'll never go for that shit."

"You're right," Lisa relented. "But they're not the loyal people you believe, Brenda. They sacrificed your son RJ and made a deal with the people who killed him, you know?"

"You're lying. You tryna get me to go against my family."

"I'm bringin' you truth, Marshall," Lisa retorted as she stood up from her seat. "If you wanna rot in this prison? Fine by me. Just know the people you deal with can't be trusted. If they would make a deal with the people who killed your son, what's that's saying about how they feel about you, huh? You need to start thinking about yourself because they damn sure are," she ended as she began walking off.

"Sit down." Brenda ordered. "Tell me what went down with my son."

Lisa paused with her back to Brenda and smiled. She'd known for some time who to play between the two women she and Tammy had busted and her plan of manipulation was going along accordingly. She turned around and took a seat once more, leaned over the table and said, "Your son was killed by someone named Bena Holland."

"Holland? The same people my crew made a deal with," Brenda remarked.

"Deal? What kind of a deal?" Lisa asked inquisitively. Although having an angle to play, Lisa wasn't fully aware of the fact that Brenda's people had contracted the hit on Tammy Moto, and Brenda was no less clued in on the fact.

"Never mind the deal right now. How soon can you get me out?" Brenda asked.

"Depends on what do you have to offer me in return. I can have you walk by next week being I'm over the case. I can make it look as if Tammy had nothing of substance and the bust was conducted without proper warrant. I can get you off on a technicality. What deal are you referring to?" Lisa asked a second time.

"If I tell you about that deal, you have to promise to get me and Vivian outta here."

"You think your partner will join us?" Lisa asked suspiciously. "I came to you and you alone. Anybody you bring in on this deal is your responsibility and you will have to answer for their actions."

"I never said I was joining you, Lisa. But if I do, Vivian will follow my lead," Brenda declared. "Just tell me if you can get us out or not."

"I can get you out next week," Lisa let it be known. "Now, tell me about this deal."

Brenda rested her elbows on the table and said, "Tammy had a contract put out on her by my crew."

"Who took the contract?"

"I don't know the name, but it came from somebody inside the Holland family—the same people who you claim killed my son. The hit was given to some Asians out west."

"Who's your boss?"

"I don't have a boss. And if I did I wouldn't tell ya' they name because I'm already risking my life just by talking to you," Brenda answered with a scowl on her face. She was feeling disrespected by the mere thought of working for people she'd brought in and had protected when the entire thing she had going with Faye and Tanya began over twenty-five years ago.

"Okay, okay," Lisa relented. "Keep their names to yourself for now, but you seem to have a lot of animosity towards them whoever they are."

"I controlled shit when we all started," Brenda told Lisa. "I brought them bitches in on what I had going on down in New Orleans and now they act like they been running this whole operation? Fuck that!"

"They were your students back in the day," Lisa patronized in an attempt to further endear herself to Brenda Marshall, a woman she knew was on the verge of switching sides given all she'd recently loss. "Now, they've become your tutors. This is what happens when ungrateful people become too big for their britches. They forget where they started. As if the past has no accountability or bearing on the present."

"You're right," Brenda nodded in agreement. "We all worked together once upon a time, but it's a new day. You get me and Vivian outta this place and I'll help you get back at the people responsible for your partner's death."

"Without a name? We have no deal and I won't get you out," Lisa countered. "But if you give me a name, any name on who was in on that hit against Tammy? You'll walk out of here next week."

Brenda was now faced with a conundrum workable to her own Cause. If Lisa was on the up and up, she now had a chance to get back at the people who'd let the death of her son be used as a bargaining chip to fulfill a contract on Tammy Moto. Several options lay before her. The first was Tanya Weinberger—the uncontested leader of the Germans who was a pure novice and had been nearly worked over by the King Sisters when she first arrived in New Orleans back in 1978. Over time, she became an all-wise and calculating woman whose only concern was keeping the family in the black when it came to finances.

The second option was Faye Bender—the Germans' violent diplomat whose last resort was bloodshed for the sake of business. Faye was backed by a police force consisting of a dozen Germans back over to Cherryvale, Kansas and she was the Sheriff by all accounts so she was practically untouchable for the moment in Brenda's mind. Besides that, Brenda knew Faye would battle to very end, and if she were to survive, the repercussions would be devastating as Faye would surely crucify her before ending her existence.

The third option for Brenda was her friend of three-plus decades—Willameena 'Willie' Slack—Miss Untouchable herself. The dirt she had on Willie could surely ruin the politician if ever brought to light and it would serve her well given she'd remained on the sidelines ever since she'd become a respected member of Congress if Brenda had to tell the story. The Senator would be a hard bargain, though, so she opted for someone inside the crew she felt would be of no significance in the big scheme of things and whose death could easily be downplayed.

Upon learning the name, Lisa Vanguard nodded and pushed her chair back from the table. "I have associates that will be in town in the upcoming week. I will let them know who to go after for Tammy Moto. In the meantime? You keep off the phones and say nothing to no one. Not even her sister Vivian."

"Wait, how you know they sisters?" Brenda questioned.

"I'm working the case now, Brenda. I have access to all the files." Lisa stated in a condescending tone of voice. "Sit back and let me do my thing. You've given me the name already so you're at my mercy. Go back to your cell and wait like you've been doing. Guard!" she called out.

Brenda was left stunned. She watched in regret as Lisa walked out of the visitor's room while she was being escorted back to her tier. She'd thought about calling Lisa out on what she now knew was a scheme to decipher information from her, but she decided against it to prevent from being thrown into the hole. Once back on the tier, she was quickly greeted by Vivian.

"Who was out there?" Vivian asked.

"Nobody," Brenda placated as she walked back to her cell. "Just some public defender wanting a statement."

"A statement? He didn't wanna talk to me? We on the same case, though."

"I don't...I'm just as confused as you on all this shit alright, Vivian?" Brenda complained as she fell back onto her cot.

"Not confused enough to keep me in the dark about who it was you was talking to, though," Vivian declared. "Who came here today?"

Brenda tilted her neck up from her cot and said, "I'm looking out for me and you! Who looking out for us back here, Vivian? Nobody! I'm doing what I'm doing for us two!"

Vivian stared down at Brenda while shaking her head in disbelief. "Tanya 'nem was gone get us out," she stressed. "What did you do out there? Who visited you?"

"You paranoid," Brenda downplayed as she waved Vivian off. "You'll thank me afterwards once it's all said and done," she ended as she turned on a portable fan and closed her eyes, all-the-while wondering if she'd been played by Lisa Vanguard.

CHAPTER FORTY-TWO

FOR THAT THING SHE DID

"Y'all hoes need to hurry up, chicas! We gotta go! Streets is calling!" Zelda boomed as she sprayed glass cleaner on some of her furniture.

It was three days after Lisa had visited Brenda down in Philadelphia. Back up the Bronx, Zelda, Nadia and Eva were preparing to head out for the day and make their rounds with their Percocet pills. Business had been a little slow in Manhattan since Theron and Jaffrey had been killed so the three were now moving their product mainly throughout South Bronx and over to Harlem during the evening hours.

Zelda was a tidy woman. She moved about her apartment on 156th Street wiping down her glass end tables and dusting the wrought iron while Nadia and Eva wiped down the mirrors and windows on the third floor studio pad. She was fully dressed in a camouflage green knee-length skirt and matching camouflage three-inch heels with a camouflage scarf wrapped underneath her afro. After wiping the tables, she grabbed a Swiffer mop and began running it over her wooden floors as she toked on a blunt while jamming to Marvin Gaye's song *Got To Give It Up*.

"One of y'all wash them few li'l dishes in the zank and the other one wrap those two trash bags!" Zelda requested as she rocked in her heels. Nadia walked past her holding a rag and snatched the blunt from her lips and stepped into the kitchen

443

while swaying her hips.

Disrespectful ass!" Zelda laughed as she continued dancing behind her mop in her heels. "My perfume gone been done wore off working this hard! Marvin got a bitch in the cleaning mood this Saturday!" she joyfully added.

"When are we moving back down into Manhattan?" Eva asked as she finished wiping down the last window.

"Soon as my people get they next load of heroin in, homegirl. Maybe in a couple of weeks. It's about time, too, because shit been slow without them Jamaicans bringing in customers."

Once done cleaning, Zelda and company convened before the kitchen table where a packet of Percocet pills lay. The product was broken down into three packages containing three hundred pills each that went for ten dollars a pop. The bags were then hidden. Nadia and Eva tucking their share into their baggy jeans and Zelda stuffing hers into a small leather bag. The leader of the pack placed two .380 semi-automatic handguns in her back waistband and headed towards the front door with the Puerto Rican sisters following her lead. "Grab those trash bags, Eva!" Zelda yelled out she pulled the door open and stepped out in the hallway.

A loud banging sound was heard in the narrow corridor and Zelda jumped, placing her hand on one of her .380s while scanning the hall. "Miss Margarete," she sighed. "Woman, you gone have to stop slamming that door like that."

"Sorry, Zelda," the elderly, heavy-set black woman complained. "I been telling the slum lord that this door is hard to close, but he hasn't fixed it. I have to pull it hard to shut it and it fucks with my wrist. I have bad wrists," she declared just as her folding shopping cart tipped over, spilling her purse and its contents along with her bottled water. "Dammit!" she complained.

"Chill out, chill out, chill out!" Zelda calmed as she ran over to the woman and pulled her cart upright. "You're going grocery shopping? I would've taken you, Miss Margarete," she offered as she knelt down and picked up the woman's scattered items.

"I didn't want to bother you, Zelda."

"It's not a bother. You need a ride?"

"No," the woman answered politely as she grabbed hold of her cart a second time. "It's a beautiful day and I'd rather walk. It'll do me good."

"Okay," Zelda smiled. "Come on, girls," she then told Nadia and Eva.

"If you're riding in your pretty car today you might wanna check for a ticket on your windshield," the older woman suggested as she leaned over and rearranged the items in her cart.

"I'm not parked illegally," Zelda countered.

"Oh," the woman said as she righted herself. "I thought it was funny for an undercover to be taking down license plate numbers this morning."

"Undercover?" Zelda asked as Nadia and Eva ears perked up.

"Yeah," Miss Margarete stated. "There was a woman with red hair dressed in plain clothes, jeans and tennis and stuff like that walking around the cars. She stopped behind your pretty car and wrote down your license plate number. I saw her about an hour ago when I was taking out the trash. She's driving a short red sports car."

"Give it to me, Zelda," Nadia remarked while shaking her head as she pulled her package of pills out the front waistband of her jeans, Eva doing the same and handing her sister her package of pills.

"Somebody running they fuckin' mouth," Zelda complained as she handed Nadia her package of pills. She and Eva waited in the hall until Nadia returned after stashing the pills back inside the apartment.

The trio emerged from the building as Zelda hit the alarm on her blood red Escalade and remote started the engine while looking around in every direction. The block was quiet out and the red car was nowhere to be found. A few people moved about sweeping stoops and sidewalks and a few kids jumped rope and rode bikes. The two trash bags Eva carried out landed in the trash pile before Zelda just as she climbed into the passenger seat. "Head over to Beck Street before we head north, Eva," she stated as her friend hopped behind the wheel.

"Good," Nadia replied while jumping into the backseat. "Thought you were going to Burger King or something."

"You know I need that Chinese in my life," Zelda remarked as the SUV pulled forward. "Eh, Monday we gone ride down to Philly and see Vivian. She been tellin' me how Brenda been actin' all funny and whatnot down there. I talked to my girl Willie and she saying they should be out in like five weeks or so because the charges gone get thrown out and they gone get credit for time served. I wonder who put the law on us, though," she added as she lay back in the front passenger seat.

Eva nodded as she crossed under Bruckner Expressway and made a right turn onto Beck Street and pulled over to the right side of the curb just up from the Chinese hut Zelda loved. A white Benz had pulled in behind her, but she took no note as she walked into the building.

"You already know what time it is, homeboy!" Zelda called out over the sizzling sounds of the deep fryers as the smell of fried chicken coated her nostrils. "Let me get three chicken plates to go with the quickness! Pill heads been through here?" The Chinese cook shook his head to say no with his back turned to Zelda as he chopped bell peppers inside a large wok. "Y'all mighty quiet today, brer. I know business slow and all, but it'll pick up."

"It no the business," another Chinese man remarked as he peeled shrimp without making eye contact with Zelda. "You have trouble," he whispered.

"Excuse me?" Zelda asked as she neared the counter.

"You come early. I told them you no come here until later, but..." the guy's voice trailed off when the door to the bodega was heard opening. When he looked up, only then did Zelda see the black eye and swollen jaw he sported. The second cook turned around and she got a glimpse of his swollen lips and the blood lining the collar of his white t-shirt.

"The fuck happened here?" Zelda asked as she turned around and saw a slender, white Jamaican creeping up to her with a machete in his right hand. "Shit!" she yelled out as she moved to her left. The machete slammed into the counter and became lodged in the wood; it was enough time to allow Zelda to pull her .380 pistols and open fire on her attacker. The man was hit four times in his back before he collapsed face first onto the floor.

"How many?" Zelda frantically asked the Chinese men as she moved towards the front door.

"I don't know!" "We don't know it was a lot of them!" "You have to leave!" the men shouted out at random as they ran from behind the counter.

Zelda, meanwhile, was scanning the block through the front door. She could see a white Mercedes with tinted windows resting on chrome rims parked out front and her Escalade was just up ahead to her right. She stepped into the doorway of the bodega with her guns aimed outwards and crept over to her Escalade. "Yo, Eva, Nadia? I think Theron and Jaffrey people..."

Zelda paused in her speech when she laid eyes on the interior of her pristine SUV. There behind the wheel sat Eva. She was clutching her throat as blood oozed out through her fingertips. She made brief eye contact with Zelda, but was unable to speak as her throat had been slit from ear to ear.

Nadia was in the back seat slumped over with a blade planted in her left temple. "Fuck! Oh, fuck!" Zelda fretted as she backed away from her SUV and ran back to the bodega. She had intentions on running back inside and barricading herself behind the steel double doors, but just as she reached the doorway, the black steel doors were shut tight.

"This me, bitches!" Zelda screamed as she banged on the door. Guns being racked caught her attention and she slowly turned and found herself staring at three white Jamaicans, a woman and two men, all of whom were holding chrome twelve-gauge shotguns on her.

"Did you not think we would learn what you did, Zelda King?" the woman spoke as she held her shotgun on Zelda.

"Bridgette!" Zelda exclaimed. "What, what the fuck you doing here?" she asked through a pretentious laugh. "I was, I was meaning to call you."

"Only after I've buried my brothers? You were der dat night. I hear Theron talking to you. Nadia and some woman named Krause on the phone. The next day? They're dead and I hear nothing from yuh!"

"They dead?" Zelda asked as her heart raced.

Bridgette Fischer, wife to Rafael Gacha, took offense over Zelda's attempt to play her for a fool. "One ting before I murk ya' bloodclot! Who dat gave the order?"

Zelda knew even if she talked, she would not walk away alive. She knew why Bridgette had come to town and it wasn't to just ask who'd killed her brothers. She was out for blood and Zelda knew it. She gripped her .380 pistols and raised the guns. "Fuck you!" she screamed into the afternoon air.

Before Zelda could let off a round, she was hit with countless buckshot as she stood in the barricaded doorway of her favorite eatery. The powerful pellets stood her up against the steel. The guns she carried were aimed downwards, and as she squeezed the triggers while being pumped full of lead, the bullets she fired off ricocheted off the concrete, some of the shells shooting back up into her legs as she remained upright while absorbing shell after shell from three shotguns.

Bridgette Fischer and her two goons fired off eighteen rounds, striking Zelda King over and over again. When the smoke cleared, forty-four year-old Zelda was left standing in the doorway with her .380s clutched in her lifeless hands. She died standing up with her mouth and eyes wide open, a shocked expression frozen onto her face after being gunned down in broad daylight in one of the most violent parts of the Bronx. Her death would spark a wave of violence and bring about a realignment for all involved in this ongoing battle for control of America's drug trade as the bosses of each family involved were now being dragged into what could only be described as that of a battle of attrition.

The gunners all climbed back into their Mercedes and sped off the block with Bridgette taking note of the red Mustang that was now tailing them. Just before they made a turn to get onto the Bruckner Expressway, Bridgette and company were hit with flashing lights from an unmarked red car following them. The driver was about to press on the gas, but Bridgette stopped him. "She sat and watched us on Beck Street," she told the man. "She wants something."

Lisa climbed from her car just as the white Jamaican woman she'd witnessed kill Zelda King climbed from the passenger side of her car. "Glad you didn't speed off. I was hoping you noticed me," she told the woman. "My name is Lisa Vanguard and I'm a federal agent."

"State your case. I have a bird to fly on," Bridgette remarked.

"Why'd you kill King back there?"

"For dat ting she dun waan she killed my brother," Bridgette said as she turned to hop back in her Benz.

"There's more of them, you know?" Lisa stated.

"How many?"

"Ohh, I don't know, but they have political connections. Once this thing gets out about Zelda? They'll be sure and track you down. I think you're going to need my help."

"What can you offer?" Bridgette asked in wonderment.

"Let me take you to the airport. We'll talk on the way." Lisa suggested.

"We will follow you," Bridgette told her driver before walking over to Lisa's Mustang. She pulled her gun and waited for Lisa to open the door. When Lisa walked around and climbed behind the wheel, Bridgette held her gun on her and said, "Talk," as Lisa pulled back out into the traffic.

CHAPTER FORTY-THREE

THEY WILL ANSWER

"Secrets...stolen...from deep inside....the drum beat's out of time...if you're lost you can look and you will find me...time after time...if you fall I will catch you...I will be waiting...time after time..."

Cyndi Lauper's song *Time After Time* was being sung by a large choir inside Franklin Avenue Baptist Church down in New Orleans, Louisiana. Tanya and Boogie sat in the back of the building as scores of parishioners sat and wept for Zelda King, an infamous woman with many loyal friends who were still around from back in the day. Her death hadn't really come as a surprise and many were expecting her to have been killed years ago. With that aside, many were saddened by a New Orleans original and had to pay their respects and say a final goodbye.

The choir ended the song and the pastor took the stage briefly. When he did, Tanya and Boogie excused themselves and quietly walked out of the building towards a black limousine with mirror tint. The two climbed inside and sat before Senator Slack, who was needless to say, in a somber mood having loss her friend of nearly thirty years. The sunshades she wore did nothing to hide the tears falling from her eyes and rolling down her cheeks.

"Faye advised me not come, as did my son and closest campaign managers," Willie stated as she choked back tears.

"They, they said if I was to show up and reporters linked me with Zelda, my opponent could use it against me in 2014."

"But you came anyway," Tanya comforted. "You did the right thing, Willie. Don't worry about 2014. That's over four years from now, this will all be swept under the rug by that time."

"It don't matter," Willie replied lowly. "Ever since I became a politician it's been nothing but death. I never had these problems when I was a common street chick."

"Crime is synonymous with politics," Tanya remarked as Boogie nodded in agreement. "You do what many others inside the beltway do and have been doing now for decades. Did you find out anything about who was behind this?"

"They were Jamaican. White Jamaicans."

"The same people who Sascha took down," Boogie stated. "Maybe relatives."

"That's the only angle I could see right now," Willie remarked. "Zelda wasn't in on the Sheinheimer job so it couldn't be for that. It has to be someone associated with the Fischer brothers. How's Vivian and Brenda holding up?"

"Vivian couldn't get out to attend the funeral and she is tore up," Boogie stated. "She called last night and said her and Brenda may be getting out. Since Agent Moto went down, the case appears to be falling apart."

"That's good news. We get enough strength back to replace Zelda and the Puerto Ricans up in the Bronx," Tanya remarked.

"Okay," Willie stated as she removed her sunshades and rubbed her wet eyes. "I guess the show must go on. Popeye checking all flights in and out of New York a week prior and after Zelda was killed to see if any names stand out. That's gone take time."

"Time we have," Tanya followed. "And Faye got word from our guy in Saint Louis that Dawk Holland will be in Chicago in the next few days. We still have that job to execute."

"Thereby proving my point that this business has devolved into a killing contest," Willie sighed in frustration as she looked over to the church's entrance and checked her watch. "The pastor should be done in a few minutes. Time to eulogize my friend. You ladies can have this limousine. I don't want any photo ops."

"Me and Helen have a flight to catch back to Ohio anyhow," Tanya stated as Willie exited the car and walked by her lonesome up the sidewalk leading to the church just as the choir was beginning to sing a hymn.

****

"Zelda war ein guter Freund, dessen Geist ich für immer vermissen. Ich erinnere mich daran, wie Sie mit mir spielen in Tanyas altes Haus, das Französische Viertel." (Zelda was a good friend whose spirit I will forever miss. I remember how she used to play with me in Tanya's old house down the French Quarters.) Maggie McPherson said to Faye as the two sat on the patio reflecting on the loss of their friend.

"Sie machen ihren großen Kopf." (She used to make fun of your big head.) Faye laughed.

Maggie laughed along with the woman who'd been her mother for over twenty-five years just as Sascha emerged onto the patio with a rotor phone that had a long extension cord eating a red apple. *"Sie schnurlose Telefone jetzt wissen Sie? Und auch diese,"* (They make cordless phones now, you know? And these, too,) she said as she held up a cell phone.

"Technologie macht Sie fit." (Technology makes you lazy.) Sascha retorted. *"Das ist der Grund, warum Sie ihre Hüften verbreiten sich wie die Flügel eines Adlers. Sie möchten eine der Kühe, wenn Sie hier um mit Ihrem Esel so riesig."* (That's why your hips are spreading like the wings of an eagle. You like one of the cows here when you turn around with your ass so huge.)

"Sie erhielten, dass Apple von der Waldung heute? Über die von der Holzhacker?" (You got that apple from the grove today? Over by, over by the wood chipper?) Maggie asked with a smirk.

"Ich habe," (I did,) Sascha remarked as she handed the phone to Faye and bit into the fruit. *"Warum?"* (Why?) she asked as Faye took the phone and slapped the apple from her hands.

"Sie haben über zwolf Menschen in der DNA, die Sie jetzt." (You got about twelve people DNA inside you now.) Maggie laughed.

Sascha spit out the bitten portion of the apple and ran back into the house to rinse her mouth. *"Sie sind wie ein Kind, Maggie!"* (You're such a child, Maggie!)

"Sie wissen besser als zu essen von Obst!" (You know better than to eat from fruit over there!) Maggie yelled out loud, tickled that Sacha had eaten fruit that'd been fertilized by human remains.

"Hello," Faye remarked as things settled back down.

"How's it going?"

"Good, Natalia. Where do we stand?" Faye asked as Maggie ceased her giggles.

"Our friends will be in Chicago the day after tomorrow. The same night his crew passes through your town. We're all set on this thing now if you're ready."

"It's about time," Faye stated seriously as she stood and stretched. "I have your cell number. I'll leave for Chicago tomorrow and call you when I get there."

"We're on," Natalia III replied as he hung up the phone inside his apartment down in the Soulard section of Saint Louis. He dabbed out the blunt he was toking on and placed a button up Polo over his silk wife beater and left his apartment to ride over to Malik's Grill just before three in the afternoon on this cloudless day, the first week of the month of May.

When he arrived, he saw Malik's Benz jeep parked out front and DeMarco and Max standing on the sidewalk talking to two Mexican females. "Where ya' boss?" he asked the two.

"Yo," Max called out after pushing the door to the empty diner open and whistling for Malik.

Malik appeared a couple of minutes later with Kantrell Luckett walking behind him straightening her clothes. It didn't take a science major to determine what the two'd been up to in the back of the diner. Natalia smirked as Kantrell walked past him and climbed into her evergreen Escalade and rode off.

"What's up homes?" Malik asked as he stepped onto the sidewalk.

"Dawk called me last night. He ready to make that trip to Chicago," Natalia let it be known while staring into Malik's eyes.

Malik licked his lips and nodded while looking over to Max and DeMarco. "I guess we gone really do this thing, huh?"

"You don't sound sure."

"Nah, I'm sure," Malik stated seriously. "I hope he understands that this is business and nothing personal."

"Yeah? Tell his ass before you send him on his way," Natalia stated coldly as he spat on the ground. "Make sure you wash your hands before touching the food after handling that pussy. It's a health code violation," he added as he walked back to his Expedition. "I'll pick you up in the morning around eight. Be ready."

Malik stood and watched as Natalia III drove off his block. He was thinking hard about not going through with such a cold-hearted plan, but like he told Natalia III, it was business, nothing personal against Dawk and the family. The Germans were backing him in his staged coup, and he also had the Italians in Chicago backing him. The magnetism of becoming Boss was too much of a temptation to resist and he couldn't turn back if he wanted to as he'd crossed the point of no return in his envy.

"Yo, Max?" Malik called out.

"'Sup, boss?" Max answered as he trotted over.

"That thing? It's happening tomorrow."

"For real?" Max asked seriously. "What you need me to do?"

"I'll be away for a couple of days, alright? Hold the diner down and keep moving the weight we're holding for the family. Act as if it's business as usual. Dawk's gonna come up missing and we'll be among the first to get questioned. You say nothing and let DeMarco speak being he not in on this thing with us."

"Si, boss," Max nodded. "I got your back on this. We be here while you handling things with Natalia," he ended as he and Malik walked back towards the diner's entrance.

****

"Boy, if this ain't Dawk all over again my name not Kimi Dawkins," Kimi stated matter-of-factly as she held two week old Sosa Holland in her arms.

It was several hours after Natalia III had met up with Malik. Night had fallen across the Midwest and the Holland family was all over to Dawk and Oneika Holland's sprawling five bedroom, two-story 7,500 square foot home located on the southern portion of the land spending time with the newest member of the family as they awaited the dinner being prepared by Naomi, Mary and Francine.

In his infancy, Sosa Holland was vanilla-skinned like his mother with jet black, curly hair and all of his father's facial features from the naturally mean-looking downward eyebrows and dark eyes. Unlike when Dawk was a newborn, Sosa smiled a lot and would let anybody hold him so long as they had a conversation to hold as he was a very alert baby.

Sosa's six aunts and nephew, his great aunts, grandmother and many others took turns holding him inside the first floor the nursery as Oneika lay on a chaise relaxing. She hadn't gotten much sleep over the past few weeks dealing with her labor and the child's birth and the downtime was appreciated. The woman was proud to bring a son forth for Dawk. She knew he wanted a boy without him ever saying so.

Dawk, meanwhile, was outside the home walking with Ben towards the lake. "I'll be leaving out for Chicago tomorrow night with Kimi and Koko," he told Ben as the two walked side-by-side puffing on cigars. "Natalia been wanting me to go up and meet with the rest of the Italians to help solidify the cocaine market up there. We gotta establish further ground with the street dealers if we wanna keep doing business."

"You sure you gone be all right going there with Kimi and Koko?"

"Yeah," Dawk answered. "They not gone be at the meeting. They going to see Sharona and talk about a marketing campaign on the shopping malls in San Francisco, Vegas and Miami. She been sick lately and my grandfather been there for a while now. They wanna see him, too. We all do."

"Most of the family flying out in the morning with Samantha back to Arizona to watch Tyke and the team play Arizona State later on that night. Katrina all amped up talkin' 'bout her Alma Mata gone run circles around Tyke 'nem," Ben chuckled.

"Yeah?" Dawk laughed. "How she and her mother getting along?"

"They good, bruh. I thought Faye was gone be a problem, but she been nothing short of phenomenal with my sons the time she been staying with us. She actually working with Katrina in one of the cafés now. It's all good on the home front."

Dawk nodded as he and Ben neared the lake. "I don't really know what to expect going up there to meet Natalia, fam. I got this, like this voice on my shoulder telling me not to go. But if I don't, then we gone look real weak on the streets."

"You won't look weak, brer," Ben replied. "A lot of men in the game went through with something they knew wasn't a good move to keep from looking weak in the eyes of men who didn't give a fuck about 'em one way or the other and they died behind not wanting to appear weak. Don't make sense to me."

"You saying I should back out?"

"If it was me I wouldn't. But I can't see what you seeing. What your gut saying? Because this not a matter of the heart, fam. You can't think with that organ on this here level."

"My gut telling me not to worry. Natalia been straight up on what he been tellin' me. The Italians got a bad history, though."

"That they do," Ben replied as he puffed on his cigar. "Either way, fam? It's gone be some cold-bloodied shit that go down in the next twenty-four hours or so. Everybody involved in this here deal gone look back on it and say this was a turning point for either the good or the bad. And when you put it in that perspective, we only left with one option."

"Play it through," Dawk replied as he puffed his cigar while looking over the moonlit waters of Kaw Lake. "If you don't hear from me by eleven 'o' clock tomorrow night, Natalia sold me out."

"And that mean the Germans done laid up there and switched sides." Ben remarked somberly.

"You don't get my text? Kill every crew in Saint Louis outside of Jay-D and his people. I already got a team up in Chicago. Just send the Ramirez family to hit that farm up there in Kansas."

"I'm gone send everything we got at all of 'em for ya', li'l brother," Ben remarked as he hugged Dawk briefly and patted his back. The two then headed back to Dawk's home to rejoin the family and have dinner before separating the following morning.

CHAPTER FORTY-FOUR

A NEW OUTLOOK

"Come on, Tyke! Knock it out on your first at bat!" Samantha yelled aloud from the bleachers of Arizona State's softball field. It was the evening after Ben and Dawk had their talk down on the ranch in Oklahoma. As the five 'o' clock hour approached, the sun beat down on the crowded ball park as the two opposing teams opened their game up in their first inning.

Spoonie was down in the dugout with her teammates cheering Tyke on while she was at home plate. The Oklahoma State softball had dedicated the entire season to Spoonie and it now came down to s single game they had to win in order to enter into the playoff tournament. This was Tyke's first time back on the field with her team since she'd been shot five months earlier. Hers was a remarkable recovery, but she was still unable to play. Just being amongst her friends, however, was therapy in itself for the eighteen year-old.

"Swing batter, batter, batter, miss!" Katrina yelled.

"Sit down!" Samantha playfully quipped as she looked over to Katrina and Faye, both of whom were laughing. "Faye, get your daughter!"

"They is not going to come to my daughter's home state and win no game!" Faye sassed as she brushed Samantha off.

"Okay!" Samantha nodded as she turned back to the game.

"Strike three!" the umpire yelled.

"Get some glasses, already!" Samantha snapped as she watched Tyke strike out swinging and dart back to the dugout.

"She threw a changeup. I thought it was a riser, but she came with a sinker!" Tyke said exasperated as she threw her helmet aside and entered the dugout.

Spoonie wheeled her chair over to her twin and said, "That's her go to pitch when she up on the count, Sinopa."

"How you know?" Tyke asked as she sat beside her sister on a wooden bench.

"I been watching film on her back home. When she up by like two strikes and have one ball, she throw what looks like a hittable ball on the changeup. It's either gone be a slider or a sinker. You gone have to adjust. Follow the ball with your eyes. If you see it rise? It's a sinker. If it stay level it's gone be a riser."

"Tyke? Next time watch for her changeup. She caught you on what you thought was a riser. That pitch is always the opposite when she's up on the pitch count. We'll work it on it before your next bat," the hitting coach said before stepping back out of the dugout.

"Told you," Spoonie smiled.

"You'd make a good hitting coach someday," Tyke stated lovingly as she pressed her head to her sister's head and laughed. "I'm gone get a hit on her before this game over, watch."

****

"I oughta mail my specs down to that umpire after calling that strike on my granddaughter. He gone cost us the game. And just what are we listening to on the stereo?" DeeDee complained as he sat in his recliner inside the living room of his Lake Shore Drive condominium that overlooked Lake Michigan watching his youngest granddaughter play her game on his sixty-three inch wall-mounted plasma screen.

"That's Mo' Thugs song, granddad," Koko answered. "You and everybody else in this family think every time Spoonie or Tyke miss a pitch the umpire messed up somehow. They could just be up against some good pitchers, yeah, granddad?" she laughed as she handed a bowl of popcorn to DeeDee and fell back onto his posh C-sectional sofa beside Kimi.

"What in the hell is a Mo' Thug? And see yourself out since you siding with these umpires," DeeDee chided as he popped a few kernels into his mouth.

"Granddad!" Koko laughed over the music. "I'm just saying, man. It's only the first inning and you ackin' like the game over already!"

"Let me tell ya' something about the game of baseball," DeeDee began as he eased his chair around. "In nineteen forty when I was just eight, umpires were—"

"No! Unt un! Not, not this time, potna!" Kimi protested as she kicked her bare feet into the plush, suede couch while waving her hands in the air. "Ain't no way I'm gone let you lay up there and take a two thousand nine softball game and turn it into a history lesson because it don't have nothing to do with what's going on with Tyke game today."

"It's relevant to the day because umpires used to go back and look at the play and make the correct call."

Kimi frowned her faced and said, "Go back and look at the play? They ain't even have *television* when you was a child, man! Who was doing the instant replay? Houdini?"

"They had film. Hollywood film."

"No wonder this game take so long," Koko chimed in while laughing.

"That ain't why," DeeDee defended. "This game allows people to bake pies and make ice cream."

"Ain't nobody baking pies and making ice cream!" Kimi laughed. "Mrs. Smith works wonders and Ben and Jerry got ya' covered on the ice cream. This a game you put on and do whatever with it playing in the background. When Tyke bat again?"

"She went first, so depending on how many hits her team get in the second inning, we might not see her again to the third or fourth inning. That music ain't too bad," DeeDee remarked as he nodded his head to the bluesy rap song coming across his system.

"Now I can understand that jargon," Koko remarked. "They play seven innings so she gone get like three bats at least."

"Who asked you? Don't feed into him, girl." Kimi laughed.

"Teach her something, Koko." DeeDee laughed just as Dawk and Sharona walked through the door with a stack of pizzas and hot wings.

Kimi and Koko jumped up and grabbed the two bags Sharona was toting into the condominium. "Miss Benson, why you ain't call when y'all made it back?" Kimi asked anxiously.

"I'm fine, Kimi," Sharona assured.

DeeDee remained seated as he watched his three grandchildren and Sharona set up the food in his dining area. Sharona said she was fine, but it was plain to see that she hadn't much time left. She'd loss and exborbitant amount of weight and her skin had darkened a few shades due to the dialysis she had to undergo three times a week. She was tired all the time, but when she heard Dawk, Kimi and Koko were coming to Chicago, she went and got an extra treatment, did her hair up and bought a new outfit just for the occasion. She wore a white all-in-one dress with a pair of orange flats as it was hard to keep her balance in heels, and had decorated the apartment in Oklahoma State gear.

"Doss, what you know about Mo' Thugs, young man?" Sharona smiled over to her love.

DeeDee snapped from his thoughts and stood up from his recliner and stretched. "My granddaughters where listening to that."

"You two ladies are in tune with my heart," Sharona smiled. "I love that song's chorus."

"I ben trying to figure out what they're saying. They rap so fast, but the music is pleasant," DeeDee chimed in as he grabbed a set of glass dishes from the dish rack.

Sharona smiled and walked over to DeeDee. Like her former love, she knew she hadn't much time left on Earth, but she was determined to make her transition as painless as possible for those she'd be leaving behind in the upcoming months. "They're," Sharona bowed her head momentarily as the reality of her imminent death filled her mind for a countless time. "The women in that song are saying, they're saying how I feel. And I feel, I feel," she paused again as she hugged DeeDee and waited for Mo' Thug's song's chorus to come around again. When it did, Sharona stared up into DeeDee's eyes and harmoniously sung, "...*Ghetto blues has got me down for the last time...ghetto blues has got me down for the last time....ghetto blues has got me down for the last time...ghetto blues has got me down...*"

Kimi, Koko and Dawk went about setting the table as their grandfather and the love of his life held onto one another. They weren't sure if DeeDee understood Sharona's reason for singing, but they knew. The woman was tired of her sickness. It wasn't a coincidence she'd only come to the ranch once since Spoonie had been shot, which was for Dawk's wedding, and even then she wasn't in the best of health.

DeeDee, however, *could* relate to the song Sharona was singing whether his grandchildren understood him or not. "It's not fair," he said as he gripped Sharona. "This ain't fair to you, baby!"

"It's got me down for the last time, Doss," Sharona smiled as she leaned back and looked up into DeeDee's eyes once more. "I promise to smile every day I have left. So many people just give up. Not me."

"I wasn't going to let you," DeeDee soothed as he ran his hands through Sharona's shiny, black hair.

"I know. And because you weren't going to let me give up? The least I could do is meet you at the finish line, baby."

DeeDee raised his hands to the side of head and frowned. "Why these things happen, Jesus? My son's mother is dying and I can't do nothing to help! I can't, I can't help!"

Kimi and Koko's eyes were watery listening to conversation

going down just feet away. No one in the family had really believed Sharona was dying, but now it was made real. Doss III would be motherless inside a year's time and many in the family were going about it as if it wasn't a reality they would have to face one day.

"My uncle won't have to ever worry about being taken care of, Sharona and granddad." Dawk stated seriously. "To be honest, I feel funny saying that there being he only seven and given the title, he should be looking after my grown self," he added.

Koko placed another plate onto the table and snorted. "Oh no!" she fretted. "I hate that!"

"Y'all laugh?" Sharona smiled as she broke away from DeeDee and walked into the dining room. "Laughter is good! And trust me, I'm not worried about little Doss because he's with the best family, and the only family he's ever known. Just, if you can? If I ask and need you to be there? Help me break the news to him? He doesn't know his mother his dying."

"Anything you need, Sharona," Dawk assured.

"The double play executed by Sinopa Dawkins was a classic play by a budding short stop in big twelve softball play. A line drive caught on the fly and a forced out on third base saved a run for the Cowboys closing out the first inning of what looks to be a memorable game for the freshman!" an announcer was heard over the television.

"Tyke made a play!" Sharona yelled excitedly as she walked back into the living room.

"Damn right she did! That's my granddaughter, dammit!" DeeDee stated proudly as he made his way over to his recliner and sunk back down into his seat before the television.

"Hit the rewind on the tv!" Kimi yelled while grabbing a slice of pizza as Koko ran and picked up the remote to rewind the play.

Dawk remained behind in the dining room while watching his family gather before the television. It was after five down in Phoenix, but after seven in Chicago. He would have to leave his grandfather's condominium in ninety minutes or so to meet up with Natalia III and the way things were going, he wasn't sure if he'd make it back.

Kimi and Koko, and Sharona herself, for that matter, was in the dark as to why Dawk had traveled to Chicago exactly. As far as they knew, Dawk was in town to visit his grandfather and watch Tyke's game with him since he was unable to make it down to Arizona with Sharona being sick and all. He kept things in line by grabbing plates and passing them around to his family before returning with pizza boxes for everyone to select a few slices before returning with the hot wings to sit and watch the game with his family, enjoying what time he had remaining with his family before he entered the realm of the unknown.

****

Back down in Phoenix, Asa Spade was beside the bleachers working a grill full of beef franks as Xiang sat beside him feeding ice cream cones to Tabby and Gabby, who would be two years-old in a couple of weeks. "Good," Tabby said as she swung her legs and licked the cone.

"Yes it is, ain't it, Tabitha?" Xiang smiled over the cheers of college ball players and supportive fans. "Here, Gabriella," she then said to the other twin.

"Mister, can I have one of your hot dogs?" a little girl ran up and asked Asa Spade.

"If your parents says it's okay you can have one," Asa said as he turned the franks. "I'm not trying to get sued out here."

"What does sued mean?"

"It means your parents will own my ass if you eat one of these and get sick," Asa replied as Xiang snickered.

The little girl covered her mouth and said, "You said the word ass. That's a bad word like the word nigger. You're a nigger and mother says we should never call black people that name."

Asa looked down at the little girl with a turgid look planted on his face as he grabbed a hot dog bun and placed a beef frank onto it. "You want some mustard?"

"No, sir."

"Okay, here ya' go, young lady. Tell your mother to kiss my black ass when you get back over for me would ya'? And if she has any problems, tell her send ya' daddy so we can umm, so we can smooth things over. You gone remember that?"

"I have a good memory for ten," the little girl said as she bit into the hot dog and walked off.

"That one there gone have many a rough day in life with asshole parents teaching her that bull," Asa stated as he watched the unmindful child disappear back into the crowd.

"Because she used the N-word?" Xiang asked as she wiped the twins' mouths with baby wipes.

Asa didn't respond. He just threw up his hands like, "*You that's what it is.*"

"I think it's more how she used it instead of what she said. She may have misinterpreted what was told to her. She was only ten," Xiang smiled.

"It's people a lot younger than me. People her own little age that'll smack her in the mouth talking like that. They not gone understand a misinterpretation," Asa remarked as he closed the lid on the smoking grill and stood beside Xiang. "Ice cream and potato chips," he chuckled. "You been spoiling Samantha's babies since we got here."

"They're adorable!" Xiang smiled while touching the toddlers at random. "You should spend more time with them. They're your granddaughters."

Asa looked over to Xiang and nodded over his epiphany. "You're right, baby," he smiled. "My granddaughters. I never looked at it like that."

"Samantha does. And so do I. I know you're restless, but you're missing out."

"I am restless. But I can say it was a good thing for Ben to keep us on the sideline for a while."

Xiang nodded as she wiped her hands free of melted ice cream. Tabby reached for the bag of chips at that moment, but she moved them away. "I'll have to ask your mother. She's going to say no, by the way."

"No?" Tabby asked while shaking her head from side-to-side. She then nodded her head up and down and said, "Yes!"

"Aww," Xiang cooed as she opened the chips.

"Didn't you just say you had to ask her mother?" Asa chuckled.

"Right," Xiang laughed. "Water?"

"Water," Tabby repeated while nodding her head up and down.

"Asa," Xiang remarked as she knelt down and pulled the lid open on an ice chest, "I like Phoenix. What about you?"

"It's different."

"Is that good or bad?"

"It's a good thing." Asa replied as he pulled the lid open on the grill and sprayed water onto the coals to lower the temperature.

Xiang pulled two small bottles of water from the ice chest and shook her hands free of liquid. "Good enough not to go back into the business?" she asked.

Asa turned and faced Xiang while wiping his hands on his apron. "I didn't say all that," he countered.

"Can you ever?" Xiang asked as she opened the bottles of water and tilted them up to Tabby and Gabby's mouths. "Because I'm starting to get used to the way life is now. I like the memories."

"We have memories, baby. Good ones," Asa reinforced over the ping of a soft ball hitting a bat and the crowd's uproar.

"But there was always a gun around on some night stand and we ran the risk of losing it all," Xiang complained as an Arizona State softball player ran past her on the other side of the fence. "I have to be honest, man—I was scared to death in

Colorado. Not because of the time I was facing, not of the people in that jail, I was afraid of losing you, Montoya. Losing you," she admitted over the cheers of college students and adults alike. "I don't, I can't go through that again. Being away from you me tears my heart apart."

"You think I enjoyed being back there?" Asa frowned. "I missed you, too, Xiang. And I been by your side ever since we got out."

"But for how long?" Xiang asked as Asa shook his head in disbelief. "Not like that," the emotional woman defended. "You're not going to step out on me—anymore—I ask how long before we have to pick the guns up again?"

"I can't answer that, Xiang."

Xiang removed hair from her face as she checked to make sure Gabby and Tabby were doing okay. The twins were sipping and splashing their water under the warm Arizona sun, nothing of trouble, just being babies. "I want a normal life Asa," she let it be known. "I want to shop for curtains, hang pictures and get up on Saturday mornings, turn on some music and clean my home. Since we been staying with Samantha? I see what a family is like. A real one. Why can't we have a normal life?"

"A normal life is for squares, Xiang," Asa remarked as he began moving the hot dogs off the grill onto the top rack to keep them from burning.

"Being normal doesn't make you a square, Montoya. It makes you grown."

"So, you saying I'm not a grown—"

"Of course you're a grown man, Montoya. More man than a dozen men in my book. I only have eyes for you, baby," Xiang stated seriously. "But being here in Phoenix showed me something different and for the first time, I found something, maybe the only thing that will give me the strength to walk away from you if you do not agree. And that one thing is normal. Normal is pets, it's Sunday dinner, a bad hair day, and maybe, maybe a Montoya Spencer Junior running through the house I don't know. All I know is I want to be normal."

"You asking me to make serious changes in my—"

"I'm not asking you to decide today, love," Xiang interrupted. "Just think about it. Really, really think about it. I've been following you around since I was a little girl doing whatever it is you wanted because it was what I wanted to do. I wanted to make you happy. I think for once, you should at least consider doing something that would make me happy," the soul-bearing woman declared. "The babies need changing," she ended as she placed Gabby and Tabby into their double stroller and wheeled them off, leaving Asa Spade alone with his thoughts and smoking grill.

CHAPTER FORTY-FIVE

GAME OVER

"This has to be like a freshman's dream come true, or a very terrifying experience depending on who you are in this sport. And having watched Sinopa Dawkins for most of the big twelve softball season, I'm willing to bet my life savings it's the afore mentioned. The only question is, can she, or rather will she do it?" an announcer broadcasted over the airwaves as Tyke stood at home plate giving check swings before the next pitch.

The game was now in the bottom of the seventh inning and Tyke was the last person up to bat. Oklahoma State was down 3-0 and the bases were loaded. The pitch count was two balls and three strikes, giving the pitcher for the Arizona Wildcats the upper hand in the deal. Arizona players were playing close to the infield. Any out would give them the victory and send Oklahoma State home in defeat and without a playoff berth.

Tyke could maybe hit a fly ball for a double and bring two runners in, but the chances of doing it a second time to tie and then a third to take the lead when all Arizona had to do was get a single out, were astronomical. She felt she had no choice but to hit a walk off grand slam and ice the game, but there was more to Tyke's reasoning.

In March of 2002, Spoonie was facing a similar at bat up to Kaw Lake Park. She needed to hit a double during the last at bat to help their little league team get into the playoffs.

Spoonie struck out swinging, though. Tyke never forgot how sad her sister was that day and her constant cry that she may never get a chance to redeem herself. Their father was also at that game that day. And on Walee's suggestion, the entire family recreated the scenario for Spoonie and she got to hit her walk off double.

Nothing beats the real thing, though, was Tyke's thinking, and this one here mattered more than anything. *"Do it for Spoonie. Do it for Spoonie,"* the dark-skinned and petite eighteen year-old told herself as she touched the tip of her bat to the edge of home plate and readied her swing. She watched as the pitcher placed the ball in her glove before winding up the pitch and releasing her throw.

Tyke was expecting a riser or a sinker, but the ball had some serious heat on it and she couldn't get a bead on the pitch. She had no choice but to foul it. The ball hit the fence over near Asa's grill as Tyke walked off from home plate.

Back up in Chicago, one could hear a rat piss on cotton it was so quiet up in DeeDee's condominium. Koko and Kimi were dozing off, and Sharona had gone upstairs and fallen asleep. Dawk and DeeDee were the only two watching, both on the edge of their seats as Tyke walked back up to home plate.

"It's a good thing Dawkins fouled that pitch because the Wildcat pitcher was coming in with a sinker. Dawkins seemed to be expecting a riser and hadn't the time to adjust her swing to keep the ball in play," the announcer stated over the airwaves as Tyke's stats appeared on the screen. "Dawkins hit twenty-two homers and had thirty-one RBIs. She was a one woman wrecking crew for a good portion of the season. Let's see if she can add to those numbers and make it all worthwhile," she added in near whisper as Tyke touched the edge of home plate and readied her swing.

The ball left the pitcher's hand and stayed level. Tyke's eyes widened and she swung, hitting the ball's underside and forcing it to foul behind the catcher. *"Quit looking for the sinker! That was the pitch, Sinopa! Walk it in!"* Tyke said to herself through gritted teeth as she slapped her helmet a couple of times and then removed it, putting her lush, black afro on display.

Frustrated, yet focused, Tyke placed her helmet back onto her head and walked back over to home plate. She was reaching out to touch the edge of the diamond when she caught glimpse of an orange flash in her peripheral vision. It was Spoonie waving a cap inside the dugout. Tyke rose and looked over to her twin and saw that she was motioning her hand in a curve motion. She nodded, touched the heels of her cleats with the top of her bat in order to stall for time and digest what Spoonie had just told her before touching the edge of home plate and readying her swing.

The crowd roared, Wildcat players were all eyeing the batter, and Cowboy players on base were easing off the squares to get a lead, just in case Tyke hit the ball into play. The ball left the pitcher's hand and curved inward. At first glance, it appeared to be an inside sinker. Tyke, however, kept in mind what Spoonie had told her, and had also taken her own advice to walk the pitch in. It was as if she could see the seams on what was understood to be a curve ball rather than an inside sinker. In a split second, Tyke choked down on her bat to give herself more power, bit her bottom lip and swung the hardest swing she'd ever swung in her life.

The time she'd hit that ball, Tyke knew. She dropped the bat and began skipping sideways down the first base line in her orange uniform and black cleats while pointing to the ball as it soared across centerfield. Oklahoma State players picked Spoonie up in her wheel chair and left the dugout, some running out to home plate flipping their hats off and tossing their gloves aside to greet their teammates as they crossed the diamond.

Tyke ran past first base pumping her right fist as tears of joy filled her eyes. By the time she crossed second base she was in a full sprint. She just had to get to Spoonie. Rounding third base, her teammates stepped aside and Tyke's twin awaited her arrival.

"You did it, Shima!" Tyke screamed aloud while laughing and running towards home plate. "You did it, girl!"

"*You* did it, Tyke!" Spoonie screamed back as her sister crossed home plate and slid down to one knee before her. "You did it, girl!"

"*We* did it!" Tyke said out of breath as she hugged her twin's neck. "*We* did it!"

"Dad would be so proud of you, Sinopa! He would be sooo proud!" Spoonie said as the team started to pick Tyke up to carry her off.

Tyke played it off like she didn't know what her teammates was trying to do by getting behind her sister's wheelchair as she didn't want to show up her twin. "Shima, how you knew she was gone throw a curve ball?" one of their teammates asked excitedly.

"I counted her pitches in the fourth inning. She lull you to sleep with the same pitch. Tyke fouled twice on a full count which gave her seven throws. The eighth pitch in the fourth inning was a curve. She struck us out in the fourth like that. I knew it was coming because she hadn't used it since."

"OOO—KKK!" half the team shouted as they skipped off the field.

"COWBOYS!" the other half yelled as they all lined up to touch hands with the opposing team.

Spoonie was allowed to wheel across the field and shake hands with Arizona's team. When she got to the pitcher, the young woman leaned down and said, "That was a good call you gave your sister, freshman. You'll make a helluva batter when you get back on the field."

Spoonie thanked the player and the biggest smile crept across her face. Although not on the field, she'd been acknowledged as having helped win the game by the opposing team. Her teammates and coaches kept her involved, and Tyke always sought her advice. All these things combined to further help Spoonie in her recovery. She never had a doubt that she would get the chance to play again, and what'd happened today, only made her more determined to get back on the field. With her focus solidified in the realm of sports, there was one more thing Spoonie needed to do in the future once she returned to the ranch, but for now, it could wait. Her sister had just hit a walk off grand slam to send their team to the playoffs.

****

"Heyyy," Kimi sang as she snapped her fingers above her head, having just watched her sister hit a walk off grand slam. "That's my family actin' a donkey down in Arizona!"

Dawk was easing up off on the couch at that moment. He nudged a sleeping Koko's feet off his legs and stood up and stretched. "I knew she could do it," he smiled as he looked around for his suit jacket.

"You right about that grandson," DeeDee laughed as he got up from his recliner. "This calls for a glass of wine."

"I know that's real!" Koko snapped.

"Wait," Kimi laughed. "Wasn't you like sound asleep two seconds ago, Koko?"

"I wasn't sleeping, Kimi. I was resting my eyes."

"And sucking all the air out the room snoring and carrying on," Dawk joked as he grabbed his suit jacket.

"Where you going this late, Dawk?" Kimi asked as she grabbed wine glasses for everybody.

"Gotta look into something right quick before we leave out tomorrow afternoon."

"I'm gone tell Oneika on you!" Koko chided, believing Dawk was going visit another woman while in town.

"It even like that," Dawk laughed as he headed for the door.

Koko was busy pouring wine, but Kimi was paying close attention. "Dawk?" she called out softly as she walked towards the front door. "Where you going, man? For real?"

"I'm just going look into something, Kimi," Dawk assured.

"The way daddy used to do when he came here on business?" Kimi asked matter-of-factly. "You need to tell me what's going on. We just getting Spoonie back on track, man. What you doing?"

475

"Something I can't let get pass the family, Kimi."

"Are you in danger?"

"Yeah," Dawk answered, leaving behind a stunned Kimi.

The ride over to The Cicero Hot Dog Deli was a quiet one for Dawk as he thought about all that was about to go down. He was taking a gamble on his life, but he couldn't turn back. The family's respect and reputation was on the line and he knew it.

Arriving over to the deli, he saw the block was still, dark and quiet. Only that of Natalia III's Expedition sat in front of the building and there was dim-lighting on the inside. He climbed from his car and walked into the building and saw Natalia sitting at the bar counter watching the highlights of the softball game.

"Eh, look who's here," Natalia smiled as he eased off the bar counter and shook Dawk's hand. "Man, Tyke is a baller, huh? Knocked that sucker clean out into the parking lot. I think she broke somebody's windshield," he joked.

Dawk smiled slightly as he took a seat at the bar. "Where everybody else at?"

"My boys out making their rounds. It's still business for us up here, ya' know?"

"I was hoping to meet 'em."

"We'll do so later on tonight. I know this club. Real laidback. We can have a few drinks and you can meets some of the people we deal with. How's that sound?"

"Like a plan," Dawk replied. "What's on the stove back there?"

"I was warming up some chili. It's a new recipe I'm trying out for the menu. I'm thinking of naming it, but I don't know what to call it. Any suggestions?"

"I would have to try it first."

"Yeah," Natalia nodded. "Make yourself at home. Look around while I whip ya' up a bowl."

"Where ya' bathroom?" Dawk asked.

"All the way in the back, il mio amico," Natalia answered as he disappeared into the kitchen.

Dawk eased up from the bar stool and placed his suit jacket over the back of the chair. He walked through the dark, quiet deli, found the bathroom stalls and entered and went stood before the sink. He stared at himself in silence for several seconds before turning and vomiting into one of the toilets. "*I gotta be crazy doing this shit!*" he thought to himself as he began to panic.

The thought of what he was about to put himself through had brought about a pressure the young gangster hadn't anticipated. Dawk had always prided his self on being calm under pressure, but the circumstances were putting everything into new perspective. He wiped his mouth and loosened his silk slacks and took a long piss. Before long, he was sitting emptying his bowels, sitting on the throne in shame over his actions. But death has a way of bringing out unknown actions of any human being when they're up against it.

After he'd done his business, Dawk walked back over to the sink, washed his hands and then splashed water onto his face to bring back some form of dignity. Regaining his composure, he straightened his clothes and walked out of the bathroom and sat at a table in the center of the deli.

Natalia emerged from the kitchen at that moment with a tray and a bowl of chili and presented it to Dawk. "Here ya' go, boss," he said as he stepped back from the table with his hands clasped before his body.

Dawk unrolled a silver spoon and began stirring the concoction. "You not gone have a bowl?" he asked.

"Not really my thing, boss," Natalia replied nonchalantly as he looked past Dawk.

Dawk noticed the Italian's eye movement and sat his spoon down as a shadow appeared behind him. "This is why you wanted me to come to Chicago," he declared as Malik Gomez walked past the table and stood beside Natalia.

"It's about to be a new day inside the family," Malik stated as he eyed Dawk callously.

"Says who?"

"Says me," Malik stated.

"And me," Natalia III quickly followed. "And it's been a long time coming."

"You were my brother." Dawk told Malik. "My brother. And you sell me out? You come up here to my birthplace to take me out the game, boy?"

"I was your brother, but you sold me out when you made the deal with the Germans," Malik countered. "You never asked my opinion because you didn't care about how I felt about Peppi being killed by those people. You avenged everybody's death except hers."

"We killed RJ for what went down. We got Indianapolis now because of that." Dawk said as he stirred his bowl of chili once more.

Malik looked off as he laughed. "Money. It's always been about the money. I don't care about no Indianapolis, Dawk. And I'm gone get that anyway now. Me and Natalia? We gone run things now. Your reign is over," he added as Natalia III went into his suit jacket and pulled a .9mm from his shoulder holster.

"You want me to do it?" Natalia asked as he racked the pistol and aimed it at Dawk just as Faye Bender walked out from the kitchen eating a bowl of chili.

"No," Malik answered as he held out his hand. "I want this one for myself." Natalia III passed the gun to Malik and he gripped the handle while pointing the gun at Dawk's head. "It's nothing personal, boss," he said as he squeezed the trigger.

Dawk didn't know which way Natalia III was going to go really given the past history of the Italians, which was the reason for his anxiety inside the bathroom. For all he knew, Natalia III could've been playing him all along, but he chose to believe what he was told about an attempted coup inside the family by him and had decided to put both men to the test using his own life. When the gun didn't fire, Natalia III had proven his loyalty. That also meant that the Germans were holding true to the agreed upon peace.

Dawk jumped up at that moment and charged at Malik as Natalia III grabbed the Mexican around the neck. He kept squeezing the trigger as Natalia tightened his grip and forced him to drop the gun and remain calm. A powerful jab to the face by Dawk buckled his knees. Out of breath, he looked up at Dawk as he now stood before him with the gun in his hand.

"When I first met you I kept placing a gun before you to see what you would do. You passed the loyalty test back then," Dawk stated as he stared Malik in the eyes. "You wanna be a boss, but you don't know how to move like one. This is why your plan failed, because all you were ever meant to be was my employee. You can't go no higher. It's not in you—brother."

"Boss," Malik panicked as Faye walked up to the group licking her fingers.

"This chili good, but it's cold," Faye remarked as she eyed the men. "You okay, Malik?"

"We had a deal, Faye!" Malik cried out. "Boss, they were in with me on this! Faye was taking payments from me, and Natalia was telling me how to get at you! He tried to set you up at that McDonald's on Jefferson Avenue the day you came to traps on Ann Avenue! He was in on it!"

Natalia laughed and said, "You don't know how glad I was you made the decision to go to another restaurant that day, Dawk. It was hard enough keeping this bum on a string while trying to make it look like a coincidence every time he tried ta' kill ya' and things didn't work out in his favor," he let it be known as he held a tight grip on Malik.

"Faye?" Malik pleaded. "Get me out of this!"

Faye scooped another helping of chili up onto her spoon and took a bite. She licked her lips and asked, "Can I call my people so they can go ahead and take out the rest of his crew? They been keeping them at bay for the last hour."

"Give 'em the green light," Dawk nodded.

"Great," Faye smiled as she walked off while reaching for her cell phone. "This is some good chili. It's just cold, Natalia," she reiterated as she disappeared into the darkness of the deli.

Malik now understood that his entire plan to overtake the family by killing Dawk and aligning himself with the Germans and Natalia was nothing more than a game of manipulation. Whereas he thought he was making all the right moves in a figurative game of chess, it was now plain to see that he was a mere pawn the entire time. "Dawk!" he begged. "I'll be your employee, man! Make me a runner! I'll be a lookout for Ann Avenue, just don't kill me, please," he cried as Natalia held him up.

Dawk extended his hands with the gun in one hand and said, "You have no place no more inside this family, Malik. In my head, man. You were going to shoot me in my head right where I sat! Sit your ass down!" he commanded as his voice boomed throughout the deli.

"Boss," Malik pleaded.

"You heard the man! Take a seat!" Natalia III growled as he shoved Malik down into the chair before the bowl of chili.

Dawk and Natalia now stood on the opposite side of the table staring at Malik as he now sat where Dawk was once seated. "Pick up the spoon," Dawk commanded as he set the empty gun down before Malik.

"Boss, please."

"Pick...up...the spoon." Dawk sternly ordered. Malik did as commanded. "Now eat," he stated as Natalia III went into his back waistband and passed him a chrome .45 caliber.

"You wanted a picture, right?" Natalia asked Dawk as he pulled out his phone.

"Yeah," Dawk answered. "I got a name for this meal, but I don't want it on the menu. It'll be an inside thing with the family."

"What you got?" Natalia asked.

"Call it Cold Chili. Because revenge is a dish best served cold. Malik Gomez tried to cross me out. It's only right I return the favor and do it right."

Malik sat at the table with a blank stare. Tears rolled down his face as he held onto the spoon, having resolved himself to the fact that tonight was going to be his last night on Earth. A flash from Natalia's phone camera had caught his shocked image for all times.

"Let me show you how it's done, Malik," Dawk stated as he held onto the gun. "See? You gotta rack it," he said as he racked the psitol and allowed a live round to jump out from the chamber. "And rack it again, and again, and again. That way, you know it's fully loaded because ain't no telling if you being passed an empty gun or not, ya' understand?" he asked as the live rounds rolled along the wooden floor.

Malik remained silent as he looked up to Dawk with his chin held high. From his seated position, he watched as Dawk raised the gun, and pointed it at his head.

Dawk Holland was looking Malik Gomez square in the eyes when he fired a single round, sending a bullet crashing through the center of his forehead and blowing his brains out of the back of his skull. He died sitting upright in the chair with the back of his head blown out and his eyes open before a cold bowl of chili. He'd come on the scene in September of 2002, and had his run dismantled in May of 2009. His body would be placed inside of the trunk of a stolen car and driven over to Gary, Indiana where it would be crushed by Natalia III inside his family's scrap yard.

"You got Minneapolis now, fam," Dawk told Natalia as he stared at Malik's corpse. "Call Jay-D and give the green light on Max," he ended as he walked off and sent a text to Ben to let him know he was okay. Then one to Kimi to calm her nerves.

"Gotcha, boss," Natalia answered.

Dawk then sent a text to Siloam, who was waiting just down

the block with Montenegro and three ranch hands, just in case the call didn't come. "Dawk's fine," Siloam told Montenegro. "We can head back to Ponca City now," she let it be known.

****

"Flush, mutherfucka!" Maggie laughed as she spread her cards out on the table she and the driver of the RV that held Malik's crew were sitting in as it sat parked inside of Biscuitville's parking lot down in Cherryvale, Kansas.

"Full house!" the driver countered as he spread his cards and laughed.

For the past hour or so, the Germans down in Cherryvale had been holding the RV up by telling them that there were two roadblocks north of town that were going to last for another couple of hours and there was no way around it. Over the past few months, the six men aboard the bus had become endeared to their 'cop' friends as they kept them bust-free during their ride up to Minnesota.

Bonita was at the table when her phone chimed. She checked the message and read the words, *Waste them all*.

"My deal," a second Mexican said as he scooped up the cards. "How long before the road block clears, Bonita?" he asked.

"Let me go check," Bonita said as she tapped Maggie's leg and nodded. "I have to use the bathroom first."

"You should really hire a better plumber for that diner," the driver laughed as he stood to allow Bonita to exit the table.

Bonita went into the RV's bathroom and removed her Glock .40 from her hip holster. She waited a few moments before flushing the toilet and racking it over the swooshing sound.

Back outside, Maggie was using hand signals to notify Sascha and Cikala. The two started easing over to RV's opened door with their hands on their service pistols while dressed in their black Sheriff deputy uniforms. Just before they stepped onto the bus, Bonita stepped out of the bathroom and opened fire on two men sitting down listening to music on MP-3 players with her Glock .40. The gunfire startled the four

482

remaining men.

Maggie pulled her service pistol and shot the driver and the second Mexican sitting at the table before her as Sascha and Cikala waited outside the door. When the two remaining men ran off the RV, they gunned them both down in the parking lot and began dragging their bodies back onto the RV. In under a minute's time, six men had been murdered down in Cherryvale. Malik's crew was completely wiped out save for Max, and Jay-D was soon to take care of that job.

Once the men were inside the RV, Sascha closed the door after allowing Bonita and Cikala to leave. Together, she and Maggie rode back over the Bender farm with the six dead corpses and the RV was parked before the barn.

Bonita and Cikala pulled up behind the RV in their patrol cars and climbed out and pulled the barn doors open. The RV was driven inside and the barn doors were closed as the four women set about chopping the men's bodies up into pieces small enough to fit inside the wood chipper out near the apple groves.

CHAPTER FORTY-SIX

THE NEXT BIG THING

Lisa Vanguard stood on the docks of Seattle watching as men offloaded from a freighter labeled Red Dragon on May 29th 2009. Two weeks after Malik Gomez and his crew had been taken down. The men she were looking for were amongst the last of the men to walk off the ship and she was there to greet them. "Raiden! Arata!" she called out.

The men turned and eyed a red-haired, slender woman approaching them.

"Who's asking?" Raiden inquired.

"Lisa Vanguard. Federal agent and friend of Tammy Moto."

"Good," Raiden smiled as he looked around. "Where is she?"

"I'm sorry to inform you, Mister Moto, but your sister was killed nearly three weeks ago in Philadelphia, Pennsylvania. "

The Moto brothers stood stoic as they eyed Lisa. "Who... would kill a federal agent? Have they been captured or killed?" Raiden asked as Arata made a call back to Japan.

"No they haven't, but the who is a group of Germans from Cincinnati, Ohio. The same people responsible for killing your parents back in January of 1984, Mister Moto," Lisa let it be known.

"How do you know all of this? And who are you, exactly?"

"Tammy never told you about me I see," Lisa nodded. "I was the one who got her through boarding school and put her in college. I helped manage her finances and gave her her start inside of the Federal Bureau of Investigations. She was my partner, but more importantly, she was friend. She told me what you two were involved in, but I'm not here to make a bust. I'm here to help you get your revenge on Tanya Weinberger and her daughter Helen. They ordered the death of your sister. But I have more," Lisa stated.

"Continue," Raiden listened intently.

"Please," Lisa stated as he she extended her hand towards a waiting limousine. "Let's sit and talk."

"It's been confirmed," Arata told Raiden as he ended his call. "Tammy's dead. More of us are on the way."

"Miss Vanguard," Raiden nodded as he extended his hand. The two walked over to the limousine and climbed inside.

Lisa crossed her legs and nodded over to two women sitting with her and the Asians. "These are my associates Brenda Marshall and Bridgette Fischer," she let it be known as the party of five began to lay out a plan to get back at the people responsible for Tammy's death and much, much more...

To be continued

Made in the USA
Monee, IL
30 August 2021

76869674R00272